New York Times bestselling author **Christine Feehan** has over 30 novels published and has thrilled legions of fans with her seductive and sensual 'Dark' Carpathian tales. She has received numerous honours throughout her career including being a nominee for the Romance Writers of America RITA, and receiving a Career Achievement Award from *Romantic Times*, and has been published in multiple languages and in many formats, including audio book, e-book, and large print.

For more information about Christine Feehan visit her website: www.christinefeehan.com

Praise for Christine Feehan:

'After Bram Stoker, Anne Rice and Joss Whedon,
Feehan is the person most credited with
popularizing the neck gripper'
Time magazine

'The queen of paranormal romance'
USA Today

'Feehan has a knack for bringing vampiric Carpathians
to vivid, virile life in her Dark Carpathian novels'
Publishers Weekly

christine
FEEHAN

Magic before Christmas

The first two books in the
DRAKE SISTERS SERIES

piatkus

PIATKUS

The Twilight Before Christmas first published in the US in 2003 by Pocket Books,
a division of Simon and Schuster, Inc.
Magic in the Wind first published in 2005 by Berkley Books, a division
of Penguin Group (USA) Inc.
First published in Great Britain in 2013 by Piatkus

A CIP catalogue record for this book
is available from the British Library.

ISBN 978-0-349-40218-5

Printed and bound by CPI Group (UK) Ltd, Croydon, CR0 4YY

Papers used by Piatkus are from well-managed forests
and other responsible sources.

MIX
Paper from
responsible sources
FSC
www.fsc.org   FSC® C104740

Piatkus
An imprint of
Little, Brown Book Group
100 Victoria Embankment
London EC4Y 0DY

An Hachette UK Company
www.hachette.co.uk

www.piatkus.co.uk

Thank you to Heather King and Rose Brungard for the wonderfully chilling Christmas poem they so graciously provided to me to use for this book!

The Twilight Before Christmas
by
Heather King and Rose Brungard

'Twas the twilight before Christmas and all through the lands,
Not a thing has occurred that was not of my hand.

The snowglobe they hold has a secret inside,
Where the mist rolls in place of the snow that's outside.

A chill, colder still than the air they will feel,
As I rejoice in release as I slip past the seal

A wreath of holly meant to greet,
Looks much better tossed in the street.

A town dreams of sweet thoughts while nestled in bed,
Until nightmares of me begin to dance in their heads.

The time, it was right, for a present or two,
And the fog on the sand holds a secret, a clue

As lovers meet beneath mistletoe bright,
Terror ignites down below them this night

And the blood runs red on the pristine white snow . . .
While around all the houses the Christmas lights glow.

A star burns hot in the dead of the night,
As the bell tolls it's now midnight

Beneath the star, that shines so bright,
An act unfolds, to my delight

In the stocking hung with gentle care,
A mystery, I know, is hidden there.

A candle burns with an eerie glow,
As it melts, the wax does flow,

My last gift now, is a special one,
A candy cane for a special son,

He watches and tends and knows the land,
But not enough to evade my hand.

All deeds are now done, forgiveness is mine,
As two people share a love for all time.

THE
TWILIGHT
BEFORE
CHRISTMAS

This book is dedicated to my sister Lisa,
who has a special magic all her own.

Chapter One

'Twas the twilight before Christmas and all through the lands
Not a thing has occurred that was not of my hand.

"Don't say it. Don't say it. Don't say it," Danny Granite muttered the mantra under his breath as he sat in the truck watching his older brother carefully selecting hydro-organic tomatoes from Old Man Mars's fruit stand. Danny glanced at the keys, assuring himself the truck was running and all that his brother had to do was leap in and gun it. He leaned out the window, gave a halfhearted wave to the elderly man, and scowled at his brother. "Get a move on, Matt. I'm starving here."

Matt grimaced at him, then smiled with smooth charm at the old man. "Merry Christmas, Mr. Mars," he said cheerfully as he handed over several bills and lifted the bag of tomatoes. "Less than two weeks before Christmas. I'm looking forward to the pageant this year."

Danny groaned. A black scowl settled over Old Man Mars's

1

face. His craggy brows drew together in a straight, thick line. He grunted in disgust and spat on the ground.

The smile on Matt's face widened into a boyish grin as he hurried around the bed of the pickup truck to yank open the driver-side door. Almost before settling into his seat, he cranked up the radio so that "Jingle Bells" blared loudly from the speakers.

"You'd better move it, Matt," Dan muttered nervously, looking out the window, back toward the fruit stand. "He's arming himself. You just had to wish him a Merry Christmas, didn't you? You know he hates that pageant. And you know very well playing that music is adding insult to injury!"

The first tomato came hurtling toward the back window of the truck as Matt hit the gas and the truck leaped forward, fishtailing, tires throwing dirt into the air. The tomato landed with deadly accuracy, splattering juice, seed, and pulp across the back window. Several more missiles hit the tailgate as the truck tore out of the parking lot and raced down the street.

Danny scowled at his brother. "You just had to wish him Merry Christmas. Everyone knows he hates Christmas. He kicked the shepherd last year during the midnight pageant. Now he'll be more ornery than ever. If you'd just avoided the word, we might have gone unscathed this year, but now he'll have to retaliate."

Matt's massive shoulders shook as he laughed. "As I recall you played the shepherd last year. He didn't hurt you that bad, Danny boy. A little kick on the shin is good for you. It builds character."

"You only think it's funny because it wasn't your shin." Danny rubbed his leg as if it still hurt nearly a year later.

"You need to toughen up," Matt pointed out. He took the highway, a thin ribbon of a road, twisting and turning along the cliffs above the ocean. It was impossible to go fast on the switchbacks although Matt knew the road well. He maneuvered around a sharp curve, setting up for the next sharp turn. It ran uphill and nearly doubled back. The mountain swelled on his right, a high bank grown over with emerald green grasses and breathtaking colors from the explosion of wildflowers. On his left, a narrow ribbon of a trail meandered along the cliffs to drop away to the wide expanse of blue ocean with its whitecaps and booming waves.

"Oh, my God! That's Kate Drake," Danny said gleefully, pointing to a woman on a horse, riding along the narrow trail on the side of the road.

"That can't be her." Matt hastily rolled down his window and craned his neck, gawking unashamedly. He could only see the back of the rider, who was dressed all in white and had thick chestnut hair that flamed red in the sunshine. His heart pounded. His mouth went dry. Only Kate Drake could get away with wearing white and riding a horse so close to the side of the road. It had to be her. He slowed the truck to get a better look as he went by, turning down the radio at the same time.

"Matt! Watch where you're going," Danny yelled, bracing himself as the truck flew off the road and rolled straight into the grass-covered bank. It halted abruptly. Both men were slammed back in their seats and held prisoner by their seat belts.

"Damn!" Matt roared. He turned to his brother. "Are you all right?"

"No, I'm not all right, you big lug, you ran us off the road gawking at Kate Drake again. I hurt everywhere. I need a neck brace, and I think I might have broken my little finger." Danny held up his hand, gripping his wrist and emitting groans loudly.

"Oh shut up," Matt said rudely.

"Matthew Granite. Good heavens, are you hurt? I have a cell phone and can go out to the bluff and call for help."

Kate's voice was everything he remembered. Soft. Melodic. Meant for long nights and satin sheets. Matt turned his head to look at her. To drink her in. It had been four long years since he'd last spoken with her. She stood beside his truck, reins looped in her hand, her large green eyes anxious. He couldn't help but notice she had the most beautiful skin. Flawless. Perfect. It looked so soft, he wanted to stroke his finger down her cheek just to see if she was real.

"I'm fine, Kate." It was a miracle he found his voice. His tongue seemed to stick to the roof of his mouth. "I must have tried to take the turn a little too fast."

A snort of derision came from Danny's side of the truck. "You were driving like a turtle. You just weren't looking where you were going."

The toe of Matt's boot landed solidly against his brother's shin, and Danny let out a hair-raising yowl.

"No wonder Old Man Mars wanted to kick you last year," Matt muttered under his breath.

"Daniel? Are you hurt?" Kate sounded anxious, but her fascinating lower lip quivered as if close to laughter.

Determined to get her away from his brother, Matt hastily shoved the door open with more force than necessary. The door thumped soundly against Kate's legs. She jumped back, the horse half reared, and Danny, damn him, laughed like the hyena he was.

Matt groaned. It never failed. He was a decorated U.S. Army Ranger, had been in the service for years, running covert missions where his life depended on his physical skills and his cool demeanor, yet he always managed to feel clumsy and rough in front of Kate. He unfolded his large frame, towering over her, feeling like a giant. Kate was always perfect. Poised. Articulate. Graceful. There she was, looking beautiful dressed all in white with her hair attractively windblown. She was the only person in the world who could make him lose his cool and raise his temperature at the same time just by smiling.

"Is Danny really hurt?" Kate asked, turning her head slightly while she tried to calm the nervous horse.

It gave Matt a great view of her figure. He drank her in, his hungry gaze drifting over her soft curves. He'd always loved watching her walk away from him. Nobody moved in the same sexy way she did. She looked so proper, yet she had that come-on walk and the bedroom eyes and glorious hair a man would want to feel sliding over his skin all night long. He just managed to stifle a groan. How had he not known, *sensed* that Kate was back in town. His radar must be failing him.

"Danny's fine, Kate," Matt assured her.

She sent him a quick smile over her shoulder, her eyes sparkling at him. "Just how many accidents have you been in, Matt? It seems that on the rare occasions I've seen you, over the last few years, your poor vehicle has been crunched."

It was true, but it was her fault. Kate Drake acted as some sort of catalyst for strange behavior. He was good at everything.

Everything. Unless Kate was around—then he could barely manage to speak properly.

The horse moved restlessly, demanding Kate's immediate attention, giving Matt time to realize his jeans and blue chambray work shirt were streaked with dirt, sawdust, and a powdery cement mixture in complete contrast to her immaculate white attire. He took the opportunity to slap the dust from his clothing, sending up a gray cloud that enveloped Kate as she turned back toward him. She coughed delicately, fluttering her long feathery lashes to keep the dust from stinging her eyes. Another derisive hoot came from Danny's direction.

Matt sent his brother a look that promised instant death before turning back to Kate. "I had no idea you were in town. The town gossips let me down." Inez at the grocery store had mentioned Sarah was in town, as well as Hannah and Abigail, three of her six sisters, but Inez hadn't said a word about Kate.

"Sarah came back for a visit, and you know how my family is, we get together as often as possible." She shrugged, a simple enough gesture, but on her it was damned sexy. "I've been in London doing research for my latest thriller." She laughed softly. The sound played right down his spine and did interesting things to his body. "London fog is always so perfect for a scary setting. Before that it was Borneo." Kate traveled the world, researching and writing her bestselling novels and murder mysteries. She was so beautiful it hurt to look at her, so sophisticated he felt primitive in her presence. She was so sexy he always had the desire to turn caveman and toss her over his shoulder and carry her off to his private lair. "Sarah's engaged to Damon

Wilder." She tilted her head slightly and patted the horse's neck again. "Have you met him?"

"No, but everyone is talking about it. No one expected Sarah to get married."

Matt watched the way the sunlight kissed her hair, turning the silky strands into a blazing mass of temptation. His gaze followed her hand stroking the horse's neck, and he noted the absence of a ring with relief.

Danny cleared his throat. He leaned out the driver's side. "You're drooling, bro." He whispered it in an over-loud voice.

Without missing a beat, Matt kicked the door closed. "Are you going to be staying very long this visit?" He held his breath waiting for her answer. To make matters worse, Danny snickered. Matt sent up a silent vow that their parents would have one less child to fuss over before the day was out.

"I've actually decided to stay and make Sea Haven my home base. I bought the old mill up on the cliffs above Sea Lion Cove. I'm planning on renovating the mill into a bookstore and coffee shop, and to modernize the house so I can live in it. I'm tired of wandering. I'm ready to come home again."

Kate smiled. She had perfect teeth to go with her perfect skin. Matt found himself staring at her while the earth shook beneath his feet. He stood there, grinning at the thought of Kate living in their hometown permanently.

A shadow swept across the sky, black threads swirling and boiling, a dark cauldron of clouds blotting out the sun. A seagull shrieked once. Then the entire flock of birds overhead took up the warning cry. Matt was so caught up in Kate's smile, he didn't realize the ground was really rolling, and it wasn't just her

7

amazing effect on him. The horse backed dangerously close to the road, tossing its head in fright, nearly dragging Kate from her feet. Matt swiftly reached past her and gathered the reins in one hand to steady the animal. He swept his other arm around Kate's waist, anchoring her smaller body to his, to keep her from falling as a jagged crack opened several feet from them and spread rapidly along the ground, heading right for Kate's feet. Matt lifted her up and away from the gaping hole, dragging her back several feet, horse in tow, away from the spreading crack. It was only a few inches wide, but it was several inches deep, very long, and ran up the side of the embankment.

"You all right, Danny?" he called to his brother.

"Yeah, I'm fine. That was a big one."

Kate clung to Matt, her small hands clutching at his shoulders. He heard the sharp intake of her breath that belied her calm demeanor, but she didn't cry out. The ground settled, and Matt allowed her feet to touch the path but retained his hold on her. She was incredibly warm and soft and smelled of fresh flowers. He leaned over her, inhaling her fragrance, his chin brushing the top of her head. "You okay, Kate?"

Appearing as serene as ever, Kate murmured soothingly to the horse. Nothing ruffled her. Not earthquakes and certainly not Matthew Granite. "Yes, of course, it was just a little earthquake." She glanced up at the boiling clouds with a small frown of puzzlement.

"It was a fairly good one. And the ground opened damn near at your feet."

Kate continued to pat the horse's neck, seemingly unaware that Matt was still holding her, caging her body between his and the animal. He could see her hands tremble as she struggled to maintain composure, and it made him admire her all the more. She lifted her face to the wind. "I love the sea breeze. The minute I feel it on my face, I feel as if I'm home."

Matt cleared his throat. Kate had a beautiful profile. Her hair was swept up in some fancy knot, showing off her long, graceful neck. When she turned, her breasts thrust against the thin shirt, full and round and so enticing it was all he could do to keep from leaning down and putting his mouth over the clinging white fabric. He tried to move, to step away from her, but he was drawn to her. Mesmerized by her. She'd always reminded him of a ballerina, with her elegant lines and soft, feminine curves. His lungs burned for air, and there was a strange roaring in his head. It took three tries opening his mouth before a coherent word came out. "If you're really serious about renovation, Kate, it just so happens my family's in the construction business."

She turned the full power of her huge eyes on him. "I do recall all of you are builders. That's always struck me as a wonderful occupation." She reached out and took his hands. He had big hands, rough and callused, whereas her hands were soft and small. "I always loved your hands, Matthew. When I was a young girl I remember wishing I had your capable hands." Her words, as much as her touch, sent little flames licking along his skin.

Matt was certain he heard a snort and probably a snicker coming from the direction of his younger brother.

"I think you've held on to her long enough, bro," Danny called. "The ground stopped pitching a few minutes ago."

Matt was too much of a gentleman to point out to his

brother that Kate was holding *his* hands. Looking down at her, he saw faint color steal under her skin. Reluctantly, he stepped away from her. The wind tugged at tendrils of her hair, but it only made her look more alluring. "Sorry, Kate. This is the first time in a while we've had an earthquake shake us up so hard." He raked his fingers through his dark hair in agitation, searching for something brilliant to say to keep her there. His mind was blank. Totally blank. Kate turned back to her horse. He began to feel desperate. He was a grown man, hardworking, some said brilliant when it came to designing, and most women quite frankly threw themselves at him, but Kate calmly gathered the reins of her horse, no weak knees, completely unaffected by his presence. He wiped the sweat suddenly beading on his forehead, leaving a smear of dirt behind.

"Kate." It came out softly.

Danny stuck his head out the window on the driver's side. "Do you want a little help with the old mill, Kate? Matt actually is fairly decent at that sort of thing. He obviously can't drive, and he can't talk, but he's hell on wheels with renovations."

Kate's eyes lit up. "I would love that, Matthew, but I really wouldn't want to presume on our friendship. It would have to be a business arrangement."

Matt hadn't realized she thought of them as friends. Kate rarely spoke to him, other than their strange, brief conversations when they'd run into one another by chance during her high school years. He liked the idea of being friends with her. Every cell in his body went on alert when she was near him, it always happened that way, even when she'd been a teenager and he'd been in his first years of college. Kate had always brought out his protective instincts, but mostly he'd felt he had to protect her from his own attraction to her. That had been distasteful to a man like Matt. He had taken his secret fantasies of her to every foreign country he'd been sent to. She had shared his days and nights in the jungles and deserts, in the worst of situations, and the memory of her had gotten him home. Now, a full-grown man who had fought wars and had more than enough life experience to give him confidence, he found he could speak easily and naturally to any other woman. Only Kate made him tongue-tied. He'd take friendship with her. At least it was a start. "Tell me when you want me to take a look, Kate, and I'll arrange my schedule accordingly. Being my own boss has its advantages."

"Then I'm going to take advantage of your generous offer and ask if you could go out there with me tomorrow afternoon. Do you think you can manage it that soon? I wouldn't ask, but I'm trying to get this project off the ground as soon as possible."

"It sounds great. I'll pick you up at the cliff house around four. You are staying there with your sisters, aren't you?"

Kate nodded and turned to watch the sheriff cruise up behind the pickup truck. Matt watched her face, mainly because he couldn't tear his gaze away from her. Her smile was gracious, friendly even, but he was aware even before he turned his head that the man getting out of the sheriff's cruiser was Jonas Harrington. It occurred to him that he knew Kate far too well, her every expression. And that meant he had spent too much time watching her. Kate was smiling, but she had stiffened just that little bit. She always did that around Jonas. All of her sisters did. For the first time he wondered why Kate reacted that way.

"Well, Kate, I see you caused another accident," Jonas said in greeting. He shook Matt's hand and clapped him on the back. "The Drake sisters have a tendency to wreak havoc everywhere they go." He winked at Matt.

Kate simply lifted an eyebrow. "You've been saying that since we were children."

Jonas leaned over to brush a casual kiss along Kate's cheek. Something black and lethal, whose existence Matt didn't want to recognize, moved inside of him like a dark shadow. He put a blatantly possessive hand on Kate's back.

Jonas ignored Matt's body language. "I'll still be making the same accusation when you're all in your eighties, Kate. Where is everyone?" He looked around as if expecting her sisters to appear galloping over the mountaintop.

"You look a little nervous, Jonas," Danny observed from the safety of the truck. "What'd you do this time? Arrest Hannah and throw her beautiful butt in jail on some trumped-up charge?"

He subsided when Kate turned the full power of her gaze on him. The wind rushed up from the sea, bringing the scent and feel of the ocean. "I had no idea you were so interested in my sister's anatomy, Danny."

"Come on, Kate, she's gorgeous; every man's interested in Hannah's anatomy," Danny pointed out, unrepentant.

"And if she doesn't want them to look, what is she doing allowing every photographer from here to hell and back to take pictures of her?" Jonas demanded. "And just for your information, I wouldn't have to trump up charges if I wanted to arrest Hannah," he added with a black scowl. "I ought to run her in for indecent exposure. That glitzy magazine in Inez's store has her on the cover . . . naked!"

"She is not naked. She's wearing a swimsuit, Jonas, with a sarong over it." Kate sounded as calm as ever, but Matt noted that her hand tightened on the reins of her horse until her knuckles turned white. He moved even closer to her, inserting himself between her and the sheriff.

"She might try a decent one-piece and maybe a robe that went down to her ankles or something. And does she have to strike that stupid pose just to make everyone stare . . . " Jonas broke off as the wind gusted again, howling this time, bringing whispers in the swirling chaos of leaves and droplets of seawater. His hat was swept from his head and carried away from the group. The wind shifted direction, rushing back to the ocean, retreating in much the same manner as a wave from the shore. The sudden breeze took the hat with it, sailing it over the cliffs and into the choppy water below.

Jonas spun around and looked toward the large house set up on the cliffs in the distance. "Damn it, Hannah. That's the third hat I've lost since you've been home." He shouted the words into the vortex of the wind.

There was a small silence. Matt cleared his throat. "Jonas. I don't think she can hear you from here."

Jonas glared at him. "She can hear me. Can't she, Kate? She knows exactly what I'm saying. You tell her this isn't funny anymore. She can stop with her little wind games."

"You believe all the things people say about the Drake sisters, don't you, Jonas?" Danny said. He imitated the opening theme of *The Twilight Zone*.

Matt stared down at Kate's hand. The reins were trembling. He covered her hand with his own, steadying the leather reins she was clenching. "I'll be happy to come look at the mill tomorrow, Kate. Would you like a leg up?"

"Thanks, Matthew. I'd appreciate it."

He didn't bother with cupping his hands together to assist her into the saddle. He simply lifted her. He was tall and strong, and it was easy to swing her onto the horse. She settled into the saddle as if born there. Elegant. Refined. As close to perfection as any dream he could conjure up and just as far out of reach. "I'll see you then. Say hello to your sisters for me."

"I'll do that, Matthew, and you give my best to your parents. It was nice to see you, Danny." Her cool gaze swept over Jonas. "I'm sure you'll be by the house, Jonas."

Jonas shrugged. "I take my job seriously, Kate."

Matt watched her ride away, waiting until a curve in the road took her out of sight before turning on the sheriff. "What the hell was that all about?"

"You know all seven of the Drake women drive me crazy half the time," Jonas said. "I've told you all the trouble they get up to. You're always grilling me about them. Well—" he grinned evilly as he indicated the truck—"Isn't this the third accident you've had with Kate in the vicinity? You should know what I mean."

Jonas had grown up with Matt Granite, had gone through school, joined the Army, the Rangers, and fought side by side with him. He knew how Matt felt about Kate. It was no secret. Matt wasn't very good at hiding his feelings from his family and friends, especially since Jonas had gotten out of the service two years before Matt and Matt had continually interrogated him about Kate's whereabouts and marital status. Matt had been home three years and he'd been waiting for Kate to come home for good, too.

Danny snickered. "You were there back in his college days, Jonas, when he drove Dad's truck into the creek bed and hung it up on a rock. Wasn't Kate about three at the time?"

Matt took a deep breath. He couldn't kill his brother in front of the sheriff, even if it was Jonas. The time he had wrecked his father's truck, driving it without permission, Kate had been about fifteen, far too young for a college man to be looking at her, and he was still embarrassed that his brothers and Jonas had known why he'd wrecked the vehicle. Of course he'd known the Drake sisters, everyone in town knew them, but he'd never *looked* at them. Not in a fascinated, physical, male way. Until he'd seen Kate standing in a creek bed picking blackberries with the sun kissing her hair and her large sea-green eyes looking back at him. The second time he'd wrecked a vehicle had been four years ago. Matt had been home on leave, and he'd been so busy looking at Kate walking on the sidewalk with her sisters, he'd failed to realize he was parked in front of a cement hump and had hung up his mother's car on it when he'd gone to pull out. Now, ignoring his brother's jibe, he moved around the truck to inspect the damage. "I think I can get the truck out without a tow."

"I see you upset old man Mars." Jonas pointed to the tomato smears on the rear window.

"You know Matt, he just had to wish the old man a Merry Christmas." Danny shoved open the door. "He likes to stir the

15

old geezer up right before the pageant. He does it every year. The time Mom made me play the little drummer boy, Mars broke my drumsticks into ten pieces and threw them on the ground and then jumped up and down on them. All my brothers got a kick out of that, but I've been traumatized ever since. I have nightmares about being stomped by him."

Jonas laughed. "Mars is a strange old man, but he's harmless enough. And he gives away most of his produce to the people who need it. He takes it to some of the single moms in town and some of the elderly couples. And I know he feeds the Ruttermyer boy, the one with Down's syndrome who works at odd jobs for everyone. He persuaded Donna to give the boy a room right next to her gift shop. I know he helps that boy with his bills."

"Yeah, deep down he's a good man," Matt agreed. A slow grin spread over his face. "He just hates Christmas." He nodded toward the other side of the truck, and the other two men went to the front to scrape away the mud and dirt and push until they separated the bumper from the embankment. "I didn't appreciate you saying anything to Kate about her and her sisters being different, Jonas." Matt said it in a low voice, but Jonas and he had been friends since they were boys, and Jonas recognized the warning tone.

"I'm not going to pretend they're like everyone else, Matt, not even for you," Jonas snapped. "The Drakes are special. They have gifts, and they use themselves up for everyone else without a thought for themselves or their own safety. I'm going to watch out for them whether they like or it not. Sarah Drake nearly got herself killed a few weeks ago. Hannah and Kate and Abbey were with her and also might have been killed."

Matt felt the words as a blow somewhere in the vicinity of his gut. His heart did a curious somersaulting dive in his chest. "I heard about Sarah, but I hadn't heard the others were there. What happened?"

"To make a long story short, Wilder had people trail him here. They wanted information only he could give them. He helped design our national defense system, and the government wanted him protected at all costs. With Sarah being from Sea Haven, it was natural enough for the Feds to send her in to guard him. These people had gotten their hands on him once before, killed his assistant right in front of him, and tortured him. That's why he uses a cane when he walks. They broke into the Drakes' house, armed to the teeth when he was there, and were ready to kill Wilder and the Drakes to get what they wanted." The anger in Jonas's voice deepened.

"No one said a word about Kate being in the house at the same time. I knew Sarah was guarding Damon Wilder and that he was a defense expert in some kind of trouble, but . . . " Matt trailed off as he looked back toward the house on the cliff. It was covered with Christmas lights. Beside it was a tall full Douglas fir tree, completely decorated and flashing lights even before the sun went down. When he looked toward the house he felt a sense of peace. Of tightness. The Drake sisters were the town's treasures. He looked away from the cliff toward the old mill. It was farther up the road, built over Sea Lion Cove. A strange cloud formation hung over the small inlet and spread slowly toward land. The shape captured his imagination, a yawning black mouth, jaws opening wide, heading straight for them.

"All of them were nearly murdered," Jonas said. His eyes went

17

flat and cold. "The Drakes take on far too much, and everyone just expects them to do it without thinking of the cost to them."

"I never thought of it like that, Jonas. Now that you mention it, I've seen them all drained of energy after helping out the way they do." Matt didn't take his eyes from the sky. He watched a seagull veer frantically from the path of the slow-moving cloud, braking sharply in midair, wings flapping strongly in agitation. Wisps of fog began to rise from the sea and drift toward shore. "Maybe we all should pay more attention to what's happening with them," he murmured softly, more to himself than to the others.

Chapter Two

The snowglobe they hold has a secret inside.
Where the mists roll in place of the snow that's outside.

Inhaling the mingled scents of cinnamon and pine, Kate wandered into the kitchen of the cliff house. The sound of Christmas music filled the air and blended with the aroma of fresh-baked cookies and the fragrance of richly scented candles. "Is that Joley's voice?" Kate asked, leaning her hip comfortably against the heavily carved wood cabinet. "When did she make a Christmas collection?"

Hannah Drake spun around, teakettle in her hands. Her abundance of blond hair shimmered for a moment in the last rays of sunshine pouring through the bay window. "Kate, I didn't hear you get out of the shower. I think I was in my own little world. Joley sent the CD as a surprise, although she made a point of saying it was not to go out of the family."

They both laughed affectionately. "Joley and that band of hers. She can sing just about anything from gospel to blues, from

19

rock to rap, but she's so careful not to let anyone know. I think she likes her bad girl image. Did she mention whether she's coming home for Christmas? I know she was touring."

Hannah's face lit up, her smile brilliant. "She's going to try. I can't wait to see her. We keep missing each other in our travels."

"I hope she gets here soon. Talking on the phone just isn't the same as all of us being together." Kate swept a stray tendril of hair behind her ear. "What about Mom and Dad? Has anyone heard from them? Are they coming here for Christmas?"

Hannah shook her head. "Last I heard they sent kisses and hugs and were snuggling together in their little chalet in the Swiss Alps. Libby got in a quick visit with them before she headed out to the Congo. She said she was coming home for Christmas. Mom and Dad promised next year they'd be here with us."

Kate laughed softly as she leaned over to sniff the canister of loose tea. "Mom and Dad are still such lovebirds. What are you making?"

"I was in the mood for a little lavender, but anything is fine." Hannah scrutinized Kate closely. "But let's go with chamomile. Something soothing."

Kate smiled. "You think I need a little soothing?"

Hannah nodded as she measured the tea into a small pot. "Tell me."

"I ran into Matthew Granite and his brother Danny." Kate tried to sound casual, when her entire body was trembling. Only Matt could do that to her. Only Matt moved her. She'd never understood why.

"Matthew Granite? I thought that might be him." Hannah's

huge blue eyes settled on her sister with compassion and interest. "How did he seem?"

Kate shrugged her slender shoulders. "Wonderful. Helpful. He offered to look at the old mill for me and help with the renovations." She always enjoyed looking at her younger sister. Hannah wasn't just beautiful, she was strikingly so, exotically so, with her bone structure, abundance of pale, almost platinum hair, her enormous, heavily lashed eyes, and sultry lips. Beauty radiated from her. Kate had always thought Hannah's extraordinary beauty came from the inside out. She watched the graceful movements of Hannah's hands as she went about making tea. "Mart's always so helpful." She sighed.

Hannah reached out to her, clasping Kate's hands in a gesture of solidarity. "Was it the same?"

"You mean with his brothers laughing all the time? Well, only one was with him, Danny." Color crept up under Kate's skin. "Yes, of course. Every time I get anywhere near the Granites they all laugh. I have no idea why. It isn't the same way Jonas is with you. Matthew never needles me. He's always perfectly polite, but I seem to have some humorous effect on his family. I try as hard as I can just to be polite and calm, but the brothers laugh until I want to go check a mirror to see if I have spinach in my teeth. Matthew just glares at them, but it really draws attention to all the silly things I do in front of him." She squeezed Hannah's fingers before letting her hand go. "I've showered and changed, but I came home with my clothes covered with dirt. Poor Matthew just came from work, was dusting himself off, and I had to be two steps behind him. When he tried to open his truck door, of course I managed to get too close."

"Oh, Katie, honey, I'm so sorry. What happened?" Hannah's face mirrored her sister's distress.

Kate shrugged. "The door nearly knocked me over, and he had to apologize yet again. The poor man spends every minute apologizing to me. I'll bet he wishes he never had to see me again."

"No he doesn't," Hannah said firmly. "I think he's always been sweet on you."

Kate sighed. "You and I both know Matthew Granite would never look at me twice. He's wild and rough and an adrenaline junkie. He played every sport in high school and college. He joined the Rangers. I researched what they do. Even their creed is a bit frightening. They arrive at the 'cutting edge of battle' and they never fail their comrades and give more than one hundred percent. The creed says things like fight on even if you're the lone survivor, and *surrender* is not a Ranger word." She shuddered delicately. "He's a wild man, and he does very scary wild things. He's going to look at women who climb mountains and scoff in the face of danger. Can you see me doing that?"

"Kate," Hannah said softly, "maybe he's more settled now. He went out and did his save the world thing and now he's come home and he's working the family business. He could have changed."

Kate forced a fleeting smile. "Men like Matthew don't change, Hannah. I was telling you my tale of woe. We were just at the point where Jonas drove up. You know how he has to make his little 'Drake sisters' comments. He implied every time I was around something awful happened. It just made the situation worse." She sighed again. "I tried to look as though it didn't bother me, but I think Matthew knew."

"Jonas Harrington needs to fall into the ocean and have a nice hungry shark come swimming by." Hannah dragged the whistling teakettle from the stove and splashed water into the teapot, a fine fury radiating from her at the thought of Jonas Harrington saying anything to upset Kate. The water boiled in the little china teapot, bubbles roiling and bursting with a steady fury. Steam rose.

Kate covered the top of the teapot with her palm, settling the water back down. "You were out on the captain's walk."

Hannah nodded, unrepentant. "The earthquake bothered me. I felt something rising beneath the earth. I can't explain it, Kate, but it frightened me. I was sitting here listening to Joley's Christmas music, you know how much I love Christmas, then I felt the quake. Almost on the heels of it, something else disturbed the earth. I felt it as a darkness rising upward. I knew you were out riding, so I went out to the walk to make certain you weren't in trouble."

"And you felt the wind come in off the sea," Kate said. She leaned her hip against the counter. "I felt it too." She frowned and drummed her fingers on the tiled counter. "I smelled something, Hannah, something old and bitter in the wind."

"Evil?" Hannah ventured.

Kate shook her head slowly. "It wasn't that exactly. Well," she hedged, "maybe. I don't know. What did you think?"

Hannah leaned against the brightly tiled sink, her body so graceful the casual movement seemed balletic. "I honestly don't know, Kate, but it isn't good. I've felt disturbed ever since the earthquake and when I looked at the mosaic, there was a black shadow beneath the ground. I could barely make it out because it seemed to move and not stay in one place."

Kate glanced at the floor in the house's entryway. Her grandmother, along with her grandmother's six sisters, had made the mosaic, women of power and magic, seven sisters creating a timeless floor of infinite beauty. To most people it was simply a unique floor, but the Drake sisters could read many things in the ever-changing shadows that ran within it. "How very strange that neither of us knows precisely whether the disturbance is evil." She shrugged her shoulders and drew in a deep breath filled with cinnamon and pine. "I love the fragrances of Christmas." She tapped her foot, a small smile hovering on her face.

"You're holding back on me," Hannah guessed, her voice suddenly teasing. "Something else happened, didn't it?"

"When the earthquake started, Matthew put his arm around me to steady me, and we just stood there, even after it was over." She grinned at Hannah. "He is so strong. You have no idea. That man is all muscle. It's a wonder I didn't end up in a puddle at his feet! But I managed to look cool and serene."

Hannah pretended to swoon. "I wish I could have seen it. Matthew is definitely hot, even if he is a Neanderthal. I must have come up on the captain's walk just after that, just in time to see the slimy toad of the world arrive in his little sheriff's car." She smirked. "Too bad the wind came up, and his precious little hat went sailing out to sea."

"Shame on you, Hannah," Kate scolded halfheartedly. "Jonas means well. He's just so used to everyone doing everything he says, and we always seem to be in the middle of any kind of trouble in Sea Haven. You're beginning to enjoy tormenting him."

"Why shouldn't I? He's tormented me for years."

There was so much pain in Hannah's voice that Kate slipped her arm around her sister's waist to comfort her. Jonas had known them all since they were children, and he'd never understood Hannah. She'd been an extraordinarily beautiful, very intelligent child, but she'd been so painfully shy outside of her own home, the sisters had had to work their magic just to get her to school every day. Jonas had been certain she was haughty, when in fact, she'd rarely been able to speak in public. "Well, all in all, it was a good day. You managed to lose another hat for Jonas, and I got to be up close and personal with the hottest man in Sea Haven." Kate hugged Hannah before pouring herself a cup of tea and walking into the living room with it.

Hannah followed her. "Did you get your manuscript mailed off?"

Kate nodded. "Murder and mayhem will prevail in a small coastal town. I forgot to put the tea cozy back on the pot, will you do it?"

Hannah glanced into the kitchen and lifted her arms.

When Kate looked back, the cozy was safely on the teapot. "Thanks, Hannah. I do have to say, Jonas was invaluable to me with the research."

"I know he was, but don't credit him with doing it to be nice or anything." Hannah's large blue eyes reflected her laughter. "He was trying to get on your good side so you'd persuade me to stop messing around with his precious hats."

They both swung around as the front door burst open.

Abigail Drake rushed in, a small woman with dark eyes and a wealth of red-gold hair spilling down her back in a thick pony-tail. Her face was flushed and her eyes over-bright. The moment she glimpsed her sisters, she burst into tears.

"Abbey!" Hannah set her teacup down on the highly polished coffee table. "What is it? You never cry."

"I humiliated myself in front of the entire Christmas pageant committee," Abigail said miserably. She threw herself into the overstuffed armchair, curled her feet under her, and covered her face with her hands. "I can never face any of them again."

Hannah and Kate rushed to her side, both putting their arms around her. "Don't cry, Abbey. What happened? Maybe we can fix it. It can't be that bad."

"It was bad," Abigail muttered from between her fingers. "I accidentally used *the voice*. I wasn't paying attention. There was the earthquake, and I was so distracted because I felt something under us, something moving just below the surface seeking a way out. I *felt* it." Of all the talents gifted to the sisters, Abigail felt hers was the worst. Her voice could be used to extract the truth from people around her. As a child, before she'd learned to control the tone and the wording of her sentences, she'd been very unpopular with her classmates. They would often blurt out the truth of some escapade to their parents or a teacher whenever they were in her presence. Abigail pulled her hands down and stared at them with her sad eyes. "It isn't an excuse. I'm not a teenager. I know I have to be alert all the time."

Hannah and Kate exchanged a long, fearful look. "We felt the shadow too, Abbey. It was very disconcerting to both of us. What happened at the meeting?"

Abbey drew her legs up tighter into her body. "We were all discussing the Christmas pageant." She rubbed her chin on the top of her knees. "I felt the rift in the earth, a blackness welling up, and the next thing I knew I was asking for the truth." She clapped her hands over her ears. "I got the truth too. Everyone did. Bruce Harper is having an affair with Mason Fredrickson's wife. They were all in the room. Bruce and Mason got in a terrible fistfight, and Letty Harper burst into tears and ran out. She's six months pregnant. Sylvia Fredrickson slapped me across the face and walked out, leaving me standing there with everyone looking at me." She burst into tears all over again.

Kate frowned as she rubbed her sister's shoulders. She could feel the waves of distress pouring off of Abigail. "It's all right now, honey. You're home, and you're safe." At once a soothing tranquillity swept into the room, a sense of peace. The wicks on the unlit candles on the mantel leapt to life with bright orange-red flames. Joley's voice poured into the room, uplifting and melodic, bringing with it a sense of home and Christmas cheer. Kate leaned into her sister. "Abigail, your talent is a tremendous gift, and you have always used it for good. This was a distortion of your talent, not something any of us could have foreseen. Let it go. Just breathe and let it go."

Abbey managed a small smile, the sobs fading at the sound of her sister's voice. Kate the peacemaker. Most thought she prevented fights and solved problems, but in truth, she had a magic about her, a tranquillity and inner peace she shared with others just by the way she spoke. "I wish I had your gift, Kate," Abbey said. She pressed her hand to her cheek. "I didn't mind everyone's finding out about Sylvia—she likes to think she can get

27

any man—but poor little Letty, pregnant and loving her stupid unfaithful husband so much. That was heartbreaking. And at Christmas too. What possessed me to be so careless? I'm so ashamed of myself."

"What exactly did you say, Abbey?" Kate asked.

Abbey looked confused. "Everyone had put in a variety of ideas for acting out the play we do every year and someone asked if they really liked the old script and should we keep it as a tradition or should we modernize it. I think I said, now would be a good time to tell the truth if you want to make any major changes. I meant with the script, not in people's lives." She rubbed her temples. "I haven't made a mistake like that since I was a teenager. I'm so careful to avoid the word *truth*." She scrubbed her hand over her face a second time, trying to erase the sting of Sylvia's hand. "You know if I use that word everyone in the immediate vicinity tells the truth about everything."

"It worries me that we all felt the same disturbance," Kate said. "Hannah saw a dark shadow in the mosaic. You said something you would never have normally said, and a crack opened up nearly at my feet and ran all the way up the embankment."

Hannah gasped. "You didn't tell me that. Kate, it could have been an attack on you. You're the most ... " She broke off, looking at Abbey.

Kate lifted her chin. "I'm the most what?"

Hannah shrugged. "You're the best of us. You don't have a mean bone in your body. You just don't, Katie. I'm sorry, I know you hate our saying that, but you don't even know how to dislike someone. You're just so ... "

"*Don't* say perfect," Kate warned. "I'm not perfect. And I

think that's why Matthew's brothers always laugh at me. They think I want to be perfect and fall short."

Hannah and Abbey exchanged a long, worried look. "I think we should call the others," Hannah said. "Sarah will want to know about this. She must have felt the earthquake too. We can ask her if anything strange happened to her. And we should call Joley, Libby, and Elle. Something's wrong, Kate, I just feel it. It's as if the earthquake unleashed a malicious force. I'm afraid it could be directed at you."

Kate took a long sip of tea. The taste was as soothing as the aroma. "Go ahead, it can't hurt to see what the others have to say. I'm not going to worry about it. I didn't feel a direct threat. I'm not calling Sarah though. She and Damon are probably twined around one another. You can feel the heat right through the telephone line."

"I can go to the captain's walk and signal her," Hannah said wickedly. "Their bedroom window faces us, and for some utterly mysterious reason the curtain keeps opening in that particular room."

"Hannah!" Kate tried not to laugh. "You're impossible."

Hannah did laugh. "And you are perfect whether you want to acknowledge it or not. At least to me."

"And me," Abigail said.

Kate smiled at them. "I'm not all that perfect. I'd like to give Sylvia Fredrickson a piece of mind. She had no right hitting you, Abbey. Even in high school she was nasty."

"I'll take care of Sylvia," Hannah said. "Don't worry, Abbey. She'll spend a long time thinking about how stupid it was to hit you."

"Hannah!" Kate and Abbey chorused her name in protest.

Hannah burst out laughing. "I get the message, Kate. You'll talk to Sylvia, but you don't want me casting in her direction."

Kate grinned. "I should have known you were baiting me."

"Who said I didn't mean it? Sylvia gives women a bad name."

Kate shook her head. "Hannah Drake, you're becoming a bloodthirsty little witch. I think Jonas is having a bad influence on you." She touched Abbey's cheek gently. "Even for this we can't use our gifts for anything other than good."

Hannah made a face. "It's good for Jonas to have to chase his hat. It keeps him from becoming too arrogant and bossy. And who knows what great lesson Sylvia Fredrickson would learn if I tweaked her just a little bit." Before either sister could say anything, she laughed softly. "I'm not going to do anything horrible to her, I just love to see you both get that 'there-goes-Hannah-look' on your faces."

Kate nudged Abbey, ignoring Hannah's mischievous grin. "Guess what I'll be doing tomorrow? Matthew Granite agreed to look over the mill with me tomorrow. I'm hoping none of his brothers will be around to laugh at me, and maybe he'll notice I'm a grown woman, not a gawky teenager. You'd think the fact that I've traveled all over the world and that I'm a successful author would impress him, but he just looks at me exactly the same way he did when I was in high school."

Hannah and Abbey exchanged a quick, apprehensive look. "Kate, you're going to spend the afternoon with him? Do you really want to do that?" Abigail asked.

Kate nodded. "I like to be with him. Don't ask me why, I just do."

"Kate, you haven't been home in ages. Matthew has a certain reputation," Abigail said hesitantly. "He's always been easygoing with you, and he's very charming, but he's . . . " She trailed off and looked to Hannah for direction.

"What? A ladies' man? I would presume a man his age has dated." Kate walked across the room to touch the first of the seven stockings hung in a row along the mantelpiece. It allowed her to keep her expression hidden from her sisters. "I know he's been in relationships."

"That's just it, Kate. He doesn't have relationships. At best he has one-night stands. Women find him charming and mysterious, and he finds them annoying. Seriously, Kate, don't *really* fall for him. He looks great on the outside, but he has a caveman attitude. He was in the military so long, doing all the secret Special Forces kind of stuff, and he just expects everyone to fall in line with his orders. It's probably why he isn't impressed with your world travels. Please don't fall for him," Hannah pleaded. "I couldn't bear it if he hurt you, Kate."

"You're so certain he wouldn't fall for me? A few minutes ago you were saying you thought he might be sweet on me." Kate tried to guard her voice, to keep her tone strictly neutral when there was a peculiar ache inside. "I really don't need the warning. Men like Matthew don't look at women like me." She shrugged. "It doesn't bother me. I need solitude, I always have. And I don't have a tremendous amount of time to give to a relationship."

"What do you mean, Matthew wouldn't look at a woman

like you?" Abbey was outraged. "What are you talking about, Kate?"

Kate took another sip of tea and smiled at her sisters over the rim of her teacup. "Don't worry, I'm not feeling sorry for myself. I know I'm different. I was born the way I am. All of you stand out. Your looks, your personalities, even you, Hannah, with being so painfully shy, you embrace life. You all live it. You don't let your weaknesses or failings stand in your way. I'm an observer. I read about life. I research life. I find a corner in a room and melt into it. I can become invisible. It's an art, and I am a wonderful practitioner."

"You travel all over the world, Kate," Hannah pointed out.

"Yes, and my agent and my publisher smooth the way for me. I don't have to ask for a thing, it's all done for me. Matthew is like all of you. He throws himself into life and lives every moment. He's a born hero, riding to the rescue, carrying out the wounded on his back. He needs someone willing to do the same. I'm a born observer. Maybe that's why I was given the ability to see into the shadows at times. A part of me is already there."

Hannah's blue eyes filled with tears. "Don't say that, Kate. Don't ever say that." She wrapped her arms around Kate and hugged her close, uncaring that a small amount of tea splashed on her. "I didn't know you felt that way. How could I not have known?"

Kate hugged her hard. "Honey, don't be upset for me. You don't understand. I'm not distressed about it. My world is books. It always has been. I love words. I love living in my imagination. I don't want to go climb a mountain. I love to study how it's done. I love to talk to people who do it, but I don't want the experience of it, the reality of it. My imagination provides a wonderful adventure without the risk or the discomfort."

"Katie," Abbey protested.

"It's the truth. I've always been attracted to Matthew Granite, but I'm far too practical to make the mistake of believing anything could ever work between us. He runs wild. I remember him being right in the middle of every rough play in football both in high school and in college. He's done so many crazy things, from serving as a Ranger to skydiving for the fun of it." She shuddered. "I don't even scuba dive. He goes white-water rafting and rock climbing for relaxation. I read a good book. We aren't in the least compatible, but I can still think he's hot."

"Are you certain you want to spend time with him?" Abbey asked.

Kate shrugged. "What I want to do is to take a look at the mosaic and see if I can make out the shadows in the earth the way Hannah did."

"Maybe all three of us can figure out what is going on," Hannah agreed. She followed Kate to the entry-way, glancing over her shoulder at Abigail. "Doesn't Joley sound beautiful? She sent us her Christmas CD. She said she might be able to make it home for Christmas."

"I hope so," Abbey said. "Did Elle or Libby call?"

"Libby is in South America," Hannah said.

"I thought you said she was in the Congo," Kate interrupted.

Hannah laughed. "She *was* in the Congo, but they called her to South America. She phoned right after the quake. Some small tribe in the rain forest has some puzzling disease and they asked Libby to fly there immediately to help and of course she did. She said it will be difficult, but no matter what, she's coming home for Christmas. I think she needs to be with us. She sounded tired. Really tired. I told her we would get together and see if we could send her some energy, but she said no. She told me to conserve our strength and be very careful," Hannah reported.

Abbey and Kate stopped walking abruptly. "Are you certain Libby doesn't need us, Hannah?" Kate asked. "You know what can happen to her. She heals people in the worst of circumstances, and it thoroughly depletes her energy. Traveling those distances on top of it with little sleep won't help."

"She said no," Hannah reiterated. "I heard the weariness in her voice. She obviously needs to come home and regroup and rest, but I didn't feel as if she was in a dangerous state." She knelt on the floor at the foot of the mosaic her grandmother and her grandmother's sisters had worked so hard to make.

Relief swept through Kate. Libby always drove herself too hard, and her health suffered dramatically for it. Libby was too small, too slender, a fragile woman who pushed herself for others. Libby worked for the Center for Disease Control and traveled all over the globe. "We'll have to watch her," Kate said softly, musing aloud.

It was one of the best-loved talents of the sisters, to be able to stay in communication with one another no matter how far apart they were physically. They could 'see' one another and send energy back and forth when it was needed. Kate knelt beside Hannah in the entry-way.

Kate always felt a sense of awe when she looked at the

artwork on the floor. The mosaic always seemed to her to be alive with energy. Anyone looking into the mosaic felt as if they were falling into another world. The deep blue of the sea was really the ocean in the sky. Stars burst and flared into life. The moon was a shining ball of silver. Kate bent close to the mosaic to examine the greens, browns, and grays that made up mother earth.

Only Joley's voice poured into the room, then melted away on the last notes to leave the room entirely silent. The three sisters linked hands. Small bursts of electricity arced from one to the other. In the dimly lit room the energy appeared as a jagged whip of lightning dancing between the three women. Power filled the room, energy enough to move the drapes at the windows so that the material swayed and bowed.

Kate kept her eyes fixed on the darker earth tones. Something moved, down close to the edge of the mosaic, in the deeper rocks. It moved slowly, a blackened shadow, slipping from one dark area to the next. It had a serpentine, cunning way about it, shifting from the edges up toward the surface as if trying to break through. Kate let her breath out slowly, inhaled deeply to fill her lungs, and let her body go. It was the only way to walk in the shadow world that was invisible to most human eyes.

She felt the malevolence immediately, a twisted sneakiness, shrewd and determined, a being honed by rage and fueled by the need for revenge. The turmoil was overwhelming, spinning and boiling with heat and anger. It crept closer to her, awareness of her presence giving it a kind of malicious glee. She held herself still, trying to discern the dark force in the deeper shadows, but it blended too well.

"Kate!" Hannah shook her hard, catching her by the shoulders and rocking her until her head lolled back on her neck.

Abbey yanked Kate away from the mosaic and into her own body. There was a long silence while they clung to one another, breathing heavily, close to tears. The shrill ringing of the phone startled them.

"Sarah," they said simultaneously, and broke into relieved laughter.

Abbey jumped up to answer the phone. "I'm telling Sarah on you," she warned Kate, "and you're going to be in so much trouble!"

Kate gripped Hannah's hand, trying to smile at Abbey's dire prediction. "Did you feel it, Hannah?" she whispered. "Did you feel it coming after me?"

"You can't go into that world again, Kate. Not with that thing there. I couldn't read what it was, but you have to stay away from it." Hannah held Kate even tighter. "I know what it's like to be afraid all the time, Katie. I can't function in a crowd because the energy of so many people drains me. Their emotions bombard me until I can't think or breathe. You all protect me, you always have. I wish we'd done the same for you."

Kate smiled and leaned over to kiss Hannah's cheek. "I accepted my limitations a long time ago, Hannah, and I've never regretted my choice of lifestyles. I control my environment, and it works for me. I didn't have the need to do all the things you wanted to do with your life. My world is carefully built and has large walls to protect me. You're far more open to the assault. I'll be careful, Hannah. I'm not a risk taker. You don't have to worry that I'll try to find the answers without the rest of you."

"Katie!" Abbey called out. "Sarah has a few things she wants to talk to you about." She held out the phone.

Kate hugged Hannah again. "It will be all right, I promise you, honey. It's Christmas. Most everyone is coming home, and we'll have the best time ever, just like we always do when we're together."

Chapter Three

A chill, colder still than the air they will feel,
As I rejoice in release, as I slip past the seal

Matt stood beside the enormous Douglas fir tree decorated with hundreds of ornaments and colorful lights. The tall tree grew in the yard up near the cliffs in front of the house. It was one of the most beautiful sights he'd ever seen, but it paled in comparison to Kate. She stood on her porch, a snowglobe in her hands, smiling at him. Her eyes were as green as the sea, and her long, thick hair was twisted into some kind of intricate knot that made him want to pull out every pin so he could watch it tumble free.

He walked up the porch steps and held out his hand. "Where in the world did you get that snowglobe? The scene inside looks exactly like your house and this Christmas tree."

She put the globe in his hands. Two of her sisters were standing on the porch with her, watching him with serious expressions on their faces. He had been so busy staring at Kate he hadn't even noticed them. His hands closed over the heavy globe, his fingers brushing Kate's. A tingle of electricity sparked its way up his arm. Almost at once the snowglobe grew warm in his hands. "Afternoon, ladies."

"Hi, Matt," Hannah greeted. Abbey nodded to him.

Although he'd made every effort to clean up after work, scrubbing his hands for a good half hour to get the dirt out from under his fingernails, he noticed with dismay that he hadn't been successful. His nails seemed to be spotlighted from the strange glow coming from inside the glass of the globe. The lights of the tree blazed unexpectedly inside the glass, while an eerie white fog began to swirl. Fascinated, he held the globe at every angle, trying to see how he had turned it on, but he couldn't find a battery or a switch anywhere. Peering closer he noticed a strange dark shadow taking shape at the base of the tree and creeping up the path toward the steps of the house. His body reacted, going on alert as he watched the shadow move stealthily.

"This thing is spooky." He handed the snowglobe to Hannah and took Kate's elbow in a deliberate, proprietary action. Staking his claim. Declaring his intentions. His fingers settled around her slender arm, and his heart actually jumped in his chest. She was wearing some lacy white shirt that clung to the shape of her rounded breasts and left her lower arms bare. The pad of his thumb slid over her petal-soft skin just to feel the texture. She shivered, and he moved his body closer to block the breeze coming in off the ocean. They said good-bye to her sisters and headed for his car.

Kate cleared her throat. "I appreciate your coming to pick me up, Matthew. I could have met you there."

"That's silly, Kate, since we're both going to the same place, and you're on my way. I thought we might discuss the plans for the renovation over dinner when we're finished inspecting the mill." He pulled open the door to his Mustang convertible. The top was securely up. "What were you doing with the globe?"

She smiled up at him and just that easily took his breath away. "We're still putting out our decorations. Hannah just brought the globe down from the attic and was cleaning the glass. It's a Christmas tradition in our family to wish on it."

"What was that strange dark shadow moving in the globe?"

Kate abruptly turned back toward the house. Matt was standing close to her, holding the door open to the Mustang, and she bumped his chest with her nose. For a second she stood there with her eyes closed, then she inhaled deeply. He felt that breath right through his skin, all the way down to his bones. The tips of her breasts brushed his rib cage sending fire racing through his bloodstream and pooling into a thick heat low in his belly. She smelled of cinnamon and spice. He wanted to pull her into his arms and kiss her right there. Right in front of her sisters.

"Matthew." For the first time that he could remember, Kate sounded breathless. "What are you doing?"

He realized his arms were around her. He was holding her captive against him, and his body was growing hard and making urgent demands. He cursed silently and let her go, turning away from her. "I thought you were getting into the car." His voice was rough, even to his own ears. He had never wanted a woman the way he wanted Kate. He didn't feel gentle when he wanted to be gentle. He didn't feel nice and charming when it was usually so easy for him to be charming. He felt edgy and restless

40

and achy as hell. He had a mad desire to scoop her up and lock her in his vehicle, a primitive, out-of-character urge when she looked on the verge of flight.

"You really saw a shadow in the globe?" she asked. "What was it doing?"

It was the last thing he expected her to say, and it sent a chill skittering down his spine. "I couldn't tell what it was. The dark shadow went from the base of the tree up the path toward the porch of the house. It is your house in the globe, isn't it? There's fog or mist instead of snowflakes swirling around. It gives the globe a very eerie effect."

Kate glanced back at her sisters. Hannah set the snowglobe very carefully on the wide banister and stepped away from it. Inside the glass, heavy fog swirled. The lights from the tiny Christmas tree glowed a strange orange and red through the mist, almost as if on fire. Matt watched Kate's sister closely. He had lived in Sea Haven all of his life. He had heard strange things about the Drake sisters. Up close to them, he *felt* power and energy crackling in the air, and it emanated from them. The power filled the space around them until he breathed it. Hannah lifted her arms, and the wind swept in from the sea. With it came soft voices, whose words were impossible to distinguish, but the chant was melodious and in harmony with the things of the earth. The strange light in the snowglobe faded and diminished until it was a soft, faint glow. The voices on the wind continued until the lights behind the glass flickered and vanished, leaving the globe a perfectly ordinary Christmas ornament.

The wind swirled cool air around them. Matt tasted the salt from the sea. He looked down at his fingers curled around

Kate's arm. He had pulled her protectively to him without thought or reason. He knew he should release her, but he couldn't let go. Her slender body trembled, with power or with fear, Matt wasn't certain which, but it didn't matter to him.

Kate looked up at him. "I can't explain what just happened with the snowglobe."

"I'm not asking for an explanation. I just want you to get in my car."

She smiled up at him. "Thank you, Matthew. I really appreciate it." She relaxed visibly and allowed him to help her into the warm leather seats.

Kate felt very small beside Matt. Inside the car, he appeared enormous and powerful. His shoulders were wide enough to brush against her in the confines of the Mustang. When she inhaled, she took the masculine scent of him deep into her lungs. For a moment she felt dizzy. It made her want to laugh aloud at the thought. Kate Drake dizzy from the scent of a man. None of her sisters would believe it. The car handled the tight turns along the coastal highway with precision and ease, flowing around the corners so that she relaxed a little. Being around Matt always made her feel safe. She didn't know why, but she no longer questioned it.

He glanced over at her. "Does it bother you, the way people are always talking about your family?"

"They talk in a nice way," Kate pointed out.

"I know they do. You're the town's treasures, but does it bother you?"

Kate smiled at him. "Only you would ask me that question."

She sighed. "It shouldn't bother me. We are different. We can't exactly hide it, and of course people are going to talk about our strange ways. We grew up here, so everyone knows us and to some extent they protect us from outsiders, but yes, it does bother me that people are always so aware of us when we're around." She'd never voiced that aloud to anyone, not even her sisters.

"I miss you when you're gallivanting around the world, Kate. I'm glad you've decided to come home."

Her smile widened. "You're such a flirt, Matthew, even with me, and I've known you all of my life. You haven't calmed down much since your wild college days. When I was in high school, all the girls said you were legendary at Stanford."

"Well, I wasn't. I should have gone to a college far away from here instead of only a couple of hours. It might have cut down on the talk. And I don't flirt," he said firmly. He wanted to park the car and just look at her. Touch her soft skin and kiss her for hours. The moment the thoughts crept into his head his body hardened into a dull, painful ache. He couldn't get near her without it happening. He was a grown man, and his body responded to her as if he were an adolescent.

"Matthew, you flirt with everyone. And your reputation is terrible. If I wasn't already so talked about, I'd be worried."

"No one talks about me."

She laughed softly. "I can relate the story of you and Janice Carlton by heart, I've heard it so many times."

He groaned. "Is that still going around? That happened long ago. I was on leave, it must have been what? Six years ago? I did pick her up in the bar, she was drunk, Kate. I couldn't just leave her there."

43

"And how did her blouse get on the bushes outside the grocery store?"

Matt glanced sideways at her. "All right, I'll admit it was her blouse, but come on, Kate, I wasn't in high school. Give me a little credit for growing up. She was as drunk as a skunk and began peeling off her clothes the minute we were driving down the street. She threw her blouse out the window and would have thrown her bra but I told her I'd put her out on the sidewalk if she did. I took her straight home. And in case you want to know why my version was never told, I don't like talking about women who throw themselves at me when they're drunk. In spite of what you've heard, my mother raised me to be a gentleman. We may be a little rough around the edges, but the Granites have a code of honor."

The Mustang swung fluidly into the driveway leading to the old mill on the cliff above Sea Lion Cove. Matt drove straight up the dirt driveway to the long, wooden building and parked. He turned off the engine and slid his arm along the back of her seat. The ocean boomed below the cliffs, a timeless rhythm that seemed to echo the beat of his heart. "Most of the stories about me aren't true, Kate."

Kate stared straight ahead at the old building. Much of the wood was pitted from sea salt. The paint had long since worn away from the steady assault of the wind. She loved the look of the mill, the way it fit there on the cliff, a part of the past she wanted to bring with her into the future. She took a deep breath, composed herself, and turned to take Matt in.

Up close, Matthew Granite was a giant of a man with rippling, defined muscles and a strong, stubborn jaw. His mouth was something she spent far too much time staring at and dreaming about, and the shape of it had managed to slip into her bestselling novels on several heroes. His eyes were amazing. They should have been gray but they were more silver, a startling color that made her heart do triple time. He had the kind of thick, dark hair that made her want to run her fingers in it, and he wore it longer than most men. Kate felt a bit faint looking at his heavily muscled chest, then up into his glinting silver eyes. "Well, darn it, Matthew, all this time I thought I was in the presence of greatness." She managed to conjure up a lighthearted laugh. "It's not nice to destroy a woman's illusions."

He frowned. "I didn't say I *wasn't* the bad boy of Sea Haven."

"I thought Jonas Harrington was the bad boy of Sea Haven."

Matt looked affronted. "I never come in second place." His hand came up, unexpectedly spanning her throat.

Kate was certain her heart skipped a beat. His palm was large, and his fingers wrapped easily around her neck, his thumb tipping her head up so she was forced to meet the sudden hunger blazing in his eyes. It was the last thing Kate expected to see, and his intensity shocked her. "Matthew." She breathed his name in a small protest. It wasn't a good idea. They weren't a good idea.

He simply lowered his head and took possession of her mouth. His kiss was anything but gentle. He dragged her close, a starving man devouring her with hot, urgent kisses. The breath slammed out of her lungs, and every nerve ending in her body screamed at her. Electricity crackled between them, arcing from Matt to Kate and back again. Fire raced over her skin, melting her insides. He took the lead, kissing her hungrily, hotly, his tongue dueling with hers, demanding a response she found herself giving.

Her arms crept around his neck, her body pressing close to the heat of his. She felt so much heat, so much magic she couldn't think straight.

The blare of a horn made Kate jump away from him. Matt cursed and glanced at the highway in time to see his brothers waving, hooting, and honking as they drove by. "Damned idiots," he said, but there was a wealth of affection in his voice impossible to miss.

Kate pressed a trembling hand to her swollen mouth. Her skin felt raw and burned from the dark shadow on his jaw. She didn't dare look in the mirror, but she knew she looked thoroughly kissed. "They saved us."

"They may have saved you, but I'm in dire straits here, woman." And dammit all, he was. What was it about this woman that made him lose control whenever he was around her? Was she really a witch? He was going to have a few things to say to his brothers when he got his hands on them. He wasn't looking forward to the ribbing he was going to get after being caught necking like a teenager with Kate Drake. It didn't help matters that he saw Jonas Harrington cruising by very slowly, obviously looking for them. Damn Danny and his radio. It would be all over Sea Haven if they weren't more careful, and the last thing he wanted was for Kate to run from him because of gossip.

He touched Kate's red face. Her soft skin was raw from his whiskers. "I should have shaved, Katie, I'm sorry. I wasn't planning on kissing you." So, okay, he wanted to kiss her. He'd hoped to kiss her. He'd actually gotten down on his knees briefly last night when no one was around and asked for a Christmas miracle, but she didn't need to know how badly he wanted her.

The way he said Katie, turned her heart over, sending a million butterfly wings brushing at her stomach. "I don't mind."

He caught her face in his hands. "I mind. I need to be more careful with you." Abruptly he let her go and opened the door. It was the only safe thing to do when she looked so tempting. The chill from the sea rushed in to displace the heat of their bodies inside the car.

Kate didn't wait for him to come around and open her door. She was too shaken, too shocked by her reactions to him. It was so un-Kate-like of her. Kate the practical had just made a terrible mistake, and she couldn't take it back. She could still taste him, still had his scent clinging to her body, still felt a tremendous, edgy pressure, a need as elemental as hunger and thirst. She stood in the wind and lifted her face, hoping her skin would cool and that the raging need that was always inside of her would once again find rest.

Matt took her hand and led her up the broken and uneven path to the building. She didn't resist or pull away.

"The structure's sound," she assured him as she unlocked the door. "I want to be able to incorporate as much of the original building as possible when I expand. I was thinking decks outside with some protection against the wind for the sunnier days, and indoors, a large area with chairs and small tables for reading and drinking coffee or chocolate or whatever. There's a large stone fireplace in what must have been an office, and I'd like to keep that too if possible."

Kate covered her anxiety with talk, pointing out the rustic features she wanted to save and as many of the problem areas as she knew about. She was very aware of Matt's hand holding hers securely. Twice she tried to casually disengage, but he tugged her across the room to examine a rotted section of wood near the foundation.

"Where do the stairs lead?" He opened the sagging door and peered down into the dark interior. The stairs appeared to be very steep and halfway down he was certain the walls were dirt. "Is there a light?"

"Of sorts," Kate said. "It's over the second stair down. I can't reach the chain."

"Why wouldn't it be up here?" He pulled the chain gingerly, half-expecting the light to explode. It came on, but it was a dim yellow and made a strange humming sound. "What is that?"

"I don't know, but the fire marshal assured me it was safe in here." She smiled at him. "Isn't one of your brothers an electrician?"

"It will be a while before we need him," Matt said, starting down the stairs. The staircase was solid enough, but he didn't like the look of the wall. Several cracks spread out from the center of the wall in all directions like spiderwebs. He glanced at Kate, his eyebrow raised.

She shook her head. "The earthquake must have damaged it. It wasn't like that when I came down here with the Realtor. I actually came down twice just to make certain the entire place wasn't going to sink into the ocean. I know it's in bad shape, but it's such a perfect location. If I have to, I can pull down the mill and start from scratch. If you think that's the best thing to do,

I'll take your advice, but I really want to save as much of the original building as possible."

"It's going to cost more money than it might be worth, Kate," he warned.

Kate shivered as they went down the stairs to the dimly lit basement. It was far colder than she remembered. Always sensitive to energy, she felt an icy malevolence that hadn't been there before. She looked around cautiously, moving closer to Matt for protection. The atmosphere vibrated with unrestrained malicious amusement. "Matthew, let's leave." She tugged at his arm.

He looked down at her quickly. "What is it, Katie?" There was a caress to his voice, one that warmed her in spite of the icy chill in the basement. "You can wait upstairs while I look around." He felt her shiver and took the jacket she was holding from her to help her into it. "It won't take me very long." He pulled the edges of the jacket together and buttoned it up, his fingers lingering on the lapels, just holding her there, close to him.

Kate shook her head. "It feels unhealthy down here. I don't want to leave you alone. Matthew," she hesitated, searching for the right words. "This doesn't feel right to me, not the way it did before."

His silver eyes moved over her face. He suddenly winked, a quick sexy gesture that sent her heart thudding. "I'll make it quick, I promise."

Kate trailed after him, reluctant to be too far from him in the gloomy basement. It was long and wide and had a dirt floor. "I think this was used as the smugglers' storehouse.

There's a stairway leading to the cove through a narrow tunnel. Part of the tunnel collapsed some years ago, but I read in my grandmother's diary that the mill was used to store supplies and weapons and spices coming in off the boats." She pressed her lips together, determined not to distract him as he studied the walls and the floor of the basement.

"What's this?" Matt halted next to a strange covering in the dirt. It was at least two inches thick and looked almost like the lid of a coffin, except it was oval in shape. The surface was rough and covered with symbols, which were impossible to read with the dirt and grime over them. Running straight through the middle of the lid was a large crack.

Kate frowned. "I didn't notice it before. It must have been covered by the dirt. Could the earthquake have shifted that much dirt?" She moved closer to it reluctantly. The icy cold air was coming from the deep crack. "I don't like this, Matthew."

"It isn't a grave, Kate," he pointed out, crouching beside it and brushing at the dirt along the edges. "It's more like a seal of some kind."

She hunkered down beside him. A blast of cold air touched her palm as she passed it above the crumbling rock. She brushed the dirt away from the symbols, trying to decipher the old hieroglyphics. The language was an ancient one, but it was all too familiar to her. Her ancestors, generations of powerful witches, had used such symbols to communicate privately. Her mother had urged them to learn the language, and Kate knew a few of the symbols, but not all. "It says something about rage. The symbols are chipped and worn away. I can make out the words, 'sealed until the day one is born'—" She broke off in frustration, leaning closer to try to figure out the meaning of the words.

"Where did you learn those symbols? Are they Egyptian?" Matt asked.

Kate shook her head. "No, it's a family thing. We were all supposed to have learned. Do you think this is a well of some kind?"

Matt continued to dig around the edges of the thick lid. "It can't be a well, Kate. Maybe some kind of memorial?" He pushed at the heavy slab. It crumbled around the edges but slid slightly.

"No!" Kate caught Matt's arm, tugging hard. "We don't know what's inside. Something about this doesn't feel right to me. Can't you feel the malevolence pouring out of the crack?" She stumbled back, taking him with her, nearly sprawling on the ground so that he had to catch her as a noxious gas poured from the slit that had opened.

"It's just gas created from decomposed matter that's been trapped for a long time," Matt said, dragging her as far from the crevice as he could get them. He pushed her toward the stairs. "Sometimes the gases can make you sick or worse, Kate. Don't breathe it in." She looked pale, her eyes wide with horror. She stared at the lid without moving, one hand pressed to her mouth. Matt could see that her entire body was trembling.

At once he wrapped his arms around her and drew her close to him. He practically enveloped her entire body, yet she never looked away from the oddity in the basement, mesmerized by the yellow-black vapor streaming from the crack. "It's nothing Kate, just a hole in the ground. It's probably a couple of hundred years old." He remained calm in order to reassure her, but all of his senses had gone on alert.

Matthew obviously couldn't feel the malicious triumph pouring out of the ground, a welling-up of victory, a coup of sorts. She couldn't identify it, had no idea what it was, but she was terrified they might have unleashed something dangerous. Horrified, she watched the dark, ugly vapor swirl around the room, then stream up the stairs toward freedom, leaving behind an icy cold that chilled her to her bones.

"Stop shaking, Kate. It's gas. It happens all the time in these old vents." Matt couldn't bear that she was so frightened. "We find pockets all over the place. You haven't gone into the tunnel, have you? That could have all sorts of gas pockets as well as cave-ins."

"Have you ever seen gas do that? Travel around the room?"

"We're getting some kind of wind off the ocean, Kate. Can't you feel the draft in here? It's very strong."

"I have to take a look at those symbols, Matthew. I think something was sealed beneath that lid, and the earthquake disturbed it." She knew she sounded utterly ridiculous. She probably appeared a crackpot to him, but she was certain she was right. Something had slid out of that vent, something not meant to inhabit the world.

Matt studied her serious face, the fear in her eyes. "Let me make certain it's safe, Kate." He gently set her aside and made his way across the uneven dirt floor to the crumbling rock lid.

"Be careful, Matthew." When he looked at her, she wished she'd kept her mouth shut. She was sounding more and more paranoid.

He sniffed the air cautiously. The odor was foul, but he could breathe easily without coughing. "I think it's safe enough, Kate. I'm not keeling over, and I don't feel faint. I don't know what the hell you think just happened, but if it has you so afraid, I'm going to believe it. Jonas says never to doubt any of you Drakes."

She was grateful that he was trying to understand, but she knew he couldn't. Kate ducked her head, avoiding his gaze, afraid to see the way he was looking at her. She sank down beside the lid and dusted lightly with her fingers, afraid of crumbling the old rock even more.

Matt waited silently as long as he could. There was the sound of the sea booming in the background. The echo of it pounded off the walls eerily. "Does it mean anything to you?" He tried to keep impatience from his voice when all he wanted to do was snatch Kate up and carry her out of the place.

Kate peered closer to decipher the words. Seven sisters. Seven Drake sisters. Her ancestors. They had bound something to earth, committed its spirit to the vent hole to protect something. She couldn't read it exactly as parts of the letters were smashed and worn away, but she was afraid it was the towns-people who needed to be protected. She could also make out something to do with Christmas and fire and one who would be born who could bring peace. Kate looked up at Matt. There was no way to hide the terror in her eyes, and she didn't bother to try. "I need to go home right now."

Chapter Four

A wreath of holly meant to greet.
Looks much better tossed in the street.

Matt sat in his car with the heater running and his favorite CD playing low. Joley Drake's unique, sultry voice had taken her up the charts fast. He loved this particular collection, usually finding it soothing, but it wasn't doing him any good now. He gripped the steering wheel and stared up at the blazing lights of the Christmas tree in front of the cliff house. The fog was beginning to roll in off the sea, stretching white fingers toward land and the house he was watching. There were no electric lights in the windows, yet he could see the flicker of candlelight and an occasional shadow as one of the Drake sisters moved past the glass.

The passenger door jerked open, and Jonas Harrington slid into the seat beside Matt, shutting the door against the cold.

"Dammit, Jonas, you scared the hell out of me!" Matt snapped. He hadn't realized just how jumpy he was until Jonas had pulled the door open.

"Sorry about that." Jonas sounded as pleasant as ever. Too pleasant. Matt turned his head to look at his childhood friend. "What are you doing out here? It's cold, and the fog's coming in. You aren't stalking our Kate, are you?"

Matt studied his friend's face. He was smiling, looking amicable, but his eyes were ice-cold. "Of course I'm stalking Kate. Do you think I've lost my mind? That woman belongs with me." He grinned to relieve the tension gathering between them. "I just have to figure out how to convince her of that. What are you doing here? And why didn't I see the headlights of your car?" He glanced in the rearview mirror and noted Jonas had cruised silently up behind him.

"I ran without headlights, didn't want to scare you away. What happened tonight? Why are they all upset?" There was no obvious accusation in the voice, but Matt had been around Jonas his entire life, and he recognized the underlying note of suspicion.

"What the hell are you trying to say, Jonas? Spit it out and quit beating around the bush." Temper was beginning to flare. "I've had a hell of an evening, and you aren't helping."

Jonas shrugged. "I did just spit it out. They're upset. I can feel it. All of them, every single sister. Does it have something to do with you and Kate?"

"What kind of question is that? Hell, yes, I want Kate. And yes, I'd do just about anything to get her, but I sure wouldn't lay a finger on her if she didn't want me to, and I wouldn't *ever* hurt her. Is that what you want to know?"

Jonas nodded. "That's about what I was looking for. I'd hate to have to kick your ass, but if you hurt that girl, I'd have to do it."

"As if you could." Matt tapped his finger against the steering wheel, frowning while his temper settled. "What do you mean, you can feel they're all upset?"

"I've always been able to feel when something's wrong with the Drakes. And right now, something's very wrong." Jonas continued to look at him with cool, assessing eyes.

Matt shook his head. "It wasn't me, Jonas. Something weird happened at the old mill, and Kate was very distressed. She asked me to take her home, and I did." He raked his fingers through his hair, not once, but twice. "I didn't even have a chance to ask her out again. I was just sitting here, trying to figure out whether I should go up to the house and ask her what happened, or go back to the mill and try to figure it out."

"There they are!" Jonas muttered an ugly word beneath his breath. "What the hell do they think they're doing going out in the middle of the night with the fog rolling in?"

Matt could just make out the three Drake sisters swirling dark, hooded cloaks around them as they hurried down the steps. The fog was heavy and thick, an invasion of white mist that hid the women effectively as they rushed down the worn pathway that wound down the hill toward the road. Matt leaped out of his car, losing sight of them in the curtain of fog. He was aware of Jonas swearing under his breath, keeping pace as they angled to cut off the Drakes before they could reach the highway.

Jonas beat him to the women, catching Hannah's arm and yanking her around to face him. "Are you out of your mind?"

Kate's expression went from startled to troubled when she caught sight of them. "Matthew, I thought you went home."

She looked uneasily around her at the fog. "You shouldn't be out here. I don't think it's safe. And neither should you, Jonas."

Hannah glared at the sheriff. "Has anyone ever told you you have bad manners?"

"Has anyone ever turned you over their knee?" Jonas countered. "If you don't think it's safe out here, what are you doing running around in the dark?"

Kate indicated the heavy wall of fog. "It isn't like we're going to get very far in this stuff. We have an errand, Jonas, an important one."

"Then you should have called me," Jonas snapped impatiently. Hannah stirred as if to say something but Jonas's fingers tightened around her arm. "I'm really, really angry right now, Hannah. Don't make it worse."

"Jonas." Kate's voice was placating. "You don't understand."

"Then make me understand, Kate," he snarled.

Matt immediately stepped between Jonas and Kate. "I don't think you need to talk to her like that, Jonas. Let her explain."

Kate's fingers curled around Matt's arm. "Jonas worries about us, Matthew. We probably should have called him."

Matt didn't want her calling Jonas; he wanted her to call him when something was wrong. And something was obviously wrong. Before she could pull her hand away from his arm, he covered her fingers with his. "We're already here, Kate. Tell us what you need to do."

Her sea-green eyes moved over his face. He had the feeling she could see more deeply into him than most people, but it was always like that with Kate. He tightened his hold on her hand. "Kate. You trust Jonas. He can vouch for me."

Kate closed her eyes briefly. Matthew Granite was her dream man, and after he witnessed what really went on around the Drake sisters she wouldn't even be able to sustain the fantasy of a relationship with him. She sighed but she squared her shoulders. Some things were just more important than romantic dreams. She took a deep breath. "Something was unleashed today, something malevolent. We think." She looked at her sisters for courage before continuing. "We think the earthquake may have awakened it or at least provided it with the opportunity to rise. It was the shadow you saw in the globe, Matt, and my sisters and I saw in the mosaic. It's very real, and it feels dangerous to us." She stared up at him, clearly expecting him to laugh.

Matt kept his face completely expressionless. He knew the Drakes were different; some said they performed miracles, some said they were genuine witches. Sea Haven was a hotbed of gossip, and the Drake sisters were always at the forefront. But not Kate. Never Kate.

"So it felt dangerous to you, and the first thing you do is rush out into the night in the middle of one of the worst fogs we've ever had," Jonas snapped. "Dammit, Kate, Abbey and Hannah might rush headlong into danger, but you usually show some trace of sense." He hauled Hannah back against him when she tried to squirm away. "I'm not playing around with you, Hannah. Keep it up, and I'll lock you away for the night."

Hannah's beautiful face radiated fury, but instead of taking Jonas to task as Matt expected, she was gasping for breath.

Abbey leaped to her side. "Breathe, Hannah, very slow."

Hannah shook her head, fear filling her eyes. Abbey extracted a paper bag from her purse and handed it to her sister. "Breathe into this."

Looking alarmed, Jonas wrapped his arm around Hannah's waist to support her as she doubled over, clearly unable to breathe adequately. "What the hell is wrong with her? Should we get an ambulance?"

"Would you please stop swearing at her?" Abbey snapped. "Be very careful, Jonas, or I'll ask you questions you don't want to answer."

"Shut up, Abbey, don't you dare threaten me," Jonas growled back.

"Stop it, all of you, stop it," Kate pleaded.

Seeing the anxiety on Kate's face, Matt stepped closer to her and put his arm around her. Hannah breathed into the paper bag for a couple of minutes and lifted her head. She looked ready to cry. "Abbey, if you want to take Hannah back to the house, I'll go with Kate to do whatever it is you all think is so important." He made the offer before he could stop himself. Kate was shivering in the cold fog. She didn't need to be out on such a night. He wanted just to pick her up and take her home and lie down with her by the fireplace.

Jonas pushed back Hannah's wealth of blond hair. "Are you all right, baby doll?" His choice of words should have been insulting, but the gentle concern in his voice made them an endearment.

Hannah nodded but didn't look at any of them, still clearly fighting for air.

"Maybe that's a good idea, Hannah. I'll go with Matt and just look around a little, and you and Abbey pull out the diaries and see if you can find anything that might help us figure this out," Kate said. "Matthew, are you certain you don't mind? I want to walk around town and just get a feel for what's going on."

"I don't mind. Are you going to be warm enough?"

"Just how dangerous is this, Kate?" Jonas asked.

"I honestly don't know," she replied. "I wish I knew. We thought if we went out together, all of us might be able to pick something up, but I already feel it. I think I can track it."

Matt cleared his throat. "Track a shadow?" If they weren't all so serious, he would be thinking it was a Halloween prank. He glanced up at the house. The fog was a heavy shroud, almost obliterating the house. He could see the lights of the Christmas tree, but only as pale, orange-glowing haloes distorted by the blanket of grayish white. He went still. The fog was changing color, darkening from white to a charcoal gray. Just as the fog had done in the snowglobe when he'd picked it up to examine it.

"The fog is bad, Kate. I've never seen it like this," Jonas said. "Stay close to Matt. I'll take Hannah and Abbey back to the house."

Hannah stiffened and looked at Abbey. Abbey smiled. "We'll make it home fine, Jonas. It's just up the hill. We know the path."

"I'm coming with you, Abbey, so don't argue." Jonas turned resolutely toward the house. "Matt, if it feels wrong to you, or you think Kate's in any danger at all, get her back here and don't let her give you any nonsense."

Kate smiled at Jonas. "I never talk nonsense. You take care of my sisters because if anything happens to them . . . "

"I know, I've heard it all before." Jonas waved at her, and the fog swallowed them up, even muffling the sound of their footsteps on the path, leaving Kate alone with Matt.

She looked up at him. "You don't have to do this, you know. I'm capable of walking up and down the streets of Sea Haven."

Matthew stared down into her beautiful sea-green eyes. "But I'm not capable of leaving your side when there's even a hint of danger near you." He lowered his head slowly to hers, drawn as if by a magnet, expecting her to pull away, giving her plenty of time to think about it.

Kate watched his eyes change, go dark with desire, right before his mouth took possession of hers. It didn't matter that the air was cold, and the wind chilled them, their bodies produced a remarkable heat, their mouths fused with fire. He dragged her against his body, his muscular arms enveloping her, holding her as if she were the most precious person in the world to him. He was exquisitely rough, yet impossibly gentle, voraciously hungry, nearly devouring her mouth, yet so tender he brought tears to her eyes. She had no idea how he did it, but she wanted more.

"You're not good for me," she whispered against his mouth.

His tongue slid along the seam of her lips, teased her tongue into another brief, but heated tango. "I'm absolutely perfect for you." He tugged at her cape until her body was pressed tightly against his. "I was born to be with you, Kate. You're supposed to be some kind of a magical woman, filled with the second sight, yet you don't see what's right in front of you. Why is that?" He didn't give her the opportunity to debate, he just kissed her long and thoroughly.

Kate felt her insides melting, turning to a warm puddle and settling somewhere in her lower region as a frustrating and unrelenting ache. Her knees actually went weak. "I can't think straight when we're kissing, Matthew."

"That's a good thing, Kate, because neither can I," he answered, his lips drifting into the hollow of her neck and back up to find her ear.

Heat pulsed through her, but she forced herself to pull away from him. He wasn't for her. She knew that, and once he found out what she was really was like, he'd know it too. She might seem courageous and strong, but when it came to losing him, she knew she'd be very fragile. Starting up with Matthew Granite was a decidedly ridiculous thing for her to do. "Matthew, really, I have to find this malevolent shadow and hopefully help it find some peace or get my sisters to help me seal it back up."

Matt silently cursed dark shadows and evil entities and every other thing that went bump in the night. She obviously believed they had let something harmful loose on the small town of Sea Haven. He was certain it was a pocket of gas; but if it meant walking around town with her at night, holding hands and kissing her every chance he got, well, hell, he was her man. He could do that. And he would even try to keep an open mind.

"Then let's go." He wrapped his arm around her. "I've got a flashlight in my car. This fog is really thick."

"We won't need a flashlight, Matthew. I have a couple of glow sticks. My sister Elle makes them. They work very well in the fog." She pulled several thin tubes from the inside pocket of her cape and handed him one. "Just shake it."

"I forgot about little Elle and her chemistry set. She blew up more missiles on the beach than any other kid at Sea Haven. Didn't she get a full scholarship to Columbia or MIT or some other very prestigious school? One very brave to take her on?"

Kate laughed, warmth spreading through her. "They were very brave, but fortunately they turned out a remarkable physicist able to do just about anything she wants to do. Elle is a genius and utterly fearless. She's not afraid to crawl around in caves looking at strange rock formations, and she's not afraid of taking apart a bomb when she's needed. Unlike me."

"What do you mean?" Matt tightened his fingers around hers.

"My sisters do incredible things and people expect it of us, but I wouldn't want you to think I'm capable of climbing mountains or jumping out of planes because you've heard of all of their exploits." She was feeling her way in the fog rather than following the glow stick. She lifted her face to the droplets of sea moisture, inhaling to try to catch the scent of something foul. "We have to cross the highway."

With the fog so thick there was virtually no traffic. Matt moved with her across the coastal highway and took the shortcut that led to the center of town. She was so serious all of a sudden, so distant from him, that he was actually beginning to believe she was on the trail of something evil. He could sense the stillness in her, the gathering of energy.

The survival instincts he'd honed during his years as a Ranger kicked in. His skin prickled as he went onto alert status. Adrenaline surged, and his senses grew keener. He felt the need for complete silence and wondered if he was beginning to believe in supernatural nonsense. Matt eased the glow stick inside his jacket without activating it. The fog muffled the sound of Kate's footsteps. He was aware of her breathing, of the eerie feel of the fog itself, of everything.

By mutual consent they were silent as they walked along the street. He became aware of a slight noise. A puffing. It was distant and hushed, barely audible in the murky blanket of mist. Matt found himself straining to listen. There was a rhythm to the sound, reminding him of a bull drawing air in and out of its lungs hard before a charge. Breathing. Someone was breathing, and the sound was moving, changing directions each time they changed directions.

Matt pressed his lips to her ear. "There's someone in the fog with us." He was certain someone was watching them, someone quite close.

Kate tipped her head back. "*Something*, not someone."

Kate turned toward the residential area. The town looked strange shrouded in the gray-white fog. Heavily decorated for Christmas, the multicolored lights on the stores and office buildings, the houses and trees gave off the peculiar glow of a fire in the strange vapor, giving the town a disturbing infernal appearance rather than a festive one. Matt wished he had brought a weapon with him. He was a good hand-to-hand fighter because he was a big man, strong, with quick reflexes and extensive training, but he had no idea what kind of adversary they faced.

Something hit him in the back, skittered down his jeans, and fell to the street. Matt whirled around to face the enemy and found nothing but fog.

"What is it?" Kate asked. Her voice was steady, but her hand, on the small of his back, was shaking.

Matt hunkered down to look at the object at his feet. "It's a Christmas wreath, Kate. A damned Christmas wreath." He looked around carefully, trying to penetrate the fog and see what was moving in it. He could feel the presence now, real, not imagined. He could hear the strange, labored breathing, but he couldn't find the source.

As he stood, a second object came hurtling out of the fog to hit him in the chest. He heard the smash of glass and knew immediately that the wreath had been decorated with glass ornaments. "Let's get out of here, off the street at least," he said.

Kate was stubborn, shaking her head. "No, I have to face it here."

Matt pulled Kate to him, shielding her smaller body with his own as more wreaths came flying through the air, hurled with deadly accuracy at them from every direction. He wrapped his arms around her head, pressing her face against his chest. "It's kids," he muttered, brushing a kiss on top of her head to reassure her. "Always playing pranks; it's dangerous in this fog, not to mention destructive."

He hoped it was kids. It had to be an army of kids, tearing wreaths off the doors of the houses and throwing them at passersby as a prank. He heard no laughter, not even running footsteps. He heard nothing but the rough breathing. It seemed to come out of the fog itself. The nape of his neck prickled with unease.

"It isn't children playing a prank, Matt." Kate sounded close to tears. "It's much, much worse."

"Kate." He stroked a caress down the back of her head. Her hair was inside the hood of the cape, but his palm lingered anyway. "It isn't the first time a group of kids decided to play around, and it won't be the last."

The Christmas wreaths lay around them in a circle, some smashed or crushed and others in reasonably good shape. Kate lifted her face away from his chest and took a breath. "I can smell it, can't you?"

Matt inhaled deeply. He recognized the foul, noxious odor of the gases in the old mill. His heart jumped. "Dammit, Kate. I'm beginning to believe you. Let's get the hell out of here before I decide I'm crazy."

She pulled free of his arms. "Is that what you think about me? That I'm crazy?"

"Of course not. This is all just so damned odd."

Her sea-green eyes moved over his face, a little moody, a little fey. "Well, brace yourself, it's going to get damned odder. Stay still."

The fog swirled around them, their faces, their feet, and bodies, spinning webs of charcoal gray matter. As at the cliff house, Matt got the impression of bony fingers, and this time they were trying to grab at Kate. Without thinking, he caught her up and started to run, the urge strong to get her away from the long gray tentacles, but the blanket of fog was thick around them.

Kate pressed her lips to his ear. "Stop! I have to try to stop it, Matthew; it's what I do. We can't outrun the fog, it's everywhere."

"Dammit, Kate, I don't like this." When she didn't respond,

he reluctantly put her down and stayed very close to her, ready for action.

She turned in the direction of her home, her face serene, thoughtful, yet determined. She radiated beauty, an inner fire and strength. She whispered, a soft, melodic chant that became part of the night, of the air surrounding them. She wasn't speaking English but a language he didn't recognize. Her voice was soothing, tranquil, a soft invitation to a place of peace and harmony with the earth.

The fog itself breathed harder, in and out, a burst of air sounding like a predatory animal with teeth and claws. The mist seemed to vibrate with anger, roiling and spinning and growing darker. Gray fog whirled around the Christmas wreaths at Matt's feet, spinning fast enough to lift them into the air. Bright green wreaths withered and blackened as if all the life was being sucked out of them. The objects reminded Matt of the garlands at funerals rather than the cheery decorations for a holiday, and each of them seemed to be aimed straight toward Kate.

His breath caught in his throat, and his heart pounded. Kate looked small and fragile under the onslaught of the vicious gray-black vapor. He moved, a fluid glide that took him into the path of the blackened garlands so that they smashed into his larger frame. Kate ignored the fog and the wreaths, concentrating on something inside of herself. She stared toward the house on the cliffs and abruptly lifted her arms straight up into the air. The wind rushed in from the ocean with wild force. It carried the crisp scent of the sea, the taste and feel of the waves, and a spray of salt. It also carried voices, soft and melodious and very feminine. The wind swept through the fogbank, the voices swelling in strength, Kate's voice joining theirs until they were in perfect harmony, in total command.

The spinning Christmas wreaths dropped to the road. The fog receded, heading inland, blanketing the residential homes; but the wind was persistent, shifting directions and herding the fog back toward the ocean. Kate looked translucent, her skin pale and beaded with moisture, wisps of hair clinging to her face, but she didn't falter. Her voice brought a sense of peace, of tranquillity, of something beautiful and satisfying. It filled Matt with longing for a home and a family of his own. It filled him with a deep sense of pride and respect for Kate Drake.

He watched the fog reluctantly retreat until it was far out over the ocean, dissipated by the force of the wind. There was a silence left behind in the vacuum of the tempest. Kate dropped her arms as if they were leaden. She staggered. He leaped forward to catch her before she collapsed, swinging her into his arms and cradling her against his chest.

"It's growing in strength. I couldn't have sent it away if my sisters hadn't helped." Kate looked up at him with frightened eyes.

Matt kissed her. It was the only thing he could think to do. She seemed weightless in his arms. He kissed her eyes and the tip of her nose and settled his mouth, feather-light over hers. "It's all right now, Kate. Rest. You sent it away. Tell me what you need." He could see that every drop of her strength had been used up in fighting the unseen enemy in the fog. She'd made a believer out of him. He was a man of action, having spent several years in the service training to protect his countrymen, yet there had been nothing he could do to stop the evil shadow in the mist. "What is it?"

She rubbed her face tiredly against his jacket. "I don't know, Matthew, I honestly don't know."

"How did you know what to say to it? What language it would understand?"

"I didn't know. I was using a healing chant my family has passed down from generation to generation. I was attempting to heal its spirit."

He stared at her, trying not to look shocked. The dark shadow seemed beyond any sort of redemption to him, something dark and dangerous, looking for a chance to strike out at anything or anyone around it.

Kate looked at the wreaths strewn all over the road. "Strange that he would choose to attack us with the wreaths."

"Strange that it could use them at all. Do you think it's a he?"

She shrugged. "It felt male to me."

The adrenaline was beginning to subside, but he continued to eye the cliffs warily. "I'm never going to look at fog again in the same way."

"A wreath is a continuous circle, Matthew, and it symbolizes real love, unconditional, true affection that never ceases." Her voice was thoughtful.

"I didn't feel love flowing out of the fog," he answered. He began walking back in the direction of her house, Kate in his arms.

"But he tore the Christmas wreaths off every door on the street and threw them."

"At *us*," he said grimly. "I'm used to looking my enemy in the eye, Katie, fighting him with weapons or my bare hands. I couldn't exactly grab the fog and throttle it, although I wanted to."

"Put me down, Matthew, I'm too heavy for you to carry all that way."

"I was a Ranger for ten years, Katie, I think I can pack your weight with no problem."

She wasn't going to argue, she was just too drained. "Ten years. That's right, you joined right out of college. I've been wandering around so much, and I knew you didn't live here, but your family always made it seem as if you were here."

"I spent my leave here, every chance I could. I picked up my life here again immediately after I got out of the service because the family business was waiting for me. My father and brothers kept me a part of it, even though they did all the work."

"Why did you join the Rangers, Matthew? As soon as I heard, I researched what they were all about. It was very—" she hesitated, searching for the right word—"intense. And frightening. Why would you want to do something like that?"

"I've always needed to push myself to find out my limits. And I believe in my country, so it seemed a perfect fit for me. The Rangers embody everything I believe in. Move farther and faster and fight harder than any other soldier. Never surrender, never leave a fallen comrade, survive and carry out the mission under any conditions."

Kate sighed heavily and turned her face into his shoulder, hiding her expression from him. Something about that sigh gave Matt a sick feeling in the pit of his stomach. He wanted to ask her about it, but by the time he reached the path leading to the house, Kate was asleep.

Chapter Five

A town dreams of sweet thoughts while nestled in bed,
Until nightmares of me begin to dance in their heads.

"Kate. Katie. Wake up, hon." The soft voice beckoned Kate from layers of sleep. "You need to eat now, wake up."

Kate opened her eyes and stretched, blinking drowsily up at her sister. "Sarah. What are you doing here?" She pushed at the heavy fall of hair tumbling around her face. She always braided her hair before she went to bed, yet it was everywhere. She turned her head and went still. Matthew Granite was sprawled in a chair beside her bed, his silver gaze trained intently on her face. Her stomach did a funny little flip.

A slow smile softened his tough features, lit his gray eyes, and stole her heart. "You're finally awake. I was getting worried."

"You slept in the chair?" Kate couldn't imagine his large body finding a relaxing position in her bedroom chair.

"Well, I did want to share your bed, but I was worried about your sisters giving me the evil eye." His smile widened into a teasing grin. "Jonas slunk out of here a couple of hours ago afraid even to drink a cup of coffee. He warned me one of you might slip an eye of newt into my coffee, so I thought it best to stay in everyone's good graces."

"You like coffee that much, do you? Enough to stay in our good graces?" She couldn't stop looking at him. There was a blue-black shadow along his jaw, and his clothes were rumpled, but it didn't make him any less attractive to her. "Just so I'm not the one slipping the eye of newt to you, why are you sleeping in my room?" She glared at Sarah rather than at Matt.

Sarah held her hands up, palm out. "We all tried to get him to leave last night, Kate, but he wouldn't go. Granite might be his last name, but it's also what he's made of. No one could budge him. Jonas tried scaring him off, but that didn't work either."

Kate tried not to be pleased. She tried to frown at Matt, to pretend displeasure, but there was no way she could carry it off, so she gave up. He just winked at her anyway, looking sexier than ever with the dark stubble shadowing his jaw.

Sarah sat on the edge of the bed. "I hate interrupting, but you have to eat. You expended far too much energy last night. Even Joley called and was feeling drained." She waved a hand toward the drapes, and, to Matt's astonishment, the curtain slid open to allow the morning light to pour in. "I know you don't feel hungry, you never do afterward, but you have to eat for all of us."

Neither Kate nor Sarah seemed to think anything was unusual. Matt blinked several times to test his eyesight.

"How's Hannah?" Kate sat up, thankful she was still wearing

her clothes. Matt and her sisters must have removed her cape and her shoes and socks before putting her in her bed, but at least she was safely clad in her slacks and blouse. "I couldn't believe with all of us working on her, she still had an attack. That's the first time I can remember that our joining together failed her."

Sarah glanced at Matt and hesitated. He raised his hands. "If you need to be alone with Kate, I'll go on down to the kitchen and see what kind of trouble I can get into." He stretched out his hand to Kate, resting it palm down on the bed.

"It's just that Hannah is such a private person, Matthew." Kate placed her hand over his. "She was embarrassed that it happened in front of you and Jonas. Especially Jonas."

"It? You mean her asthma attack?" He turned his hand to circle hers with his fingers, knowing she was trusting him with something private. "It was an asthma attack, wasn't it?"

"Not exactly." Kate sighed. "I wish Jonas would let up on her a little bit."

"She seems to be able to dish it right back to him." Matt leaned over to brush strands of hair from her face. "I don't quite get your relationship with Jonas, but I served with him in the Rangers. Jonas, me, and Jackson Deveau. Jonas is a good man."

"Jackson Deveau is the deputy who scares the hell out of everyone," Sarah informed Kate when she frowned. "You must have seen him a few times. He doesn't ever say much, but he looks lethal. He came to Sea Haven with Jonas when he returned from the Army."

"Jackson's a good man too," Matt said.

Kate hadn't met the deputy because she hadn't been back

long, and she tended to wrap herself up in the cocoon of her own world. "I take it Jackson isn't from here originally."

"No, but he often came to Sea Haven on leave with us. He had no family and nowhere else to go when he left the service, so we asked him to come back with us. This town is friendly and tolerant, and Jackson needs tolerance. He's family to us. As for Jonas, you have to understand him. I saw him go in under heavy fire to drag a wounded man out of a battle zone. He carried that man for miles on his back. And Jackson . . ." He broke off, shaking his head. "I know Jonas watches over you all."

"Like a hawk," Sarah interjected dryly.

Matt shrugged. "Maybe it's because he really cares about all of you."

"Don't worry about our relationship with Jonas," Kate said. "We all love him dearly, even when we want to conjure up a spell to turn him into a toad."

Matt cleared his throat, rubbed the bridge of his nose, and sat back in his chair. "Can you really do that?"

Kate exchanged a mischievous grin with Sarah. "You never know about the Drake sisters. Really, Matthew, Jonas is intertwined deeply with our family. He always seems to know when something is wrong. He's sensitive to things not seen with the human eye."

Sarah leaned toward Matt. "You felt it last night, didn't you, when you were in the fog with Kate, and we joined with her? You knew something was wrong."

Matt sighed. "I don't know what happened last night, but I sure as hell don't want Kate facing anything like that again." His gray eyes smoldered with something dangerous as he looked at

Kate. "I didn't like the way the fog seemed to be attacking you."

Sarah gasped. "What do you mean attacking her?"

"Nothing came at me," Kate denied hastily. "Really, Sarah, it was just throwing Christmas decorations around and Matthew was actually hit a few times. I was never touched."

Sarah looked at Matt steadily. "Why did you think it was after Kate?"

"I stepped in front of her to protect her. The wreaths were thrown, but not very hard in the beginning, yet when Katie began to talk to it, whatever it is, the Christmas wreaths were thrown much more forcefully and with greater accuracy."

"Were you hurt?" Kate looked suddenly anxious, coming up on her knees on the bed to look at him. "Libby's the best at healing, but Sarah . . . "

"I'm fine," Matt said, but wished he didn't have to admit it. She looked incredibly beautiful leaning toward him with her hair tousled and her eyes enormous with concern for him.

"Kate—" Abbey stuck her head in the room—"Gina over at the preschool says something's wrong, and she needs you. I could hear the children crying in the background. I told her you weren't well, but she said it was an emergency. She said she needed your help. I'll go if I absolutely have to go."

Abbey was clearly apprehensive about going in Kate's place. Matt looked at Sarah. "What does Kate have to do with the preschool?"

"Haven't you noticed Kate has a gift for calming people with her voice? She's able to bring peace to even the most distressed person or situation," Sarah answered.

"Is that what your lives are like? People need you, and it doesn't matter if you're tired or not, you just go to them."

"We were born with certain gifts, Matt," Kate said. "We've always known we were meant to serve others. Yes, it isn't always easy, and all of us have to have ways of protecting ourselves but when we can help, we have to go."

"How do they know to call you?"

Sarah smiled. "You were older than us, Matthew, ahead of us in school, so you really weren't around when our talents began to develop. I'm sure you've heard the rumors, but you didn't witness what we could do the way other people in town did. Jonas has always connected with us in some way, so it was easy enough for him to believe."

"Kate?" Abbey prompted.

"I'll go. Give me a few minutes to shower and have a cup of tea."

Matt followed her to the bathroom door. "I don't like this, Kate. You look fragile to me. I think Sarah's right. You need to stay home."

Sarah's eyebrow shot up. "Did I say that?"

Kate rubbed a caress along Matt's stubbly jaw right in front of her sisters, then closed the bathroom door on his startled expression. When he turned around, Sarah and Abbey were grinning at him. "She doesn't listen, does she?" he asked.

"Not very well," Sarah agreed. "Kate may be quiet about it, but she goes her own way and does what she thinks is right."

"Do you have another bathroom so I can clean up really fast?"

Sarah grinned at him. "I even have an extra toothbrush. You've got that look in your eye when you look at her."

He followed her down the hall. "What look?"

"You look at her like you can't wait to kiss her," Sarah said. "A toothbrush is definitely in order."

"Does she have something against the Rangers?" Matt asked, remembering the small sigh from the night before. It had haunted him most of the night.

Sarah pushed open a door to a powder blue bathroom. "Of course not. Why would you think that?"

"No reason. Thanks, Sarah." Matt didn't want to think about that strange little sigh of Kate's. She wasn't the type of woman to react that way unless she had a reason. He'd ask her about it later. He hurried through his shower wanting to get back to her.

Kate was still in the bathroom when he returned to her room. He rested his palm on the door, the exact level as her head. "Come out of there, Katie, you're beautiful enough without working at it."

From behind the door she laughed. "How do you know? You took a terrible chance staying. You could have woken up and my mask could have slipped off in the middle of the night."

"I didn't go to sleep. I watched over you."

There was a small shocked silence. Kate jerked the door open and stared up at him. "You must be exhausted. Go home and go to bed."

"I'd rather go with you." He reached out and pulled her to him. Her body fit perfectly against his, as if made to be there.

"Matthew." There was hesitation in Kate's voice.

He kissed her. He didn't want her to voice her reservations. Kissing her was a much better and far more enjoyable idea. It was magic, if there was such a thing, and he was beginning to believe there was. He meant for it to be a brief, good morning kiss, a gentle shut-up-and-just-kiss-me kiss, but she caught fire, or he did, and they both just went up in flames. He wanted more than to kiss her, he wanted to touch her, to claim her soft body, to feel her moving beneath him, her hands clinging . . .

"Stop!"

Matt and Kate drew apart, their hearts racing, and blinked at each other, then looked around in surprise to see Sarah, Hannah, and Abbey in the doorway glaring at them.

"Kate," Sarah said, taking a deep breath. "You know we're all connected in some way. You can't be in such close proximity to us and carry on like that. We're all in overdrive, thank you very much."

Unrepentant, Matt grinned at them as he pulled Kate tight against him. "Sorry about that. We're off to see some preschoolers." Kate hid her face in his shoulder, trying not to laugh. He did the gentlemanly thing and got her out of there quickly, waving at Damon, Sarah's fiancé, as they hurried past him.

"The man should thank us," he whispered, and pretended to wince when Kate smacked his arm.

Kate stared out the window of the Mustang at the white-capped ocean as they drove along the highway toward the exit to the street where the preschool was located. "The fogbank is very thick out over the ocean," she said, a note of apprehension in her voice. "See how dark it is, more gray than white, and it seems to be churning." She turned her gaze on Matt. "I should have been more careful. Somewhere in the diaries there has to be something about this strange phenomenon."

"What diaries? You've mentioned the diaries before. How can they help?"

"My family keeps a history, books handed down generation to generation. Somewhere this event had to be recorded. The problem is, all of us were supposed to learn the earlier languages used, but we gave it a half-hearted attempt. All of us know a little, but Elle really can read it. We have to decipher the books."

Matt turned the car onto the exit. "You think this thing is coming back."

"I know it is. Can't you feel it on the wind?"

He could only feel how close he was to her. How just out of his reach she always seemed to be. Matt parked the car in the lot at the preschool, and they sat for a moment, absorbing the unnatural silence. There were no children playing in the small yard.

Kate squared her shoulders. "Do you want to wait out here?"

For an answer, he got out of the car and went around to open her door. He wasn't about to miss his opportunity to see more clearly what Kate's life was all about.

Gina Farley greeted them with obvious relief as they entered. Many of the children were sobbing and sniffling as if they'd been crying a long time. Some of the children stared silently at Kate and Matt with large, frightened eyes. Others hid their faces. In the room were several adults, many of whom Matt recognized and nodded to.

There was tension and fear in the room, but Kate smiled at everyone and went directly to the children. "Hello, everyone. I'm Kate Drake." She sat down in the circle and looked at the little ones in invitation.

Matt stood back and watched her. She looked utterly serene, a center of calm in the midst of a violent storm. Immediately the children were drawn to her, pushing and shoving to sit as close to her as they could get. She began talking to them, and a hush fell over the room so that only Kate's magical voice could be heard, bringing a sense of peace and contentment.

"So most of you had a bad dream last night?" Kate's smile was a starburst, radiating light and warmth. "Dreams can be very frightening. All of us have had them. Haley, would you tell us about your dream?" She asked the little girl who had been sobbing the hardest. "Dreams are like stories we make up in our imaginations. I make up stories and write them down for people to read. My stories can be very frightening sometimes. Was your dream scary, Haley?"

It wasn't so much her actual words that were magic as it was her voice. It became apparent to Matt that somehow Kate drew the intensity of the children's emotions out of them. As the room grew calm, and the children quieter, the tension dropped dramatically. It was only Matt who could see the effect on Kate. How draining it was to accept the backlash of emotion not only from the children but their parents as well.

Haley revealed her dream in halting sentences. A skeleton-like man in a long coat and old hat with glowing eyes and bony fingers came out of the fog. He burned the Christmas tree and stole the gifts, and he did something awful to the shepherd in the Christmas pageant. Matt stood up straight when the shepherd was mentioned. His brother, Danny, always played the shepherd in the Christmas pageant. His alarm grew as child after child revealed they'd had a similar dream.

Kate didn't seem the least bit alarmed. Her smile never wavered, and her voice continued to dispel the trauma the nightmares had caused. She told several Christmas stories and soon had the children laughing. As she stood up to leave, Matt saw her sway with weariness. Without a word, Matt waded through the children and slipped his arm around her. She leaned heavily into him as they spent the next ten minutes trying to leave gracefully.

"You look a bit on the fierce and forbidding side," she said once they were back in the car. "I've never quite seen that expression before."

"I was contemplating picking you up and carting you out of there."

Kate laughed softly. "That would have given everyone something to talk about, wouldn't it?" She pressed her fingers to her temples. "Where are you taking me?"

"To the Salt Bar and Grill. You need to eat. Danny's been dating the waitress there, Trudy Garret, so we've spent quite a bit of time sampling the food. It's not bad." He glanced at her and noted that her hands were shaking. "You were using some sort of magic, weren't you? With your voice, and it drained your strength."

"There's always a cost to everything, Matthew." She shrugged without looking at him, closing her eyes and leaning back against the leather seat. "I'm not certain I'll be able to eat, but I'll try."

"You're already too thin, Katie."

She laughed. "A woman can never be too thin, Matthew, don't you know that?"

"That's what women like to think, but men think differently."
He parked the car. "I don't mind carrying you."

She opened her eyes then. "Don't you have work to do?"

"I am working. I'm courting you the old-fashioned way.
Showing you what a great guy I am and impressing you." He
opened the car door for Kate and helped her out, happy to see
her laughing. Some of the shadows had disappeared from her
eyes.

"You think you're impressing me?"

"I know I'm impressing you."

"Only when you kiss me. I'm really impressed when you kiss
me," she admitted, deliberately tempting him. She needed the
comfort of his arms more than she needed anything else.

Matt didn't need a second invitation. He pulled Kate's slender body into the shelter of his and lowered his mouth to hers.
He brushed her lips gently, back and forth, giving her teasing
little kisses meant to prolong the moment. Then his mouth settled over hers, and he kissed her hungrily, like a man starving for
more.

Kate's slender arms circled his neck, and her body pressed
tightly against his. He knew she couldn't help but feel his body's
stark reaction to her, but she didn't seem to mind, burrowing
even closer to him so that he felt the warmth of her breasts and
the cradle of her hips beckoning with heat.

Tendrils of fog floated in from the sea, ghostly gray strands
drifting past them as they stood together on the steps of the
restaurant. Kate stiffened, her fingers gripping Matt's shoulders.
"Did you hear the weather report? Did they say there would be
fog?"

Matt scowled at the mist floating lazily into the parking lot. "We get fog all the time here in Sea Haven, Kate." But it didn't make the hair on his arms rise or his reflexes leap into survivor mode as it had the night before. "I don't smell that noxious odor, do you?"

She shook her head. "But the sun should have burned this fog off. The sky isn't that overcast, Matthew."

"Let's go inside." He held the door open for her to precede him. At once they could hear the wailing of a child in terror. The tension in the restaurant was tangible.

"Oh, Kate! I'm so glad you're here." Trudy Garret beckoned to them from behind the counter, her expression anxious. She was tall and pretty even with the apron she was wearing. Her youthful face was lined with worry.

Danny Granite stood behind her, his arm wrapped around her. He looked relieved to see them. There were a few people in the Salt Bar and Grill, but they were obviously tense and upset over the continual unrestrained sobs coming from somewhere in the back.

"Danny, why aren't you at work?" Matt asked. "Is everything all right at home?"

"Trudy's son had a bad nightmare last night. She can't seem to calm him down, so I offered to come over and see what I could do for him. He's only four years old, a cute little tyke, and I could hear him crying when I called her. I couldn't stand it."

"We haven't been able to calm him down," Trudy said. She was wringing her hands and looking imploringly at Kate. "I'm so glad you came in. Would you talk to him, Kate? Please?"

The cook stuck his head out of the kitchen. "Kate, thank heaven you're here!"

A few of the local patrons broke into applause.

Matt looked at Kate. Her face was pale, her eyes too big for her face, and there were shadows under her eyes. He stirred protectively but didn't speak when Kate put a light, restraining hand on his forearm. She smiled at Trudy. "Of course, I'll be happy to talk to him, Trudy. He isn't alone, many of the children at the preschool had nightmares last night."

Matt slid his hand down her arm, circling her wrist with his fingers. Her pulse was very fast, her skin cool. "While Kate talks to your son, Trudy, maybe you can heat a bowl of soup for her."

"Of course, be happy to," Trudy said. "Right this way, Kate, he's in the back."

Matt followed Kate behind the counter to the back room. The wails grew louder as they approached the small room. Kate opened the door. Matt winced at the high-pitched shrieks, but he stepped inside with her. It was the same scenario as at the preschool. Little Davy Garret sat in Kate's lap, telling her the details of a skeleton in a long coat and old hat in between gulping and tears, finally listening to the sound of her magical voice. Kate replaced the boy's memory of the terrifying nightmare with several funny Christmas stories. She rocked him while she talked, using her talent, her gift, to bring him peace, to soothe him, and make him feel that his world was right again.

After Kate spent twenty minutes sitting on the floor with the boy, Matt reached down and took the child from her arms and set him aside to play happily with his toys. "Danny can take over, Kate. Come eat the soup, then I'll take you home. You're exhausted." He pulled her gently to her feet.

Kate nodded. "I am tired. I wish I knew what was going on, though. I've never seen anything like this. How could all these children have the same dream? At the preschool, at first I thought maybe Haley told her dream to the others, and they all became upset because she was; but the parents said, no, the children had woken up that way. And Davy certainly didn't have contact with any of them. I don't like it at all." She slipped into a booth near the window and peered out. "The fog seems to be rolling in again, Matthew." She couldn't keep the apprehension she felt out of her voice.

"I noticed," he said grimly. The bright, blinking Christmas lights and cheerful music couldn't quite dispel the tension in the air. "Tell me more about the diaries."

Kate sipped at the hot tea Trudy brought her and stared out the window, avoiding his gaze. "Each generation in our family records our activities in journals, or diaries as we sometimes call them. They're considered the history of the Drake family. The earlier journals were recorded using a language or code of symbols like the ones we saw in the mill. I could read part of what was written on the seal. Someone in my family sealed that malevolent force in there. If it was that dangerous that they decided to seal it without laying it to rest, it was because they couldn't give it peace. And that's very frightening."

"And Elle's the only one who can read the language?"

"Sarah knows a little, just as I do. The others have some working knowledge as well, but there's a lot of history to go through when you don't have a good understanding of the language. We need Elle, but I'm certain Sarah and the others will keep trying to find the proper entry and hopefully decipher it."

The wind whirled through the room as the door to the restaurant was thrust open and Jonas strode in, coming directly to them, his face etched with deep lines. Without asking, he slid into the booth beside Kate. "It's Jackson, Kate. I've never seen him like this. I need you to come and talk to him."

A chill went down Matt's spine. "What's wrong with him?"

At Matt's tone, Kate looked up quickly and caught an expression passing between the two men. "What is it? Why are you both so worried?"

There was a small, uncomfortable silence. "You know how you said Hannah was a private person and wouldn't want people to find out what happened the other night? Jackson is the same way," Matt said.

Jonas sat up straight. "What doesn't Hannah want talked about?"

"We're talking about Jackson," Kate reminded him. "What's wrong with him, and why are you both so worried?"

The two men exchanged another long look. Jonas sighed and shrugged in resignation. "I need your help or I wouldn't be telling you this, Kate. I expect you to keep it confidential."

She nodded because he had actually waited for her answer.

"Jackson is—was—is a specialist for the Rangers."

There was another silence. Kate watched their eyes. They looked grave, more than a little worried. When neither was more forthcoming she took a guess. "He's trained in things I don't want to know about, and you don't want to talk about.

Right now he's in a bad way and both of you are concerned for his mental well-being. And what do you mean by is—was—is?"

"That about sums it up, Kate. Let's go," Jonas said.

"Once a Ranger always a Ranger," Matt added. "And she needs to eat her soup. Give her a few minutes."

"Do you have any idea what's going on, Kate?" Jonas asked. "Your sisters are all upset, and whatever happened last night to you and Matt sounds bizarre. You were so drained, even I could feel it."

She shook her head. "My sisters are still looking in the old family diaries for an explanation, but I don't have any answers, Jonas. I wish I did."

Chapter Six

The time, it was right, for a present or two,
And the fog on the sand holds a secret, a clue.

Jackson Deveau paced back and forth in complete silence. That was the first thing Kate noticed, how very silent he was. His clothes didn't rustle, and the soles of his shoes didn't make any noise. His eyes were as cold as ice, as bleak and as dead as she had ever seen in a human being. She sat down in the one good armchair and tried to repress a shiver. If the man had any gentleness in him, she couldn't detect it.

"I told you I didn't need a damned psychiatrist, Jonas," Jackson snapped, without looking at her. "Get her out of here. You think I want anyone to see me like this?" Sweat beaded on his forehead, dampened his dark, unruly hair.

"I'm not a psychiatrist, Mr. Deveau," Kate said. "I'm simply a friend of both Jonas and Matthew. I have a gift, and they thought it might help you in some way. Neither meant to upset you."

"Stop growling like a Neanderthal, Jackson, and let her talk," Matthew said. "You'd think you didn't have a civilized bone in your body."

"How strange that you would choose that particular description when my sisters said the same thing about you, Matthew," Kate replied. "Did you have a particularly disturbing dream, Mr. Deveau?"

Jackson whirled around and stalked toward her from across the room, his body moving like a large predatory cat's. "What'd they tell you about me? That I'm crazy? That I have nightmares and can't sleep? What the hell do you want me to say?"

Kate noted both Jonas and Matt were close to her, ready to defend her if necessary. In spite of the shiver of fear, she calmly looked up at the deputy. "They didn't say anything. They've told me next to nothing about you. Most of the children in town seem to have had a collective nightmare. So far, none of the adults have admitted to it, but everywhere we've been today, there's unexpected tension. I thought maybe you would be able to tell me about it. I'm getting garbled accounts from the children, and so far no adult has been courageous enough to admit they had the dream too."

Jackson raked both hands through his dark hair, the muscles rippling under his thin, tight tee shirt. He looked from Jonas to Matthew as if expecting a trap. "Kids have been having nightmares?"

Kate nodded. "Last night, after the fog rolled in, something bizarre happened. This morning, children from all over town were distressed and in tears, some traumatized by a dream they all seem to have shared."

"About what?" For the first time since she'd entered the room, Jackson sat down, his hands still gripping his head as if he had a violent headache.

"They described a skeleton man in a long coat and old hat."

Jackson hesitated, clearly reluctant to discuss his problem with her. He looked from Jonas to Matt and finally capitulated. "The coat and hat were old-fashioned, a heavy wool, maybe. There was no real face, just white-gray bones. There was a woman and a baby and a shepherd, or at least someone with a shepherd's staff." He scrubbed his hand over his face. "I go after real people, real threats, but this thing, this was from a place I can't get to, and I sense that everyone is in danger." He looked at Kate. "More than the actual dream, it was the feeling the dream left me with that's disturbing. The danger was real. I know it sounds crazy, but dammit, it was real!"

Matt stiffened. Jackson Deveau had never feared very much, certainly not his own mortality, yet he was deeply shaken by the nightmare.

"Then you felt it too. That the threat is real," Kate said, leaning toward Jackson.

Jackson drew back. Matt had forgotten to tell Kate the deputy didn't like physical contact. "I know it is." He looked at Jonas and Matt. "You two probably think I've finally gone around the bend, but I swear, whatever that thing was in my dream, he's looking for a way to walk among us."

"He uses the fog," Kate explained. He was no child to be soothed with Christmas stories and loving smiles. He was a grown man, a warrior, and what he needed was the naked truth. It was the only thing he would accept. He needed facts to assure him he was not losing his mind. "Whatever he or it is, he's growing stronger. I think the earthquake cracked a seal locking him deep in the earth, and he managed to escape. Matthew and I found a broken lid in the basement of the old mill. Something came out of a crack in the form of a noxious vapor. I've smelled the same odor in the fog." She met Jackson's gaze steadily. "If you're losing your mind, so am I. So is Matthew. And so are all the children of Sea Haven."

Matthew heard it then, that magical note that brought absolute peace to a troubled mind. He had become attuned to it, aware of the surge of energy in the room, going from Kate to the person she was speaking with. He was also aware of her absorbing the negative energy, taking it in and holding it away from its victim.

"That's a relief. I thought this time I was really losing my mind. I have nightmares, and I can deal with them, but this was something out of a horror film." Jackson shook his head. "I'm not going into an institution."

"You're the only one who ever thinks that way," Jonas said quietly. "So do your sisters have any ideas, Kate? This is more your field than ours." He nodded toward the other two Rangers. "We can be your soldiers, but you're going to have to give us a direction."

Kate leaned back in the chair, fatigue in every line of her body. "We're working on it. Abbey and Sarah and Damon were going through the diaries this morning. We'll find the reference and at least have a starting point."

"I notice you didn't mention Hannah," Jonas observed. There was a challenge in his voice. "Is she ill? Is that what's wrong with her?" When Kate didn't answer, Jonas swore. "Dammit, Kate, if she's ill, you owe it to me to tell me. Something's wrong with her."

"Something's always been wrong with her, Jonas, you just never noticed before." Kate folded her arms. "I'm not going to be bullied into telling you something that is Hannah's private business. Ask her."

Jonas swore again and stormed out. Kate rolled her eyes. "His temper hasn't improved much with age."

"Come on, Kate, I'm taking you to dinner at my house. I'm a great cook." Matt reached down and drew her up from the chair. "I think it's the only sanctuary left to us."

"I should go home and help the others."

Jackson stood up too. "You made me feel better. How did you do it?"

Kate smiled at him and offered her hand. "It was a pleasure finally to meet you, Mr. Deveau. Jonas and Matthew speak so highly of you."

He hesitated but took her hand. "Please call me Jackson."

Kate felt the jolt of his heavy burden go up her arm. It was difficult to maintain her smile when she felt the brooding darkness in the man. She wasn't Libby. She couldn't heal the sick, and in any case, she didn't sense that Jackson Deveau was physically ill so much as spiritually so. "I wish you peace, Jackson," she murmured softly, and allowed Matthew to draw her from the house out into the cool air.

"He didn't have a Christmas tree up, or any decorations at all," she said sadly. "If anyone needs Christmas, it's that man."

"He'll work it out, Kate," Matthew assured her. "He has his

demons, but the bottom line is, honor and integrity rule his life. He would never do any of the things he's afraid he will, and, just like Jonas, he would protect this town and the people in it with his last breath."

"I'm glad you brought him to Sea Haven. You were right about this place. There's just something about the way the people are here—they're welcoming to outsiders." The interior of his car was warm after the chilling wind blowing in off the ocean.

"Did your sisters really call me a Neanderthal?"

She burst out laughing. "Well, yes, but in a good way. I think they could easily picture you beating your chest and tossing your woman over your shoulder to carry her off to somewhere private."

He nodded. "I can understand that. I do have those urges. Often." He looked at her, his hand still around the key. "I really want to take you back to my house, Kate." He waited a heartbeat before starting the engine.

"Are your brothers going to be there? Because, honestly, I think I'm too tired to have them all laughing at me today. I'd probably burst into tears."

He pressed a hand to his heart. "Don't even say that. I think I'd rather take a bullet than see you cry. And my brothers don't laugh at you." He glanced at her to see if she was serious.

"They *always* laugh at me," she said. "I'm always doing these idiotic things whenever I'm around you. Like the other day when you had that accident and you tried to get out of the truck and I was standing too close." She looked down at her hands. "Danny just about fell out of the truck laughing."

"At *me*, Katie, never at you. My entire family knows how I feel about you, and they think it's a riot that I can make such a complete fool of myself every time you're near."

Kate sat very still, her gaze fixed on his face. "How do you feel about me?"

"I've made that pretty damn clear, Kate."

"Have you? I know you're attracted to me physically."

He gave a small snort of derision. "Is that what you call it? I haven't had a good night's sleep since I looked at you when you were fifteen years old. I hate admitting that. I shouldn't have been looking at you, but I did, and I just knew. I've had more dreams about you, more fantasies, than any man should admit to having." He pulled the car into the driveway of his yard and turned off the engine before facing her. "Hell, Kate, if you didn't know, you're the only person in this town who didn't. Jonas asked me last night if I was stalking you."

"He wouldn't do that. You're his friend. He must have been kidding."

"With his hand on his gun. Afraid not, and here you are, at my house, all alone with me. Are you coming in?"

"Am I supposed to be afraid now?"

"I thought my fantasies might scare you off."

"Did you?" Kate slid out of the car. The wind whipped her hair around and tugged at her clothes. "Actually I'm intrigued."

His entire body reacted to her sultry tone. Maybe she didn't mean it the way it sounded, but he was going to take her words as an invitation to love her every way a man could love a woman.

Kate smiled to herself as she went up the stairs to his home.

It was situated on the bluff above the ocean, his deck wrapping around the house providing a view from every direction. The house itself was obviously built for a man of Matt's size. The ceilings were vaulted, there were few walls, so the space seemed enormous, one room running directly into the next. His furniture suited the house, casual, yet overstuffed to go with the dimensions of the house.

"It's so beautiful, Matthew. I love all the bay windows and the alcoves and the way everything is so spacious. Did you design it?"

He felt a little glow of pleasure. "Yes, I wanted a home I was comfortable living in day in and day out. I need space. Even the doorways are wider and taller than normal, so I don't always feel as if I might have to duck."

"I love the open beams and the rock fireplace. This is what I had in mind for my house, or at least something very similar. I love the beams and the natural-looking fireplace in the mill." She turned to smile at him. "We do have very similar taste."

His heart did a curious somersault in his chest. He gripped the edge of the door. "I think so. It should be easy to come up with a design you'll really fall in love with." He said the words deliberately.

Kate stilled and turned her head to look at him. The movement was graceful and elegant. So Kate. He ached, just looking at her. Color swept her face. She glanced from him to the tall Christmas tree in his front room. It was a silver tip, beautiful and decorated with lights and a few ornaments. "Did you put up your tree?"

"I brought in the tree and hung the lights. Mom insisted I get ornaments. She said I was supposed to have a theme, but I just picked up ones I liked."

Kate wandered around the tree. One of the ornaments was a wooden house carved by a local artist. She was surprised and pleased to see it was her cliff house. She didn't comment on the ornament, but she hoped it meant he'd been thinking of her when he'd bought the miniature replica of her home.

"This is my favorite room. I spend a lot of time in here. My office is straight ahead, and I have a large library. I call it a library; Danny and Jonas call it my den." He grinned at her. "They talked me into a pool table."

She laughed. "Of course they did. I'll bet they had to twist your arm."

Matt hastily gathered up a few shirts he'd tossed aside earlier in the week. There was an old pizza box on the coffee table along with an empty doughnut box overturned beside a half-full coffee cup.

Kate grinned at him. "I see you're into health food."

"I actually like to cook. I used to cook all the time for the men in my unit." He opened a door, tossed his shirts inside without looking where they landed, and hastily closed the door to gather up the dirty boxes and coffee cup. "I haven't been home much. Dad's running a big job, and all of us have been working to bring it in on time."

"Matthew." Kate put her hand lightly on his arm. "Are you nervous?"

He stood there looking down at her upturned face. Her enormous soft eyes. Her tempting mouth. Could she be any more beautiful? "Hell, yes, I'm nervous. I don't even know what a woman like you would be doing in the same house with a man like me."

"A woman like me?" She looked genuinely puzzled.

Matt groaned. "Come on, Kate. Are you telling me you haven't known I've been wild about you for years? I can't even have a good time with another woman. I've tried dating numerous women. We have one date, and I know it isn't going to work."

"You're wild about me?" she echoed.

He tossed the boxes on the couch and pulled her into his arms. Hard. Possessive. Commanding Ranger style. "I can't even think straight around you."

There was no way to think when his mouth took hers, hot and hungry and devouring her. Her body melted into his, her arms sliding around his neck, her fingers brushing the nape of his neck intimately, creeping into his hair while she met his ravenous hunger with her own.

He couldn't kiss her and not touch her soft, tempting skin. Without conscious thought, he slid his hand beneath her blouse to move up the soft expanse of skin. Just that slight contact brought him such deep pleasure it bordered on pain. He trembled, his hand actually shaking as he brushed the pads of his fingers over her rib cage, and up to cup the soft weight of her breast in his palm. His body went into overdrive, his heart slamming in his chest and his jeans growing uncomfortably tight.

"Aren't you going to stop me, Kate? One of us should know what we're doing." He wanted to be fair with her. She was exhausted and obviously not thinking straight, arching into his hand, pushing closer, rubbing her body against his. Soft little moans came from her throat, driving him right over the edge.

He found himself kissing her again and again, long hot kisses that pushed their temperatures even higher.

Her lips smiled under the assault of his. "I know exactly what I'm doing, Matthew, you're the one who's unclear." Her hands dropped to the buttons of her blouse.

There was a strange roaring in his ears. He had waited years for this moment. Kate Drake in his home. In his arms. Kate's body open to his exploration. It would take a lifetime to satisfy him. More than that. Much more. Her blouse fell open, exposing the creamy swell of her breasts. White lace cupped her skin lovingly.

Matt stared down at her body, mesmerized by the sight of his large hand holding her, his thumb brushing her nipple through the white lace. For one moment, it occurred to him he was making the entire thing up. Kate Drake. His Christmas present. He bent his head to her breast, his mouth closing around soft flesh and lace. His tongue teased and danced over her nipple while his arms enfolded her closer.

The pounding on the front door was abrupt, loud, and unexpected. Kate cried out, and he felt her heart beneath her skin jump with fear.

Matt lifted his head, his gray eyes appearing silver as they smoldered with a mixture of anger and desire. "Don't worry, Katie." He pulled the edges of her blouse together. Why couldn't the world leave them alone for one damned hour? Was that too much to ask?

Kate buttoned her blouse and tried to finger comb her hair. He caught her wrist and brought her hand to his mouth. "You look beautiful. Whoever it is can just go away."

She waited in the middle of his living room while he yanked the door open. The sheriff stood there, his fist poised for another assault. "Jonas, I'm beginning to think our friendship is going to suffer," Matt greeted with a scowl.

Jonas pushed right past him. "Come on out here and take a look at this." His voice was grim. He stalked through the house to the ocean side, pushing open the double doors leading to the deck overlooking the sea. "What the hell is going on, Kate?"

The fog whirled around the house as if alive. Dark and gray and gloomy, the mist was thick, almost oily. It crept up the walls and swirled around the chimney. Jonas glared at the fog. "No one can drive anywhere. Car accidents are happening all over town. Your sister Elle called. She's in the islands and yet she had *the exact same dream as Jackson and the children*. How could she have the same dream? She said to tell you the symbols meant something. When I asked her what they meant she said you would know."

Both men looked at Kate. She hesitated, trying to remember, but there was nothing that seemed to be of great significance. "There were symbols on the seal, but the only thing of importance I could read was that a locking spell had been placed on the lid to hold something in the ground. I'll call Elle and ask her to give me details. Is she on her way home? She was going to try to make it back for Christmas."

"She said she'd be catching a late flight." Jonas stared at the thick gray blanket of mist, frowning as he did so. "The worst of the fog seems to be centered here. It's much heavier around your house, Matt. People are going to start dying if we don't figure out what's going on. We've been lucky, most people pulled their cars over to wait it out and the accidents that have occurred have been minor. But it would be very easy to drive off the cliff in this dense fog. We've asked the radio stations to alert everyone to the driving hazards."

"I'm guessing you called the weather station and the meteorologists there told you this fog is unnatural," Matt said with a small sigh. The supernatural wasn't his realm of expertise, but he had the feeling he was going to have to learn more about it very fast. A part of him had hoped it would all go away. Instead, the fog was wrapped tightly around his house. He glanced at Kate. She stood very still, her hand to her throat, staring out into the dark gray mist. There was fear on her face.

Anger began to smolder in the pit of his belly, not hot and fiery, but ice-cold and clear, dangerous and deadly, an emotion he recognized from his combat days. Matthew took Kate by the shoulders and pulled her back, away from the deck and into the safety of the house. "Did Sarah say whether or not they found anything in the diaries, Jonas? They were all looking, hoping to find an explanation."

Jonas shook his head. "Sarah said she doesn't have a clue as to what's going on, but she thought with all the sisters concentrating, they might be able to drive this fog back to sea to give us more time to figure it out."

Matt's hands tightened on Kate's shoulders. "I don't want you to do it again, Katie. I think you're making it angry, and it's striking back at you. Why else would it have followed us to my house and stayed here?" He couldn't articulate the emotions the fog gave off, but there was something dark and ugly about it that reeked of pitiless hostility. He didn't want Kate anywhere near it.

"We can't take chances, Matthew," Kate said, her voice trembling. She pressed her lips together. Instinctively she moved back toward Matt as if for protection. "Jonas said there have already been traffic accidents."

Matt could feel her reluctance. Whatever was in the fog had grown in strength and intensity. The previous night it had been an eerie annoyance; now it seemed darker . . . more aggressive and dangerous.

"The fog swept through town, Kate, right after the two of you left Jackson's house," Jonas explained. "People came out of their houses to stand there and watch it. The sheriff's office logged well over a hundred calls. When it receded, it left behind a mess. All over town gifts left outside, everything from bicycles and ATVs to garden furniture, were smashed and covered with sea trash—sand, kelp, driftwood, smashed seashells, you name it. Even crabs crawling around." Jonas pushed back his hat and rested his gaze on Kate's face. "The worst damage was done to the town square. The three wise men statues were all but destroyed, and the gifts they carried were ground into the lawn. The statues had kelp wrapped around their necks and wrists and ankles. It was bizarre and ugly and it scared everyone enough that the folks on the committee are concerned about the safety of the men playing the parts of the wise men in the pageant. Do you think it was a warning?"

Kate rubbed at her throbbing temples. She was already so tired. She felt drained and just wanted to lie down for a few hours. "I honestly don't know, Jonas, but the entity is accelerating its destructive behavior."

"Dammit, Kate, what the hell could be alive in the fog?" Matt burst out, wanting to throttle the thing. "I don't want you any-where near this stuff. Why do you have to be the one to face it?"

"My voice. The others can channel through me. And Hannah can call up the wind to drive it back to sea."

He wasn't touching that. It sounded like witches and spells and things he saw in movies, not in real life.

Matt began a slow massage at the nape of Kate's neck to help ease the tension out of her. "Katie, why would this thing smash gifts? If it's capable of destroying things and moving objects as it did with the wreaths on the doors, why such a silly, almost petty display? Why do the gifts bother it? What would be the significance?"

Jonas followed them back to the sliding glass door. "That's a good question. Is that all it can do? When the calls started coming in I thought it was kids and childish pranks. Smashing gifts and outdoor ornaments and leaving behind dead fish are relatively harmless acts of vandalism a kid might do. Well, at least I thought a kid might be the culprit until I saw the three kings smashed to pieces. Jackson came out to the square to take a look at the damage, and he said the scene was reminiscent of his nightmare."

Kate shook her head. "I think it's growing stronger, testing its abilities. It doesn't feel childish to me. It used wreaths, a symbol often associated with Christmas, and now gifts. Elle said the sym-bols matter. Gifts obviously are another symbol of Christmas." She sighed and rubbed at her temples. "Obviously this thing does not like Christmas at all. Any guesses as to why?"

"I have no idea," Matt said. He used his body to gently

shepherd her farther back into the room, wanting to close the doors against the fog.

She turned in his arms and pressed her body close to his for strength and comfort. "My sisters are waiting. Even Libby. It isn't easy to sustain a channeling for any great length of time."

Matt tightened his arms around her, holding her captive, holding her safe. He buried his face against her neck. "I hate this, Kate. You have no idea how much. I want to pack you up and take you far away from this place. I know you're in danger."

"If I don't do this, Matthew, one of my sisters will try, and they don't have my voice." She hugged him hard and slowly pulled away from him.

Matt allowed her to slip from his arms, taut with fear for her when she stepped onto the deck. He stepped beside her. Close. Protective. Daring the thing to come through him to get to her. Jonas took up a position on her other side. Kate closed her eyes and raised her face to the sky.

A breeze from the sea fluttered against her face. She felt the cooling touch. She felt the joining of her sisters. All seven, together yet apart. Strength flowed into her, through her. She lifted her arms and knew Hannah stood on the battlement of their ancestral home and simultaneously did the same.

Matt heard the moaning of the wind. Out on the ocean, the caps on the waves reached high and foamed white. The fog became frenzied, whirling and spinning madly, winding around Kate so that for a moment it obscured Matt's vision of her. He reached out blindly, instinctively, and yanked her into the protection of his body. "This is bullshit, Kate." He pressed her face against his chest and wrapped his arms around her head to keep the fog from getting at her.

Kate didn't struggle. She didn't act in any way as if she noticed. Her voice was soft, barely above a whisper, yet the wind carried it into the bank of mist, and it vibrated through the vapor, taking on a life of its own. Kate remained against him, her eyes closed but her chanting continuing, a gift of harmony and peace, of contentment and solidarity. She called on the elements of the earth. Matt heard that clearly.

Voices rose on the wind. Seawater leaped in response to the chant, waves rising high, bursting through the fogbank and breaking it into tendrils out over the ocean. The wind howled, gathering strength, rushing at them, bringing the taste of salt and droplets of water to brush over their faces. Thunder crashed, shaking the deck. Still the voices continued, and the tempest built.

"Hannah." Jonas said her name softly, slightly awed by the raw power forged and controlled between the sisters.

Kate took a deep breath and let go. Let go of her sisters and her body and the physical world she lived in to enter the shadow world. Far off, she heard the echo of Hannah's frightened cry. The world wasn't silent as one would expect. She never got used to that. There were noises, moans and cries, not quite human, unidentifiable. Static, the sound of a radio not tuned properly. And the terrible howl of the wind endlessly blowing. It was cold and bleak and barren. A world of darkness and despair. She looked around carefully, trying to find the one she was seeking.

She wasn't alone. She could feel others watching her. Some

were merely curious, others hostile. None were friendly. She was a living being, and they were long gone. Something slithered close to her feet. She felt the touch of something slimy against her arm. Kate took another breath and called out softly. At once she saw it. A terrifying sight. Tall, bare white bones, the skull ghastly with a gaping mouth and empty sockets for eyes. It wasn't fully formed. A great hole was in the chest cavity. The ribs were missing. It came striding toward her, and she noticed that the skeleton wore old-fashioned boots stuck at the end of the sticklike bones of its legs. She might have laughed had it not been so frightening. The bones rattled as it rushed toward her, deadly purpose in every bone.

"Kate!" Abigail's cry echoed Hannah's and Sarah's.

Kate held up her hand to ward the thing off as it reached her.

Matt felt Kate's energy crackling in the air around them, a fierce force never wavering, yet her slender body shook with the effort, or maybe with fear, crumbling beneath the strain. Without warning he felt every hair on his body stand up. Kate went sickly pale. Afraid for her, he swept her up into his arms and held her tight against his chest, the only thing he could do to shelter her from the onslaught of the wind and the menace of the fog.

Kate wrenched herself from the shadow world, opened her eyes, expecting to see Matt. Empty sockets stared back at her. The skull's mouth gaped wide, the jaw loose, bony fingers wrapping around her throat. She screamed and pulled away, trying to run when there was nowhere to go. The pressure on her throat increased. She choked.

The wind rose to a howl. Feminine voices became commanding. The bony fingers slid from Kate's throat. She fell to the ground and stared in horror as the voices of the Drake women forced the skeleton away from her one dragging step at a time. Those pitiless empty eye sockets stared at her with malice. Kate tried to scoot crablike in the opposite direction, feeling sick as the entity clacked white bones together in a dark, ugly promise of retaliation.

The wind blew sand into the air, obscuring Kate's vision. She squeezed her eyes closed tightly against the new assault. At once she felt Matt's body pressed close to hers. Afraid to look, she lifted her lashes, hands out in front of her for protection. Matt's reassuring face was there, the planes and angles familiar to her. She buried her face against his throat, felt the warmth of his body leaching some of the icy cold from hers.

The fog crept back toward the ocean slowly, almost grudgingly, retreating from around the house and deck to the beach, with obvious reluctance. With Kate safely in his arms, Matt stared in horror at the wet sand. Distinct footprints were left behind, as if someone had backed toward the ocean with short, dragging steps, a man's boots with run-down heels. A cold chill swept down his spine. His gaze went from the prints in the sand to Jonas. "What the hell are we dealing with here?"

Chapter Seven

As lovers meet beneath mistletoe bright,
Terror ignites down below them this night.

Matt stared down at Kate's face. She lay in his bed, sound asleep, the signs of exhaustion present even as she slept. She looked more fragile than ever, as if fighting back the entity in the fog had taken most of her spirit and drained all of her strength. The curtains over his sliding glass door were pulled back to allow him a clear view of the ocean. He had always enjoyed the sight and sound of the waves pounding, but now he searched the horizon for signs of the fog. Kate was worn out. He worried that if the entity returned, she wouldn't have the strength to fight it, even though she'd slept for hours. The day had disappeared, and night had fallen.

He rubbed his hands over his face to wipe away his own exhaustion. He hadn't slept the night before, standing watch at Kate's bedside, and he was feeling the effects. He had stripped her of her clothes and wrapped her in one of his shirts. It was far too big for her and covered every curve. He'd tucked her in his bed and all the while she lay passively, making little effort to do anything but close her eyes. He had the feeling she'd faced something far worse than the fog, but she hadn't been ready to talk about it with him. Recognizing the signs of exhaustion, he hadn't pushed her.

Matt removed his shirt and shoes and socks and stretched out beside her. He had built his home in the hopes of finding a wife when he returned from serving his country, but no matter how many women he had dated, there had been only one woman for him. Kate had been in his dreams from the moment he'd first laid eyes on her. He would never forget that moment, driving his father's truck, his rowdy brothers cranking up the music and laughing happily. He had glanced casually to his right not realizing that his life was about to change forever. Kate was standing in the creek bed with her six sisters, her head thrown back, laughing, her eyes dancing, totally oblivious to his gaze. A jolt of electricity had sizzled through his entire body. In that one moment, Kate Drake had managed to burn her brand into his very bones, and no other woman would do for him.

"Matthew?" Her voice was drowsy. Sexy. It poured into his body with the force of a bolt of lightning, heating his blood and bringing every nerve ending alive.

"I'm here, Katie," he answered, wrapping his body around hers as he slipped his arm around her waist.

"Didn't Sea Haven always seem like home to you? When you were far away, in another country, in danger, didn't you dream of this place?"

"I dreamed of you. You were home to me, Kate." There in

the darkness with the ocean pounding outside his bedroom he could admit the truth to her. "You got me through the gunfire, and the ugliness, and it was the thought of you that brought me back to Sea Haven. My family always kept track of you for me."

Kate turned her face into his shoulder, snuggling closer to him. "I heard you were doing things that seemed so scary to me. I have such an imagination, and I would wake up in the middle of night picturing you rising up out of the desert sand in your camouflage fatigues with your rifle and enemies all around you. Sometimes the dreams were so vivid I'd actually get sick. I've never told that to anyone, not even my sisters. They saw the differences in us and knew we weren't right for each other."

"Kate." He said her name tenderly. With an aching need in it. "How can you say that? Or even think it? I was made for you. To be with you. I feel it so strongly, the rightness of it. You feel it too. I know you do." He held her possessively, his arms locking her to him. Matt buried his face in the soft warmth of her neck. "Katie, you can't hand a man his dream, then take it away. Especially not a man like me. I stood back and gave you all the room in the world when you were too young for me. Later, when you were grown, you were busy and happy with your life, traveling around the world doing what you do. I never once made a move on you. I knew you needed your freedom to pursue your writing. But now you're home, telling me you're ready to settle down, and I can't just step back and pretend we don't feel anything for one another. Every time you looked at me, you had to know we belonged. You should never have kissed me if you weren't willing to give a relationship between us a try."

Kate closed her eyes, feeling tears welling up. His lips moved over her neck, drifted lower to nudge the collar of the shirt aside. Her pulse pounded frantically. Her heart went into overdrive. "I'm not brave the way you are, Matthew," she admitted in a small voice. "I can't be like you. I'm not at all a person of action. In a few months when you realize that, you'll be so disappointed in me, and you'll have too much honor to tell me."

Matt lifted his head and looked down at her. Tears shimmered in her eyes, and his heart nearly stopped beating in his chest. "What the hell are you talking about, Kate?" He bent his head to kiss the tears away. He tasted grief. Fear. An aching longing. "Dammit." He muttered the words in sheer frustration, then kissed her hard, his mouth claiming hers. A ravenous hunger burst through him, over him. There was a strange roaring in his head. His chest was tight, his heart pounding with the force of thunder. He had faced enemy fire without flinching, but he couldn't bear the idea of Kate walking away from him.

He poured everything he felt into his kiss. Everything he was. His hands framed her face, held her to him while he ravaged her mouth. Heat spread like a wildfire, through him, through her, catching them both on fire until he thought he might ignite. She melted into him, her arms sliding around him, nearly as possessive as he was. He lifted his head to look at her, memorizing every beloved line and angle of her face. He was gentle, his fingertips stroking caresses and tracing her cheekbones, the shape of her eyes, the curve of her eyebrows. The pad of his thumb slid back and forth over the softness of her lips. He loved her mouth, loved everything about her. "Kate." He kissed her gently. Once. Twice. "How could you think I don't know you?

We've lived in the same town practically all our lives. I've watched you. I've listened to you. Do you know how many times I've dreamed of you?"

"Dreams aren't the same as reality, Matt," Kate said sadly.

Her gaze moved over his face, examining every inch of his features. Matt waited, holding his breath. He was rough and she was elegant. He was a man who protected the ones he loved. And he loved Kate Drake.

"Matthew ..." There was that catch in her voice again. Need. Caution.

Matt couldn't imagine why Kate would fear a relationship with him, a life with him, but the thought that she might pull away had him bending his head. His teeth tugged at her delicate ear. His tongue made a foray along the small shape. She shivered in reaction. He grew harder. Thicker. His body was heavy and painful, straining against the confines of his jeans. "Katie, unzip my jeans." He breathed the words into her ear, his lips drifting lower to find her neck. Her soft, sensitive neck.

Kate closed her eyes as his teeth nipped her chin, her throat, as his lips found her collarbone, his chin nudging aside the shirt collar again. She ached with wanting him, her body hot and sensitive. Her breasts felt swollen, begging for his attention. What was so wrong with reaching for something, just this one time? He was everything she'd ever wanted, yet was always out of her reach. Matthew Granite was a fighter, larger-than-life. He'd done things she would never comprehend, never experience. He felt like a hero from one of her novels, not quite real and too good to be true. She knew she'd thought of him when she'd written each and every one of her books. She'd used him as her role model because, to her, he was everything a man should be. Why would he ever choose to be with a woman who looked at life, wrote about life, but refused to participate in it?

Kate was certain she was going to leap from the bed and run, but her body had a mind of its own. She was already working on the button at the waistband of his jeans, finding the zipper and dragging it down. The air left his lungs in a rush when her hand shaped the thick, heavy bulge, caressed and stroked with loving fingers. "You're wearing too many clothes, Matthew," she pointed out, determined to have her time with him, even if it couldn't be forever.

"So are you." His hands dropped to the buttons of her shirt, sliding them open so that the edges gaped apart. He raised his upper body in order to stare down at her, to drink in the sight of Kate Drake in his bed. She shrugged out of the shirt and allowed it fall to the floor before lying back. His mouth went dry.

Outside, the continual booming of the sea seemed to match the pounding of his heart. In the soft light, her skin was flawless, inviting. Her breasts were full and round, her nipples taut inviting peaks. Kate's long hair spilled around the pillows, just as he'd always fantasized. For a moment he was caught and held by the sight of her, unable to believe she was real. "There was more than one night out in the desert when I was lying half-buried in the sand, surrounded by the enemy. It was important to get in and out without being seen. The enemy showed up and set up camp virtually on top of us. It was the fantasy of you lying just like this in my bed, waiting for me at home, that got me through it."

"Then I'm very glad, Matthew." She tugged on the loop at the waistband of his jeans. "Get rid of those things."

He didn't wait for a second invitation. "I've always loved you, Kate. Always." She would never know how often he thought of her, in the hot arid desert and the freezing nights, in the painful sandstorms. Lying in a field with the enemy not ten feet from him. He had been all over the world, performing high-risk covert missions in places no American leader would ever admit to sending troops, and Kate had gone with him every single time.

He stroked his hand down her leg, more to ensure she was real than for any other reason. He felt her shiver in response. Her lips parted slightly. Her sea-green eyes watched his every move. Matt knelt on the bed, tugging on her ankles, a silent command to open her legs. She complied, parting her thighs wide enough to allow him to slide between her legs.

Matt was a big man. At once Kate felt vulnerable, the cool night air teasing the tiny curls at the junction of her legs. His hands, sliding up her thighs, were gentle, removing her anxiety as fast as it rose. She loved the way he looked at her, almost worshiping her skin, her body, his hot gaze exploring in the same thorough way as his hands. A wave of heat rushed through her, of anticipation. Matt took his time caressing every curve along her slender leg, even the back of her knee as if memorizing the texture of every inch of her was terribly important.

His touch sent darts of fire racing over her skin, penetrating every nerve ending until she could hardly lie still beneath his touch. Her breath was coming in a gasp, and heat coiled deep inside her, a terrible pressure beginning to build.

Matt couldn't contain himself another moment. She lay there like a beautiful offering. He bent over her, kissed her enticing navel, his tongue swirling in the small, sexy dip, his hands continuing their foray lower. He felt her reaction, a warm, moist welcoming against his palm as he pushed against her. He kissed his way up her smooth body to the underside of her breast. Kate gasped and arched her body, her hips moving restlessly. She flushed, her luminous skin taking on a faint peach-colored glow.

He groaned. His body reacted with another swelling surge. Fire raced through his veins. His tongue flicked her nipple, once, twice, and his mouth settled over her breast. Kate cried out, her hands grasping handfuls of his hair, tugging him closer to her. She was magic. He could think of no other word to describe her. His body pressed into the softness of hers, while he lavished attention on her breasts. He'd dreamed of her skin, of the feel and shape of her every curve, and his imagination hadn't come close to the real thing. He cupped her other breast, teasing her nipple, feeling the response in Kate. She was very sensitive to his touch, to his mouth, to every caressing stroke. And she showed him she loved his touch.

Her soft moans heightened Matt's pleasure. He hungered for the sounds and responses Kate showed him. He needed them. She was generous in her reception, her hands moving over him, her body restless with the same hunger. He flicked her nipple one more time with his tongue and took possession of her lips, swallowing her moan, robbing her of breath.

Matt kissed her mouth over and over because no amount of kissing Kate would ever be enough. He trailed kisses down her throat, in the valley between her breasts. Her fingers dug into his hips, urging a union, but he took his time. He rained kisses across her stomach, pausing to dip again into her fascinating belly button.

"Matthew, really, I don't think I'm going to live through this." Her breath came in a series of ragged gasps.

"I waited a long time, Kate. I'm not rushing things." He ducked his head, his tongue sliding wickedly over her wet, hot sheath. She nearly jumped out of her skin. He grinned at her. "I may only have this one chance to prove my worth to you. I'm not about to blow my chances by charging the battlefield." He bent his head and blew softly against her sensitive body. He caught her hips more firmly, dragged her closer to him, and bent his head to taste her.

Kate screamed and nearly rose off the bed. He held her hips firmly, locking her to him while he feasted. She was hotter than he had ever imagined, a well of passion, and he had just begun to tap into it. He felt the first strong ripple of her muscles rushing to overtake her, and his body swelled even larger in response.

"I think you're ready for me, Kate." He didn't bother to hide the satisfaction in his voice. It was still a miracle to him that she chose to be with him. He pushed her thighs a little wider to accommodate his hips, pressing against her so that the sensitive tip of his penis slipped into her hot, welcoming body. The breath slammed out of his lungs. He pushed deeper so that she swallowed the tip, her tight muscles gripping with soft relentless pressure that sent violent waves of pleasure shooting through his body.

Kate gasped and clutched at the bedsheets. Matt froze, understanding dawning. He bit back a string of swear words, took a deep breath, and let it out. "Relax, honey, just relax. I swear, we fit together perfectly."

She smiled at him. "I'm not afraid, you idiot, I've never felt this before, and it's amazing. I want more, Matthew, all of you. Stop being so careful." If he didn't quit moving so slowly, she was going to spontaneously combust. She wanted to push her body over his. It was difficult to hold back when every instinct demanded she lift her body to receive his.

"Dammit, Kate, you're not experienced." He was sweating now. It was impossible to hold back. She was squirming, her hips pushing hard into his, and he was inching his way deeper into the hot core of her. Pleasure was building at such a ferocious rate he was losing all control just when he needed it the most. She was so damned tight, squeezing and gripping him, the friction like a hot velvet fist pumping him dry. Matt thrust deeper because he had no other choice. It was that or risk death. He was certain of it. She took him in, gasping with pleasure, when he'd been so worried.

Matt let go of his fears and took the ride, thrusting deep, tilting her body until she could take all of him. He moved the way he wanted, the way he needed, hard and fast and deep, joining them together in a rush of heat. The ocean pounded the shore just outside the glass door. Matt was unaware of it, unaware of anything but Kate and her body and the way she gave herself so completely to him. She came over and over, crying out, clutching his arms, lifting up to meet him as eagerly as he surged into her. The explosion started somewhere near his toes and blew through his entire body. His voice was hoarse, a roar of joy, as he emptied himself into her.

He sank on top of her, completely spent, completely sated, his lungs burning for air and his heart pounding out of his chest. And it was a perfect moment in time. Her body was soft and welcoming beneath his. He turned his head to capture her breast in his mouth, to lie there in contentment, to have her with him. He had been in hell many times in his life. But he had never been in paradise until now. His arms tightened around her possessively. "Dammit, Katie, don't ask me to give you up." He said the words around her tantalizing breast.

Kate combed her fingers through his hair, lying back with her eyes closed, savoring every aftershock while his mouth pulled strongly at her breast, and his tongue did delicious things to cause fiery sparks zinging in her deepest core. "Silly man," she murmured, clearly amused by his reaction. "I'm right here. Did you think I was going to grab my clothes and go slinking off?" The smile faded from her mind. There was a small part of her that wanted to do just that, run while she still had the chance. Self-preservation was strong in her. Everything about Matthew appealed to her. His lovemaking dazzled her, but she wasn't so far gone that she couldn't look ahead to the future and realize they couldn't spend every moment in bed.

Matt shifted position enough to take most of his weight off of her smaller body, but his arms held her in place and he turned her so he could keep access to the temptation of her breasts. His tongue flicked her nipple. "I want you forever, Kate. I want to grow old and have you here in my arms. I want children. I've wanted you for so long. I don't think that's about to change." He noticed that when he drew her breast into his mouth her hips moved restlessly. It was a wonderful find and one he intended

117

to spend time exploring. He stroked her stomach and moved his hand between her thighs to cup her heat. She jumped but pushed against his hand. His thumb caressed her, his finger pushed deep to find the one spot that could give her another release.

Kate was Kate. She didn't try to pull away or pretend she wasn't ready for another orgasm, she rode his hand, gasping with pleasure, her fingers digging into his shoulder with one hand and the other curled in his hair directing his mouth. He wanted this every damn day of his life. Not just a Christmas present. He wanted to go to sleep with her breast in his mouth. He wanted to wake up with his body buried deep in hers. He wanted to be the man to bring her pleasure in every way possible.

"Marry me, Kate. Stay with me."

She heard him through a haze of piercing fulfillment, so sated with contentment, with the throbbing fire spreading through her like a storm, she could only lay there dazed by the gift he was holding out to her. The temptation.

Matt lifted his head to look at her, his fingers still buried deep inside of her. "Kate. I'm serious. Marry me. I'll make you happy."

"I am happy, Matthew," she said. "I lead a relatively quiet life. I work hard, meet my deadlines, and I'm looking forward to renovating the old mill."

Sensing her withdrawal, he turned to lie over the top of her, his head resting on her stomach. He pressed a series of kisses along her sensitive skin and flicked her enticing navel with his tongue. "We can renovate the old mill together, Katie."

"You're moving a little too fast for me, Matthew."

His Kate was becoming cautious again. He should have known she would. He nibbled his way down her body to her thigh. "We don't have to move fast. We don't have to go for the wedding and children and the entire package if that's too much for you right now." His teeth nipped as his fingers moved deep inside of her. He wasn't above a little persuasion. "We can keep it to great sex. Incredible sex."

She heard the note of pain in his voice, and it upset her. "Matthew, I'm not normal. I'll never be normal. You think you know me, but you don't. You can't. My sisters and I inherited a legacy that we have no choice but to use. It comes with a price. Sarah has phenomenal athletic abilities, and she can sense things before they happen. Abigail can demand the truth. I can bring peace to people in need. Libby heals people. Joley has incredible powers, and so does Hannah. Both command the wind and the sea. And our Elle." Kate shook her head. "Elle's legacy is tremendous and important and very frightening. She has it all, along with the responsibility to bring the next generation into the world. We each have gifts, but when we're together, we are very powerful. We try to lead our own lives, but we keep the cliff house so we always can be together."

He lifted his head, his silver eyes darkening to smoldering charcoal. "You think I can't understand honor and commitment? You live by a code the same as I do. I understand codes. You have a way of life that's important to you. Why would you think it would be any less important to me? I don't mind sharing you with your sisters, Kate."

She sighed. "I'm sorry. I didn't mean to upset you, Matthew. I just want you to know what we do isn't going to go away, even if we wanted it to. And it isn't only sharing me with my sisters, but with a lot of other people as well." But it was more than that. She wasn't like her sisters, embracing life in the way they did. In the way he did.

"I know a lot of ways to be happy with you," he promised, dipping his head to her breasts, not wanting her to see his face. "We'll take it slow if that's what you need, Katie. Just don't shut me out because you're afraid."

She tried not to react to his words. Of course she was afraid. She was afraid of everything, and that was *exactly* why she couldn't agree to marry him.

He kissed her ribs, her belly button. The phone rang, startling them both. He ignored it, dropping kisses over her stomach. The shrill ringing of the telephone persisted. Matthew sighed heavily and reached lazily across her small body, deliberately brushing across her bare breasts. "Hello." It was the middle of the night. He didn't have to be polite. He didn't want to waste a single moment of his time with Kate, especially when she needed persuasion to stay with him.

"This is Elle Drake. I need to speak with Kate." It was Kate's youngest sister, reputed to be traveling home for Christmas. There was anxiety in her voice. Without a word, Matt passed the phone to Kate.

She sat up, dragging the sheet over her breasts. "Elle? What's wrong, hon?"

"Something's there, Kate. Something's where you are. Below you. It's dangerous, and it's below you."

"Are you certain?" Kate leaned over the bed to examine the floor. Matt could clearly hear the terrified voice on the other end of the phone. "Calm down, Elle, I'm fine. We're both fine."

"Kate, I'm really afraid for you. What's going on? I saw you clearly. You were kissing Matthew Granite. There was mistletoe very close to you, but not directly over your head. And then something bright burst out from under you, a flash and flames and it was truly frightening. What is it?"

"I don't know, but we'll find out."

Matt was already out of the bed, pulling on his jeans, his eyes searching every inch of the floor. Moonlight pouring through the sliding glass door provided enough light for him to search every corner of the room. With his training ingrained in him, Matt chose not to turn on the light and give their position away to the enemy. He might have dismissed the phone call as hysteria or a nightmare, but he had been around the Drake sisters long enough now to see the strange things Jonas sometimes spoke of and to know to take them seriously.

"I'll call you later, Elle," Kate said, her eyes mirroring her fright. "Thank you for the warning." She placed the receiver in its cradle and looked up at Matt. "She's never wrong, Matthew. Do you have a basement? Maybe whatever it is has found a way to get in through the basement."

He shook his head. "There is no actual basement. I did take the space beneath the deck and create storage rooms and a lab to develop photographs." Their eyes met in sudden silence.

Kate slid out of bed and caught up his shirt, the nearest article of clothing she could wrap herself in. "Do you have mistletoe in the house, Matthew?"

"No, but it grows in several of the trees outside near the

121

deck. I've stood on my deck to knock it out of the branches a few times."

Quickly buttoning the shirt, she followed him on bare feet. He didn't like her exposed to danger, but at least he could keep an eye on her if she were with him. He reached back to take her hand. She looked small and vulnerable in his too-large shirt with her hair tousled from their lovemaking. He bent his head and kissed her, a brief hard kiss of reassurance. Kate's public image was always neat and elegant. He liked that Kate very much. He loved the one with him now. His sexy, passionate, private Kate, with her hair mussed and her delicate skin red from his five o'clock shadow. Nothing was going to harm her. *Nothing*.

Kate felt her heart beating wildly in her chest. She tightened her fingers around Matt's hand. Matt slid open the glass door leading outside. The wind rushed in, bringing a cold chill and the scent of the salty air. The roar of the ocean was loud, whereas before the walls of the house had muffled it. She glanced nervously out toward the open sea, afraid of seeing the gray fog, but the ocean's surface was clear.

"Kate." Matt said her name as a warning.

Kate froze and dropped her gaze to the sand below them. It was wet from the continual pounding of the waves, rolling up onto the beach and receding according to the tide. There was a clear trail of boot prints, coming out of the ocean, and marks alongside them that indicated something heavy had been dragged. Kelp lay in tangles along the path toward the stairs leading up to Matthew's home. There was a heavy dark stain, much like oil in several spots in the sand. Kate wanted a closer look and stepped out onto the deck.

Matt pulled her back and thrust her behind him. "It doesn't feel right to me." He had long ago learned to rely on his survival instincts when something wasn't right. "Stay in the house, Kate."

"The fog isn't out there anymore," she pointed out, but she stayed behind him, holding tight to his hand. "Should we call Jonas?"

Matt sighed. "I imagine Elle called him. Don't all your sisters call him when something supernatural happens? I don't think the poor man's had a night's sleep since Sarah came home."

"Supernatural? I never thought of it like that. We've always had certain gifts. We were born with them, and using them seems as natural as breathing. Some people call us witches, and others just think we're able to use magic, but it's different. More. And less. I wish I could explain it." Kate frowned up at him. "It's natural to us."

Matt pushed her hair from her face, his fingers lingering in the silky strands. He tucked her hair behind her ear, the gesture tender. "You don't have to explain it. I'm a believer, Kate." He paused and drew in a deep breath. "Something's wrong. We're not going out on the deck. Come through the house with me." Matt silently slid the glass door closed, lifting his gaze to the night sky, where patches of dark, ominous clouds floated lazily.

Deliberately he didn't turn on any lights as he led her through the house. He paused long enough to slip a leather sheath around his calf. Kate's eyes widened as he shoved a long knife down into it. "Do you think that's necessary?"

"I believe in being safe. You're with me, Kate. Nothing's going to take you away from me. I don't care if it's a monster in the fog or something crawling out of the ocean." He pushed open the door to his house and stepped outside. His eyes searched the terrain restlessly, never stopping. "Do you smell something burning?"

The breeze shifted again, but Kate caught the peculiar pungent odor. "Oily rags?"

Matt hurried over the stepping-stones leading around to the back of the house. He had a good ocean view on three sides, but the bedroom was to the back. The dark stains led from the beach to the stairs and straight to the small photography laboratory he had built. The door was closed and appeared locked, but there were oily smudges all over the door, the same oily smudges they'd seen on the beach.

Kate's heart began to pound. She felt the danger swamping her. Glancing up, she could see the branches of the tree spread over the top of the deck, reaching over the bedroom where she and Matt had been kissing. In the branches were nests of mistletoe and the base of the tree was covered in the oily substance. "Matthew, let's wait for Jonas."

"I have photo-developing chemicals in there, Kate. I'm not losing my house to this thing." He set her away from him. "You stay back. I mean it, Kate. If I have to run, I'll need the way clear. Drag the hose over here for me, but don't get too close."

Matt felt the door. It wasn't hot to the touch. He opened it cautiously. The stench was overpowering, smelling of the sea, dead fish, and heavy oil. Black smoke seeped from a pile of photo paper and rags piled with smashed glass and a mixture of what he knew was lethal chemicals. He dragged some of the papers from the pile, trying to stop the inevitable. Tiny flames licked up the sides of the pile. There was a flash of white and a popping sound.

Kate thrust the hose into his hands. The water was running full out. He turned it on the greedy flames. "Get out of here, Kate," he ordered.

Kate stifled a scream when Jonas emerged out of nowhere and pulled her back, away from the deck. "Call the fire department," he snapped. "Use my car radio and stay out of the house." He pointed to the driveway, where he'd pulled in and left the door on the driver's side open. "I have a jacket it in the car, put it on, you aren't wearing very much."

Kate heard the wail of a siren and saw the deputy's car tear up the driveway. She ran to Jackson as he stepped out of his car. "Jonas says to call the fire department."

He made the call from his radio, pointing silently to the car, as if that was enough to make her stay, then he quickly joined Jonas and Matt. Kate dragged on Jonas's jacket, nearly sagging with relief. There was something utterly reassuring about the three men being together. They exuded complete confidence and worked as a team, almost as if each knew what the others were thinking. They had the fire out before the fire trucks even arrived. It took longer to go through the mess in the photo lab, searching for evidence. She was grateful to be able to return to the house where it was warm. Kate curled up in a chair and waited for Matt to return to her.

Chapter Eight

And the blood runs red on the pristine white snow . . .
While around all the houses the Christmas lights glow.

Matt stared out the large bay window of his kitchen at the pounding sea. He frowned at the foaming waves, peering toward the darkness far out in the distance, almost at the horizon where a mass seemed to be congealing. Dark clouds had spread across the entire sky by the time the three men had sifted through the mess in his photography lab. Matt had taken calls from his parents and his brothers making certain he was alive and well and the house was still standing. Kate had received calls from her sisters.

Kate, fresh from her shower and wrapped in his robe, sat in the chair nearest him. "It's out there, isn't it?" she asked quietly. "I'm sorry about all your equipment."

He spun around to look at her. "Do you think I blame you for this?"

She hesitated. "I don't think he would have come here if I

126

hadn't been here. I don't know why I draw him," she said, shaking her head. "Maybe he got my scent in the old mill, or maybe he perceives me as a threat."

"So it's definitely a he. I think it's taking shape, gaining a form," Matt said.

"I need to go home and help find the appropriate entry in the diaries. There are quite a few written in the symbols, and my sisters will need help. I don't think we have a lot of time to figure this out, Matthew. It's only a few days until Christmas, and I think this thing means to stop the town from having a Christmas." It sounded melodramatic even to her own ears. How could she expect to have any kind of a relationship with Matthew Granite and still be who and what she was?

"Time enough, Kate. We'll go right after we take care of things here. I promise."

She lifted an eyebrow. "What things? I thought you and Jonas and Jackson took care of everything."

Matt padded over to her on his bare feet and simply lifted her in his arms. "It takes some getting used to."

Kate clasped her fingers at the nape of his neck. "I'll admit I've never faced anything like this before." She wanted him. Suited or not, for just this space of time, Matthew belonged to her.

"I wasn't referring to our foggy fiend. I was referring to you. Having you in my house. Having you right here where I can look at you or touch you." He set her on the tiled counter and slid his hand inside the warmth of the robe.

He loved her instant response, the way she pushed into his hand. Welcoming him. "Remind me to thank your sister for the warning." Matt leaned forward to take her offering into the warmth of his mouth.

"I think you're a breast man," she teased.

"Mmmm, maybe," he agreed, his hands sliding down her waist and over her hips inside the robe. "But you also have a beautiful butt, Kate. I absolutely love the way you walk. I used to get behind you just to breathe a little life into my fantasies."

He was wedging himself between her legs, and Kate opened her thighs wider to accommodate him. "You've had fantasies about my rear end?"

"More than you'll ever know." He leaned in to capture her mouth. To spread heat and fire. Her fingers tangled in his hair. His fingers tangled in hers. Their mouths welded together so that they breathed for one another. He pulled her bottom closer to the edge of the counter and yanked her robe all the way open. "I've had fantasies about every separate part of you." Very gently he slid her legs apart.

"Matthew." There was a gasp in her voice. Kate stared at the long bank of windows, her hands still in his hair. "What are you doing?"

"Having you for breakfast. I've always wanted you for breakfast."

If Kate had thought to protest, it was far too late. He was already devouring her, and she was too far gone to care where they were. It was a deliciously decadent moment, and she reveled in it as wave after wave of pleasure crashed over her and rushed through her. The room spun dizzily, and colors mixed together, while his tongue and his fingers worked magic on her body. Her hands grabbed the edge of the smooth-tiled counter to keep herself anchored when she was flying so high, but then he was lifting her and laying her on the table, his body buried deep inside of hers, and there was no room for thought. No room for anything but feeling. The sound of his body joining with hers, their pounding hearts and heavy breathing, was a kind of music accompanying the strong orgasms as they broke over her and through her. His heat was so deep inside of her, she felt as though she were melting from the inside out.

She stared up into his face, the hard angles and planes, the rough shadow on his jaw. His eyes held secrets, things he had seen that should never have been witnessed. She realized how alone he seemed, even in the midst of his family. Like Jonas. Or Jackson. A man apart, not by choice, but by experiences. Kate framed his face with her palms, her thumb sliding in a caress over his faint whiskers. "You're a very wonderful man, Matthew Granite. I hope you know how special you are."

He gathered her to him as if she were the most precious being on the face of the earth, carrying her tenderly to the bathroom so they could shower. He said little, but he watched her all the time, would reach out and touch her body, her face, his fingers lingering against her skin, almost as if he couldn't believe she was real.

"My clothes are dirty," she said, pulling them on. At least she managed to tame her hair, braiding the long length and swirling the braid around the back of her head in an intricate knot.

He smiled at her. "Your clothes are never dirty, you just think they are." He dragged out a fresh pair of jeans from his drawer. "How can we find out what this thing is, Katie? I need to know what we're facing."

"My sisters are poring over the diaries, and I think Damon is helping them. I can try as well, and Elle's on her way home. We should be able to find some clue."

"What's your gut telling you?"

She pressed her lips together to keep from smiling. There was something raw about the way Matt talked, something that always intrigued her. "I think it has to do with the history of our town, possibly an event that happened around Christmas, maybe the pageant itself. I think whatever is in the fog is gaining strength and becoming more destructive, but I'm not entirely certain why. The tree beside the deck with the mistletoe in it is a fir tree, and you had lights strung in it. You didn't have them on, but the dark stain, which seemed to be oil of some kind, was all around the bottom of the tree and going partially up the trunk."

"I noticed that," he agreed. "But there was nothing to ignite it."

"If Elle hadn't called and warned us, we never would have gone outside, Matthew. We would have been above the room when the fire took off, and it might have exploded. I think the fire would have raced to the tree, and he was hoping it would go up in flames as well."

"Strange way to kill us."

"Maybe not just us. Maybe it was the fir tree." She sat on the edge of the bed to watch him dress. He moved with such power, so fluidly, with a masculine grace he didn't seem aware of having. "Each symbol attacked so far has been attached to the Christian belief. There were ancient beliefs far before Christianity ever celebrated Christmas. It's widely believed the birth of Christ was in April, not December."

He paused in the act of buttoning his shirt. "I didn't know that."

She nodded. "I'm not Elle, or the others who sometimes are able to see things clearly, but I *feel* it's connected in some way."

"I get feelings when there's danger near." He suddenly grinned, transforming his face from man to boy. "Unless I'm otherwise occupied."

Kate couldn't help smiling back. In spite of everything, he looked more relaxed than she'd ever seen him. She always thought of him as a great tiger prowling through town. "We can forgive you that." She stood up. "The fir tree's needles rise toward the sky, and the fir tree stays green all year round."

"And that means something?"

"Everlasting hope, and, of course, the raised needles are reputed to represent man's thoughts turning toward heaven. If I were right, why would he want to destroy those symbols? He's not attacking Santa Claus. He isn't someone thinking Christmas is too commercial, he's actually destroying the symbols themselves." She looked up at him, rubbed her temple, and smiled a bit tiredly. "Or not. I could be way off base."

"I doubt it, Katie. I think your guess is as close as we can get right now." Matt looked across the room at her, still astonished that she was in his bedroom. "Let's go shopping for groceries. We can take them to your house and spend the day going over those diaries until we find something."

"Sounds good. I want to get home and put some decent clothes on."

She wandered out of the room while he pulled on his socks and boots. The house was so open, it beckoned her to walk the length of it. Entering the kitchen, she found herself smiling. In her wildest dreams she had never considered making love on a tabletop. A character in one of her novels might do such a thing, but not Kate Drake, with her every hair in place and her need for order. She'd never be able to look at a kitchen counter or table in quite the same way again.

Matt listened to Kate moving around his home. He liked the scent of her, the soft footfalls, the way her breath would catch when she looked at something she liked.

"Matthew?" Kate called out to him. "You have a very interesting kitchen. I wanted to put the cups in the dishwasher, and it seems to be a bread bin."

There was a small silence. Matt cleared his throat. "I've never actually used the dishwasher, Kate. I just do dishes by hand."

"I see. I guess that makes sense. But why would you put all the fruit in the microwave?"

He hurried into the kitchen. "It's convenient. What are you looking for?"

She grinned at him. "You don't really cook much, do you?

He rubbed the bridge of his nose. "I do a mean barbecue."

"I'll just bet you do. Are you ready?"

Matt took her hand and drew her close to him as they went out into the morning air. She fit with him, belonged with him. She didn't believe it. He could see the reservations in her eyes, but he was determined to change her mind.

All the regulars considered the grocery store the center of town. Inez Nelson had a way with people. She didn't know the meaning of the word *stranger* and nearly everyone shopped at the local market, more to catch up on all the news and see Inez than for any other reason. She had known every one of the Drake sisters since their births and considered them akin to family.

Matt parked his car in front of the town square just to the left of Inez's store. "The Christmas pageant is growing, so many people want to participate that I think we're going to have to get a larger town square. The actors can barely get through the crowd as they walk up the street to the manger."

"I love the fact that everyone participates. It's so fun for the children afterward, when Santa shows up with his reindeer and gives out candy canes." Kate took the hand Matt held out to her. They stood together looking at the nativity scene in the town square, astonished that the statues, minus the wise men, had already been cleaned and the scene put back together. It would be reenacted with humans Christmas Eve, but a local sculptor had created the beautiful statues and several artists had done woodwork for the manger and life-size stable, and others had painted the entire backdrop. This year, Inez had managed to find a powdery substance that looked exactly like snow and had sprinkled it on the roof of the stable and on the surrounding ground, to the townspeople's delight and amusement. Snow was rarely seen in their coastal town.

"How many kids do you think have snuck into the square for a snowball fight?" Matt lowered his voice and looked around, half-expecting Inez to hear him even though she was a safe distance away inside the store.

Kate turned her laughing gaze on him. "You would have, wouldn't you?"

Fast-moving shadows slid across the ground, blocking out the sun's rays. "Damn right. Jonas and I would have made a snow fort and pelted everyone within throwing distance." His smile faded even as he finished his sentence. His hand gripped her arm to draw her attention. He nodded toward the sky. Seagulls filled the air overhead, winging their way fast inland. The birds were eerily silent, their great wings flapping as they hurried away from the ocean.

Kate shook her head and looked out toward the sea. The gray fog was rolling in fast. It roiled and churned, a turbulent mass, displaying raw energy. Lightning arced, chains of red-orange flashing within the center of the gray mist.

Matt swore and tugged her toward the store. "Let's get inside."

"It's growing stronger," Kate said.

Matt could feel her trembling against him. He pulled her closer to him. "We knew he would get stronger, Kate. You'd think the damned thing would take a vacation and give us a break. We'll figure this out."

"I know." She walked with him to the store. The entity was growing stronger and she felt stretched and tired and breakable. She couldn't very well tell Matt. He was already worried about her. She could read it in his eyes. How had she never managed to see the stark loneliness in him before? The aching desire? It was deep and intense and swamped her sometimes when he looked at her. Yet still, as he walked beside her, a tall, formidable man with wide shoulders and a thick chest and eyes that were never still, she could barely take in that he loved her.

Matt slid his arm around Kate's shoulders as they entered the building. As always, the small store had more than its share of customers. Inez greeted them loudly, gazing at them speculatively with bright eyes and a cheerful smile. "Kate, how lovely to see you, dear. And with Matt. I swear you grow taller every day, Matt."

Her comments effectively turned him into a boy again. Only Inez could manage to do that. "I feel a little taller today, Inez." He winked at Kate.

"Are you two coming to the pageant practice?" Inez asked. "I organized another one after the big fiasco the other night. No one blames Abbey, Kate. It certainly wasn't her fault that rat Bruce Harper is having an affair with little miss hot pants Sylvia Fredrickson."

"Abbey felt terrible, Inez," Kate said. "I'm sure it must have caused problems."

"Well, Bruce's wife left him. You know she's due to give birth any day now. They all dropped out of the production, and I had to find replacements." Inez glared at Matt. "Danny was in a fine snit saying he wasn't certain he could work with *amateur* actors. I told him he was an amateur actor."

"Inez," Kate protested. "You probably broke his heart."

For a moment Inez pursed her lips, looking repentant. "Well, he deserves it. I've got enough trouble without that boy complaining about his part. The three wise men are nervous, and I'm afraid they're fixing to drop out. I don't want to cancel the pageant. It's been put on every year since this town was founded."

"Danny won't drop out. He likes to herd those sheep around," Matt said.

Inez scowled. "He likes to chase them toward the kids and get a huge reaction."

"That is the truth." Matt grinned at her, but his eyes were on the wisps of gray-white fog slipping into town. He moved away from the women toward the plate-glass window, where he studied the fog. The enemy. It was strange to think of the fog, a nearly everyday occurrence on the coast, as the enemy.

The dark tendrils stretched toward houses, reached with long, spiny arms and bony fingers. The image was so strong Matt took a step closer to the window, narrowing his eyes to peer into the fog. "Katie, come here for a minute," he said softly, and held out his hand without taking his eyes from the fog. Something was moving inside of it.

Kate immediately put her hand into his and stepped up beside him. "What is it?"

"Look into the fog and tell me what you see."

Kate studied the rapidly moving vapor. It was darkening and spinning, almost boiling with turbulence. She shivered as long streaks stretched across the highway and began to surround the residences. It made her think of a predator hunting something, sniffing for the right scent. She thought something moved in the middle of the thick fogbank, something shaped vaguely like a tall man in a long, flowing coat and an old hat. She glimpsed a form, then it disappeared in the seething mass, only to reappear moments later, fading into the edges of the whirling mists. It was tall with bare white bones, pitiless eyes, and a wide, gaping mouth. She stepped back, gasping. The skeleton had more than taken shape. This time the entire chest was intact, and small pieces of flesh hung on the body, making it more grotesque than ever.

Kate put a hand protectively to her throat to stifle the scream welling up as she backed completely away from the window. She realized the store was eerily silent. Inez and the patrons stared out the window fearfully.

"It's taking shape, isn't it?" Matt asked.

Jonas and Jackson stalked into the store, Jonas's expression grim. "Kate, get out there and get rid of this before we start having fatalities," Jonas snapped without preamble, ignoring everyone else. "No one can see to drive the highway. I issued a warning on the radio, but we're going to have people not only driving over cliffs but also walking over them. Unfortunately, not everyone listens to the radio."

"Go to hell, Jonas." Matt was furious. *Furious.* At the thing in the fog. At Jonas, and at his own inability to stop the entity. "You're not sending Kate out there to battle that damned thing alone again. She's scared and tired, and I'll be damned if you bully her into thinking she's responsible for taking this thing on by herself. You want someone to fight it, be my guest."

"Dammit, Matt, don't start with me. You know I would if I had a chance in hell, but I don't. This is the Drakes' territory, not mine," Jonas bristled.

Kate put a restraining hand on both men's arms. "The last thing we need is to fight among ourselves. Jonas, I can't manage it alone. I really can't. I need Hannah." She leaned her head against Matt's chest. "I don't bring the wind, Hannah does. She's exhausted with fighting this thing. My sisters have been working with me the entire time. Without Hannah, we can't do anything."

Matt glanced down at her face, saw the lines of weariness there, the look of far too much energy expended, and for the first time, uncertainty. He wrapped his arms more tightly around her, and addressed Jonas. "How bad is it out there? Can they pass on this one and get some rest?"

"I'm getting damned sick of this secrecy where Hannah's concerned," Jonas said, obviously trying to get his temper under control. He felt every bit as impotent against the entity as Matt did, and it was clearly wearing on him. "We may have a running battle going; but if she's ill, it matters to me, Kate. You've been my family for as long as I can remember."

Kate felt Matt stirring, a fine tremor of anger rippling through his body at the tone Jonas used with her. She rubbed her head against his chest. "I know that, Jonas. Hannah is aware you're angry too. You know we all have a difficult time after we use our gifts. Hannah has to expend a tremendous amount of energy controlling something as capricious as the wind. Using our gifts is very draining. And whatever is in the fog has been growing in strength and resisting us, so we're having to expend more effort to contain it."

"Can you get rid of it, Kate?" Inez asked.

Everyone in the store seemed to hold their breath, waiting for her answer. Kate could feel the hope. The fear. All eyes were on her. "I honestly don't know." But she had to try. She could already hear the feminine voices whispering in the soft breeze heading inland from the sea. She felt her sisters calling to her to join with them. Hannah was already on the battlement, drooping with weariness, but facing the fog, waiting for Kate. Sarah and Abbey stood with her, and Joley had arrived. She'd been traveling for two days, yet she stood shoulder to shoulder with her sisters, waiting for Kate.

Kate closed her eyes and drew in a deep breath in an effort to summon her strength. Her courage. A paralyzing fear was beginning to grip her, one she recognized and was familiar with. Like Hannah, she suffered from severe panic attacks. Unlike Hannah, she was not a public figure. As a writer, her name might be known, but not her face. She could blend into the background easily, yet now everyone was watching. Waiting. Expecting Kate to work some kind of magic when she didn't even know what she was dealing with.

Matt felt the fine tremors that ran through Kate's body and turned her away from everyone in the store, his larger body shielding her. "You don't have to do this, Katie." He whispered the words, his forehead pressed against hers.

"Yes, I do," she whispered back.

Jonas instinctively stepped in front of her to protect her from prying eyes. Jackson spoke. His voice was utterly low, so soft one felt they had to strain to hear his words, yet his voice carried complete authority. "Inez, move everyone to the center of the store away from the windows, and let's give Kate some room to work. We have no idea what's going to happen, and we don't want to take chances with injuries."

Kate was grateful to the three men. She took another breath and pulled away from Matt, deliberately yanking open the door and slipping outside before her courage failed her. At once she felt the malevolence, a bitter, twisted emotion beating at her. The dark fog wrapped around her body, and twice she actually felt the brush of something alive sliding over her skin. She pressed her teeth together to keep them from chattering. Strength was already flowing into her—her sisters, reaching out from a distance, calling to her with encouraging words.

Matt joined her outside, slipping behind her, circling her waist with his arms, drawing her back against his hard, comforting body so that she had an anchor. Jonas took up a position on her right side, and Jackson was at her left. Three big men, all seasoned warriors, all ready to defend her with their lives. It was impossible not to find the courage and the strength she needed when it was pouring into her from every direction.

Kate faced the dark, boiling fog, lifting her arms to signal to Hannah, to signal to bring in the wind. She began to speak softly, calmly, using the gift of her soothing voice in an attempt to bring peace to the swelling malevolence in the fog. She spoke of peace, of love, of redemption and forgiveness. Gathering every vestige of courage she possessed, Kate made no attempt to drive it away. Rather she summoned it to her, trying to find a way to pierce the veil between reality and the shadow world where she could see into the soul of what was left behind and, hopefully, find a way to heal the broken spirit.

The fog spun and roiled in a terrible frenzy, a reaction to the sound of her voice. Her sisters protested for a moment, frightened by what she was trying, but joining with her when they recognized her determination. Jonas made a small sound of dissent and moved closer to her, ready to jerk her back into reality.

Moans assaulted her ears. The shadow world was vague and gray, a bleak hazy place where nothing was what it seemed. She chanted softly, her voice spreading through the world with little effort, stilling the moans and alerting whatever lived there to her presence. Kate felt the impact when the entity realized she'd once again joined him in his world. She could feel his blazing rage, the fierce anger, and the intensity of his guilt and sorrow. The thing turned toward her, a tall skeleton of a man, blurred so that he was nearly indistinct in the gray vapors surrounding him. He wore a long coat and shapeless hat, and he shook his head and pressed his bony hands over his ears to stop the enchantment of her voice. Flesh sagged from the bones, a loose fit in some places, stretched tight in others.

Kate whispered softly to him, calling, beckoning, trying to coax him to reveal the pain he suffered, the torment of his existence. She used her voice shamelessly, cajoling him to find peace. The shadowy figure took a few steps toward her. Kate held out her hand to him, a gesture of camaraderie. *There is peace. Let yourself feel it surround you.*

The being took another cautious step toward her. Her heart pounded. Her mouth was dry, but she kept whispering. Speaking to him. Promising him rest. He was only a few feet from her, his arm stretching out toward her hand. The bony fingers were close. Inches away from her flesh. She remembered the feel of the finger bones closing around her throat, but she stood her ground and kept enticing him.

Something slithered around his boots. Snakelike vines wrapped around bony ankles. Out of the barren rocks bounded a huge creature with matted fur and yellow eyes. In the cold of the shadow world, she could see the creature's vaporous breath mingling with the fog. The eyes fixed on her, an intruder in their world.

The tips of her fingers touched the bony ends of the skeleton as it reached toward her. The creature howled, sending a shiver of fear down Kate's spine. Her sisters held their collective breath. Jonas stiffened, communicating his apprehension to Matt and Jackson.

Kate continued to whisper of peace, of aid, of a place to rest. The being took more shape, the pitiless eyes swimming with tears, extending its hand as far as the snakelike vines allowed. Abruptly the skeleton threw back its head and roared, rejecting her. Rejecting the idea of redemption and forgiveness. She glimpsed a raging hatred of self, of everything symbolizing Christmas, of peace itself. *There can be no peace.* She caught that as the being began to whirl around, furious, using the vortex of its wild spinning to hurl objects at her. The moans rose to shrieks. The huge creature bounded toward Kate, breathing as loudly as any bull. Kate made one last grab for the hand of the skeleton, but it had turned on her completely, rushing at her along with the beast.

"Get her out of there!" Jonas shouted, catching the collective fear that ran through the Drake family. He gripped Kate's arm hard, shaking her. "Matt, pull her back to us!"

"Kate," her sisters cried out, "leave him, leave him there."

"Hannah!" Jonas cried the name desperately. "The wind, Hannah, bring in the wind."

Kate stared at the terrible figure coming straight at her, fury in its every line. The eyes glowed red through the dark fog; the face was made of bones, not flesh. The mouth gaped open in a silent scream. She was trapped there in the world of shadows, real, yet not, unable to find her way back. The worst of it was, she caught sight of a second insubstantial figure coming at her from the left.

"Kate." Matt whispered her name, lifted her into his arms. Her body was an empty shell, her mind caught somewhere else.

"Kate, darling, go with the other one, he'll lead you out." Elle's soft voice pushed everything else away.

The dark demon was almost upon her. Kate felt a hand on her arm. She looked down and saw Jackson's fingers circling her wrist like a vise. She didn't have time to go voluntarily; he yanked her out of the shadows, back into the light. She heard a roar of rage, shuddered when she felt bones brush against her skin. Matt was real and solid, and she gripped him hard, needing to feel grounded. She felt physically ill, her stomach a churning knot. She closed eyes, sliding into a dead faint.

The wind swept in from the sea, a strong tempest of retaliation. Hannah's fear added to the strength of the storm. Rain burst down on them. The dark fog swirled and fought, not wanting to give ground. For a brief moment there was a confrontation between the entity and the Drake sisters, sticks and debris flying in the wind. The three men could hear the desperate cries of seagulls. And then it was over, the fog retreating to the sea, leaving behind silence and the rushing wind and rain. Matt stood there on the sidewalk, Kate, safe in his arms, staring in shock at the mess left behind.

Clouds overhead obscured the sun, the day overcast and gloomy. Christmas lights twinkled on and off where they hung over the buildings in rows of vivid colors, a terrible contrast to the scene left behind in the town square. Feathers were everywhere and in the pristine white snow by the manger there was a bright red pool of blood.

Chapter Nine

A star burns hot in the dead of the night,
As the bell tolls it's now midnight

"Never again. Never again." Matt shoved both hands through his hair and glared at the Drake sisters. "I swear, Kate, you are never doing that again." He paced restlessly back and forth across the living room floor.

Sarah, Kate's older sister, rested her head against her fiancé's knee, and watched Matt in silence. Abbey sat on the couch, Joley's head resting in her lap. Joley lay stretched out, her eyes closed, appearing to be asleep in spite of his tirade. Hannah lay on the couch closest to the window, lines of exhaustion visible on her young face.

"It doesn't do any good to get upset," Jonas said. "They do whatever they want to do without a thought for the consequences."

Sarah sighed loudly. "Don't start, Jonas. That's not true, and you know it. If you were the one trying to get rid of this thing, you wouldn't worry about your own safety, and you know it. You'd just do whatever had to be done."

"That's different, Sarah," Jonas snarled back. "Dammit anyway. Look at Hannah. She can't even move. I think she needs a doctor. Where the hell is Libby when we need her?"

"Are you ever going to stop swearing at us?" Sarah asked. She rubbed her face against Damon's knee. "Hannah needs rest and maybe some tea."

"I'll make tea," Damon offered. "I think all of you could use it."

"Damon, you are a darling," Sarah said. "The kettle's boiling."

Matt glanced into the kitchen, and, sure enough, the kettle was steaming. He knew very well it hadn't even been turned on minutes earlier.

Damon leaned down to brush a kiss across Sarah's temple before making his way into the kitchen. "This feels like old times," he called out, reaching for the tea kept for just such occasions.

"We could use a little more festive atmosphere," Abigail decided. She stared at the row of candles on the mantel until they spluttered to life, flames leaping and flickering for a moment, then taking hold. At once the aroma of cinnamon and spice scented the air.

"Good idea," Sarah agreed and focused on the CD player. Instantly Joley's voice filled the room with a popular Christmas carol.

"Not that one," Joley protested. "Something else."

"Are you all insane?" Jonas demanded. "Kate could have been killed. Are we going to pretend it didn't happen and have a little Christmas get-together?"

145

"Jonas, it does no good yelling at them. What do you want them to do?" Damon returned, carrying a tray with several cups of tea on it. He distributed them among the Drake sisters.

"And you were the one asking me, no, telling me to get out there and stop the fog," Kate pointed out.

Jonas muttered something ugly under his breath and reached down for Hannah's limp wrist to take her pulse. As he did a breeze swirled around the room, and his hat sailed from the chair where he'd placed it and landed in the middle of the room. Jonas straightened and glared down at Hannah, who didn't stir.

"Jonas, we didn't know the entity was going to try to hurt Kate," Abbey pointed out. "We have to know what his motivation is."

Sarah shoved a heavy book across the floor. "Trying to read this thing without Elle is impossible. She's the only one that can read the language our ancestors used. The writing is in that strange hieroglyphic language we were all supposed to study back when we were teens. Mom told us to learn it, but we kept putting it off, wondering why we needed to delve that far back into the past. With the little bit we know, it's impossible to find a single entry in all of this."

Matt stopped pacing, coming to a halt beside Kate, his hand resting on the nape of her neck. "Elle's on the way home, isn't she? It shouldn't be long. How come she learned the language when the rest of you only know a little?"

Abbey blew on her tea. "She learned it in order to teach the next generation, just as our mother did."

"Speaking of Elle, how did she connect with you, Jackson?

How did she know you were able to go into the shadows and bring Kate out?" Sarah asked.

There was a sudden silence, and all eyes turned to regard the man sitting in absolute stillness just to the side of the window. His cool dark eyes moved over their faces, a brooding perusal. "I don't know what you're talking about. I don't even know Elle."

Abbey sat up straighter. "That's not the truth, Jackson."

Jonas sucked in his breath sharply. "Don't, Abbey!" His warning came a heartbeat too late. She'd already said it, her voice pitched perfectly to turn people inside out, to reach into their darkest depths and pull the truth from them.

Jackson stood up slowly, his eyes hard steel. He walked across the floor without a single sound. Joley sat up and blinked at him. Matt moved in on one side of Abbey, Jonas on the other. Ignoring the two men, Jackson bent down until he was eye level with Abbey. "You don't ever want to ask me for the truth, Abbey. Not about me and not about Elle." He hadn't raised his voice, but Abbey shivered. Joley put her arm around her sister.

"I'll be outside," Jackson said.

"He's never met Elle," Sarah said, after the door closed behind the deputy. "Jonas, he hasn't, has he?"

Jonas shook his head. "Not to my knowledge. And he's never mentioned her. They both had the same nightmare, but so did half the kids in Sea Haven."

"He scares me," Abbey said. "I don't want Elle near him. She's so tiny and fragile and so sweet. And he's . . . "

"My friend," Jonas said. "He saved my life twice, Abbey."

"And mine too," Matt added. "You shouldn't have done that."

Abbey looked down. "I know. I don't know why I did. It's just that he's so frightening, and the thought that Elle was out there in the shadow world too . . . "

"But she wasn't," Kate interrupted. "She wasn't there. I heard her voice, but she wasn't in the world, she was in my head." Her voice trailed off in sudden speculation. The sisters exchanged a long look. "Jonas, is Jackson telepathic?"

"How the hell would I know?" Jonas asked.

"Well, because you are. Sort of." The sisters looked at one another again and burst out laughing. Their bright laughter dispelled the air of gloom in the room.

Jonas made a face at Matt. "See what I have to put up with?" He stomped across the room to reach down and retrieve his hat. Before his fingers could close around the rim, the flames on the candles flared from a sudden gust of wind, and the hat leaped away from him to land dangerously close to the fireplace. Jonas straightened slowly, his hands on his hips, glancing suspiciously around the room at the Drake sisters. They all wore innocent expressions. "You are not going to get me to believe that the wind is in the house without a little help."

Unexpectedly the logs in the fireplace burst into flame. Jonas took a step toward his hat. It went up on the rim and rolled a few inches toward the burning logs. "My hat had better not go into that fire," Jonas warned.

"Really, Jonas." Joley didn't open her eyes. "You're becoming paranoid. Hannah's already asleep."

He continued to study their faces and finally crossed to the couch where Hannah lay asleep, looking almost a child. "I'm taking the baby doll to bed. It's the only safe thing to do." He simply lifted her in one quick movement and, before anyone could protest, started out of the room.

"The tower," Sarah called after him.

"What a surprise there. I can see Hannah as the princess in her tower," Jonas called back.

The sisters looked at one another and burst out laughing. Matt shook his head. "You all are downright scary."

Joley leaned her head back and grinned at him. "I'd like to know what's going on with my sister and you all alone up in that house of yours. I was going to help Hannah whip up a little love potion and stick it in your drink the next time I saw you, but they tell me you've been playing fast and loose with her already."

Kate turned a particularly fetching shade of crimson. "Joley Drake, that will certainly be the last we hear on that subject."

Joley didn't look impressed with the stern tone. "In case anyone is interested, I took a good look at Kate's neck, and she has a particularly impressive love bite."

Kate clapped her hand over her neck and shook her head. "I most certainly do not. Drink your tea."

"What's even more impressive," Joley continued, "is that Matt seems to be sporting one of his own."

A collective gasp went up. "We want to see, Matt," Abigail pleaded.

"Only if I get to make a wish on the snowglobe," he bargained.

There was instant silence. Sarah sat up straighter. "Matt," she paused and glanced at Kate. "Wishing on our snowglobe is not like making a silly, frivolous wish. It's very serious business. You have to know what you want and really mean it. You have to have weighed your decision very carefully."

"I can assure you I have. If you want to see the love bite, you can produce the snowglobe." Matt folded his arms across his chest.

"Matt," Kate cautioned, "if you're thinking about wishing for anything we already discussed—don't. It wouldn't work."

Joley lifted her head off the back of the couch and eyed them both. "This sounds very interesting. Does anyone else want Christmas snacks to go with the tea, because I really could go for those little decorated sugar cookies." She waggled her fingers in the direction of the kitchen. "Tell us more, Matt. The snowglobe is right over there by the fireplace. Please do step on Jonas's hat. It always livens things up when he does his sheriff he-man routine." She turned her head to glance at the stairs. "He's been up there a long time. You don't suppose he's taking advantage while Hannah is asleep, do you?"

Sarah nudged Joley with her foot. "You're terrible, Joley."

Matt skirted around Jonas's hat and reached for the snowglobe. It felt solid in his hands. He glanced at Kate. She shook her head, looking fearful. The globe warmed in his hands. He stared at the scene, the snowflakes whirling around the house until they all blended together to become fog. The lights on the tree sprang to life.

"You activated it," Sarah said. "That's nearly impossible."

"Not unless he's . . . "

"Joley!" Kate interrupted her sister sharply. "Matt, really, it isn't something to play with."

"I've never been more serious. Tell me what to do." He looked at Sarah.

She glanced at Kate, then shrugged. "It's relatively easy, Matt, but be sure. You look into the fog and picture what you want most in the world and wish for it. If you meet the criteria, the globe will grant your wish."

"And it works?"

"According to tradition. Family is allowed one wish a year, no more. And you can't wish for harm to anyone."

"That's why we don't allow Jonas access to it," Joley said.

Matt inhaled the fragrance of the candles and fresh-baked cookies wafting from the kitchen. He didn't question who made the cookies. He wasn't even surprised by the fact that there were cookies. He stared into the fog inside the snowglobe and conjured up the exact image of Kate. With everything in him, body, soul, heart, and mind, he made his wish. The fog was still for a moment, then swirled faster, dissipating until the globe was once more clear and the lights on the tree dimmed. He placed the globe back on the shelf carefully and grinned at Kate.

"Let's hope you know what you're doing," Joley said.

Suddenly in a much better mood, Matt flashed her a smile. "At the risk of sounding like an adoring fan, I love your collection of blues. You have the perfect voice for blues." He grinned at her. "Or Christmas music."

Joley winced. "I just sent that to my family for fun."

"It's beautiful," Abbey said. "Are you having fun on your tour?"

151

Joley frowned. "Yes, it's tiring, and there are always the freaks out there, but there's nothing quite like the energy of forty thousand people at a concert."

"What freaks?" Jonas demanded, walking back into the room. "Hannah didn't even wake up, not even when I called her Barbie doll. Are you certain she's okay, Sarah?"

Sarah paused for a moment, seeking inside herself, reaching out to her sister. "She's exhausted, Jonas, and needs sleep. We'll have to find a way to get some food into her soon."

Jonas rolled his eyes. "We can't have Miss Anorexic gaining an ounce. She's probably worried the camera won't love her, and she won't be able to parade around half-naked on the cover of a magazine for the entire world to see."

Kate tossed her napkin at Jonas. "Go away, you're annoying me. We have to have clear heads to decide how to handle this, and you just stir everyone up."

Jonas shrugged, in no way perturbed. "I have to go back to work anyway. But I want to hear about these freaks of yours, Joley. You haven't been getting any nutcases stalking you, have you?"

Joley took a sip of tea and looked up at Jonas. "I don't know. I hired a couple of bodyguards, bouncers really, just to protect the stage. Each concert hall has a security force, of course, but I thought if these two traveled with us, we'd have a little extra protection. Stalkers come with the territory, you know that. The more famous you get, the more crazies you attract."

Matt sat down beside Kate. "Do writers have that kind of problem?"

Before Kate had a chance to deny it, Jonas answered. "Of

course they do. Anyone in the public eye does, Matt. Writers, musicians, politicians, and—" he glanced toward the stairs— "supermodels."

Joley laughed. "You worry so much, Jonas, you ought to go into law enforcement. It's right up your alley."

"Ha-ha, very funny. I'll call you later to see if anything new has happened." Jonas glanced out the window. "I never thought I'd dread nightfall."

Matthew looked out the window to the pounding sea. "Is Elle expected tonight?"

"She said around midnight. She's flying into San Francisco and renting a car to drive here. I offered to pick her up," Abbey said, "but she didn't want any of us on the road with the fog. She promised she'd check the weather station before she came into Sea Haven."

Jonas scooped up his hat. "I'll keep an eye out for her. You all rest and stay out of trouble." He left, banging the door behind him.

At Sarah's urging, Damon nodded toward the kitchen and Matt obliged.

Abbey waited until the men were out of the room. "I didn't mean to challenge Jackson like that." She pressed her hand to her mouth, her eyes enormous. "That's twice now. And the house should have protected me. How could that happen in our home?"

"You were relaxed," Sarah said. "You let your guard down."

Abbey shook her head. "I haven't let my guard down since I caused such a problem during the committee meeting. Poor Inez called me this afternoon and told me no one realized it was me, but Sylvia knew."

"She went to school with us," Joley pointed out.

Hannah walked back into the room. Tall and blond and beautiful, she looked so fragile she could have been made of porcelain. "Don't worry about Sylvia. I'm certain she's very sorry she hit Abbey."

Joley held out her arms. "Come here, baby, sit by me. You look done in. You were very bad teasing poor Jonas that way and making him think you were sleeping." Joley kissed Hannah. "You really should be in bed."

"I couldn't sleep," Hannah admitted. "I needed to be with all of you."

Joley stroked back her hair. "You didn't do anything awful to Sylvia, did you?"

Hannah's eyes widened in a semblance of innocence. "You all think I'm so bent on revenge all the time."

Sarah paused in the doorway to the kitchen. "That's not an answer, you bloodthirsty little witch. Exactly what did you do to Sylvia?"

Hannah leaned against Joley. "I'm glad you're home. You don't give me that stern face like Sarah does."

"Hannah Drake, what did you do to Sylvia?"

Hannah shrugged. "I *heard* from a reliable source . . . "

"Inez at the grocery store," Abbey supplied.

"Well, she's reliable," Hannah pointed out. "I heard Sylvia developed a bright red rash on the left side of her face. It appears to be in the shape of a hand. I couldn't help but think it was fitting."

Sarah rubbed her hand over her face, trying to stare down her younger sister without smiling. "You know very well you can't use our gifts for anything other than good, Hannah. You're risking reprisal."

Hannah stretched her legs out in front of her and gave Sarah a sweet smile. "You never know what a humbling experience can do for someone's character."

"I'm getting your tea for you, but I hope this is a big joke, and I won't hear about it later at the store." Sarah turned away quickly to keep Hannah from seeing her laughter.

Abbey squeezed Hannah's hand. "You didn't really do anything to Sylvia, did you?" There was a hopeful note in her voice she couldn't quite hide.

"Drink your tea," Sarah said. "And eat some cookies. You're too pale. Matt and Damon are making us dinner tonight."

"Did I miss anything important while I was making Jonas carry my deadweight up those long and winding stairs?"

"Only Matt wishing on the snowglobe," Joley said. "And we're all fairly certain what he wished for."

"You're so brave, Kate," Hannah said. "I could never be with a man so absolutely frightening. They have those cold eyes and those scary voices, and I just want to curl up and fade away." For a moment tears shimmered in her eyes. She looked over the rim of her teacup at Kate. "You thought I was so brave to go out into the world and be seen, while you chose to stay out of sight and share your wonderful stories with the world, but you're willing to try with a man to have a real life with him."

"I haven't made up my mind yet," Kate admitted. "I'm afraid he'll wake up one day and realize what a coward I am. You'll find someone though, Hannah."

Hannah shook her head. "No, I won't. I don't want some

man snarling at me because I forgot to put the dishes in the dishwasher, or angry because I had to fly to Egypt to do a photo shoot. And I could never live with a man who always seemed on the edge of violence, or even capable of violence. I'd be so afraid I'd be paralyzed."

Kate laid her hand on Hannah's knee. "Matt isn't capable of violence against a woman. He's protective, there's a difference."

"That's how everyone describes Jonas, as protective, but he's really a bully. He'll order his wife around day and night."

"If Jonas ever falls in love with a woman, I think he would move heaven and earth to make her happy," Kate said. "He looks after all of us, and we're sometimes very aggravating. He has a job to do, and he works hard at it. We often make his job much more difficult. And it must be very disconcerting to be so connected emotionally to us. He senses when we're in trouble or hurt, and unfortunately we're in trouble quite often."

Hannah sighed. "I know. He's just so annoying all the time. I closed the window in the entryway; too much fog was drifting in, and it scared me." She forced an uneasy laugh. "I never thought I'd be afraid of the fog."

Kate stood up and looked around the house. "What do you mean too much fog was drifting in?" She stared out the window toward the sea. "You *saw* it? You weren't dreaming? What did it look like?"

Sarah stood up too and began to move uneasily about the room, checking the windows.

"It looked like fog," Hannah said. "I came down the stairs and, to be honest, was a little unsteady, so I sat on the floor in the entryway for a couple of minutes. I could see fog drifting in through the open window. It appeared to be normal fog, a long wisp of it, but the fact that I could see it in the house upset me. So I closed the window."

"Nothing can get into the house, Sarah," Abbey said. "It's protected. You know that the house has always protected us."

Sarah shook her head. "Mom told us we needed to know the ancient language of the Drake sisters, and we all shrugged it off with the exception of Elle. She also told us we needed to renew our safeguards every single time we came home, but did we do that? No, of course not—we've become complacent. Mom has precog, we all know it. It was a foreshadowing, but we didn't take her instructions seriously."

Abbey put a hand to her throat. "Do you think the entity was influencing me to use my voice on Jackson as well as at the committee meeting?"

Sarah nodded. "There's a good chance of it. We have to be very careful. None of us are handling this very well. We've never faced such a thing before."

"And I never want to again," Kate said fervently.

"Dinner," Matt called from the kitchen. "Come eat. And bring Hannah with you. Jonas said she had to eat something."

Hannah rolled her eyes. "There's my point exactly, Kate. Men always try bossing women around. It's their nature, they can't help themselves. We know the thing in the fog is a male, and I'll bet he's seriously upset with a woman."

They all started into the kitchen. Sarah and Kate helped steady Hannah. "Actually, I felt guilt and sorrow and rage coming from him," Kate said. "I could feel the connection, but he tossed it away because he feels he doesn't deserve forgiveness.

Something terrible happened, and he believes he's to blame for it."

"Why is he causing terrible things to happen now?" Hannah asked.

"I don't know," Kate admitted. "But it has something to do with Christmas. Sarah's right. We have to really pay attention to every detail now. He can't get any stronger, or we won't be able to stop him."

Matt spent the rest of the day poring over the entries in the diaries and listening to the easy teasing back and forth between the sisters. The women slept on and off throughout the day. Damon and Sarah spent a lot of time kissing every chance they could steal away, and he was a bit jealous that he didn't have the right to be as openly demonstrative with Kate. As the hours slipped by, all he could think about was Kate and being alone with her.

He slipped his arm around her shoulders. "It's late, let's go back to my house."

"Elle's driving in tonight. I'd like to wait for her. She's supposed to be here any minute, and we slept most of the day after that horrible encounter this morning," Kate replied.

"The fog is coming in," Matt announced. He opened the door and wandered out to the wide, wraparound veranda to stare out over the ocean.

"Elle should be here any minute; she told us midnight," Kate said, studying the wisps of fog as they drifted toward land. "She'll make it before the fog hits the highway."

"Who decorated your Christmas tree?" Matt indicated the huge tree covered in lights and adorned with a variety of ornaments.

Kate went down the porch stairs to stand in front of the tree. She touched a small wooden elf. "Isn't it beautiful? Frank, one of the local artists, did this carving. Many of these ornaments have been handed down from generation to generation."

"Don't you worry about them out in the weather?" The tree was inside the yard, and two large dogs protected the area. Sarah's dogs. No one would sneak in and steal the ornaments, even the more precious ones, but the sea air and the continual rain could ruin the decorations.

"We never worry about weather," Kate said simply. "The Drakes have always decorated a tree outside and, hopefully, we always will."

The fog burst over them in a rolling swirl, wrapped around the tree, and filled the yard, streaming in from the ocean as if pushed by an unseen hand.

"I think our old nemesis is attacking another Christmas symbol," Matt said, pointing to the top of the huge Christmas tree in the front yard. "What does the star stand for? There has to be a meaning."

The fog tangled around the branches, amplifying the glow of the lights through the vapor. Kate looked up at the star as it shorted out, sparks raining down through the fog. It brightened momentarily, then faded completely. She was looking up and saw through the wisps of clouds a hot, bright star streaking across the sky, plunging toward Earth. She went still, the color draining from her face. "Elle." She whispered her sister's name. "He's coming for Elle. That's what he was doing in the house. He's after Elle." The fog was choking the road, making it impossible to see.

"What the hell do you mean, it was in the house?" Matt

raced back inside the house just as her sisters hurried outside to join Kate. He caught up the phone and called Jonas. He had no idea what Jonas could do. No one could see in the fog. They didn't know exactly where Elle was, only that she was close. She had said she'd arrive sometime around midnight. It was close to that now. She might be on the worst section of narrow, twisting highway leading to Sea Haven.

Kate whirled around, facing toward the town as a bell began to ring loudly. The sound reverberated through the night. "The bell is the symbol for guidance, for return. She's here now. She's coming up the highway now, returning to us. Returning to the fold. Sarah—" she caught her sister by the hand—"she's nearing the cliffs right now. Even if Hannah had the strength to bring in the wind, it's too late. He's warning us, telling us what he's going to do. Why would he do that?"

Kate reached for her youngest sister, mind to mind. She wasn't the most telepathic of her siblings, but Elle was a strong telepathic. Kate heard music, Joley's voice filling the car with her rich, warm tones. Elle's voice joining in. Elle drove slowly, crawling through the thick fog, knowing she was only a mile from her home. It was impossible to see in front of the car; she had no choice but to pull off the road and park until the fog lifted.

Elle peered at the side of the road, trying to see where the shoulder was wide enough to get her car off the highway in case another vehicle came along. She steered slowly over, aware the cliff was high above the pounding sea. Joley's voice was comforting, a sultry heat that kept the chilling cold from entering the car. Elle turned off the engine and pushed open the door, needing to get her bearings. If she could see the lights from any

160

direction, she would know where she was. She knew she had to be close to her home. The fog surrounded her, a thick, congealed mass that was utterly cold.

Kate drew in her breath, tried to touch Elle, tried to warn her of the impending danger. Elle kept her hand on the car. *What is it, Kate?*

Kate cursed the fact that she couldn't form an answer and send it to her sister. She could only send the impression of danger very close. They all knew when their siblings were in danger, or tired or upset. But Kate didn't have the ability to actually tell Elle something was in the fog, something that was taking enough of a form that it could cause bodily harm. She didn't even know whether to tell her to stay in the car or to get away from it. She could only hope that Elle was sufficiently tapped in to all of her sisters and would know what was transpiring. Elle turned in the direction of their home and began to walk along the narrow path.

Matt rushed past Kate, heading toward the highway. The fog swallowed him immediately. "Try to clear it out, Kate," he called back. His voice sounded muffled in the thick mist, even to his own ears. He knew the trail; he'd walked it enough times over the years and was certain Elle would do the same.

Jonas and Jackson were converging from their locations as well, all of them running to Elle's aid from three different directions, but Matt had no idea if any of them would be in time. He only knew that his heart was in his throat, and he had such an overwhelming sense of imminent danger, he wanted to run flat out instead of carefully jogging his way along the steep, uneven path.

Chapter Ten

Beneath the star, that shines so bright,
An act unfolds, to my delight

Matt heard voices, the rise and fall of feminine voices. He knew Kate and her sisters were doing their best to fight against the wall of fog crouched so malevolently on the highway. He picked his way as fast and as carefully as he could. The ocean pounded and roared beneath him, waves slapping against the cliff and leaping high so that every now and then, as he jogged, he could feel the spray on his face. Rocks and the uneven ground impeded his progress. The wind picked up, blowing fiercely against the fog, taking chunks out over the roiling sea.

"Matt!" Jackson's disembodied voice called to him from deep inside the fog, somewhere ahead of him. "She's gone over the cliff. She's not in the water, but she's not going to be able to last much longer. Search along the edges." The voice was muffled and distorted by the fog.

"Watch yourself, Jackson, the cliff is crumbling in places," Matt cautioned. He didn't ask how Jackson knew Elle had gone over. Hell, he was beginning to believe he was the only person in the world without some kind of psychic talent. "Dammit, dammit, dammit." He couldn't return to Kate and tell her Elle was dead, that they'd been too late. He'd never be able to face her sorrow.

Matt inched toward the cliff, testing the ground every step of the way, making certain it would hold his weight. "Elle!" He shouted her name, heard Jackson, then Jonas echo his call. The ocean answered with another greedy roar, lifting higher, seeking prey. "Dammit, Elle, answer me." He felt desperation. Rage. Fear for Elle was beginning to swirl in the pit of his stomach. He detested inaction. He was a man who took charge, got the job done. He could have endless patience when needed, but he had to know what he was doing.

It seemed a hundred years until Jackson called out. "Found! I'll keep calling out so you both can get a direction. She's not going to be able to hang on, so I'm going down after her. I've tied off a safety rope."

Even with the fog distorting the voice, Matt got a sense of Jackson's direction and moved toward him. Jackson's voice was far more distant the second time he called out, and Matt knew he'd gone over the side of the cliff to try to get to Elle before she plunged into the sea. He'd been in combat with Jackson, had served on many covert missions with him. He wasn't a man to rush headlong into anything. If he was already going over the cliff to get to Elle, she needed the help. He was counting on Jonas and Matt to rescue them both. He knew they'd come for him.

163

Matt felt the crushed grass with his hand and flattened his body, belly down, reaching along the crumbling edge of the cliff until he found the rope. Jackson had tied off the end, using an old fence post. Matt sucked in his breath. The fence post was rotted and already coming out of the ground. "I'm tying off again, Jackson, give me a minute," Matt called down to him. He peered over the cliff.

Jackson was climbing down almost blind, feeling with his hands and toes for a grip. Elle lay sprawled out on a small ledge, clinging to a flimsy tree. He caught only glimpses of her as the fog was pushed out toward the sea. The heavy mist crawled down below the cliff line, hovering stubbornly in the more protected pocket to obscure the vision of the rescuers.

"Pass the rope back to me," Jonas said, coming up behind Matt.

Matt did so immediately, not taking his eyes from the scene unfolding below him. The fog was thick and churning, but the wind kept attacking it, driving it out in feathery clumps. It was the only thing that provided him with glimpses of the action. Jackson made his way, with painstaking care, down the sheer side of the cliff. Jonas tied off the rope to a much more secure anchor behind them, where Matt couldn't see.

"We're ready up here, Jackson, say the word," Matt called when Jonas signaled him the rope was safe to use. "Elle, I'm not hearing anything from you." He hadn't. Not a moan, not a call for help. It was alarming. He thought he could see her actively holding on to the small tree growing out of the side of the cliff, but the more he tried to pierce the veil of the fog, the more he was certain Elle wasn't moving.

As Jackson reached her, Matt held his breath, waiting. Afraid to hear, afraid not to hear. His heart beat loudly over the sound of the sea.

"She's alive," Jackson called up. "She has a nasty bump on the head, and she's bruised from head to toe, but she's alive."

Matt leaned farther over the cliff to hear the conversation below him. Jackson's voice drifted up to him. "Lie still, let me examine you for broken bones. I'm Jackson Deveau, the deputy sheriff."

"This ledge is crumbling." Elle's voice trembled. "Someone pushed me. I didn't hear them, but they pushed me."

"It's all right. Don't move. You're safe now." Jackson's voice was soothing. "Do you remember me? We met once a long time ago."

Matt recognized instantly the calming quality to Jackson's voice. He was talking to keep her from being agitated. "Jonas, I think Elle's injured. I can tell by the way Jackson's acting." Keeping his voice low, he gave the news to the sheriff, aware that Jonas was anxious to know Elle's condition.

"I heard your voice, in a dream," Elle said. Her words blurred around the edges, sending Matt's heart tripping. "You were in pain. Terrible pain. Someone was torturing you. You were in a small closet of a room. I remember."

Matt went still. Jonas froze behind him, obviously hearing Elle's response.

"Then you know you're safe with me. You helped me when I needed it. I'll get you out of this. That's the way the buddy system works."

It was the most Matt had ever heard Jackson say to anyone.

He glanced back to look at Jonas's face. The fog along the highway was clearing. The wind gusted, careening off the cliff face in order to push the heavy mist away from Elle and Jackson. Jackson never talked about being captured. Never talked about the treatment he'd endured. He never spoke of the escape that followed or how difficult it had been as he led a small ragtag group of prisoners back through enemy lines to join their forces.

That a Drake sister might be aware of details Matt and Jonas weren't privy to no longer surprised either of them.

"Can you hold on to me as I climb up?" Jackson asked. "I can send you up by the rope. Matthew Granite and Jonas Harrington are up top waiting for you. You're bound to accumulate a few more bruises being hauled up that way."

"I'd feel safer going up with you, but I seem to keep fading in and out. Things sort of drift away," Elle answered.

Matt felt the tug of the rope, knew Jackson was tying the safety line around Elle.

"Then we'll go up together," Jackson said. "I'm not going to let anything happen to you."

"I know you won't." Elle circled his neck with her arms and crawled carefully onto his back. Matt felt more tugs with the rope and knew Jackson was tying her body to his.

"Your arm is broken. Can you hold on?"

"I don't exactly like the alternative, and Libby is blocking the pain for me."

Matt shook his head. Libby Drake, the doctor. A woman reputed to have a gift for healing the impossible. "Did you know Libby was anywhere near here?" he asked Jonas.

Jonas shook his head. "I knew she was coming home for Christmas, but not that she was on the way. But that isn't unusual for the Drakes. They're all connected somehow, and they tend to do things together."

Jackson's voice drifted up to them. "Good. I'm going to start climbing, Elle. It's going to hurt."

Elle pressed her face against Jackson's broad back. Matt watched Jackson start up the cliff, testing each finger- and toe-hold carefully before committing to the climb. Matt and Jonas kept the rope just taut enough to allow him to scale the vertical rock face. When Jackson was halfway to the top, the fog simply gave up, retreating before the onslaught of the wind. Matt leaned down to grasp Elle, as Jackson gained the top of the cliff.

Matt untied the rope and gently laid Elle on the ground. "I'll get to a car and radio for an ambulance," Jonas said.

Elle shook her head. "Libby's on her way. She'll fix me up." She turned her head to look at Jackson. "Thank you for coming for me. I didn't think anyone would find me." She touched the bump on her forehead. "I know the fall knocked me out."

Jackson shrugged and glanced at Matt and Jonas, shook his head, and remained silent. A car pulled up beside them and Libby Drake leaped out, dragging a black leather case with her. "How bad is she hurt, Jonas?"

"I'm fine, Libby," Elle protested.

Libby ignored her, looking to Jonas for the truth as she knelt beside her sister. Jackson answered her. "I think her left arm is broken. She definitely has a concussion, and she's either bruised her ribs or possibly fractured them. She's very tender on the left

167

side. There's one laceration on her left leg that looks as if it could use a few stitches. Other than that, she's a mass of bruises."

"I don't want to go to the hospital, Libby," Elle protested.

"Too bad, baby, I think we're going to go and check you out."

Libby's word was obviously law. Elle protested repeatedly, but no one paid any attention to her. Matthew found himself holding Kate's hand in the waiting room while Libby went through all the required tests with Elle and finally settled her in a hospital bed for the remainder of the night.

Kate leaned into Matt's hard frame, looking up at him. "Thank you. I don't know what we would have done if you, Jonas, and Jackson hadn't found her. She looks all cut up." There was a little catch in her voice.

Matt immediately put his arms around her. "I'm taking you home. To my home, where you can get some rest, Kate. Elle's in good hands, you've kissed her ten times, and Libby's going to stay overnight with her. She can't be safer than that. Jackson brought her car to your house and left it for her, so everything's taken care of. Come home with me, Katie. Let me take care of you."

"You need a shave," she observed, her hungry gaze drinking him in.

They walked together to his car, their steps in perfect harmony. Matt smiled because he loved being with her more than anything else. He rubbed his jaw. "You're right, I do. You're not only going to have whisker burn on your face, but if I'm not more careful, you'll have it other places too."

She blushed beautifully. "I already do."

He opened the door for her, caught her chin before she could slide in. "Seriously?" Just the idea of it made his body hard.

Kate nodded. "It's nice to have a constant reminder." It was more than nice. Just the thought of how the marks had gotten there made her hot with need.

Matt dragged her close to him, his mouth taking command of hers. It seemed far too long since he'd been able to kiss her. To have her all to himself. "I want to get you home where I can put you into my bed. I still have such a hard time believing you're with me."

She laughed. "Imagine how I feel."

Kate leaned her head back against the seat of his car and looked at him, the smile fading from her face. "Matt, you shouldn't have wished on the snowglobe. It isn't an ordinary Christmas globe."

He glanced at her, then back at the road, his expression settling into serious lines. "Nothing about you or your family is ordinary, Katie. I knew what I was doing."

She opened her mouth to speak, shook her head, and stared out the window into the night.

Matt searched for something to say to reassure her. Or maybe it was he that needed the reassurance. Kate was still resistant to the idea of a long-term relationship, and he wasn't certain he could change her mind. He couldn't begin to explain the sense of rightness he felt when he drove up to his house with Kate beside him. He sat in his car, looking up at the house with its bank of windows for the view, and the wide, inviting decks going in every direction. "I built this house for you. I even put in a library and two offices, just in case you wanted your own office. I asked Sarah a few years ago, when I first came back, if you had a preference where you wrote, and she said you preferred a room with a view and soft music. I added a fireplace just in case you needed the ambience."

Kate blinked back tears, leaned over, and kissed him. What could she say? Everyone in town knew Sarah. Sarah was magic. She could scale cliff walls and she knew things before they happened. She could leap out of airplanes and climb tall buildings. Sarah lived her life. She didn't dream the way Kate did or live in her imagination.

Matt took her hand and pulled her out of the car. "I soundproofed your office so the noise wouldn't bother you."

"What noise?" She knew better than to ask, but she couldn't stop herself.

"Our kids. You do want kids, don't you? I'm afraid the Granites tend to throw males. I don't have a single female cousin. You do like boys, don't you?"

Kate looked away from him, out to the booming sea. Sarah would have children. All of her sisters would have them. She'd probably tell them all stories. Maybe she should have been the one to wish on the snowglobe. Maybe she should have wished for the courage to do the right thing.

"Katie, if you don't want children, I'll be happy with it being just the two of us. You know that, don't you?" He unlocked the door to the house and stepped back to let her in. "Children would be wonderful, but not necessary. If we can have them. Sometime in the future, after I've spent endless time making love to you all over the house."

Kate went straight to the Christmas tree. She wanted him. She wanted him for as long as she could have him. She swallowed her tears and lifted her chin, smiling at him. "I like that idea. Making love to you all over the house. Would you turn on the Christmas lights? I love miniature lights like these."

Matt plugged in the lights for her. His house was dark and quiet and a bit on the cool side. He'd never bothered with heavy curtains in the living room because he had no close neighbors, and the bank of windows faced the sea. Kate dropped her purse on the nearest chair and kicked off her shoes. "It's nice to come home. Just for tonight, I want to think about Christmas and not some awful thing coming out of the fog to hurt everyone." She looked up at him, her large eyes sad. "Do you think we'll manage to get one night together, Matthew?"

"I don't know, Katie. I hope so. I'm going to check the house and downstairs, and I'll be right back." He didn't think he could sleep, not even holding her in his arms, until he checked the sand outside for any peculiar footprints.

"That's a good idea. I'll make us up a bed. You don't mind if we sleep out here by the tree do you?"

Matt looked around the huge, spacious living room. The miniature lights winked on and off, colors flickering along the walls and the high ceiling. "I'd like that, Kate."

He circled the house, checked the rooms beneath the deck and the beach for any signs of intrusion. He had the feeling the enemy was as fatigued as they were. He glanced out to sea. "How about giving us a break, buddy," he murmured softly. "Whatever has you all upset, Kate had nothing to do with it."

Above his head the skies opened up and poured down rain.

Matt grinned wryly and hurried back to the house. Back to Kate. The gas fireplace was lit, the "logs" burning cheerfully. On the mantel were several lighted candles. The scent of berry permeated the air. In the flickering lights, he saw Kate, lying naked on the sheets, her body beautiful, sprawled lazily on the covers while she watched the lights of the Christmas tree. His breath rushed from his lungs, so that he burned for air, just standing there in the doorway staring in surprise at the most incredible Christmas present he could imagine. That was how he thought of her. His Christmas present. He would love this time of year forever.

"Matthew." She turned over, smiled at him. "Come lie down with me."

He could see the real Kate Drake. On the outside, she seemed flawless, perfect, out of reach, yet she was really vulnerable, and as fragile as she was courageous. Kate needed a shield and he was more than happy to be that shield, for her. He could stand between her and the rest of the world. "Give me a minute, Kate."

Kate turned back to the tree, watching the lights blinking on and off, so many colors flickering across the wall. It was heaven just to lie down and rest. To relax. More than anything she loved to feel Matt's heated gaze on her. He made her feel beautiful and incredibly special. He was a large man, and the feel of his hands on her body, the way his body came alive at the sight of her, was a gift. A treasure.

Kate lay with the sheets cool on her skin and the lights playing over her body. She imagined his hands on her. His eyes on her. Thinking about him made her grow hot with need. A small sound alerted her, and she looked up to see him towering over her. For a moment she couldn't breathe. She drank him in. His strong legs and muscular thighs. His amazing erection. His flat stomach and heavily muscled chest. Finally, his eyes. His eyes had turned smoky, seductive, and now they smoldered with intensity and heat. "You take my breath away." It was a silly thing to say, but it was true. She patted the blanket beside her. She wanted to touch him, to know he was real. To feel him solid and strong beneath her fingertips.

"I'm supposed to say that to you." He stretched out beside her, gathered her into his arms to hold her to him. "I want to lie here with you for a very long time."

She rested her head on his shoulder, fitting her body more closely to his. "I wouldn't mind staying here for the rest of the winter, locked away in our own private world." She stretched languidly, pleased to be able to relax. To have him holding her with such gentleness.

Matt knew she was tired, and it was enough to hold her in his arms, even with his body raging at him and her body so soft and inviting and open to his. His mouth drifted down the side of her neck. She snuggled closer, turning her head toward the Christmas tree, giving him even better access.

"I love the way you smell," he said. Because he couldn't resist, he slid his palm over her skin. He'd never felt anything so soft. He traced her ribs, a gentle exploration, not in the least demanding, simply wanting to touch her. Her soft belly called to him, a mystery for a breast man, but he loved the way she reacted each time he caressed her there.

Kate smiled. "I love the feel of your hands."

"I've always hated my hands. Workingman hands, rough and big and meant for manual labor."

"Meant to bring pleasure to a woman, you mean," she contradicted, and caught his hand to bring it to her lips. She kissed the pads of his fingers, nibbled on the tips, and drew one into her mouth.

He caught his breath, aching with love, burning up with need. "Everything about you is so damned feminine, Kate. Sometimes I'm afraid if I touch you, I'm going to break you." He measured her wrist loosely by circling it with his thumb and index finger.

She laughed and rubbed her body against his affectionately, almost like a contented cat. "I doubt you have to worry about breaking me. This thing with the fog is draining, but I recover quickly." She frowned, even as she ran her fingertips along the hard column of his thigh. "I am a little worried about Hannah though, and now Elle."

He was very much aware of her fingers so close to his throbbing erection. She was tapping out a little rhythm on his upper thigh. His stomach constricted, and his blood thickened. The lights on the Christmas tree blinked on and off in harmony with the drumming of her fingers. Every tap brought a surge of heat through his body. "The doctors said Elle was going to be fine. She'll have a whale of a headache, though, and Jackson was right about her ribs and arm, but she'll heal fast with Libby around."

Matt cupped her breast in his hands, his thumbs teasing her nipples into taut pebbles. He felt her response, the swift intake of breath. The flush that covered her body. "It seems such a

174

miracle to me to be able to touch you like this. I wonder if every other man knows what a miracle a woman's body is."

"And all this time, I thought the miracle was a man's body." Kate ran her fingernails lightly along his belly.

"Maybe the miracle is just that I finally managed to stop you from hiding from me," Matt decided. He bent his head, flickered her nipple with his tongue, made a lazy foray around the areola. She moved slightly, turning to give him better access.

"I've been thinking about the fog. Something isn't quite right."

"Quite right?" He lifted his head to look at her, arching his eyebrow. The Christmas lights were playing red and green and blue over her stomach. A bright red light glowed across the small triangle of curls at the junction of her legs. It was distracting and made it hard to concentrate on conversation. He slipped his hand in the middle of the flashing light, watched his fingers stroke the nest of curls, felt Kate shiver, and pushed his fingers deep into her warm wet sheath. She pushed back against him, a soft moan escaping. He dipped his head to find her breast, suckling strongly. "What are you thinking, Kate?" His tongue swirled over her nipple, and he pushed deeper inside her until her hips began a helpless ride.

"He isn't going after Hannah. Why attack me? Or Elle? Or even Abbey? He should go after Hannah. She summons the wind to drive him out to sea. She stops him." Her words came in little short bursts. She gasped as she pushed against his hand, as her body tightened with alarming pressure, with the pure magic of passion shared with Matthew.

"Take the pins out of your hair," he whispered, his voice raw.

"I love your hair down. You look very sexy with your hair down."

"You think I look sexy no matter what," she pointed out.

His teeth teased her nipple, nibbled over her breast. "True, but I love the hair."

"You won't love it when it's falling all over you." But she was lifting her arms, pulling out pins and scattering them in every direction while he shifted her, lowering his body into the cradle of her hips, thrusting deep inside her.

She cried out when he surged forward. Whips of lightning danced through her blood. "Matthew." There was a plea for mercy, and he hadn't even gotten started.

"We have all the time in the world, Katie," he whispered, his lips sliding over her throat, her chin, and up to her mouth. His strong hips paused, waiting. She held her breath. He thrust hard, a long stroke surging deep to bury himself completely within her. A coming home. She was velvet soft and tight and fiery hot. He wanted a long slow night with her. His hands shaped her body, stroking and caressing every inch of her.

"I don't feel like we have all the time in the world." She protested, breathless, arching her hips to meet the impact of his. "I feel like I'm going to go up in flames."

"Then do it," he encouraged. "Come for me a hundred times. Over and over. Scream for me, Kate. I love you so much. I love watching you come for me. And I love your body, every square inch of it. I want to spend the night worshiping you."

Kate wanted the same thing. She did scream, clutching at the bedcovers for an anchor as her body fragmented, and she went spinning off into space. She couldn't tell if the whirling colors were behind her eyes or from the Christmas tree lights. She found it didn't matter when he caught her hips firmly, held her still, and began surging into her once more with his slow, deep strokes.

Chapter Eleven

In the stocking hung with gentle care,
A mystery, I know, is hidden there.

Matt woke already aroused. He was thick and aching, so tight he thought he'd burst through his own skin. The blankets had fallen onto the floor as if he had spent a long, restless night. His body was stark naked and mercilessly aroused. He looked down at Kate. She smiled up at him, her sea-green eyes sultry, her hands moving gently over his flat stomach. Her long hair spilled over his hips and thighs, teasing every nerve ending. He knotted a long strand around his fist. "I dreamed of you, Kate."

Her smile was that of a temptress. "I hope it was a good dream." She bent her head to her task, lovingly stroking her tongue over the thick inviting length of him, sliding the velvet knob into the heated tightness of her mouth.

Matt gasped as the pleasure/pain of it rocked him. "How could it not be?" he asked when he got his breath back. Her tongue made a teasing foray along the rigid length and stroked over him before she once again slid her mouth around him.

He closed his eyes, his hips surging forward, wanting more, needing more, as waves of heat spread through his body, as every muscle clenched and tightened. Kate's fist wrapped him up while her mouth performed miracles. "I don't know if I'll survive this, Kate."

Her answer was muffled, her breath warm and enticing, her mouth hot and tight. He was certain he felt her laughter vibrate through his entire body. There was joy in Kate. That was her secret, he decided. Joy in everything she did with him. She didn't pretend not to enjoy his body, she reveled in exploring him, teasing him, driving him to the very edge of his control.

Kate kissed her way up his belly and over his chest. She mounted him, the way an accomplished horseback rider smoothly slides aboard a horse, settling her body over his with exquisite slowness. She put up her hands and he took them so she could use leverage as her body rose and fell, stroking his. Her hair spilled around her, adding to her allure as her full breasts bounced and beckoned with every movement. She threw her head back, arched back, moving differently, tightening muscles until he was certain he would explode.

"Kate." Her name was a husky, almost hoarse sound, escaping from his constricted throat. His lungs burned. A fire spread through his belly, centered in his groin, and gathered into a wild conflagration. He couldn't take his gaze from her. There was a sheen to her skin, a flush over her body. She moved with a woman's sensuous grace and mystery. "The feel of your hair on my legs and belly makes me crazy." It should have tickled his skin, but the silky fall brushed over sensitive nerve endings and added to the heat and fire building in the deep within him. He felt as if every part of his body was being pulled in that direction.

Kate moved with exquisite slowness, undulating her body, sending him right out of his mind. The erotic visual only increased his raging hunger for her. In the soft morning sunlight, her hair flashed red streaks, and her pale skin seemed made of dewy petals. Most of all, the expression on her face, deeply absorbed in the ride of lust and love and passion, shook his entire being. He could read the way her body began to build pressure, her muscles clenching tightly, gripping him strongly. He could see it on her face, the rapture, the passion, the intensity of the orgasm as it overtook her. He watched her ride it out, watched the excitement and pleasure on her face, in her body. Seeing her like that heightened his own pleasure, and he wanted more, wanted her flushed body to feel it again and again and bring his body to his own explosive orgasm.

He caught her hips in his hands, taking control, guiding her ride, thrusting upward hard as she slid down over him, encasing him in a fist of hot velvet. He shuddered with pleasure, feeling the pressure building relentlessly. He could feel her body preparing for a second shock, the muscles tightening around him, adding to the intensity of his explosion. It shook him, a volcano going off, detonating from the inside out, taking everything in its path. He caught her to him, fighting for air, fighting to regain some sense of where he was, of a time and place, not fantasyland, where his every dream came true. It seemed impossible to be lying on his living room floor, his heart raging at him, his body in ecstasy, and the love of his life in his arms. His world had been guns and sand and jungles and an enemy fighting to kill him. Women like Kate were not real and they didn't wind their arms around his neck and rain kisses all over his face and tell him he was too sexy to be alive.

They lay together just holding one another, trying to get their heart rates back to normal and to push air through their lungs. Kate lay stretched out on top of Matt, pressing her soft body tightly against his. Beneath her, he suddenly stiffened.

"What the hell is that?" he growled, hearing a noise outside the house.

Kate gasped and rolled off of him, landing on the pile of blankets. "We have company, Matthew," she whispered, gathering the sheets around her.

He sat up abruptly, his breath hissing through his teeth. He'd asked for a night with Kate, he should have asked for the entire damned week. He was never going to get enough of her, never be sated. "I thought I'd at least get you for a few more hours," he groused as he padded naked across the floor. He suddenly halted halfway to the door and uttered a string of curses. "It's my parents."

Kate's eyes widened. She clutched the sheet to her naked breasts. "What?"

"My parents," he announced. He reached down to help her up. "Why is it that even when you're grown, parents can make you feel like a teenager caught in the act?"

Kate wrapped the sheet around her and hurried toward his bedroom while Matt scooped up the blankets and followed her. "Did you get caught in the act often?"

"Are you laughing at me?" he asked, a dangerous glint in his silver eyes.

"Only because I'm disappearing into the bathroom to leave you to face the music alone. You might get dressed." She grinned mischievously at him as she gathered up her clothes and retreated behind a securely locked door.

Matt caught sight of the wisp of peach-colored lace that lay on the floor and found a wicked smile stealing over his face. He stooped down and picked it up, bunching it into his hand before shoving it into the pocket of his jacket, which was lying on the back of a chair. He dragged on clothes as fast as he could, combing his hair with his fingers just as the polite knock on his door came.

He could hear Kate laughing, and it was contagious. He couldn't wipe the grin off his face as he opened the front door. Victoria Granite threw her arms around her son and hugged him hard. "You frightened us, Matt! We called and called and you never answered. First there was a fire here and Danny told us about that horrible incident at the store and then a call went out and ... "

"Victoria, take a breath," Harold Granite advised. He smiled lovingly at his wife, used to her run-on sentences. "We heard the fog came in last night, and Elle Drake went over the cliff. Victoria was worried."

Matt's mother made a face. "Really, Harold, I knew he was perfectly fine; you were the one who spent the entire morning trying to call him and pacing back and forth like a wild tiger. I was fine!"

Matt met his father's gaze over the top of his mother's head.

They both stifled a knowing grin. "I'm sorry, Dad. I should have remembered after all these years, how you worry."

Victoria smiled and patted Harold's arm. "There, dear, you see there was nothing at all to worry about. All that pacing." She shook her head, stopping in mid-sentence as she looked up at the mantel and the candles that had burned down to the holders. "Oh my goodness." She looked around carefully. "Matthew Granite, you had a woman here last night, didn't you?"

"Mom, once I turned thirty, I thought we agreed I didn't have to talk about women with you."

From the bedroom came the sound of a door closing. His parents exchanged a long, satisfied look. Victoria arched her eyebrow at her son. "She's still here?"

"As a matter of fact, yes. And don't start on her, Mom. I don't want her scared off. This is the one."

There was another startled silence. "Kate's here?" Harold asked, clearly astonished. "Kate Drake?"

"Of course it's Kate," Victoria said.

Kate came out of the bedroom with a bright smile and desperation in her eyes. She was wearing one of his shirts over her thin white blouse. Matthew was instantly mortified. He thought he would tease her, and at the same time, he'd have the added pleasure of knowing she was sitting beside him in the warmth of his car without a bra. He'd planned to slip his hand inside the white silk of her blouse and caress her soft creamy skin. The idea alone had made him as hard as a rock. It hadn't occurred to him that her blouse was sheer enough that her darker nipples would show so alluringly.

Kate always presented a near flawless appearance to the

world, and he realized immediately when he saw the desperation in her eyes that it was her armor. She wore her clothes and hair and makeup to keep people from seeing the real Kate. The vulnerable Kate. The Kate she shared only with her sisters, and now with him.

"Hello Mrs. Granite, Mr. Granite," she greeted.

Matthew drew the edges of his shirt together around her, sliding several buttons in place. He bent to kiss her, shielding her from his parents' scrutiny for a brief moment. When he was certain she was sufficiently covered, he circled her waist with his arms and held her in front of him. He could feel her soft unbound breasts pushing against his arms. Instantly his body reacted, thickening, hardening, an ache pounding through his blood. He held her close to him, covering the painful bulge stretching the material of his jeans. Kate was without mercy, slowly and sensuously rubbing her round bottom over the hard ridge. "I would very much like to visit, but Elle's in the hospital, and we have to go by Kate's house before we go to see her." Was that his voice? It sounded thick and husky to his ears. He was even afraid color burned in his face. His palms itched to cup Kate's breasts in his hands. The soft weight on his arms was driving him crazy. His mouth had actually gone dry. And if she didn't stop the way she was rubbing against him, he was going to shock everyone right then and there. "Let's have dinner tonight," he suggested, in desperation making eye contact with his father.

Harold, taking the cue, caught Victoria's elbow firmly.

"Danny will be spending the evening with Trudy Garret and her little boy at the Grange. Santa Claus is stuffing stockings and delivering presents around seven. We were going to watch," Victoria said. "Can we plan for another night?"

"Tomorrow is the pageant rehearsal," Matt said. "You all are in that. Maybe we can grab dinner afterward."

"There's never time." Harold shook his head, but headed across the living room to the front door. "The pageant rehearsal never runs smoothly, and we're always there until midnight."

"Good point," Matt agreed. "Don't worry, Mom, we'll have dinner together soon." He walked them to the door. "Who's playing Santa Claus this year?"

Harold grinned. "No one's supposed to know, Matt." He went out into the light drizzle and paused. "Jeff Burley broke his leg a couple of weeks ago. He's done it every year, and we had a bit of trouble finding a replacement. Everyone's afraid of the fog. Some of the townspeople think it's some kind of alien invasion."

Victoria put up her umbrella and made a little face. "People are so silly sometimes."

"I hope you're not trying to ask me to be Santa Claus this year, I'm more afraid of the kids than I am of aliens." Matt sounded as stern as he dared with his mother.

Kate made a move to retreat back into the house, but Matt held her firmly as if she were his only refuge. The cold air hardened Kate's nipples into tight buds, and she was acutely aware she wore no bra beneath Matt's shirt. The drizzle was penetrating straight through the material and turning the silk blouse beneath it transparent. She crossed her arms over her chest and kept her smile firmly in place.

"There aren't any aliens," Victoria said, exasperated. "And no,

185

you don't have to play Santa. I know better than to ask any of you boys. You'd frighten the children with your nonsense."

"Not Dad!" Matt suddenly sounded authoritative, and Kate looked up. "Dad, the doctor told you not to overdo."

"Playing Santa Claus wouldn't overdo anything." Harold was clearly annoyed. "And no, it isn't me. We had someone come forward, but he wishes to remain anonymous. It would ruin all of his fun if I revealed his identity."

Matt followed his parents to their car, taking Kate with him. "I'm not going to tell anyone."

"The last man you'd ever expect," Victoria said primly.

"The last man I'd ever expect to play Santa would be Old Man Mars." Matt laughed. "Can't you see Danny's face? He'd run from Santa."

Victoria and Harold looked at one another and burst out laughing. Victoria waved gaily at Kate. Matt stared after them. "You don't think they meant that that mean old man is going to play Santa."

"I can't imagine it. I think they were teasing you. Do you have the car keys? I'm getting cold, and I have to stop by my house to pick up some clothes before we go to the hospital."

"I've got them. Come on. Let's get you out of the rain." Matt drew her bra from his jacket pocket and held it out to her. "I'm sorry, Katie. I couldn't stop thinking about playing out my little fantasy of being able to touch you when I was taking you home. It was childish of me."

Kate merely looked at the peach-colored bra in his outstretched hand, but made no move to take it. "And you wanted to be able to touch me how?" She walked past him to the car.

There was a distinct sway to her beautiful rear, one he couldn't resist. Kate settled into his car, slowly unbuttoned the wet overshirt, and allowed the edges to gape open to reveal the transparent silk blouse underneath. She leaned back against the seat.

Matt drove slowly along the coastal highway, fighting for air when there was none in the car. The shape of her breasts was not only outlined beneath the see-through material, but highlighted. "Kate, you're an incredible woman."

"I'm a lucky woman. I rather like your fantasies. By all means, tell me whenever you get one."

He couldn't resist. Matt slipped his hand inside her blouse, cupped the soft, creamy flesh in his palm. His knuckle rubbed gently over her breast, the pads of his fingers possessive as he caressed her body. Right at that moment he could think of a hundred fantasies. He turned the car onto the drive leading to the bluff overlooking the sea. The moment he parked, he caught the back of her head and held her still while he devoured her mouth.

They spent an hour in the car, laughing like children, necking like teenagers, wildly happy as they held hands, touched and kissed and whispered of dreams and hopes and erotic fantasies.

When they arrived at the Drake house, no one was home; the sisters were all at the hospital. There was a note for Kate telling her Elle was doing much better and instructing her to join them when she could. Kate took the time to shower. Matt joined her and spent a long while leisurely lathering soap over her and rinsing her off. He made love to her under the spray of water, then dried her off with large towels. He couldn't take his eyes off of her while she dressed. "I've never been happier, Kate," he admitted, as she pinned the thick length of hair on top of her head into her "perfect Kate" style.

"Me either," she answered, and leaned over to kiss him.

Matt caught her hand and dragged her through the house into the living room. "Kate, do you love me? You know I love you. I tell you. I show you. I want to spend my life with you, and I've made no secret about that. Do you love me?"

Kate nearly stopped breathing. She touched his face. "How could you not know, Matthew? I love you so much I ache with it sometimes."

"Then why won't you agree to marry me? I don't think your family objects to me, and obviously my family would welcome it."

She let her breath out slowly. "I have some things to work out, Matt. I want to marry you. I do. But I have to be certain it's right for you. That I'm right for you."

"Katie. Honey. I know you're right for me." He looked around the room. "Where's that damned snowglobe anyway?" He retrieved it from the shelf.

Kate took it out of his hands. "You only get one wish, Matt, and you've had yours." She went to place the globe back on the shelf, but it came alive in her hands, the fog swirling. Waiting. Kate closed her eyes and made her wish. She couldn't stop herself. She wanted Matthew Granite more than she'd ever wanted anything in her life.

Matt said nothing, asking her no questions. He simply took her hand in a gesture of solidarity.

*

Kate and Matt spent most of the afternoon in the hospital with Kate's sisters in Elle's room. Matt and Damon played a game of chess while the seven sisters caught up on news. Joley helped Damon, and when Matt expressed disapproval, Abbey immediately took Matt's side. They did their best to entertain Elle, who looked bruised and very young. Her bright red hair tumbled around her white face and heightened her pale skin and deepened the purple in the bruises. She was in good spirits but weak and still had a headache.

Matt and Kate left the hospital in the evening to meet the Granites at the Grange, where most of the townspeople were bringing their children for photos with Santa and a small party.

The Grange hall was packed with parents and children. "Jingle Bells" blared through the building, mistletoe was hung in every conceivable place, and holly decorated the tables laden with cookies and punch. A fake mantel went along the entire length of one wall with holly, candles, and tiny sleighs filled with candy canes adorning the top. Rows of stockings hung on gleaming hooks. The silver-tipped fir tree nearly reached the ceiling and was covered in lights, ornaments, and a multitude of white angels with silver wings.

"The ladies at the arts and crafts shop have been busy," Matt whispered.

Kate shushed him, but her eyes were laughing. Several elves hurried past them, bells tinkling from their hats and ankles. Kate and Matt followed the elves through the crowd to the back of the building, where Santa Claus sat in a high-backed chair surrounded by more elves and a reindeer that looked suspiciously like a dog with plastic antlers attached to his head. The line to visit Santa was long, small children clutching parents' hands and staring with large round eyes at the jolly old man. The Santa suit fit perfectly, and the white beard and mustache seemed natural, both bushy enough to hide the face successfully. Matt tried to get close enough to get a good look at the Santa. Several pre-teenagers rushed past him laughing loudly, tossing popcorn at each other.

"Do you think it's Old Man Mars?" Matt whispered.

"How could it be?" Kate asked. "He hates Christmas."

"Right height. I could tell if he were talking loud or maybe even by the way he walks." Matt weaved his way through the small children.

"Hey!" A young boy with red hair protested. "No cutting in."

"I just wanted to ask Santa if he'd give me Kate for Christmas," Matt explained.

Unimpressed, the boy wrinkled his nose, and all of his friends made faces. "Well, you got to stand in line like everyone else."

Kate laughed and dragged Matt away from Santa Claus. He spotted Inez and pulled Kate toward her. "If anyone knows who Santa Claus is, it'll be Inez. She knows everything."

"Doesn't that come under the heading of gossip?"

"News, Katie. How can you even use the word *gossip*?" Matt stopped moving abruptly and brought her up short, staring out the window. He bit out a string of curses. "The damned fog is rolling in, Kate. It's coming right this way."

Kate looked at him, then looked around at the children. "I don't want people to panic and run for their cars to get away from here. No one would be able to drive in the fog. I'll find a way to distract the kids." She hurried toward Santa Claus, whispering softly to the children so that the throng parted like the Red Sea to give her access to the jolly old man sitting with a child on his lap. She leaned in and spoke to him.

From a distance, Matt watched Santa stiffen, listen some more, and nod. Kate straightened up and directed the children into a large circle. Santa gave out candy canes, patting heads and laughing as he did so. Several mothers began distributing cookies and punch while Kate started an enthralling Christmas story. Matt had never seen anyone hold an entire room in her hand, but there was no sound other than the faint background of Christmas music and Kate's spellbinding voice. He found himself caught up in the sheer beauty of the magical tone, even when the fog began to seep through the cracks of the doors and windows.

There was no way to keep the fog out. It was only the magic of Kate's voice, the anonymous Santa Claus's cheerful punctuation of ho, ho, ho woven cleverly into the storyline, and the Granite reputation in the community that kept panic from spreading as the gray-white vapor filled the room, bringing with it the scent and feel of the sea. Kate smoothly incorporated the fog into the storyline, having the children hold hands and interact with Santa's ho, ho, ho. The children did so with enthusiasm, laughing wildly at the antics of Kate's characters in the fog. Matt realized she was creating the illusion that the fog was deliberate, a part of the story she was telling, used for effect. He could see parents relaxing, thinking Kate had found a way to keep the children from fearing the incoming fog, a part of life for anyone who lived on the coast.

It seemed hours to Matt, watching the fog churning, swirling in deeper shades of gray, spinning when there was no breeze to create the effect, yet it was only a few minutes before the fog began a hasty retreat ... almost as if it couldn't take the sound of Kate's voice. It was a silly notion. Fog had no ears to listen, but it also shouldn't have been able to leave footprints in sand or do damage to property. He made his way closer to Kate, knowing she would pay a steep price using her energy to keep such a large crowd under the spell of her voice. As he moved toward her, he felt something in the fog, something tangible brush against his arm.

Matt whirled toward it, hands going up in a fighter's defensive position, but there were only coils of vapor surrounding him. He heard a sound, a growling voice muttering a warning. A chill went down his spine. He felt the touch of death on him, bony fingers reaching for him, or someone who belonged to him. The hair on his body stood up in reaction to the half moan, half growl that could have been wind, but there was no wind to generate the sound. Matt knew it was a warning, but the words made no sense.

Anger was impotent against fog. He couldn't fight it, couldn't wrestle it; he couldn't even shoot it. How could he protect Kate when he couldn't see or get his hands on the culprit? He stood very still as the vapor simply rolled from the building, leaving behind the soft Christmas music and the laughter of the children. He looked around the room, at the sunny faces, at the tree and decorations. Why had the fog come, only to recede without incident?

He made his way to Kate's side, slipping his arm around her

waist to lend her strength. She sent the children to the tables of food, a smile on her face, shadows in her eyes. Laughter picked up as if the fog had never been; but Matt continued to survey the room, inch by inch, concerned there had to more, something they were all missing.

Kate leaned into him as they looked out the window. "It's heading out to sea on its own. Why would it do that? Why would it come here and leave?"

Matt watched the children eating. Santa Claus was eating. "Could it have poisoned the food some way?" he asked, his heart in his throat at the thought. His parents were seated at a table with Danny, Trudy Garrett, and her young son.

"I doubt it, Matthew, how could it?"

"How could he do any of the things he's been doing?" His hands tightened on her shoulders. "Santa Claus is a symbol of Christmas, right? What does he represent?"

"You don't think he came to attack the man playing the part of Santa, then decided against it, do you?" Her anxious gaze followed the burly man in the red-and-white suit.

Matt shook his head. "I feel danger, Katie. When I feel it this strong, it's here, close by. Tell me what Santa represents."

She rubbed her throbbing temples. "Goodwill, I suppose. He represents goodwill and generosity. He gives presents, stuffs stockings, eats the children's milk and cookies."

"He spreads goodwill among the people and is generous, teaching by example to be generous." Matt tugged on her hand, moved toward the tree where Santa's pack lay. He peered inside. There were a few netted candy cane stockings holding small toys, candy, and various small personal items the town always generously donated for the event. Santa had slipped most of the candy cane net stockings into the children's stockings hanging from the fake mantel earlier when he'd first arrived, so that each child would have something to take home after the party.

Matt went to the brightly colored stockings, each with a child's name stitched in bold letters across the top. Kate's fingers tightened around his. She already knew, just as he did. They peered inside. She drew back, stifling a cry, looking at him with fear. Inside each stocking, the fog had added to Santa's generous gift. A mass of sand and sea bugs writhed in hideous black balls in the toes of the stockings. All were damp with seawater and smelled faintly of the noxious odor the fog seemed to leave behind. Crushed shells and spiny sea anemone, kelp and small crabs were mixed with the wiggling insects.

Santa Claus joined them, staring at the mess while all around them children ate and laughed and played. "We have to get rid of these. Some of these creatures are venomous."

Matt glanced quickly at the man, recognizing the voice. Old Man Mars was indeed playing Santa. "You're right. I'll get a couple of the men, and we'll get the stockings out of here before the children start trying to collect them. Kate." He pulled out a chair for her. "Sit down before you fall down. I'll take you home when we're through here."

"To my house," she said in a weary voice. "I need to go to my house."

He nodded, his gut knotting tightly.

Chapter Twelve

A candle burns with an eerie glow,
As it melts, the wax does flow,

"The thing in the fog spoke to me." Matt made the announcement after the Drake sisters had settled Elle firmly in the living room. It was late afternoon before the doctors let her go home, and her family had been so anxious, Matt had steered clear of the subject of the danger in the fog. He and Kate had gone to the mill earlier in the morning to reexamine the seal and see if she could find anything new about the spirit. He hadn't wanted to bring up the subject at the very source of the trouble.

There was a sudden silence. He had their attention immediately. Kate set down her teacup. "You didn't say anything to me about it."

"You were exhausted and worried about Elle last night, Katie, and again this morning. I didn't want to bring it up. Now that she's home and safe, I thought it was a good time to discuss it." En masse, the Drake sisters were difficult to contend with. He could feel every eye on him. There was power in the room, intangible, feminine, but a steady flow of it. An energy he couldn't begin to explain, but he knew it moved from sister to sister.

"What did it say?" Sarah asked. Her voice was gentle, non-judgmental. Practical, magical Sarah. She was the oldest and the most influential.

"It made no sense. It was a moan and a growl mixed together. The syntax was old-fashioned, but from what I got, it was a warning to keep my loved ones away from one with the staff."

"The staff? He used the word *staff*?" Kate asked.

Matt nodded. "I've thought a lot about it, and maybe it all ties up with Christianity and the staff of life or something. Anything to do with the Christian beliefs of Christmas is under attack?" He made it a question.

Elle lifted the old journal Sarah handed to her. "I'll do my best to try to find a reference to a staff in here," she said. "I don't think I thanked you for coming to my rescue the other night, Matt. One minute I was making my way home, and the next I felt something shove me over the side of cliff. I broke every fingernail on the way down, grabbing at dirt and rocks. I have no idea how Jackson climbed down to get me. I couldn't even call out with a strong enough voice for help, and I was afraid to move. The ledge was literally crumbling under me."

"I know it was frightening, Elle, but we have you, you're safe now," Joley soothed.

"Kate said something the other evening about how the entity didn't go after Hannah. It's strange because Hannah's the one providing the wind to drive him out to sea and away from the town," Matt said. "Do any of you have any idea why he's chosen not to try to harm her?"

Sarah frowned. "It really only went after Elle."

Kate shook her head. "It definitely tried for me, Sarah. And I think it tried to use Sylvia and her amorous ways to get to Abbey, then made a second attempt here in the house, pitting her against Jackson. Jackson's a mercurial man, and Sylvia's unpredictable. I think it wanted Abbey out of the way too. Of all of us, wouldn't Hannah be its main obstacle?"

"What do you all have in common?" Matt asked. He watched as Sarah moved through the living room lighting tall, thick candles at each entranceway. The candles each had three wicks and sat in wrought-iron holders. She murmured something he couldn't hear as she lit each candle. He realized the windows had arrangements of colorful flowers and herbs tied in bundles on either side of the sills and above the window frames. The bundles of dried arrangements hadn't been there before. The fragrance was a blend of outdoors and strong scents of rosemary, jasmine, and something else he couldn't quite identify. The lights of the candles flickered on the walls, dancing and leaping with every movement of the sisters, as if tuned to them.

"Abbey, Kate, and Joley all have special gifts involving their voices," Sarah answered, bending over a tall cranberry candle near the bay window. She glanced over at her youngest sister before lighting the round candle. "Elle has many talents, but she doesn't share their voice. She is, however, a strong telepath, and she can share the shadow world with Kate. Neither Joley nor Abbey has that ability."

"But nothing happened to Joley," Matt said. He sighed. "So much for my great detective work."

Joley made a small dissenting sound. "That's not exactly true." Immediately, she had the attention of all of her sisters.

"Something happened that you didn't tell us," Kate asked.

"I didn't want to worry anyone," Joley admitted. "I get all kinds of silly threats on the road, and in light of the threat to Kate, I didn't want to worry anyone."

Joley stretched, a sensuous flow of feminine muscle. Everything Joley did, every way she moved or even spoke was sultry. It was as natural to her as breathing. Matt found he could appreciate her looks and voice, yet not react in the least. It was a further revelation to him just how deeply in love he was with Kate. He sank onto the floor in front of Kate and leaned against her knees. At once her fingers tunneled into his thick hair, a connection between them.

"What happened, Joley?" Sarah prompted.

"I went up to my room after we all talked the other day. Hannah said she closed the window because the fog was slipping into the house, and it made her uncomfortable. I was so tired I just crashed on the bed, and I didn't think to pay attention to the feel of the room. I woke up choking, strangling really. At first I thought I'd wrapped a scarf around my neck in my sleep and somehow pulled it tight. But the fog was everywhere, layers of it. I could barely see. I pulled the scarf away from my throat and turned on the fan. My throat hurt and . . . " She hesitated, sighed softly, and dragged the turtleneck sweater away from her throat. Distinct round bruises marred her skin.

"And you didn't think it was important to tell us?" Sarah

turned on her younger sister. "That we shouldn't know this thing has advanced to such a sophisticated level of violence? Joley! You weren't thinking."

"I know." Joley rubbed her palm over her thigh. "At first I was terrified, and I went through the house and began to gather the herbs and flowers for the windows, but the entire time I wondered why it just didn't kill me. If it could partially strangle me, why didn't it just do it all the way?"

"Maybe he isn't strong enough," Abbey ventured.

Sarah glanced toward the sea. "He's strong enough. He managed to take shape and, from what Matt says, even find a voice."

"Are you saying he didn't try to kill Joley? He certainly tried to kill Elle," Abbey argued. "Maybe he wasn't prepared for how hard she fought."

"*I'm* saying it didn't try to kill me," Joley said.

"Then what was it doing?" Sarah asked.

"I think it was trying to silence my voice."

Kate put a protective hand to her throat. "In the shadow world, he went for my throat as well."

Something deep inside of Matt went very still. Kate had an incredible voice. "If he wants to still the voices capable of enthrallment, Joley, Abbey, and Kate are definitely on the hit list." He looked at Elle. "But why you?

She smiled, her green eyes bright. "Maybe he doesn't like redheads."

"I think he doesn't want to be saved," Kate announced. "When I touched him, I felt rage, yes, but it wasn't his primary emotion." She leaned towards Elle. "Didn't you feel sorrow and guilt? You were there, you had to have felt it."

Elle looked down at the journal, her expression sorrowful. "I felt it," she said in a small voice.

Matt raised his head sharply. "Elle shares emotions, doesn't she? You connected with Jackson when he was taken prisoner."

Elle refused to meet his eyes. "Yes."

"But he was halfway around the world," Matt protested.

Libby put her hand out to her youngest sister, and Elle took it immediately. "It's very difficult sometimes, Matthew," Libby explained. "We're different. We look the same and try to act the same, but we're not normal and sometimes the overload is . . ." She searched for the right word, looking helplessly at her sisters.

"Dangerous," Sarah supplied. "Using our talents is very draining. Each of us has to overcome by-products of her gift."

"I've seen it in Kate," Matt agreed. "Is there any way to minimize it?"

The seven women looked at one another. As usual, it was Sarah who answered. "We all handle it in different ways. Most of us find our own space and live there, as shielded as we can manage to be." She smiled at Matt. "I know it will help Kate to have you. Damon helps me."

"So far I haven't managed to keep her from wearing herself out. Every time I think we're going to get a little respite, the fog comes in again," Matt pointed out. He was extraordinarily happy that Sarah had accepted his relationship with Kate.

"You've helped enormously," Kate acknowledged.

Elle leafed through the journal. "You said there were symbols on the seal, Kate? Could you read it at all?"

"The first Drake settlers must have been the ones to seal the restless spirit, Elle. It was definitely formed around the time the town was settled. From what I could read, it was something about rage and sealing until one is born who could do something. I went back to take another look, but most of the seal was crushed and the actual writing lost," Kate admitted.

"Until one is born who can do something," Sarah repeated aloud. "Something to do with a voice."

"Here it is," Elle said triumphantly. "'He who will not receive forgiveness shall remain sealed until one is born who can give him peace.'"

There was a long silence. Matt stared at the cranberry candle as the three flames leaped and burned. Hot wax poured over the side like a lava flow, forming a thick pool around the holder. It was a fascinating sight, deep purple wax flowing almost like dark blood. "Why would he need peace?"

Elle pushed a pair of glasses on her nose and studied the faded writing. "One of the sisters who helped to seal the spirit must have had precognition the way Mom does. If that's the case, it means we should be able to find a way to allow him to rest."

"Unless the earthquake opened the crack in the ground and allowed him to escape before his time," Matt said.

"I doubt it," Sarah said seriously. "Things usually happen the way they're supposed to happen, Matthew. It's obviously our time. We have no choice but to figure this out. It's our destiny."

Matt wiped his hand over his mouth. He wasn't certain he believed in destiny. He felt Kate's hand in his hair and changed his mind. "Hannah, are you feeling any better?" She didn't look better. Without her, he wasn't positive they could have managed to get Elle back up the cliff in the midst of the thick fog or drive the entity out to sea and away from the townspeople time after time.

"I've been resting. Libby's helped."

Libby Drake. Matt looked at her. She was legendary in the small town. She was the only Drake with midnight black hair and pale, almost translucent skin. She was a natural-born healer, the real thing. He smiled at her. "It's good to see you again, Libby. Maybe you better hide out while you're home. If word gets out you're back, you'll have everyone in town lining up for a cure."

"I do want to visit Irene's son while I'm home. My sisters went to see him and did what they could to make him comfortable, but I promised I'd go see him."

"Libby—" Matt shook his head—"you know he has terminal cancer. Even you can't get rid of that." He waited. When no one said anything he looked at her. "Can you?" The idea was unsettling.

"I won't know until I visit him," Libby admitted.

"What would be the price?" Matt couldn't imagine what it would cost Libby to actually cure someone sent home to die.

Libby smiled at him. "I can see why Kate loves you so much, Matt. You're very discerning. It's a trade-off. I might save one person, but while I'm recovering, I might lose a hundred others."

"That bad?" He reached his hand for Kate. The thought of what the women had to go through on a daily basis moved him. In their own way, they were warriors, and he had a deep respect for them.

"Does anyone want more tea? I'm getting another cup," Hannah volunteered.

"I can get it," Matt offered. He felt a little useless.

Hannah paused just a few feet from the entrance to the kitchen. "I'm already up, but thank you," she said, and took two steps, halting abruptly, staring at the flickering candle in the bay window facing the sea. "Sarah, you need to come look at this."

Matt got to his feet, pulled Kate up beside him. Apprehensively, he glanced out the large window to the sea. He already knew what he would see. Anytime anything strange happened, the fog was back, settling over the town like a smoky monster crouched and waiting.

"What is it, Sarah?" Elle asked from her position on the couch. She had pillows piled around her, a comforter over her, and strict orders to remain where she was.

"The wax is forming something as it runs down the sides," Sarah explained. "It looks like a hook to me."

"Or a candy cane." Matt was more pragmatic.

"It's a staff," Hannah corrected. "A long staff, or maybe a cane. Something used to walk with."

"This is getting more bizarre by the minute," Abbey said, rubbing her hands up and down her arms. "And while we're on the subject of bizarre, Joley, I'm sorry, but there was no excuse for your not telling the rest of us what happened. You take shielding all of us way too far."

Sarah's smile at Joley was gentle. "She's right, hon. You should have told us what happened. Do you have any other bad news you don't want to worry us with?"

Joley hesitated for a brief moment, then shrugged. "I'm sorry, I should have mentioned the strangling fog. Do you have any idea how ridiculous that sounds?" She burst out laughing.

Kate joined her. "I have to admit, it threw Christmas wreaths at me."

"And no one is going to believe the fog *pushed* me over the cliff," Elle said with a small grin. "This one will go into our journal and nowhere else!"

"I plan on telling our children," Matt announced. "It's a great story for around the campfire, and they aren't going to believe us anyway. They'll think I'm a brilliant storyteller."

"Children?" Joley raised her eyebrow. "I love the idea of Kate having children. Don't the Granites produce boys? Very large hungry boys?" Her sisters erupted into laughter while Kate covered her face and groaned.

"You aren't helping, Joley," Matt said, putting his arms protectively around Kate so she could hide her face against his shoulder. "She hasn't even agreed to marry me yet. Don't be scaring her off with the idea of little boys running around."

Sarah continued to study the wax flow over the sides of the candle. "Do you see anything else that could be helpful in that book, Elle?"

Elle rubbed at the bump on her head and frowned at the thin pages. "There was no single predominant religion in the town at the time people first settled here. A faction celebrated the birthday of a pagan god. This is very interesting." Elle looked up at her sisters. "Many of the settlers here came together to celebrate their differences, unable to live anywhere else. The founding fathers wanted a safe haven by the sea, a place they envisioned would one day have a port for supplies. It actually says a lot about the town's founders and perhaps gives us insight to why the people here are so tolerant of others."

"And it explains why our own people settled here."

Kate nuzzled Matt's throat. "If I remember my grandmother and her history lessons correctly, she said Christmas was slow to catch on in America, that the colonists didn't celebrate it, and in some instances actually banned it."

"That's right." Joley snapped her fingers. "It was considered a pagan ritual in some places. But that was a long while before this town was settled, wasn't it?" She swept Elle's hair away from her face and fashioned it into a ponytail. "Does that have anything to do with all of this?"

"Thanks, Joley," Elle said. She smoothed the worn pages. "The townspeople wanted to celebrate the Christmas season and settled on a pageant. They asked everyone to participate regardless of their beliefs, just for the fun of it. They treated it more as a play, a production that included all town members, meant to be fun rather than religious." She looked up with a small smile. "Libby, our however-many-greats-grandmother has your very interesting handwriting. Aside from the language, I have to decipher the worst handwriting on the face of the earth."

"I do not have the worst handwriting on the face of the earth." Libby tossed a small pillow at her sister, missing by a great distance.

"There's something else in the wax," Sarah said. "All of you, look at this! Tell me what you see."

The sisters crowded around the cranberry candle. Kate tilted her head, studying it from every angle. "Where did you get this candle, Sarah? Is this one Mom made?"

"Yes, but I didn't know it would do this."

"Is a candle a symbol of Christmas?" Matt asked.

"Yes; some people say the light of the candle relieves the unrelenting darkness," Kate answered. "My mother makes incredible candles."

"I can imagine. Do they all do this?" Matt indicated the flowing wax.

"It's a face, I think," Sarah said. "Look, Abbey, don't you think it's a face?"

"That wouldn't surprise me." Matt peered at the thick pool of wax. "The spirit found feet, a coat and hat, and bones, why not get himself a face, even if it's made of wax. Does it have eyes? Maybe he wants to get a good look at us."

"Ugh." Kate made a face. "That's a horrible idea. It could never use one of Mom's candles for that. Mom instills a healing, soothing magic in each of them. We were the ones who forgot to guard our home. She insisted we make certain every time, but we just got complacent. I'm not forgetting this lesson for a very long time."

"Me either," Joley agreed.

"I think I found it now," Elle said in excitement. "Most everyone wanted to participate with the exception of a small group of believers in the gods of the earth. They considered the pageant a Christian holiday celebration and felt it was wrong to participate. One of the most outspoken said the pageant was evil and those participating would be punished. His brother-in-law, Abram Lynchman, went against his advice and allowed his wife and child to take part. Because he stood up to Johann, the rest of the group also decided to join the town in the pageant."

"Is this Johann angry because his flock was out of his control?" Joley asked.

Elle held up her hand for silence. Her hand went to her throat. Matt noticed that her hand was trembling. "Everyone helped with the production, bringing homemade candles and lanterns. The shepherd herded several sheep with his staff, and the sheep got away and ran through the crowd."

None of the sisters laughed. They were watching Elle's face intently. Matt glanced out the window to see the fog solidly in place. For some reason, his heart began to pound. The strange radar that always told him danger was near was shrieking at him, even there in the warmth and safety of the Drakes' home.

"The people were having fun, laughing as the sheep rushed through the crowd with the shepherd running after them. The sheep panicked and ran straight into the small shelter the town had erected to use as the stable for the play. The shelter crumpled, knocking several candles into the dry straw. Fire spread along the ground and across the wooden planks used to make the shelter. Several participants were trapped under the debris, including Abram's wife and child." Elle had a sob in her voice. She shook her head. "I can't read this. I can't read the words. Anastasia, the one writing the journal, was there, she saw the entire thing, heard the cries, saw them die. Her emotions are trapped in the book. I can't read it, Sarah." She sounded as if she were pleading.

Matt wanted to comfort her. The feeling was so strong he actually stepped toward her before he realized he was feeling the emotions of Elle's sisters. They rushed to her side, Sarah pulling the book from her hands, Kate putting her arms around Elle. The others touched her, helping to absorb the long ago, very strong emotions still clinging to the pages of the journal.

"I'm sorry, honey," Sarah said gently, "I should have thought of that. You've been through so much already. Kate, do you think you can get an idea of what happened next? I wouldn't ask, but it's important." She held the book out to Kate.

Matt wanted to yank the book out of her hands and throw it. "Kate's been through enough with this thing, Sarah. You can't ask her to do anymore." He was furious. Enough was enough. "Elle almost died out there. Without Jackson, she would have. You have no idea what a miracle it was that she didn't end up at the bottom of the ocean."

Kate put a restraining hand on his arm. Sarah simply nodded. "I do realize what I'm asking, Matthew, and I don't blame you for being angry. I don't want Kate to touch the journal, but the truth is, if we don't know why this spirit is doing the things he's doing, someone very well could die. We have to know."

Kate took the book from Sarah's hand. Matt muttered a string of curses and turned away from them, feeling impotent. All of his training, his every survival skill, seemed utterly useless in the unfamiliar situation. Not wanting to look at Kate, not wanting to witness the strain and weariness on her face, he stared hard at the cranberry candle and the eerie flow of wax. He stared and stared, his heart suddenly in his throat. He took a step closer, stared down in a kind of terror. "Katie." He whispered her name because she was his world, his talisman. Because he needed her.

Kate put her arm around him, held him. He couldn't take his eyes from the face in the wax, praying he was wrong. Knowing he was right. She looked down and gasped. "Danny. It's Danny."

Chapter Thirteen

My last gift now, is a special one,
A candy cane for a special son,

He watches and tends and knows the land,
But not enough to evade my hand.

Matt took Kate by the shoulders and set her aside. She made a grab for him, but he was already moving swiftly for the front door.

"Danny's at the pageant rehearsal," Kate reminded him. She ran after him, tossing the journal onto the floor, trying to keep up with him. Hannah grabbed Kate's coat and hurried after both of them.

The fog obstructed Matt's vision, but he could hear the women. "Go back, stay in the house, Kate. It's too dangerous." His voice was grim. Authoritative. It made Kate shiver. He didn't sound at all like her Matthew.

"I'm coming with you. Stay to the left. The path leads down

the hill to the highway. If we cross right beside the three redwood trees, like we did the other night, we'll end up quite close to the shortcut to town." Kate followed the sound of his voice. Hannah took her hand and held on tightly.

"Kate, dammit, this one time, listen to me. I have to find Danny, and I don't want to have to worry about what's happening to you."

Kate wished he sounded angry, but Matt's tone was chillingly cold. Ice-cold. She tightened her fingers around Hannah's hand but continued hurrying along the narrow path. "Hannah's with me, Matthew, and you're going to need us." She kept her voice very calm, very even. She ached for him and shared his rising alarm for the safety of his brother. The features in the wax had definitely been Daniel Granite. She had a strong feeling of impending doom.

Hannah pressed closer to her. "It's going to happen tonight, Katie." Her voice shook. "Should we try to clear the fog now?"

Matt loomed up in front of them, startling both of them, catching Kate by the shoulders. "It has never gone after me. Only you. Go with your sisters and work your magic. Clear the fog out of town, and this time get rid of it. I'll do what I can to keep Danny alive. I'm safe, Kate." His gray eyes had turned to steel. "I need to know you're as safe as possible in this mess."

She clung to him for just one moment, then nodded. "We'll be up on the captain's walk, where we can better bring in the wind."

Matt dropped a hard kiss on her upturned mouth, turned, and hurried down the narrow, well-worn trail. His mind was racing, working out the route the actors in the pageant used. Had they noticed the fog rolling in and taken shelter in one of the businesses along the parade route, or had they gone ahead with the rehearsal plans? Matt made it to the highway and stood listening for a moment in silence. He couldn't hear a car, but the fog seemed capable of muffling every sound. Still, he didn't want to wait. He felt a terrible sense of urgency, of his brother in acute danger. He cursed as he ran, nearly blind in the fog. It was only his training that kept him from being completely disoriented. He moved more from instinct than from sight, making his way toward the town square. Most of the committee meetings were held at the chamber of commerce building near the grocery store. The players were supposed to be rehearsing, though, and he doubted whether Inez would let a heavy fog and some entity she couldn't see change her plans.

He heard a shrill scream, the sounds of panic, and his heart stuttered. "Danny!" He called his brother's name, using the sheer volume of his voice to penetrate the cries coming out of the fog. He followed the sound of the voices, not toward the square, but away from it, back toward the park on the edge of town, where the river roared down through a canyon to meet the sea. The wall along the river was only about three feet high, made of stone and mortar. He nearly ran into it in his haste to reach Danny. At the last moment he sensed the obstruction and veered away, running parallel with it toward the cries.

He was getting closer to the sounds of the screams and calls. He heard Inez trying to calm everyone. He heard someone shout for a rope. The river, rushing over the rocks, added to the chaos in the heavy fog. "Danny!" Matt called again, trying to beat down his fear for his brother. Danny would have heard him, would have answered.

Right in front of him, Donna, the owner of the local gift shop, suddenly appeared. Her face was white and strained. He caught her shoulders. "What happened, Donna? Tell me!"

She grabbed both of his arms to steady herself. "The wall gave way. A group of the men were sitting on it. Your brother, the young Granger boy, Jeff's son, I don't know, more maybe. They just disappeared down the embankment, and all the rocks followed like a miniavalanche. We can't see to help them. There were some groans, and we heard cries for help, but we can't see them at all. We tried to form a human chain, but the bank is too steep. Jackson went over the side by himself. He was crawling. I heard a terrible crack, now he's silent. I was going to try to find a telephone to call for help. The cell phones just won't work here."

"What was Jackson doing here?" He knew the deputy never participated in the town pageant. "Is Jonas here?" As he talked he was moving along the wall, feeling with his hands for breaks, taking Donna with him.

"Jackson happened to be driving by when the fog thickened. He was worried about us, I think, so he stayed. I haven't seen Jonas."

"Don't wander around in this fog. Hopefully, Kate and her sisters will move it out of here for us." He patted her arm in reassurance and left her, continuing the search for the break in the wall with an outstretched hand. When he found it, he swore softly. He knew the section of wall was over a steep drop and the river below had a fast-moving current running over

213

several submerged boulders. The bank was littered with rocks of every size, with little to hold them in place should something start them rolling.

"Danny! Jackson!" His call was met with eerie silence. He began to crawl down the bank, distributing his weight, on his belly, searching with his hands before sliding forward. It was painstakingly slow. He didn't want to displace any more of the rocks in case his brother or any of the others were still alive and in the path of an avalanche.

Matt's fingertips encountered a leg. He forced himself to remain calm and used his hands to identify the man. Jackson was unconscious, and there was blood seeping from his head. In the near-blind conditions, it was impossible to assess how badly he was injured, but his breathing seemed shallow to Matt.

Something moved an arm's length below Jackson. Matt followed the outstretched arm and found another body. The Granger boy. Matt knew him to be sixteen or seventeen. A good kid. The boy moved again, and Matt cautioned him to stay still, afraid he would disturb the rocks.

"You okay, kid?" he asked.

"My arm's broken, and I feel like I've been run over by a truck, but I'm all right. The deputy told me not to move, and the next thing I knew he was somersaulting and smashed hard into the rock right there. He hasn't moved. Is he dead?"

"No, he's alive. What about the others? What about Danny?" He crawled around Jackson to get to the boy, to take his pulse and run his hands over him to examine him for other injuries.

"Tommy Dockins fell too. Danny tried to push him clear when the slide started. We didn't really have any time. I didn't see either of them, but Tommy's yelled for help a couple of times. I couldn't tell from which direction though."

The kid sounded tinny and distorted in the fog, and his voice shook, but he lay quietly and didn't panic. "Your name's Pete, right? Pete Granger?" Matt asked.

"Yes, sir."

"Well, I'm going to slide on around you and see if I can locate Danny and Tommy. Don't move. The fog will be gone soon, and Jonas is on the way with the rescue squad. If you move, you'll send the rest of those rocks right down on top of the others and me. Got it?"

"Yes, sir."

"I'll be back as quick as I can." Matt glanced in the direction of the cliff house, where the Drake family had lived for over a hundred years. He needed the modern-day women to work their magic, to remove the fog so he had a semblance of a chance to save his brother and Tommy and to get Jackson and Pete to safety.

"Come on, baby," he whispered, hoping the swirling clouds would take his voice to her. "Do this for me. Clear this mess out of here."

As if they could hear his words, the seven Drake sisters moved together out onto the battlement and faced the sea. Libby and Sarah both had their arms wrapped around Elle to aid her as they stood in the midst of the swirling fog.

Sarah looked up at the sky, to the roiling clouds gathered over Sea Haven and back to her sisters. "This troubled spirit is in terrible pain and does not believe there can be forgiveness for his mistake. He cannot forgive himself for what he believes to be bad judgment. I am certain his motive was to save others his sorrow. He believes that by halting the pageant, history will not repeat itself. He has lived this unbelievable nightmare repeatedly and needs to be able to forgive himself and go to his rest." She looked at Kate. "Your gift has always been your voice, Kate. I think the journal is referring to you. One born who can bring peace."

Kate could think only of Matt, somewhere out in the fog. She didn't want to be up on the captain's walk facing another struggle, she wanted to be with him. It was the first time in her life she had ever felt so divided around her sisters. She knew at that moment that she belonged with Matthew Granite. It didn't matter that she was an observer and he was a doer, she loved him, and she belonged with him.

As if reading her mind, Hannah took her hand, squeezed it tightly. "He's counting on you to do this, Kate. He's counting on all of us."

Kate took a steadying breath and nodded. She stepped away from Hannah, knowing Hannah would need room. Facing the small town invaded with the fog, Kate began to chant softly. An inquiry, no more, a soft plea to be heard. Her voice was carried on the smallest of breezes as Hannah faced the sea and lifted her arms, directing the wind as she might an orchestra.

Behind Kate, Joley and Abbey began to sing, a soft melody of love and peace, harmonizing with Kate's incredible voice so they produced a symphony of hope. Power began to build in the wind itself, in the sky overhead. Lightning forked in the spinning clouds. Kate spoke of forgiveness, of unconditional love. Of a love of family that transcended time. She beckoned and cajoled. She pleaded for a hearing.

"You've touched him," Elle reported. "He's fighting the call. He's determined to keep the accident from happening. There is no past life or future life as he understands it, only watching his wife and child die a horrible death over and over, year after year." She staggered under the burden of the man's guilt, of his loss.

Kate didn't falter. Matt was out there somewhere in the fog, and she felt him reaching for her, counting on her. And she knew he was in danger. She talked of the townspeople coming together with every belief represented. Of the elderly and the young given the same respect. She spoke of a place that was a true haven for tolerance. And she spoke of forgiveness. Of letting go.

Power spread with the building wind. The ocean leaped in response. A pod of whales surfaced, flipping their tails, almost in unison, as if creating a giant fan. Joley's voice, a sultry purity that couldn't be ignored, swelled in volume, taking over the lead, while Abbey's voice joined in perfect harmony.

Hannah's voice called on the elements she knew and loved. Earth. Wind. Fire. Rain. Lightning flashed. The wind blew. Rain poured from the clouds. And still the power continued to build. Her hands moved in a graceful pattern as if conducting a symphony of magic.

Kate lured the spirit to her with promises of peace. Rest. A family waiting with open arms, holding him dear, not placing blame. An accident, not the hand of an ancient god angry that he had allowed his loved ones to participate in something different. Simply an unfortunate accident. Joley sang of Christmas, past, present, and future. Of a town committed to all the members celebrating together in a variety of ways. Of festivals for ancient gods and a gala for those who didn't believe. The two voices blended, one in song, one in storytelling, weaving a seamless creation to draw the lost soul back home.

Abbey lifted her voice finally, a call for those lost to welcome loved ones. As she could draw truth, so did she speak truth. She added her voice to the tapestry, promising peace and rest and final sleep in the arms with those he loved most.

"He's coming. He's beginning to believe, to want to take the chance," Elle said. "He's hesitant, but he's so utterly weary, and the idea of seeing his wife and child and resting in their arms is irresistible."

Libby raised her arms with Hannah, sending the promise of healing, not the body, but mind and soul. She added her power to the force of the wind, added her healing energy to Kate's soothing peace.

The wind increased in strength, blowing with the force of a small gale, tearing through Sea Haven, herding the fog, guiding it toward the sea. Toward the house on the cliff and the seven women who stood on the battlement, hand in hand. The feminine voices carried unbelievable power throughout the air, land, and sea. Rising on the wind. Calling. Promising. Leading.

And the fog answered. The thick gray vapor turned toward the sea, drifting reluctantly at first, tendrils feeling the way, hesitant and fearful. The voices swelled in strength. The wind blew through the fog.

Elle reached for Kate. "Now, Kate. Go to him now."

Kate never stopped talking in her beguiling voice, but she closed her eyes and deliberately entered the world of shadows. He was there. A tall, gaunt man with sorrow weighing him down. He looked at her and shook his head sadly. She held out her hand to him. Beside her, Elle stiffened as a beastly creature with glowing eyes and fur stared down at Kate with hate. As the snakelike vines slithered and coiled and hissed as if alive, wanting to get to her sister, Elle moved them, holding them back with the sheer force of her power, giving Kate the necessary time to lure the spirit of Abram to her.

Kate told a story of the love of a man for his wife and children. A man who made a courageous decision to go against what others said was right and allowed his family to participate in a production designed to bring people together. She spoke of laughter and fun and his pride in his family as he watched them. And the horror of a terrible accident. The candles and dry straw, the heavy planks coming down on so many. The man watching his loved ones die. The guilt and horror. The need to blame someone . . . to blame himself.

Joley and Abbey sang softly, the voice of a woman and child calling for the one they loved to join them. Kate used the purity of her voice, silver tones to draw him closer. The woman and child waited. Loved. Longed for him. His only job was to go to them, to forgive himself. There was no one to save but himself.

Kate kept her hand extended and pointed behind him. Clouds of dark gray fog drifted aside. He turned to see the shadows there. A woman. A child. Far off in the distance waiting.

There was a sharp cry like that of a seagull. The waves crashed against the cliff, rose high and frothed white. Lightning veined the clouds, forked into the very center of the fog. The flash lit up the shadows, throwing Kate out of that world and back into the reality of her own. She landed heavily on the wet surface of the captain's walk, in the middle of her sisters. Libby held her close.

"You're all right. It's all right now. You did it, Kate. You gave him peace," Sarah said.

"We did it," Kate corrected with a wan smile.

They sat together, too weary to move, the rain lashing down at them. Sarah turned her head to calculate the distance to the door. "Damon will be here with tea, but I don't think he can carry us back inside."

Elle draped herself over Abbey. "Who cares about going inside? I want to just lie here and look up at the sky."

"I want to know Matt's safe and that he was able to get to Danny," Kate said. "When Damon comes up, please have him call Jonas."

Matt scooted carefully down the steep bank, skirting rocks until it became impossible to go farther. He had no choice but to go over them.

"I'm Tommy, not Kate," a voice called weakly from his right side.

Matt didn't realize until that moment that he was whispering her name over and over like a prayer. He glanced up at the sky, felt the wind in his face, the first few drops of real rain. He felt power and energy crackling in the air around him. "Thank you, Katie, you are unbelievable." He said it fervently, meaning it. Already the fog was beginning to thin so that he could make out the boy lying a few feet from him. "Are you hurt?"

"I don't think so. I don't know what happened though. One

minute I was falling off the fence and rolling, and the next Danny shoved me. I woke up a few minutes ago and when I tried to move, I dislodged several rocks. I didn't know where anyone was, so I thought I'd better just wait until help came."

Matt remained lying flat, searching carefully for Danny. The wind drove down through the canyon and shifted abruptly, coming back off the river. He caught sight of his brother a few yards away. Danny was lying facedown on the cliff over the water's edge, partially buried under debris. He wasn't moving. The pulse pounded in Matt's temples. He forced himself to go to the boy and examine him first. "You'll be fine. Just stay down until we can get help to you. I'm checking on Danny."

He took a deep breath and called toward the top. "Donna? Is Jonas here yet?"

"He's on his way along with the rescue squad," she yelled back.

"I'm working my way down to Danny. Everyone else is alive. Jackson looks the worst. Could be a concussion. The entire mountainside is unstable. Tell them to be careful moving around up there until I can get Danny out of the avalanche zone."

Matt patted the teenage boy and proceeded to make painfully slow progress through the rocks. The smallest trickle of pebbles could bring down a tremendous storm of boulders on his brother. He inched his way through the rubble until he reached Danny's side.

Danny was precariously balanced at the edge of the bank. It was actually the rocks that saved his life, holding him pinned in the dirt. Matt was very gentle as he examined his brother. He couldn't find a single broken bone, but there were several lacerations, particularly on Danny's hands. His face was pushed hard into the dirt. He carefully turned Danny's head, scooping dirt from his mouth. Danny coughed, and the rocks slid. Some dislodged and one fell to the river below. "Don't move, Danny, don't even cough if you can help it," Matt instructed.

"Tell us what you need, Matt," Jonas shouted down to him.

"I've got to move Danny. When I do, everything above him is going to slide. You'll have to get Pete out of there and Jackson. When you move them, Jonas, don't disturb the rocks. If I take Danny now, there's a chance we'll lose those two. I'll shield my brother, just work fast."

Matt knew Jonas wouldn't bother to argue with him. There was no way Matt would leave his younger brother hanging out over the edge of the fast-moving river with an avalanche of boulders poised to slide. The Drake sisters had managed a miracle removing the fog, but there was still dangerous work to be done.

"Don't forget about me," Tommy called.

"We'll get you," Jonas promised.

"You're going to be just fine, Danny boy," Matt said, brushing more dirt from the lacerated face.

"Get out of here, Matt," Danny barely mouthed the words. "Breathing moves the rocks. If they're working up above, the boulders will smash us both."

"Have a little faith, bro, that's Jonas up there. Are you hurt?"

"What does it look like?"

Matt heard the ominous rumble above him. "Incoming," Jonas yelled from above them. Matt shifted so his upper body protected Danny's head. He put his arms over his own head and tried to shrink as rocks bounced down, knocking a few more loose. The rocks rained down and splashed into the river below. One glanced off his calf and rolled away, dislodging more rocks before it hit the water.

"Dammit, be careful." Matt could hear Jonas snarling at the rescue team. "If you can't move them without setting off a landslide, get the hell back up here and let someone else do that! You all right down there, Matt?"

"We're fine. Just be careful," he called back.

"You weigh more than the rocks do," Danny complained.

"You deserve it, scaring the hell out of me like this. Anything broken?"

"Naw. I'm a Granite. We're tough."

Matt rubbed his brother's head in a rough, affectionate gesture. He glanced up. "They've got Jackson and the boys out, and they're on the way to us. When we move you, Danny, the entire side of the bank is going to come down. I won't be able to be very gentle, but I'm not going to let anything happen to you."

"Just get me the hell out of here."

It was not an easy task. The rescuers inched their way down and worked out a coordinated plan to move Danny, knowing once they pulled him from under the pile of rocks it would set off an avalanche. Matt stayed beside his brother, joking, keeping Danny's spirits up. The men cleared as many of the rocks from Danny as they could without triggering the landslide. It was only the soft damp dirt that saved Danny from terrible injury or death. His body was pressed deep into the muck. They dug around him with painstaking slowness, careful not to disturb the precarious balance of boulders poised over their heads.

"Ready, Danny boy?" It was Matt who locked arms with his brother.

"More than ready." There was fear in Danny's eyes, but he winked at his older brother and managed a weak smile.

Matt didn't wait. They had cleared as much of the ground as possible out of the way of the landslide path so that Matt had a clear trail on the steep embankment to drag Danny quickly out of harm's way. He exerted his great strength, pulling his brother out from under the rocks, moving as fast as humanly possible. The rocks immediately crashed into the river, starting the avalanche. The boulders above, with nothing to hold them, rolled down, taking most of the embankment with it. Matt covered Danny's body a second time, waiting until the debris had cleared.

Danny tried to stand, but his brother held him down. "You made me come down here and play mud-cakes with you, you can just get on the stretcher and let the medics carry your butt to the hospital and check you out."

"I'm fine," Danny protested, as they strapped him into a litter. "I feel like an idiot," he said.

"That's good, Danny. You are an idiot." Matt took up a position at the head of the stretcher to help carry him up the steep bank. They were still cautious, worried about the unstable conditions, but managed to get him to the top without incident.

Danny protested more when they put him in the ambulance, but no one paid him any attention. Matt jumped in beside him, keeping one hand on his brother's shoulder. It wasn't until the doctors pronounced Danny bruised, but fine that Matt left him to go check on Jackson and the teens.

By the time he returned to the cliff house, he was tired and only wanting to hold Kate to him. The Drake sisters were sprawled in every chair of the living room, pale and drawn, all greeting him with their brilliant smiles.

Matt gathered Kate to him, holding her close. All he wanted to do was take her home with him where she belonged. She looked exhausted and in need of a hot meal and two or three days of sleep. Kate clung to him, turning her face up for his kiss, burrowing against him.

"I heard there was an accident on the river wall," she greeted.

"Everyone's fine. Shook up, but fine. Did Jonas stop by?"

She shook her head. "Inez called to make certain we were all right. She knew we must have cleared out the fog and that we would be exhausted. She told us what happened. Jackson's in the hospital, but the two boys were treated and released. She said Jackson's going to be fine." Her smile was slow coming but bright. "I have a feeling he'll make a terrible patient."

"Somehow I think you're right. Danny was treated and released also. He's bruised from head to toe, but he didn't have a single major injury." There was elation in Matt's voice. "He's hoping Inez will upgrade his part next year in the pageant due to his, quote, 'heroism.' It was pretty dicey, Kate. Thanks for all you did."

"We all did it. I could never have managed without my sisters. I'm so glad your brother is fine. The pageant just wouldn't be the same without him in his annual role as the shepherd. Speaking of the pageant—" She broke off as her sisters burst out laughing.

Matt's head went up suspiciously. He was beginning to know

the Drake sisters, and their laughter heralded trouble for him. He was certain of it.

"Inez sent over a costume she made for the third wise man. A king," Kate said brightly. "She asked if you would be willing to fill the role at the last minute and of course, with Inez being so distressed, we said we were certain you'd want to help out."

He stiffened. "I'd rather be boiled in oil."

"Acting runs in your family," she pointed out.

He held up his hand. "You can't look at me with those eyes while you're weak and tired, it's unfair tactics."

"I know, Matthew," she said. "I'm trying not to, but Inez is such a good friend, and I couldn't bear her being so upset. The pageant is important to the town after all the near accidents. We need to get our confidence back."

"And I have to be in the pageant in order for our town to do that?" He raised one eyebrow skeptically.

"All you have to do is walk through the town. No lines, nothing awful. You don't mind, do you?"

"Does wanting to be boiled in oil instead sound like I want to do this?"

She turned her face into his chest. Pressed her lips against his skin.

He growled, deep in his throat. The growl turned into a groan. "I can see what my life's going to be like. I'll do it. This one time. Never again."

"Thank you." She kissed him again. "I just want to go home with you and sleep in your arms," she said, uncaring that her family could hear her. "Let's go home, Matthew."

Matt kissed her gently, her lips, her throat, bringing her hand

226

to his mouth as elation swept through him. She had said, "Let's go home." He lifted her with ease. "I'll take good care of her," he promised her family.

Sarah nodded. "We have every confidence that you will, Matt."

Chapter Fourteen

All deeds are now done, forgiveness is mine,
As two people share a love for all time.

"We're going to be late," Kate said, evading Matt's outstretched hand. "We promised the committee you'd be on time. We didn't make rehearsals, and everyone's worried you're going to mess up their play."

"I wasn't the one who agreed to wear that silly-looking robe Inez made. *You* agreed I'd wear it! Is it my fault they lost a couple of their stars to a scandalous affair?" He stalked her through the house, one slow step at a time.

Kate laughed and dodged around the table, putting a chair between them. "You theater people are always involved in scandals."

He moved the chair out of the way and proceeded to back her into a corner. "I'd be more than willing to cause a scandal. Just let me get my hands on you."

"I don't think so. Inez is probably watching her clock and

tapping her foot. I'm not about to get a lecture about the benefits of being on time. Put on your costume!"

"I am in my costume. What king travels by starlight from one country to another and wears a satin bathrobe with cheesy lightning bolts sewn all over it? And I doubt very much if he sat on that camel naked under the robe."

Kate held her stomach, laughing so hard she could barely manage to squeak through a small opening he'd left beside the counter. "Somehow I think Inez might object to the idea that you were running around naked in her kingly robes. I, however, am rather intrigued by the idea." She backed down the hallway, holding her hand palm out. "Seriously, Matthew, she'll reprimand you in front of the entire town if you're late."

She was nearing the entrance to the bedroom. His silver eyes gleamed with anticipation. "If you think that's more humiliating than wearing this damned robe, which, by the way, is two sizes too small, you're sadly mistaken. I think Bruce had the affair with Sylvia just to get out of wearing it."

She pressed her hand to her mouth to keep an undignified giggle from emerging. "I think it looks dashing on you." He was right; the robe looked utterly ridiculous on him. His huge muscles strained the material so that it stretched tight over his wide shoulders and back. Instead of reaching the ground, it was halfway up his calves, and the front gaped open to reveal . . . She laughed. "I think it has interesting possibilities."

He spread his arms wide and rushed her, using an old football tackle. She screamed and turned to run, but he caught her up and carried her across the floor to the bed, where he unceremoniously dropped her. The kingly robe made its way to the floor. "I'm the king, and I demand my rights."

Kate pushed one hand against his chest to fend him off. "You have no rights. Inez has you under contract, and you're supposed to be *on time.* Do you want the entire town waiting for you?"

"I wouldn't mind in the least." He caught her legs, pinning her to the bed, stopping her from scooting away from him. "I think everyone should wait on me. I have this tremendous need to see your breasts. Why don't you unbutton your blouse for me?"

"It doesn't have buttons, oh mighty King."

"Who the hell cares," he growled. "Get rid of the shirt."

"I think that robe went to your head." Excitement raced through her, curled heat in her deepest core. She drew the blouse obediently over her head so that her full breasts spilled over the fine white cups of her bra. "Is this what you're look-ing for?" She slid her hand over her skin, drawing his attention to the taut peaks.

Matt reached to draw the zipper of her jeans down. "Exactly like that." There was a husky catch to his voice, the playfulness slipping away as he tugged the material from her body. He left her sexy little thong. "Every time I see that thing, I want to take it off with my teeth," he admitted, and bent to the task.

Kate enjoyed the feel of his hands on her body. Big hands. Capable. Nearly covering her buttocks as he lifted her hips and teased her skin with his teeth. Just that fast she was swamped with heat, her body flushed and alive and in desperate need. The thought of the Christmas pageant went out of her head, and much more erotic thoughts took its place. His mouth was everywhere, his tongue teasing and dancing, his teeth pulling at the only barrier between him and his goal.

She felt the sudden release as the material parted, the cool air mingling with her own heat, then the plunging of his tongue going deep while she nearly came off the bed, air bursting from her lungs in a wild rush. It was only his hands holding her down that kept her open to him while he made certain she not only was prepared for him, but that she hungered for him. Laughing, he slid his body over hers, settling over her soft form, gripping her hips to pull her to meet the hard thrust as he joined them together.

"I think that kingly robe works just fine," Kate managed to say, in between gasps of pleasure.

"Maybe I'll keep it if it gets this kind of results," he teased. He began to move, a slow assault on her senses, driving deep, needing her body, needing to feel the way she welcomed him. The heat and fire. Flames licking over his skin. "I love watching you when we make love," he admitted. She was so completely abandoned in the way she gave herself to him.

Kate loved the way he watched her. There was desire etched into the lines of his face. There was hunger in the depths of his eyes. There was steel in his body and a fine hot heat that made her flame, catch fire, and burn with passion. "I love making love with you," she told him, sliding her arms around his neck to draw his head down to hers.

"That's a good thing, Katie." His teeth nibbled at her chin, her full bottom lip. "Because I think we're going to be spending a lot of time doing just that."

Kate gave herself up to the sheer glory of his body driving so deeply into hers. The pressure built and built, and she dug her fingers into his shoulders, holding on as they soared together in perfect unison.

He lay over her, fighting for his breath, trying to slow his heart rate.

"You're laughing," she observed. "I told you, your entire family laughs at me."

"I can't help it, Kate. And I'm laughing at me. I feel like one of those sappy men who run around with a big grin on his face all the time. I feel like grinning all the time around you, and it's so idiotic."

Kate's answering smile was slow. She rubbed her face against his chest. "I'm just beginning to realize how much I mean to you, Matthew."

He kissed her tenderly, his hands framing her face. "I adore you. Why else would I ever put that horrible robe on in front of the entire town?"

Kate looked smug. "And you know what I'll be thinking about when you come walking down the street looking sexy and kingly."

"I'll tell you what you'd better be thinking, Katie." He took a deep breath. "You'd better be thinking, 'here comes the man I intend to marry.'" He feathered kisses along the corners of her mouth. "Marry me, Kate. Spend your life with me."

She looked up at his beloved face. Her fingers slid through his hair in a loving caress. "I don't climb mountains or swim seas, Matthew. I sit in the corner and read books. I'm not at all brave. You have to be very sure that it's me you want."

"More than anything in the world, Kate. You. With you I have everything."

"Well, I guess that kingly robe is lucky after all." She kissed his throat, his chin. Found his mouth with hers and poured heat and fire and promises into her kiss.

He responded just the way she knew he would, his arms wrapping her close, his body coming alive, growing hard and thick deep inside her. He made love to her slowly, leisurely, as if they had all the time in the world and the entire town wasn't waiting on them. He made a thorough job of it. Kate felt like the most important person in the world. And the happiest.

They lay on the bed in a tangle of arms and legs, fighting to breathe. She turned her head to look at him. "I'm thinking you should wear that robe more often, Matthew."

He snorted his derision and glanced at his watch. "Kate! We're late."

"I told you we were late."

"Not this late, we're holding up the parade." He hastily leaped off her, looking around for his clothes. Kate laughed at him through the entire drive to the park where the members of the production were assembling. He caught Kate by the hand and ran across the lawn to the pavilion.

"Where have you been?" Inez demanded, gesturing toward the huge crowd assembled along the streets. "We've all been waiting for you."

"*And,*" Danny added, "you didn't answer your cell phone." He shook his head, hands on his hips, clucking like an old hen. "You aren't even in that lovely costume Inez made for you. What have you been doing?" He wiggled his eyebrows at Kate.

"Are you feeling all right, Danny?" Kate asked.

He tugged her hair affectionately. "I'm fine, but don't tell Trudy, she's babying me. And Mom's worse."

Inez all but stamped her foot. "Why are you late?"

"Kate made me late," Matt told Inez, and the interested group of actors crushed together to see the fireworks when Inez told Matt off. Matt exchanged a long, slow smile with Kate while he listened to Inez politely.

"I believe him," Jonas said. "You know how the Drake sisters are. Barbie doll alone takes three hours to get ready for anything. Put them all together, it could take days."

Kate glared at both former Rangers and took Hannah's hand. "Why aren't you participating this year, Jonas?" she asked sweetly. "Inez, didn't he promise you last year? I could have sworn Sarah told me Jonas really wanted to play a major role."

"He likes to stand out," Hannah added, smiling at Inez. "If you don't offer him a lead, he won't cooperate. You know Jonas. He has to be the star."

Inez turned to the sheriff. "Why didn't you sign up this year?"

"I didn't sign up," Matt pointed out.

"We don't have time for this argument," Jonas said, glaring at Kate. "Traffic is going to be backed up from here to hell and back. Get this show on the road, Inez, or we'll have to shut it down."

Inez began barking orders like a drill sergeant. Hannah nudged Jonas. "Don't look so smug. I'm putting your name in for the role of donkey next year. I'm certain Inez will come up with a suitable costume."

Deliberately the sheriff leaned into her, so close her body was pressed up against his. "That's great, baby doll, as long as you're the one riding me." He breathed the words against her ear, then stalked away from her.

The wind rushed over him and sent his hat sailing toward the river. He glanced back, his grin wide. "You have such a bad temper, Hannah. Merry Christmas."

Matt tried to cling to Kate but was dragged firmly away and forced into his satin costume. He did his best not to notice the other actors hiding their smiles behind their hands as they looked at him, or that Inez and Donna looked horrified. The streets were lined with townspeople, from the oldest to the youngest. Even Sylvia had turned up, with one side of her face covered in a red rash.

The parade began, and Matt was forced to endure trudging through the streets where everyone could see Inez's bizarre creation. The other two wise men went before him. He thought they looked somewhat ridiculous in their robes of velvet, but if he squinted enough, he could use the word *regal*. Cursing the fact that his costume looked more like a woman's bathrobe than a king's robe, Matt thought it took an eternity to get through town, with everyone singing slightly off-key, and to finally catch sight of the town square. Worse, he couldn't prevent the silly grin from breaking out on his face. It just wouldn't go away, and he knew it had to look like he was enjoying parading through town in a woman's bathrobe. He knew Kate and her sisters had grabbed a spot near the makeshift stables to wait for him, and he kept a sharp eye out for them. He let out a sigh of relief when he finally spotted them.

"You look really good in that satin robe, bro," Danny declared, nudging his brother with the hooked end of his staff.

"Shut up, Danny, or I'm going to kick your butt," Matt threatened out of the side of his mouth. He kept his eyes straight ahead, trudging like a man doomed, carrying his gift of frankincense on a white satin pillow out in front of him. He'd argued the wise men hadn't had white satin pillows to use carrying the foul-smelling stuff, but not a single person had listened, and his protests had earned him a black scowl from Inez. He kept his eyes straight ahead, not looking at the waving townspeople as he marched stoically onward to the town square with his silly grin on his face.

Danny whistled at him. "That robe manages to show your butt off nicely, Matt." He tapped the offending part of Matt's anatomy with the staff again. "Sorry, little accident, couldn't help myself."

"I hope you have life insurance," Matt said in his most menacing voice. He made the mistake of looking up to judge the distance to the square. He had to know the exact amount of time he would have to suffer further humiliation. Kate stood there with her sisters. Every last one of them had a huge smile on her face. Matt entertained the idea of throwing the frankincense at their feet and hauling Kate over his shoulder like the Neanderthal they all thought he was. He'd keep the robe, it might come in handy.

Danny poked him with the staff again. "Get along there little dogie," he teased.

Matt's furious gaze settled on Old Man Mars. He stood slightly apart, watching the pageant with a peculiar look on his face, somewhere between mortification and shock. It was obvious he shared Matt's view of the idiotic robes. The old man caught his eye, read the pain on Matt's face, and stepped closer to commiserate. He walked alongside Matt.

"She made you do this, didn't she?" Mars asked.

"Damn right. Otherwise, I wouldn't be caught dead in this getup," Matt replied, hope beginning to stir.

Mars nodded as if he understood Matt's total misery and stepped back away from him with his arms folded. Behind him, Danny began the mantra. "Don't say it. Don't say it. Don't say it." He glanced nervously at the old man as he approached him.

"Merry Christmas." Matt turned back with a cheerful grin. "Merry Christmas, Mr. Mars," he said happily.

A black scowl settled over Old Man Mars's face. His craggy brows drew together in a straight thick line. He made a single sound of disgust and spat on the ground. The old man delivered his yearly kick right to Danny's shin and shuffled off, muttering something about tomatoes. Danny howled and jumped around, holding his injured shin. The staff swung around in a wide circle so that the participants had to break ranks and run for safety. Matt kept walking straight past Inez and the outraged look on her face. Kate met him at the stable, lifting her face for his kiss, while Inez followed Danny, giving him her annual Christmas lecture on behavior.

"All in all, Katie," Matt said, holding her close, "I'd say this was a very satisfactory pageant."

Epilogue

"So, did your wish come true?" Sarah asked.

Matt reached out to take the snowglobe from her, turning it over and over in his hands. He looked across the room at Kate. His Kate. The flames leaped and danced in the fireplace. The Drake sisters were decorating a live tree they'd brought in for Christmas Day. The next day they would plant it on their property near the many other trees that marked the passing of the years.

The house smelled of cedar and pine and cinnamon and spice. Berry candles adorned the mantel and the aroma of fresh-baked cookies drifted from the kitchen. Jonas appeared in the doorway of the kitchen. Red and green frosting smeared his face and fingers, and an apron covered his clothes. "No one asked me if my wish came true," he complained.

"You're such a baby, Jonas," Joley informed him with a little sniff. She caught the apron strings and dragged him backward. "You were the one who said there was nothing to baking cookies, and we should try our hand at doing it the old-fashioned way."

Jonas escaped and raced back into the living room. "*You! You!*" he protested. "*Women* bake cookies. That's what they do. They sit around the house looking pretty and hand their man a plate of cookies and a drink when he comes home."

Jonas grinned at the women tauntingly. Matt groaned and covered his face with his hands, looking between his fingers. He already felt power moving in the air. Curtains swayed. Hair stood up. Crackles of electricity snapped and sizzled. The flames on the candles and in the fireplace leaped and danced. Jonas watched the sisters, clearly expecting reprisal. It came from behind him. The small fish tank lifted into the air and tilted part of the contents over Jonas's head. Water rushed over his head. He stiffened, but he didn't turn around, nor did he attempt to wipe it off.

"I just want to point out that this is Christmas Day," he said. "And you all just came back from church."

Joley sat down at the upright, perfectly tuned piano. "And we're all feeling full of love and goodwill, Jonas. Which is why you aren't swimming in the sea with the sharks right now. Shall I play something cheerful?"

"Oh, please do, Joley," Hannah entreated wickedly. "I'm feeling *very* cheerful."

"You would be," Jonas muttered. He took the towel Libby handed him and wiped off his face and hair.

Hannah blew him a kiss.

"Matt didn't answer my question," Sarah persisted.

"The globe only works for family," Abbey said.

Music swelled in volume, filling every corner of the house with joy. Matt heard the sound of feminine laughter, felt his heart respond. Kate walked around the tree, an ornament in her hand. She moved with grace and elegance, his perfect Kate. Feeling the weight of his gaze, she looked across the room at him and smiled.

"Yes, that's true, Abbey," Sarah said. "It only works for family. Matt? Did the globe grant your wish?"

He cleared his throat. "Yes." The affirmation came out on a husky note.

Joley's fingers stilled on the piano. She turned to look at him. Libby put her hand out to Hannah. Abbey put her arm around Elle. All of the Drakes looked at Matt. Kate's sisters. The magical witches of Sea Haven. He thought he fit in rather nicely.

"What did you wish for, Matthew?" Sarah asked. She sat down in Damon's lap, wrapping her arms around his neck.

"I wished for Katie, of course," he answered honestly.

Kate walked over to him, leaning down to kiss him. "I wished for you," she whispered aloud.

"So that little jewelry box in your jacket pocket means something?" Elle asked.

"It means Kate said yes," Matt said. He believed his grin was a permanent fixture on his face.

Jonas shook his head, still mopping up the water. "You got her to say yes just by wishing on that snowglobe?"

"That's what it took," Matt said. "But they say it only works for family. I guess it acknowledged that Katie belonged with me."

"Really? It can reason all that out, can it?" Jonas stared at the snowglobe sitting so innocently on the shelf. "Family huh? Well, I've been family for about as long as I can remember."

A collective gasp went up from the seven Drake sisters as Jonas reached for the snowglobe.

"No! Jonas, don't touch that." Hannah sounded frightened.

"You can't, Jonas," Sarah said.

His hand hovered over it. Matt could swear he heard hearts beating loudly in the sudden silence. Jonas picked up the globe. Almost at once it sprang to life, the tiny lights on the tree glowing, the fog beginning to swirl.

"Jonas, put it down right now and step away from it," Joley warned.

"You can't play with things in this house," Elle added. "They can be dangerous."

"Jonas," Abbey said, "it isn't funny."

Jonas turned toward the women, his hands absently cradling the globe. "Aren't you all supposed to be cooking dinner for us? Jackson's going to be here any minute, expecting the full Christmas fare, and all he's going to get is some cookies I made." As he spoke, he kept his gaze on Hannah. All the while his palm rubbed the globe as if he could conjure up a genie.

"Don't you *dare* wish on that globe, Jonas Harrington," Hannah hissed. She actually backed a step away from him. "I'm sorry about the fish tank. And the silly hat thing as well. Just put the globe down and keep your mind blank. We'll call it even."

"Are you watching this, Matt?" Jonas asked, clearly taunting Hannah. "This is called power."

"Not for long," Kate said. She held out her hand for the globe. "Hand it over and stop tormenting Hannah. We're liable to serve you up dragon's liver for dinner."

"All right," Jonas agreed. He looked into the glass. "It's certainly beautiful." Instead of giving it to her, he stared into it for a long moment. The fog swirled into a frenzy, obliterating the house until only the lights on the tree blazed, then it slowly subsided, leaving the glass clear and the lights fading away. Only then did he hand it over to Kate.

There was a long silence. Jonas grinned at them. "I'm teasing. You all take things so seriously." He nudged Matt. "I'm not a dreamer like my friend here. I wouldn't let a snowglobe decide my fate. Come on, let's get that turkey carved."

Kate accepted Matt's kiss and watched him go into the kitchen with Damon and Jonas. She joined her sisters as she did each year in surrounding the tree, hands connecting them in a continuous circle. The overhead lights went off, leaving them in the shadows with the flickering candles and Christmas lights. She felt the familiar power running up and down her arms. Running through her. Tiny sparks leaped into the air like little fireflies. Electricity crackled around them. She could feel the minuscule threads in the tapestry of power that wove them together. Energy sprang from one to the other.

Matt stood in the doorway with Damon and Jonas and Jackson, who had come in through the kitchen, and watched the seven women as they stood hand in hand circling the Christmas tree. The women looked beautiful and fey, with their heads thrown back and the sparks leaping around them like miniature fireworks.

Jonas nudged him. "Welcome to the world of the Drake sisters, Matt. And Merry Christmas."

Matt couldn't imagine a better one.

MAGIC
IN THE
WIND

For my sisters . . . Thank you for the magic and
the love that has always been in my life.

Chapter One

"Sarah's back. Sarah's come home." The whisper was overly loud and tinged with something close to fear. Or respect. Damon Wilder couldn't decide which. He'd been hearing the same small-town gossip for several hours and it was always said in the same hushed tones. He hated to admit to curiosity and he wasn't about to stoop to asking, not after he had made such a point of insisting on absolute privacy since he arrived last month.

As he walked down the quaint narrow sidewalk made of wood, the wind seemed to whisper, "Sarah's back." He heard it as he passed the gas station and burly Jeff Dockins waved to him. He heard it as he lingered in the small bakery. *Sarah*. The name shouldn't carry mystery, but it did.

He had no idea who Sarah was, but she commanded such interest and awe from the townspeople he found himself totally intrigued. He knew from experience the people in the sleepy little coastal town were not easily impressed. No amount of money, fame, or title earned one deference. Everyone was treated the same, from the poorest to the richest, and there seemed to be no prejudice against religion or any other preferences. It was why he had chosen the town. A man could be anybody here and no one cared.

All day he had heard the whispers. He'd never once caught a glimpse of the mysterious Sarah. But he'd heard she'd once climbed the sheer cliffs above the sea to rescue a dog. An impossible task. He'd seen those crumbling cliffs and no one could climb them. He found himself smiling at the idea of anyone attempting such an impossible feat, and few things amused him or intrigued him.

The only grocery store was in the center of town and most of the gossip originated there and then spread like wildfire. Damon decided he needed a few things before he went home. He hadn't been in the store for more than two minutes when he heard it again. "Sarah's back." The same hushed whisper, the same awe and respect.

Inez Nelson, owner of the grocery store, held court, spilling out gossip as she normally did, instead of ringing up the groceries on the cash register. It usually drove him crazy to have to wait, but this time he lingered by the bread rack in the hope of learning more of the mysterious Sarah who had finally returned.

"Are you sure, Inez?" Trudy Garret asked, dragging her four-year-old closer to her and nearly strangling the child with her hug. "Are her sisters back, too?"

"Oh, I'm certain, all right. She came right into the store as real as you please and bought a ton of groceries. She was back at the cliff house, she said. She didn't say anything about the others, but if one shows up the others aren't far behind."

Trudy Garret looked around, lowered her voice another octave. "Was she still . . . Sarah?"

Damon rolled his eyes. Everyone always annoyed the hell out of him. He thought moving to a small town would allow him to find a way to get along to some extent but people were just plain idiots. Of course Sarah was still Sarah. Who the hell else would she be? Sarah was probably the only one with a brain within a fifty-mile radius so they thought she was different.

"What could it mean?" Trudy asked. "Sarah only comes back when something is going to happen."

"I asked her if everything was all right and she just smiled in that way she has and said yes. You wouldn't want me to pry into Sarah's business, now would you, dear," Inez said piously.

Damon let his breath out in a hissing rush of impatience. Inez made it her life's work to pry into everyone's business. Why should the absent Sarah be excluded?

"Last time she was here Dockins nearly died, do you remember that?" Trudy asked. "He fell from his roof and Sarah just happened to be walking by and . . . " She trailed off and glanced around the store and lowered her voice to a conspirator's whisper. "Old Mars at the fruit stand said Penny told him Sarah . . . "

"Trudy, dear, you know Mars is totally unreliable in the things he says. He's a dear, sweet man, but he sometimes makes things up," Inez pointed out.

Old man Mars was crotchety, mean, and known to throw fruit at cars if he was in a foul enough mood. Damon waited for lightning to strike Inez for her blatant lie, but nothing happened. The worst of it was, Damon wanted to know what old Mars had said about Sarah, even if it was a blatant lie. And that really irritated him.

Trudy leaned even closer, looked melodramatically to the right and left without even noticing he was there. Damon sighed heavily, wanting to shake the woman. "Do you remember the time little Paul Baily fell into that blowhole?"

"I remember that, now that you say. He was wedged in so tight and no one could get to him, he'd slipped down so far. The tide was coming in."

"I was there, Inez, I saw her get him out." Trudy straightened up. "Penny said she'd heard from her hairdresser that Sarah was working for a secret agency and she was sent to some foreign country undercover to assassinate the leader of a terrorist group."

"Oh, I don't think so, Trudy. Sarah wouldn't kill anything." The store owner's hands fluttered to her throat in protest. "I just can't imagine."

Damon had had enough of gossip. If they weren't going to say anything worth hearing, he was going to get the hell out of there before Inez turned her spotlight on him. He plunked his groceries down on the counter and looked as bored as he could manage. "I'm in a hurry, Inez," he said, hoping to facilitate matters and avoid Inez's usual attempts at matchmaking.

"Why, Damon Wilder, how lovely to see you. Have you met Trudy Garret? Trudy is a wonderful woman, a native of our town. She works over at the Salt Bar and Grill. Have you been there to eat yet? The salmon is very good."

"So I've heard," he muttered, barely glancing at Trudy to

acknowledge the introduction. It didn't matter. They'd all made up their minds about him, making up the history he refused to provide. He felt a little sorry for the returning Sarah. They were making up things about her as well. "You might tell me about that beautiful old house on the cliffs," he said, shocking himself. Shocking Inez. He never gave anyone an opening for conversation. He wanted to be left alone. Damn Sarah for being so mysterious.

Inez looked as if she might faint and for once she was speechless.

"You must know the one I'm talking about," Damon persisted, in spite of himself. "Three stories, balconies everywhere, a round turret. It's grown over quite wild around the house, but there's a path leading to the old lighthouse. I was walking up there and with all the wild growth, I expected the house to be in bad shape, dilapidated like most of the abandoned homes around here, but it was in beautiful condition. I'd like to know what preservatives were used."

"That's private property, Mr. Wilder," Inez said. "The house has been in the same family for well over a hundred years. I don't know what they use in the paint, but it does weather well. No one lurks around that house." Inez was definitely issuing a reprimand to him.

"I was hardly lurking, Inez," he said, exasperated. "As you well know, the sea salt is hard on the paint and wood of the houses. That house is in remarkable condition. In fact, it looks newly built. I'm curious as to what was used. I'd like to preserve my house in the same way." He made an effort to sound reasonable instead of annoyed. "I'm a bit of a chemist and I can't figure out what would keep a house so pristine over the years. There's no sign of damage from the sea, from age, or even insects. Remarkable."

Inez pursed her lips, always a bad sign. "Well, I'm certain I have no idea." Her voice was stiff, as if she were highly offended. She rang up his groceries in remarkable time without saying another word.

Damon gathered the bags into one arm, his expression daring Inez to ask him if he needed help. Leaning heavily on his cane, he turned to Trudy. "The hairdresser's dog walker told the street cleaner that he saw Sarah walk on water."

Trudy's eyes widened in shock, but there was belief on her face. Inez made some kind of noise he couldn't identify. Disgusted, Damon turned on his heel and stalked out. Ever since the first whisper of Sarah's name he had been unsettled. Disturbed. Agitated. There was something unfamiliar growing inside of him. Anticipation? Excitement? That was ridiculous. He muttered a curse under his breath at the absent Sarah.

He wanted to be left alone, didn't he? He had no interest in the woman the townspeople gossiped about. Sarah might not walk on water but her house was a mystery. He saw no reason why he shouldn't pay her a neighborly visit and ask what preservatives were used in the wood to achieve the nearly impossible results.

Damon Wilder was a man driven to the edge of sanity. Moving to this tiny town on the coast was his last effort to hang onto life. He had no idea how he was going to do it, or why he had chosen this particular town with all its resident eccentrics, but he had been drawn here. Nothing else would do. He had stepped on the rich soil and knew either this place would be home or he had none. It was hell trying to fit in, but the sea soothed him and the long walks over million-year-old rocks and cliffs occupied his mind.

Damon took his time putting his groceries away. The knowledge that this town, this place, was his last stand had been so strong he had actually purchased a house. His home was one of the few things that gave him pleasure. He loved working on it. He loved the wood. He could lose himself in the artistry of reshaping a room to suit his exact needs. For hours at a time the work occupied him such that nothing else could invade his brain and he was at peace for a time.

He stared out his large bay window, the one that looked out over the sea. The one that had an unobstructed view of the house on the cliff. Damon had spent more hours than he cared to think about staring up at the dark silent windows and the balconies and battlements. It was a unique house from another century, another time and place. There were lights on for the first time. The windows shone a bright welcome.

His leg hurt like hell. He needed to sit and rest, not go traipsing around the countryside. Damon stared at the house, drawn to the warmth of it. It seemed almost alive, begging him to come closer. He went outside onto his deck, intending to sit in the chair and enjoy his view of the sea. Instead he found himself limping his way steadily up the path toward the cliffs. It was nearly a compulsion. The path was narrow and steep and rocky in places, almost no more than a deer trail and overgrown at that. His cane slipped on the pebbles and twice he nearly fell. He was swearing by the time he made it to the edge of the private property.

He stood there staring in shock. Damon had been there not two days before, walking around the house and the grounds. It had been wildly overgrown, the bushes high and weeds everywhere. The shrubbery and trees had drooped with winter darkness on the leaves. A noticeable absence of sound had given the place an eerie, creepy feeling. Now there were flowers, as if everything had burst into blossom overnight. A riot of color met his eyes, a carpet of grass was beneath his feet. He could hear the insects buzzing, the sound of frogs calling merrily back and forth as if spring had come instantly.

The gate, which had been securely locked, stood open in welcome. Everything seemed to be welcoming him. A sense of peace began to steal into his heart. A part of him wanted to sit on one of the inviting benches and soak in the atmosphere.

Roses climbed the trellis and rhododendrons were everywhere, great forests of them. He'd never seen such towering plants. Damon started up the pathway, noting every single weed was gone. Stepping stones led the way to the house. Each round of stone held a meticulously carved symbol. Great care had been taken to etch the symbol deep into the stone. Damon leaned down to feel the highly polished work. He admired the craftsmanship and detail. The artisans in the small town all had that trait, one he greatly respected.

As he neared the house, a wind rose off the sea and carried sea spray and a lilting melody. "*Sarah's back. Sarah's home.*" The words sang across the land joyously. It was then he heard the birds and looked around him. They were everywhere, all kinds of birds, flitting from tree to tree, a flutter of wings overhead. Squirrels chattered as they rushed from branch to branch. The sun was sinking over the ocean, turning the sky into bright colors of pink and orange and red. The fog was on the far horizon, meeting the sea to give the impression of an island in the clouds. Damon had never seen anything so beautiful. He simply stood there, leaning on his cane and staring in wonder at the transformation around him.

Voices drifted from the house. One was soft and melodious. He couldn't catch the words but the tone worked its way through his skin into his very bones. Into his vital organs. He moved closer, drawn by the sound, and immediately saw two dogs on the front porch. Both were watching him alertly, heads down, hair up, neither making a sound.

Damon froze. The voices continued. One was weeping. He could hear the heartbreaking sound. A woman's voice. The melodious voice soothed. Damon shifted his weight and took a two-handed grip on his cane. If he had to use it as a weapon, that would give him more leverage. Concerned though he was with the dogs, he was more centered on the voice. He strained to listen.

"Please, Sarah, you have to be able to do something. I know you can. Please say you'll help me. I can't bear this," the crying voice said.

Her sorrow was so deep Damon ached for her. He couldn't remember the last time he'd felt someone's pain. He couldn't remember how to feel anything but bored or frustrated. The dogs both sniffed the air and, as if recognizing him, wagged their tails in greeting and sat down, hair settling to make them appear much more friendly. Keeping one eye on the dogs, he strained to catch the words spoken in that soft lilting tone.

"I know it's difficult, Irene, but this isn't something like putting a Band-Aid on a scraped knee. What do the doctors say?"

There was more sobbing. It shook him, hurt him, tore up his insides so that his gut churned and a terrible weight pressed on his chest. Damon forgot all about the dogs and pressed his hand over his heart. Irene Madison. Now he recognized the voice, knew from Inez at the grocery store that her fifteen-year-old son, Drew, was terminally ill.

"There's no hope, Sarah. They said to take him home and make him comfortable. You know you can find a way. Please do this for us, for me."

Damon edged closer to the house, wondering what the hell she thought Sarah could do. Work a miracle? There was a small silence. The window was open, the wind setting the white lacy curtains dancing. He waited, holding his breath. Waited for Sarah's answer. Waited for the sound of her voice.

"Irene, you know I don't do that sort of thing. I've only just come back. I haven't even unpacked. You're asking me . . . "

"Sarah, I'm begging you. I'll do anything, give you anything. I'm begging on my knees . . . " The sobs were choking Damon. The pain was so raw in the woman.

"Irene, get up! What are you doing? Stop it."

"You have to say you'll come to see him. Please, Sarah. Our mothers were best friends. If not for me, do it for my mother."

"I'll come by, Irene. I'm not promising anything, but I'll stop by." There was resignation in that gentle voice. Weariness. "My sisters will be coming in a day or so and as soon as we're all rested we'll stop by and see what we can do."

"I know you think I'm asking for a miracle, but I'm not, I

just want more time with him. Come when you're rested, when the others have come and can help." The relief Irene felt spilled over to Damon and he had no clue why. Only that the weight pressing on his chest lifted and his heart soared for a moment.

"I'll see what I can do."

The voices were traveling toward him. Damon waited, his heart pounding in anticipation. He had no idea what to expect or even what he wanted, but everything in him stilled.

The door opened and two women emerged to stand in the shadow of the wide, columned porch. "Thank you, Sarah. Thank you so much," Irene said, clutching at Sarah's hands gratefully. "I knew you would come." She hurried down the stairs, straight past the dogs, who had rushed to their mistress. Irene managed a quick smile for Damon as she passed him, her tearstained face bright with hope.

Damon leaned on his cane and stared up at Sarah.

Chapter Two

Sarah stood on the porch, her body in the shadows. Damon had no idea of her age. Her face seemed timeless. Her eyes were old eyes, filled with intelligence and power. Her skin was smooth and flawless, giving her the appearance of extreme youth, very much at odds with the knowledge in her direct gaze. She simply stood there quietly, her incredible eyes fixed on him.

"How did you get through the gate?"

It wasn't what he expected. Damon half turned to look back at the wrought-iron masterpiece of art. The gate was six feet high and an intricate piece of craftsmanship. He had studied it on more than one occasion, noting the symbols and depictions of various animals and stars and moons. A collage of creatures with raw power mixed with universal signs of the earth, water, fire, and wind. Always before when he had come to stare at the house and grounds the gate had been firmly locked.

"It was open," he replied simply.

Her eyebrow shot up and she looked from him to the gate and back again. There was interest in her gaze. "And the dogs?" Her hand dropped to one massive head as she absently scratched the ears.

"They gave me the once-over and decided I was friendly," he answered.

A faint frown touched her face, was gone in an instant. "Did they? You must get along well with animals."

"I don't get along well with anything," he blurted out before he could stop himself. He was so shocked and embarrassed at the admission he couldn't find a way to laugh it off, so it remained there between them.

Sarah simply studied his face for a long while. An eternity. She had a direct gaze that seemed to see past his physical body and delve straight to his soul. It made Damon uncomfortable and ashamed. "You'd better come in and sit down for a while," she said. "There's a blackness around your aura. I can tell you're in pain, although I can't see why you've come yet." She turned and went into the house, clearly expecting him to follow her. Both dogs did, hurrying after her, pacing at her heels.

Damon had been acting out of character ever since he heard that first whisper of gossip. He stood, leaning on his cane, wondering what had gotten into him. He'd seen the mighty Sarah. She was just a woman with incredible eyes. That was all. She couldn't walk on water or move mountains. She couldn't scale impossible cliffs or assassinate heads of terrorist organizations. She was just a woman. And probably as loony as hell. His aura was black? What the hell did that mean? She probably had voodoo dolls and dead chickens in her house.

He stared at the open door. She didn't come back or look to see if he was following. The house had swallowed her up. Mysterious Sarah. Damon lifted his eyes to the gathering darkness, to the first stars and the floating wisps of clouds. It irritated him but he knew he was going to follow her into that house. Just like her damn dogs.

Damon consoled himself with the fact that he was extremely interested in the preservation of wood and paint. He had been interested in her house long before she arrived back in town. He couldn't pass up a genuine opportunity to study it up close, even if it meant trying to make small talk with a crazy stranger. He raked his hand through his dark hair and glared at the empty doorway. Muttering curses beneath his breath, he stalked after her as best he could with his cane and his damaged hip and leg.

The porch stairs were as solid as a rock. The verandah itself was wide and beautiful, wrapping around the house, an invitation to sit in the shade and enjoy the view of the pounding sea. Damon wanted to linger there and continue to feel the peace of Sarah's home, but he stepped inside. The air seemed cool and scented, smelling of some fragrance that reminded him of the forests and flowers. The entryway was wide, tiled with a mosaic design, and it opened into a huge room.

With a sense of awe, Damon stared down at the artwork on the floor. There was a feeling of falling into another world when he looked at it. The deep blue of the sea was really the ocean in the sky. Stars burst and flared into life. The moon was a shining ball of silver. He stood transfixed, wanting to get on his knees and examine every inch of the floor. "I like this floor. It's a shame to walk on it," he announced loudly.

"I'm glad you like it. I think it's beautiful," she said. Her voice was velvet soft, but it carried through the house back to him. "My grandmother and her sisters made that together. It took them a very long time to get it just right. Tell me what you see when you look into the midnight sky there."

He hesitated but the pull of the floor was too much to resist. He examined it carefully. "There are dark shadows in the clouds across the moon. And behind the clouds, a ring of red surrounds the moon. The stars connect and make a bizarre pattern. The body of a man is floating on the sea of clouds and something has pierced his heart." He looked up at her, a challenge on his face.

Sarah merely smiled. "I was about to have tea; would you care for a cup?" She walked away from him into the open kitchen.

Damon could hear the sound of water as she filled the teakettle. "Yes, thank you, that sounds good." And it did, which was crazy. He never drank tea. Not a single cup. He was losing his mind.

"The pictures of my grandmother and her sisters are to your left, if you'd like to see them."

He had always considered looking at pictures of people he didn't know utterly ridiculous, but he couldn't resist looking at the photographs of the women who had managed to create such beauty on a floor. He wandered over to the wall of memories. There were many photographs of women, some black-and-white, others in color. Some of the pictures were obviously very old, but he could easily see the resemblance among the women. Damon cleared his throat. He frowned when he noticed a strange pattern running through every grouping. "Why are there seven women in each family picture?"

"There seems to be a strange phenomenon in our family," Sarah answered readily. "Every generation, someone produces seven daughters."

Startled, Damon leaned on his cane and studied each group of faces. "One out of the seven girls has always given birth to seven daughters? On purpose?"

Sarah laughed and came around the corner to join him in front of the wall of photographs. "Every generation."

He looked from her to the faces of her sisters in a picture near the center of the wall. "Which one carries the strain of insanity?"

"Good question. No one's ever thought to ask it before. My sister Elle is the seventh daughter so she inherits the mantle of responsibility. Or insanity, if you prefer." Sarah pointed to a girl with a young face, vivid green eyes, and a wealth of red hair pulled carelessly into a ponytail.

"And where is poor Elle right now?" Damon asked.

Sarah inhaled, then let her breath out slowly, her long lashes fluttering down. At once her face was in repose. She looked tranquil, radiant. Watching her did something funny to Damon's heart, a curious melting sensation that was utterly terrifying. He couldn't take his fascinated gaze off of her. Strangely, for just one moment, he felt as if Sarah was no longer in the room with him. As if her physical body had separated from her spirit, allowing her to travel across time and space. Damon shook himself, trying to get rid of the crazy impression. He wasn't an imaginative person, yet he was certain Sarah had somehow touched her sister Elle.

"Elle is in a cave of gems, deep under the ground where she can hear the heartbeat of the earth." Sarah opened her eyes and looked at him. "I'm Sarah Drake."

"Damon Wilder." He gestured toward his house. "Your new neighbor." He was staring at her, drinking her in. It didn't make sense. He was certain she wasn't the most beautiful woman in the world but his heart and lungs were insisting she was. Sarah was average height, with a woman's figure. She wore faded, worn blue jeans and a plaid flannel shirt. She certainly was not at all glamorous, yet his lungs burned for air and his heart accelerated. His body hardened painfully when she wasn't even trying to be a sexy siren, simply standing there in her comfortable old clothes with her wealth of dark hair pulled back from her pale face. It was the most infuriating and humiliating thing it was his misfortune to endure.

"You bought the old Hanover place. The view is fantastic. How did you come to find our little town?" Her cool blue gaze was direct and far too assessing. "You look like a man who would be far more comfortable in a big city."

Damon's fist tightened around his cane. Sarah could see his knuckles were white. "I saw it on a map and just knew it was the place I wanted to live in when I retired." She studied his face, the lines of suffering etched into his face, the too old eyes. He was surrounded with the mark of Death, and he read Death in the midnight sky, yet she was strangely drawn to him.

Her eyebrow went up, a perfect arch. "You're a little young to retire, I would have thought. There's not a lot of excitement here."

"I'll have to disagree with that. Have you hung out around the grocery store lately? Inez provides amazing entertainment." There was a wealth of sarcasm mixed with contempt in his voice.

Sarah turned away from him, her shoulders stiffening visibly. "What do you actually know about Inez to have managed to form an opinion in your month of living here?" She sounded sweet and interested but he had the feeling he had just stepped hard on her toes.

Damon limped after her like a puppy dog, trying not to mutter foul curses under his breath. It never mattered to him what other people thought. Everyone had opinions and few actually had educated ones. Why the hell did Sarah's opinion of him matter? And why did her hips have to sway with mesmerizing invitation?

The kitchen was tiled with the same midnight blue that had formed the sky in the mosaic. A long bank of windows looked out over a garden of flowers and herbs. He could see a three-tiered fountain in the middle of the courtyard. Sarah waved him toward the long table while she fixed the tea. Damon couldn't see a speck of dust or dirt anywhere in the house. "When did you arrive?"

"Late last night. It feels wonderful to be home again. It's been a couple of years since my last visit. My parents are in Europe at the moment. They own several homes and love Italy. My grandmother is with them, so the cliff house has been empty."

"So this is your parents' home?" When she shook her head with her slight, mysterious smile he asked, "Do you own this house?"

"With my sisters. It was given to us through our mother." She brought a steaming mug of tea and placed it on the table beside his hand. "I think you'll like this. It's soothing and will help take away the pain."

"I didn't say I was in pain." Damon could have kicked himself. Even to his own ears he sounded ridiculous, a defiant child denying the truth. "Thank you," he managed to mutter, trying to smell the tea without offending her.

Sarah sat across from him, cradling a teacup between her palms. "How can I help you, Mr. Wilder?"

"Call me Damon," he said.

"Damon then," she acknowledged with a small smile. "I'm just Sarah."

Damon could feel her penetrating gaze. "I've been very interested in your house, Sarah. The paint hasn't faded or peeled, not even in the salt air. I was hoping you would tell me what preservative you used."

Sarah leaned back in her chair, brought the teacup to her mouth. She had a beautiful mouth. Wide and full and curved as if she laughed all the time. Or invited kisses. The thought came unbidden as he stared at her mouth. Sheer temptation. Damon felt the weight of her gaze. Color began to creep up the back of his neck.

"I see. You came out late in the evening even though you were hurting because you were anxious to know what kind of preservative I use on my house. That certainly makes perfect sense."

There was no amusement in her voice, not even a hint of sarcasm, but the dull red color spread to his face. Her eyes saw too much, saw into him where he didn't want to be seen, where he couldn't afford to be seen. He wanted to look away but he couldn't seem to pull his gaze from hers.

"Tell me why you're really here." Her voice was soft, inviting confidence.

He raked both hands through his hair in frustration. "I honestly don't know. I'm sorry for invading your privacy." But he wasn't. It was a lie and they both knew it.

She took another sip of tea and gestured toward his mug. "Drink it. It's a special blend I make myself. I think you'll like it and I know it will make you feel better." She grinned at him. "I can promise you there aren't any toads or eye of newt in it."

Sarah's smile robbed him of breath immediately. It was a strange thing to feel a punch in the gut so hard it drove the air out of one's lungs just with a simple smile. He waited several heartbeats until he recovered enough to speak. "Why do you think I need to feel better?" he asked, striving for nonchalance.

"I don't have to be a seer for that, Damon. You're limping. There are white lines around your mouth and your leg is trembling."

Damon raised the cup to his mouth, took a cautious sip of the brew. The taste was unique. "I was attacked awhile back." The words emerged before he could stop them. Horrified, he stared into the tea mug, afraid her brew was a truth serum.

Sarah put her teacup carefully on the table. "A person attacked you?"

"Well, he wasn't an alien." He swallowed a gulp of tea. The heat warmed him, spreading through his body to reach sore, painful places.

"Why would one man want to kill another?" Sarah mused aloud. "I've never understood that. Money is such a silly reason really."

"Most people don't think so." He rubbed his head as if it hurt, or maybe in memory. "People kill for all sorts of reasons, Sarah."

"How awful for you. I hope he was caught."

Before he could stop himself, Damon shook his head. Her vivid gaze settled on his face, looked inside of him again until he wanted to curse. "I was able to get away, but my assistant"—he stopped, corrected himself—"my friend wasn't so lucky."

"Oh, Damon, I'm so sorry."

"I don't want to think about it." He couldn't. It was too close, too raw. Still in his nightmares, still in his heart and soul. He could hear the echoes of screams. He could see the pleading in Dan Treadway's eyes. He would carry that sight to his death, forever etched in his brain. At once the pain was almost too much to bear. He wept inside, his chest burning, his throat clogging with grief.

Sarah reached across the table to place her fingertips on his head. The gesture seemed natural, casual even, and her touch was so light he barely felt it. Yet he felt the results like shooting stars bursting through his brain. Tiny electrical impulses that blasted away the terrible throbbing in his temples and the back of his neck.

He caught her wrists, pulled her hands away from him. He was shaking and she could feel it. "Don't. Don't do that." He released her immediately.

"I'm sorry, I should have asked first," Sarah said. "I was only trying to help you. Would you like me to take you home? It's already dark outside and it wouldn't be safe for you to try to go down the hill without adequate light."

"So I take it the paint preservative is a deep dark family secret," Damon said, attempting to lighten the situation. He drained the tea mug and stood up. "Yes, thanks, I wouldn't mind a ride." It was hard on the ego to have to accept it but he wasn't a complete fool. Could he have behaved any more like an idiot?

Sarah's soft laughter startled him. "I actually don't know whether the preservative is a family secret or not. I'll have to do a little research on the subject and get back to you."

Damon couldn't help smiling just because she was. There was something contagious about Sarah's laughter, something addictive about her personality. "Did you know that when you came home, the wind actually whispered, 'Sarah's back. Sarah's home.' I heard it myself." The words slipped out, almost a tribute.

She didn't laugh at him as he expected. She looked pleased. "What a beautiful thing to say. Thank you, Damon," she said sincerely. "Was the gate really open? The front gate with all the artwork? Not the side gate?"

"Yes, it was standing wide open welcoming me. At least that's how it felt."

Her sea blue eyes drifted over his face, taking in every detail, every line. He knew he wasn't much to look at. A man in his forties, battered and scarred by life. The scars didn't show physically but they went deep and she could clearly see the tormented man. "How very interesting. I think we're destined to be friends, Damon." Her voice wrapped him up in silk and heat.

Damon could see why the townspeople said her name with awe. With respect. Mysterious Sarah. She seemed so open, yet her eyes held a thousand secrets. There was music in her voice and healing in her hands. "I'm glad you've come home, Sarah," he said, hoping he wasn't making more of a fool of himself.

"So am I," she answered.

Chapter Three

"Sarah!" Hannah Drake threw herself into her sister's arms. "It's so good to see you. I missed you so much." She drew back, stretching her arms to full length, the better to examine Sarah. "Why, Sarah, you look like a cat burglar, ready to rob the local museum. I had no idea Frank Warner's paintings had become valuable." She laughed merrily at her own joke.

Sarah's soft laughter merged with Hannah's. "I should have known you'd come creeping in at two A.M. That's so you, Hannah. Where were you this time?"

"Egypt. What an absolutely beautiful country it is." Hannah sat on the porch swing wearily. "But I'm wiped out. I've been traveling forever to get back home." She regarded Sarah's sleek black outfit with a slight frown. "Interesting set of tools you're sporting there, sister mine. I'm not going to have to bail you out of jail, am I? I'm really tired and if the police have to call, I might not wake up."

Sarah adjusted the belt of small tools slung low on her waist

without a hint of embarrassment. "If I can't charm a police offi-
cer out of booking me for a little break-in, I don't deserve the
name Drake. Go on in, Hannah, and go to bed. I'm worried
about our neighbor and think I'll just go scout around and
make certain nothing happens to him."

Hannah's eyebrow shot up. "Good heavens, Sarah. A man?
There's an honest-to-God man in your life? Where is he? I want
to go with you." She clasped her hands together, her face radiant. "Wait until I tell the others. The mighty Sarah has fallen!"

"I have *not* fallen—don't start, Hannah. I just have one of my
hunches and I'm going to check it out. It has nothing to do
with Damon at all."

"Ooh, this is really getting interesting. Damon. You remember his name. How did you meet him? Spill it, Sarah, every last
detail!"

"There's nothing to spill. He just waltzed in asking about
paint and wood preservatives." Sarah's tone was cool and aloof.

"You want me to believe he walked in on his own without
an invitation? You had to have asked him to the house."

"No, I didn't," Sarah denied. "As a matter of fact the gate was
open and the dogs allowed him in."

"The gate was open on its own?" Hannah was incredulous.
She jumped to her feet. "I'm going with you for certain!"

"No, you're not, you're exhausted, remember?"

"Wait until I tell the others the gate opened for him."
Hannah raised her arms to the heavens and stars. "The gate
opens for the right man, doesn't it? Isn't that how it works? The
gate will swing open in welcome for the man who is destined
to become the love of the eldest child's life."

"I don't believe in that nonsense and you know it." Sarah tried to glare but found herself laughing. "I can't believe you'd even think of that old prophecy."

"Like you didn't think of it yourself," Hannah teased. "You're just going off to do the neighborly thing in the middle of the night and just sort of scout around his house. If you say so, of course I'll believe it. Is that telescope up on the battlement directed toward his bedroom?"

"Don't you dare look," Sarah ordered.

Hannah studied her face. "You're laughing but your eyes aren't. What's wrong, Sarah?" She put her hand on her sister's shoulder. "Tell me."

Sarah frowned. "He carries Death on him. I've seen it. And he read it in the mosaic. I don't know whose death, but I'm drawn to him. His heart is broken and pierced through, and the weight of carrying Death is slowly crushing him. He saw a red ring around the moon."

"Violence and death surround him," Hannah said softly, almost to herself. "Why are you going alone?"

"I have to. I feel . . . " Sarah searched for the right word. "Drawn. It's more than a job, Hannah. It's him."

"He could be dangerous."

"He's surrounded by danger, but if he's dangerous to me, it isn't in the way you're thinking."

"Oh my gosh, you really do like this guy. You think he's hot. I'm telling the others and I'm going up to the battlement to check him out!" Hannah turned and raced into the house, banging the screen door so Sarah couldn't follow her.

Sarah laughed as she blew a kiss to her sister and started down the stairs. Hannah looked wonderful as always. Tall and tanned and beautiful even after traveling across the sea. If her wavy hair was tousled, she just looked in vogue. Other women paid fortunes to try to achieve her natural wind-blown style. Sarah had always been uncommonly proud of Hannah's genuine elegance. She had a bright spirit that shone like the stars overhead. Hannah had a free spirit that longed for wide-open spaces and the wonders of the world. She spoke several languages and traveled extensively. One month she might be found in the pages of a magazine with the jet-setters, the next she was on a dig in Cairo. Her tall slender carriage and incredibly beautiful face made her sought after by every magazine and fashion designer. It was her gentle personality that always drew people to her. Sarah was happy she was home.

Sarah made little sound as she made her way down the small deer path that cut through her property to Damon Wilder's. She knew every inch of her property. And she knew every inch of his. Her hair was tightly braided to keep it from being snagged on low branches or brambles. Her soft-soled shoes were light, allowing her to feel her way over twigs and dried leaves. She wasn't thinking about Damon's broad shoulders or his dark, tormented eyes. And she didn't believe in romance. Not for Sarah. That was for elegant Hannah or beautiful Joley. Well, maybe not the beautiful, *wild* Joley, but definitely for most of her other sisters. Just not Sarah.

Damon Wilder was in trouble in more ways than he knew. Sarah didn't like complications. Ancient prophecies and broad shoulders and black auras were definite complications. Moonlight spilled over the sea as she made her way along the cliffs, following

275

the narrow deer path that eventually wound down the back side of Damon's property. The powerful waves boomed as they rushed and ebbed and collapsed in a froth of white. Sarah found the sound of the sea soothing, even when it raged in a storm. She belonged there, had always belonged, as had her family before her. She didn't fear the sea or the wilds of the countryside, yet her heart was pounding in sudden alarm. Pounding with absolute knowledge.

She was not alone in the night. Instinctively she lowered her body so she wouldn't be silhouetted against the horizon. She used more care, blending into the shadows, using the foliage for cover. She moved with stealth. She was used to secrecy, a highly trained professional. There was no sound as the branches slid away from her tightly knit jumpsuit and her crepe-soled shoes eased over the ground.

Sarah made her way to the outskirts of the house. She knew all about Damon Wilder. One of the smartest men on the planet. A government's treasure. The one-man think tank that had come up with one of the most innovative defense systems ever conceived. His ideas were pure genius, far ahead of their time. He was a steady, focused man. A perfectionist who never overlooked the smallest detail.

When she read about him, before accepting her watchdog assignment, Sarah had been impressed with the sheer tenacity of his character. Now that she had met him, she ached for the man, for the horror of what he had been through. She never allowed her work to be personal, yet she couldn't stop thinking about his eyes and the torment she could see in their dark depths. And she couldn't help but wonder why Death had attached itself to him and was clinging with greedy claws.

Sarah rarely accepted such an assignment, but she knew her cover couldn't have been more perfect. Meant to be. That gave her a slight flutter of apprehension. Destiny, fate, whatever one wanted to call it, was a force to be reckoned with in her family and she had managed to avoid it carefully for years. Damon Wilder had chosen her hometown to settle in. What did that mean? Sarah didn't believe in such close coincidence.

She had no time to circle the house or check the coastal road. As she approached the side of the house facing her home, she heard a muffled curse coming from her left. Sarah inched that way, dropped to her belly, lying flat out in the darker shadows of the trees. She lifted her head cautiously, only her eyes moving restlessly, continually, examining the landscape. It took a few moments to locate her adversaries. She could make out two men not more than forty feet from her, on the downhill, right in the middle of the densest brush. Sarah had the urge to smile. She hoped for their sakes they were wearing their dogs' tick collars.

Lying in the shrubs, she began a slow, complicated pattern with her hands, a flowing dance of fingers while the leaves rustled and twigs began to move as if coming alive. Tiny, silent creatures dropped from branches overhead, fell from leaves, and pushed up from the ground to migrate downhill toward the thickest brush.

Sarah knew that the one window lit up in Damon's house was a bedroom. If the telescope set up on the battlements of her house happened to be pointed in that direction, it was only because it was the last room she had investigated. It just so happened that it was Damon's bedroom, a complete coincidence.

Sarah glanced back at her house overlooking the pounding waves, suddenly worried that Hannah might have her eye glued to the lens.

She hissed softly, melodiously, an almost silent note of command the wind caught and carried skyward toward the sea, toward the house on the cliff. The brush of material against wood and leaves attracted her immediate attention. She watched one of the men scuttle like a crab down the hill toward Damon's house. He crouched just below the lit window, then cautiously raised his head to look inside.

The window was raised a few inches to allow the ocean air inside. The breeze blew the kettle cloth drapes inward so that they performed a strange ghoulish dance. With the fluttering curtains it was nearly impossible to get a clear glimpse of the interior. The man half stood, flattening his body against the wall, tilting his head to peer inside.

Sarah could make out the second man lying prone, his rifle directed at the window. She inched her way across the low grasses, moving with the wind as it blew over the land. The man with his rifle trained on the window never took his gaze from his target. Never flinched, the gun rock steady. A pro, then; she had expected it but had hoped otherwise. She could see the tiny insects crawling into his clothing.

Above her head the clouds were drifting away from the moon, threatening to expose her completely. She wormed her way through the grass and brambles, gaining a few more feet. Sarah pulled her gun from her shoulder holster.

Hearing a slight noise from inside the room, the assailant at the window put up his hand in warning. He peered in the window in an attempt to locate Damon. A solid thunk sounded loud as Damon's cane landed solidly on his jaw. At once the man screamed, the high-pitched cry reverberating through the night. He fell backward onto the ground, holding his face, rolling and writhing in pain.

Sarah kept her gaze fixed on the partner with the rifle. He was waiting for Damon to expose himself at the window. Damon was too smart to do such an idiotic thing. The curtains continued their macabre dancing but nothing else stirred in the night. The moans continued from beneath the window but the assailant didn't get to his feet.

The rifleman crawled forward on his belly, slipping in the wet grass so that he rolled, protecting his rifle. It was the slip Sarah was waiting for. She was on him immediately, pressing her gun into the back of his neck.

"I suggest you remain very still," she said softly. "You're trespassing on private property and we just don't like that sort of thing around here." As she spoke, she kept a wary eye on the man by the window. She raised her voice. "Damon, have you called the sheriff? You've got a couple of night visitors out here that may need a place to stay for a few days and I heard the jail was empty tonight."

"Is that you, Sarah?"

"I was taking a little stroll and saw a high-powered rifle kind of lying around in the dirt." She kicked the rifle out of the captured man's hands. "It's truly a thing of beauty; I just couldn't pass up the opportunity to get a good look at it." There was a hint of laughter in her voice, but the muzzle of her gun remained very firmly pressed against her captive's neck. "You should stay right there, Damon. There's two of them out here and they look a bit aggravated." She leaned close to the man on the ground, but kept her eyes on his partner by the window. "You might want to check yourself the minute you're in jail. You're probably crawling with ticks. Nasty little bugs, they burrow in, drink your blood, and pass on all sorts of interesting things, from staph to Lyme disease. That bush you were hiding in is lousy with them."

Her heart was still pounding out a rhythm of warning. Then she knew. Sarah flung herself to her right, rolling away, even as she heard the whine of bullets zinging past her and thudding into the ground. Of course there had to be a third man, a driver waiting in the darkness up on the road. She had been unable to scout out the land properly. It made perfect sense they would have a driver, a backup should there be need.

The man next to her scrambled up and dove on top of her, making a grab for her gun. Sarah managed to get one bent leg into his stomach to launch him over her head. She felt the sting of her earlobe as her earring, tangled in his shirt, was jerked from her ear. He swore viciously as he picked himself up and raced away from her toward the road. The one closest to the house was already in motion, staggering up the hill, still holding his jaw in his hands. The driver provided cover, pinning her down with a spray of bullets. The silencer indicated the men had no desire to announce their presence to the townspeople.

"Sarah? You all right out there?" Damon called anxiously. Even with the silencer, he couldn't fail to hear the telltale whine of bullets.

"Yes." She was disgusted with herself. She could hear the

motor of the car roar to life, the wheels spinning in dirt for a moment before they caught and the vehicle raced away down the coastal highway. "I'm sorry, Damon, I let them get away."

"*You're* sorry! You could have been killed, Sarah. And no, I didn't call the sheriff. I was hoping they were neighborhood kids looking to do a prank."

"And I took you for such a brilliant man, too," she teased, sitting up and pulling twigs out of her hair. She touched her stinging ear, came away with blood on her fingers. It was her favorite earring, too.

The drapes rustled and Damon poked his head out the window. "Are we going to call back and forth or are you going to come in here and talk with me." There was more demand than question in his voice.

Sarah laughed softly. "Do you think that's such a good idea? Can you imagine what Inez would say if she knew I was visiting you in the middle of the night?" She reached for the rifle, taking care to pick it up using a handkerchief. "She'd ask you your intentions. You'd have to deny you had any. The word would spread that you'd ruined me and I'd be pitied. I couldn't take that. It's better if I just slink home quietly."

Damon leaned farther out the window. "Damn it, Sarah, I'm not amused. You could have been killed. Do you even understand that? These men were dangerous and you're out taking a little stroll in the moonlight and playing neighborhood cop." His voice was harsher than he intended, but she'd scared the hell out of him. He rubbed a hand over his face, feeling sick at the thought of her in danger.

"I wasn't in any danger, Damon," Sarah assured him. "This

rifle, in case you're interested, has tranqs in it, not bullets. At least they weren't trying to kill you, they wanted you alive."

He sighed. She was just sitting there on the ground with the sliver of moonlight spilling over her. The rifle was lying across her knees and she was smiling at him. Sarah's smile was enough to stop a man's heart. Damon took a good look at her clothes, at the gun still in her hand. He stiffened, swore softly. "Damn you anyway, Drake. I should have known you were too good to be true!"

"Were you believing all the stories about me, after all, Damon?" she asked. But dread was beginning even though it shouldn't matter what he thought of her. Or what he knew. She had a job. It shouldn't matter, yet she felt the weight in her chest, heavy like a stone. She felt a sudden fear crawling in her stomach of losing something special before it even started.

"Who sent you, Sarah? And don't lie to me. Whom do you work for?"

"Did you really think they were going to let you walk away without any kind of protection after what happened, Damon?" Sarah kept the sympathy from her voice, knowing it would only anger him further.

He swore bitterly. "I told them I wasn't going to be responsible for another death. Get the hell off my property, Sarah, and don't you come back." Something deep inside of him unexpectedly hurt like hell. He had just met her. The hope hadn't even fully developed, only in his heart, not his mind, but he still felt it. It was a betrayal and his Sarah, mysterious Sarah with her beautiful smile and her lying eyes, had broken him before he'd even managed to find himself.

"I can assure you, Mr. Wilder, despite the fact that I'm a woman, I'm very capable of doing my job." Deliberately she tried to refocus the argument, putting stiff outrage in her tone.

"I don't care how good you are at your damned job or anything else. Get off my property before I call the sheriff and have you arrested for trespassing." Damon slammed the window closed with a terrible finality. The light went off as if somehow that would cut all communication between them.

Sarah sat on the ground and stared at the darkened window with a heavy heart. The sea rolled and boomed with a steadiness that never ceased. The wind tugged at her hair and the clouds drifted above her head. She drew up her knees and contemplated the fact that old prophecies should never be passed from generation to generation. That way, one could never be disappointed.

Chapter Four

Sarah didn't bother to knock politely on the locked door. Damon Wilder was hurt and angry and she didn't really blame him. She was nearly as confused as he was. Curses on old prophecies that insisted on messing up lives. If they'd been two people meeting casually everything would have been all right. But no, the gate had to stand open in welcome. It was neither of their faults, but how was she going to explain a two-hundred-year-old foretelling? How was she going to tell him her family came from a long line of powerful women who drew power from the universe around them and that prophecies several hundreds of years old *always* came true?

Sarah did the only thing any self-respecting woman would do in the middle of the night. She pulled out her small set of tools and picked the front door lock. She made a mental note to install a decent security system in his house and lecture him about at least buying a dead bolt in the interim.

As a child she had often played in the house and she knew

its layout almost as well as she knew her own. Sarah moved swiftly through the living room. She saw very little furniture although Damon had moved in well over a month earlier. No pictures were on the wall, nothing to indicate it was a home, not just a temporary place to dwell.

Damon lay on his bed staring up at the ceiling. He had started out seething, but there was too much fear to sustain it. Sarah had nearly walked into an ambush. It didn't matter that she had been sent to be his watchdog, she could have been killed. It didn't bear thinking about. Sarah. Shrouded in mystery. How could he fixate on a woman so quickly when he rarely noticed anyone? If he closed his eyes he could see her. There was a softness about her, a femininity that appealed to him on every level. She would probably laugh if she knew he had an unreasonable and totally mad desire to protect her.

Damon bit out another quiet oath, not certain he could force himself to pick up and leave again. Where could he go? This was the end of the earth and yet somehow they had found him after all these months. No one would be safe around him.

"Do you always lie in the dark on your bed and swear at the ceiling?" Sarah asked quietly. "Because that could become a real issue later on in our relationship."

Damon opened his eyes to stare up at her. Sarah. Real. In his bedroom dressed in a skintight black suit that clung to every curve. His mouth watered and every cell in his body leapt to life in reaction. "It happens at those times I've been betrayed. I don't know, really, a knee-jerk reaction I can't seem to stop."

Sarah looked around for a chair, couldn't find one, and shoved his legs over to make room on the bed. "Betrayal can be painful. In all honesty I haven't had the experience. My sisters guard my back, so to speak." She turned the full power of huge blue eyes on him. "Do you believe that having friends insist on your protection is a betrayal?"

He could hear the sincerity in her voice. "You don't understand." How could she? How could anyone? "They had no right to hire you, Sarah. I quit my job, retired, if you want it neat and tidy. I have no intention of ever going back again. I cut all ties with that job and every branch of the military and the private sector."

"You tried to keep everyone around you safe by leaving." It was a statement of fact. He would think she was crazy if she told him he carried Death with him. "What happened, Damon?"

"Didn't they give you a three-inch-thick file to read on me before they sent you here?" he demanded, trying to sustain his anger with her.

Sarah simply waited, allowing the silence to lengthen and stretch between them. Sometimes silence was more eloquent than words. Damon was tense, his body rigid next to hers. His fingers were curled into a tight fist around the comforter. Sarah laid her hand gently over his.

He could have resisted most anything, but not that silent gesture of camaraderie. He twisted his hand around until his fingers laced through hers. "They hit us about five blocks from work. Dan Treadway was with me. We planned to have dinner and go back to work. We both wanted to see if we could work out a glitch with a minor problem we were having with the project." He chose his words carefully. He no longer worked for the government but his work had been classified.

"They beat us both nearly unconscious before they threw us in the trunk. They didn't even pretend to want our money. They drove to a warehouse, an old paint factory, and demanded information on a project we just couldn't safely give them."

Sarah felt his hand tremble in hers. She had read the hospital report. Both men had been tortured. She knew Damon carried the scars from numerous burns on his torso. "I couldn't give them what they wanted and poor Dan had no idea what they were even talking about." He pressed his fingertips to his eyes as if the pressure would stop the pain. Stop the memory that never left him. "He never even worked on the project they wanted information about."

Sarah knew Dan Treadway had been shot in the knee and then again in the head, killing him. Damon had refused to turn over classified information that could have resulted in the deaths of several field agents. And he had steadfastly refused to give up the newest defense system. Damon started a fire with paint thinners, nearly blowing up the building. In his escape attempt he was crushed between the wall of the warehouse and the grille of a car, severely damaging his hip and leg.

"I don't want friends, Sarah. No one can afford to be my friend."

Sarah knew he spoke the truth. Death clung and searched for victims. She wouldn't tell him, but often Death felt cheated. If that were the case, it would demand a sacrifice before it would be appeased. "Does the company know who these people are?" Sarah prompted.

His dark gaze was haunted. "You would know that better than I would. Enemies of our country. Mercenaries. Hell, who cares? They wanted something my brain conceived, bad enough to kill an innocent man for it. I don't want to think up anything worth killing over again. So here I am."

"Did you talk to anyone, a doctor?"

He laughed. "Of course I did. The company made certain I talked to one, especially after I announced my retirement. There were a few loose ends and they didn't want me leaving. I didn't much care what they wanted." He turned his head. Edgy. Brooding. "Is it part of your job to try to get me to go back?"

Sarah shook her head. "I don't tell people what to do, Damon. I don't believe in that." Her mouth curved. "Well," she hedged, "I guess that's not altogether true. There is the exception of my sisters. They expect me to boss them around, though, because I'm the oldest and I'm very good at bossing."

"Did you want to come back here, Sarah?" The sound of the sea was soothing. It did sound like home.

"More than anything. I've felt the pull of the ocean for a while now. I've always known I'd come back home and settle here. I just don't know when I'm going to manage it. Damon, your house has no security whatsoever. Did it occur to you they could waltz in here and grab you again?"

Damon tried not to read too much into that worried note in her voice. Tried not to think that it was personal. "It's been months. I thought they would leave me alone."

Sarah whistled softly. "You even lie with that straight face and those angelic eyes. I'm taking notes. That one is right up there with swearing at the ceiling. You wanted them to come after you, didn't you?" It was a shrewd guess. She hadn't known him long enough to judge his character yet, but she'd read the files thoroughly and every word portrayed a relentless, tenacious man, focused on his goals at all times.

"Wouldn't you? They forced me to make a choice between information that is vital to our nation and my friend's life. He was looking at me when they shot him, Sarah. I'll never forget the way he looked at me." He rubbed his throbbing temple. The vision haunted his dreams and brought him out of a sound sleep so that he sat up, heart pounding, screaming a denial to the uncaring night.

"What kind of a plan do you have?"

Damon felt his stomach knot up. Her tone was very interested. She expected a plan. He had the reputation of being a brain. He should have a plan. His plan had been to draw his enemies to him and dispose of them, first with his cane and then he'd call the sheriff. He doubted if Sarah would be impressed.

She sighed. "Damon, tell me you did have a plan."

"Just because you walk on water doesn't mean everyone else does," he muttered.

"Who told you I walked on water?" Sarah demanded, annoyed. "For heaven's sake, I only did it once and it was just showing off. All my sisters can do the same thing."

He gaped at her, his eyes wide with shock. She kept a straight face, but the laughter in her eyes gave her away. Damon did the noble thing and shoved her off the bed. Sarah landed on the floor, her soft laughter inviting him to join in.

"You so deserved that," she said. "You really did. Walk on water. That's a new one. Where did you hear that? And you believed it, too."

Damon turned on his side, propped up on one elbow to look

down at her. "I started the rumor myself at Inez's store. For a minute there I thought I was psychic."

"Oh, thank you so much; now all the kids will be asking me to show them. The next time you come calling I'm going to sic the dogs on you."

"What makes you think I'm going to come calling?" he asked curiously.

"I never told you about the paint preservative. You're a persistent man." She leaned her head against the bed. "Do you have a family anywhere, Damon?"

"I was an only child. My parents died years ago, first my father, then six months later my mother. They were wild about each other."

"How strange that would be, to grow up alone. I've had my sisters always and can't imagine life without them."

His fingers crept of their own accord to find the thick mass of her hair. She was wearing it in a tight braid, but he managed to rub the silky strands between his thumb and finger. How the hell did she manage to get her hair so soft? Mysterious Sarah. He was fast beginning to think of her as his Sarah. "Do you like them all?"

Sarah smiled there in the darkness. She loved her sisters. There was no question about that, but no one had ever thought to ask if she liked them. "Very much, Damon. You would, too. Each of them is unique and gifted in her own way. All of them have a great sense of humor. We laugh a lot at our house." He was tugging at her hair. It didn't hurt, in fact it was a pleasant sensation, but it was causing little butterfly wings to flutter in the pit of her stomach. "What are you doing?"

"I snagged my watch in your braid and thought I'd just take it out," he answered casually. He was lying and he didn't even care that it was a lie and that she knew it was a lie. Any excuse to see her hair tumbling down in a cloud around her face.

Sarah laughed softly. "My braid? Or your watch?" He was definitely tugging her hair out of its tight arrangement. "It took me twenty minutes to get my hair like that. I've never been good at hair things."

"A wasted twenty minutes. You have beautiful hair. There's no need to be good at hair things."

Sarah was absurdly pleased that he'd noticed. It was her one call to glory. "Thank you." She tapped her fingers on her knee, trying to find a way to get him to agree with her on his protection. "Damon, it's important to protect your house. I could set up a good security system for you. I'll let the sheriff know we have a problem and they'll help us out."

"Us? Sarah, you need to be as far away from me as possible." Even as he said it, his hands were tunneling in the rich wealth of her hair, a hopeless compulsion he couldn't prevent. He wanted to feel that silky softness sliding over his skin.

"I thought you were supposed to be brilliant, Damon. Didn't I read in your file that you were one of the smartest men on the face of the earth? Along with your swearing issues and your hair issues, please tell me you don't have idiot macho tendencies, too. If that's the case, I'm going to have to seriously study this gate prophecy. I can live with the other things but idiocy might be stretching my patience."

He tugged on her hair to make certain she was paying attention. "*One* of the smartest men? Is that what that report said? I should read the file over for you and weed out the blatant lies. I'm certain I'm *the* smartest, not *one* of the smartest. You don't have to insult me by pretending the report said otherwise. And what is the gate prophecy?"

She waved away his inquiry. "I'll have to tell you about the Drake history sometime, but right now, I think you might clear up the idiot macho issue for me," she insisted. "Brainy men tend to be arrogant but they shouldn't be stupid. I'm a security expert, Damon."

He sighed loudly. "So I'm supposed to tell all my friends that my lady friend is the muscle in our relationship."

"Do we have a relationship?" She tilted her head to look back at him. "And surely the smartest man on earth would have a strong enough ego to be fine with his lady friend being the muscle. Relationship or no."

"Oh, if there's no relationship, I doubt if any man could take that big a blow to his ego, Sarah. We need to call in an expert on this subject, consult a counselor before we make a decision. And it never hurts to get a second opinion if we don't like the first one."

Damon couldn't help the grin that spread across his face. It felt good to smile. She had thrown his life into complete confusion, but she made him smile. Made him want to laugh. Intrigued him. Turned him inside out. Gave him a reason to live. And the heavy weight that seemed to be pressing down on his shoulders and chest was lifted for just a few moments.

"You won't have to worry on that score, Damon. We'll have six very loud and long-winded second opinions. My sisters will have more to say than you'll ever want to hear on the subject.

For that matter, on every subject. You won't need a counselor for anything; they'll all be happy to oblige, absolutely free of charge."

Sarah glanced toward the cliff house. Through the bedroom window that should have had the drapes closed. The curtains were parted in the middle, pushed to either side by an unseen hand. "Sarah." There was an ache in Damon's voice.

Her heart did a funny little jump in her chest and she turned her head to look at him. Her gaze collided with his. Stark hunger was in his eyes. Raw need. Desire. He reached for her, caught the nape of her neck, and slowly lowered his head to hers. His mouth fastened onto hers. They simply melted together. Merged.

Fireworks might have burst in the air around them. Or maybe it was the stars scattering across the sky, glittering like gems. Fire raced up her skin, heat spread through her body. He claimed her. Branded her. And he did a thorough job of it. They fed on one another. Were lost in smoky desire. His mouth was perfect, hot and hungry and demanding and possessive.

No one had ever kissed her like that. She had never thought it would be like that. She wanted to just stay there all night and kiss.

Damon shifted his weight on the bed, deepening the kiss. He tumbled over the edge, sprawling on the floor, pulling her over so that she collapsed on top of him. Instantly his arms circled her and held her to his chest.

Sarah could feel the laughter start deep inside him, where it started in her. They lay in a tangle of arms and legs, laughing happily. She lifted her head to look at him, to trace his wonderful mouth with her fingertip. "Sheer magic, Damon. That's what you are. Does this happen every time you kiss a woman?"

"I don't kiss women," he admitted, shaken to his very core. His fingers were tunneling in her wealth of hair, her thick silky hair that he wanted to bury his face in.

"Well, men then. Does it happen all the time? Because quite frankly it's amazing. You're truly amazing."

The laughter welled up all over again. Damon helped her to sit up, her back against the bed. He sat next to her. Both of them stared out the window toward the cliff house.

"I could have sworn I closed those drapes," he commented.

"You probably did," Sarah admitted with a small sigh. "It's the sisters. My sisters. They're probably watching us right this minute. Hannah came home right before I left and Kate and Abigail arrived about the time the driver was shooting at me. You could wave at them if you felt up to it."

"How are they watching us?" Damon asked, interested.

"The telescope. I use it to watch the sky." She used her most pious voice. "And sometimes the ocean, but my sisters are notoriously and pathetically interested in *my* business. I shall have to teach them some manners." She waved her hand casually, murmuring something he couldn't quite catch, but it sounded light and airy and melodious.

Shadows entered the room. Moved. The drapes swayed gently, blocked the sliver of moon, the faint light reflected by the pounding sea. Damon blinked; in that split second the curtains were drawn firmly across the window.

Chapter Five

"You were kissing that man," Hannah accused gleefully. "Sarah Drake, you hussy. You were kissing a perfect stranger."

Sarah looked as cool as possible under fire. "I don't know what you thought you saw with your eye glued to the telescope lens, but certainly not that! You ought to be ashamed of yourself spying that way. And using . . . " She trailed off to motion in the air with her fingers, glaring at all three of her sisters as she did so. "To open the curtains in a private bedroom is an absolute no-no, which we all agreed on when we set down the rules."

"There are exceptions to the rules," Kate pointed out demurely. She was curled up in a straight-backed wooden chair at the table, her knees drawn up, with a wide, engaging grin on her face as she painted her toenails.

"What exceptions?" Sarah demanded, her hands on her hips.

Kate shrugged and blew on her toenails before answering. "When our sister is hanging out with a man with a black aura around him." She raised her head to look at Sarah, her gaze steady. "That's very dangerous and you know it. You can't play around with Death. Not even you, Sarah."

Sarah turned to glare at Hannah. She didn't want to talk about it, or even name Death, afraid if she gave it substance she would increase its power, so she remained silent.

Hannah shook her head. "It wasn't me ratting you out. You left the tea leaves in the cup and it was there for everyone to read."

"You still had no right to go against the rules without a vote." Sarah was fairly certain she'd lost the argument, but she wasn't going down without a fight. They were right about Death. Just the idea of facing it made her shiver inside. If she wasn't so drawn to Damon, she would have backed away and allowed nature to take its course. For some unexplained reason, she couldn't bear the thought of Damon suffering.

Kate smirked. "Don't worry, we made certain to convene a hasty meeting and vote on whether or not the situation called for the use of power. It was fully agreed upon that it was wholly warranted."

"You convened a meeting?" Sarah glared at them all with righteous indignation. "Without me? Without the others? The three of you don't make up the majority. Oh, you are in so much trouble!" she said triumphantly.

Hannah blew her a kiss, sweetly reasonable. "Of course we didn't do that, Sarah. We contacted everyone on the spot. It was perfectly legit. We told them about the gate and how it opened on its own for him. And how the dogs greeted him. Elle sent hugs and kisses and says she misses you. Joley wanted to come home right away and get in on the fun but she's tied up." She frowned. "I hope not literally, I didn't think to ask and you never know with Joley. And Libby is working in Guatemala or some other place she's discovered with no bathroom and probably leeches, healing the sick children as usual."

"I thought she was in Africa investigating that crawlie thing that was killing everyone when they tried to harvest their crops," Kate said. "She was sending me some research material for my next book."

"Wherever she is, Libby agreed totally we needed to make certain Sarah was safe." Hannah looked innocent. "That's all we were doing, Sarah. Everyone agreed that for your safety we needed to see into that bedroom immediately."

Kate and Abbey burst into laughter again. "I was a bit worried when he got so exuberant he fell on the floor," Abbey said. "But clearly you weren't in a life-threatening situation so we left you to it."

"And boy, did you go to it," Kate added. "Really, Sarah, a little less enthusiasm on your part might have gone a long way toward giving some credence to our chasing-men theory." The three sisters exchanged nods as if research were very important.

Struggling not to laugh, Sarah tapped her foot, hands on hips, looking at their unrepentant faces. "You knew I wasn't in any danger, you peeping Thomasinas. Shame on the lot of you! I'll have you know I was *working* last night."

That brought another round of laughter that nearly tipped Kate right out of the chair. "A working girl!"

"Is that what you call it? You were working at *something*, Sarah," Hannah agreed.

"She's a *fast* worker," Abbey added.

Sarah's mouth twitched with the effort to remain straight-faced. "I do security work, you horrible hags. I'm his bodyguard!"

Kate did fall off the chair laughing. Hannah slumped over the table, her elegant body gracefully posed. "You were guarding his body all right, Sarah," Abbey said, just managing to get the words out through the shrieks of laughter.

"*Closely* guarding his body," Kate contributed.

"Locked up those lips nice and safe," Hannah agreed. "Ooh, Sarah, baby, you are *great* at that job."

Sarah's only recourse was to fall back on dignity. They weren't listening to their big sister's voice of *total authority* at their antics. She drew herself up, looked as haughty as she could with the three of them rolling around together, laughing like hyenas. "Go ahead and howl, but the three of you just might want to read that old prophecy. Read the *entire* thing, not just the first line or two."

The smile faded from Hannah's face. "Sarah's looking awfully smug. Where is that old book anyway?"

Abbey sat up straight. "Sarah Drake, you didn't dare cast on us, did you?"

"I don't cast," Sarah said, "that's Hannah's department. Damon is coming over. I wanted him to meet you." She looked suddenly vulnerable. "I really like him. We talked all night about everything. You know those uncomfortable silences with strangers who can't possibly understand us? We didn't have one of them. He's so worn out from carrying Death. Of course, he doesn't know that's what he's doing and if he did, he would have sent me away immediately."

"Oh, Sarah." Hannah's voice was filled with compassion.

"I have to find a way to help him. He couldn't bear another death on his hands. His friend was killed, but he managed to save himself." She swept a hand through her hair and looked at her sisters with desperation in her eyes. "I liked everything about him. There wasn't a subject we skipped. And we laughed together over everything." She lifted her gaze to her sisters. "I really, really liked him."

"Then we'll like him, too," Kate reassured her. "And we'll find a way to help him." She opened the refrigerator and peered in, pulling at drawers. "Did you get fresh veggies?"

"Of course, and plenty of fruit. By the way, congratulations on your latest release. I read it cover to cover and it was wonderful. As always, Katie, your stories are fantastic," Sarah praised sincerely. "And thanks, Kate."

Abbey hugged Kate. "My favorite memories are when we were little and we used to lie on the balcony looking up at the stars, with you telling us your stories. You deserve all those best-seller lists."

Kate kissed her sister. "And you aren't prejudiced at all."

"Even if we were," Hannah said, "you're still the best story-teller ever born and deserve every award and list you get on."

Kate blushed, turning nearly as red as the highlights in her chestnut hair. She looked pleased. "How did the spotlight get turned on me? Sarah's the one who spent the night with a perfect stranger."

"I had to spend the night with him," Sarah insisted. "There's no security at his house. And I've asked Jonas Harrington to drop by this morning to meet Damon."

All three women groaned in unison. "How could you invite that Neanderthal to our home, Sarah?" Hannah demanded.

"He's the local sheriff," Sarah pointed out. "Come on, all that was a long time ago—we were kids."

"He was a total jerk to me and he still is," Hannah said. The mug, filled with coffee, on the table in front of her began to steam. Hannah looked down and saw the liquid was beginning to boil. Hastily she blew on the surface.

There was a small silence. "Fine!" Hannah exploded. "I'll admit he still makes me mad if I just think about him. And if he calls me Baby Doll or Barbie Doll, I'm turning him into a big fat toad. He already is one, he may as well look like it."

"You can't turn the sheriff into a toad, Hannah. It's against the rules," Abbey reminded her. "Give him a doughnut gut or a nervous twitch."

"That's not good enough," Kate chimed in. "You need imagination to pay that man back. Something much more subtle—like every time he goes to lie to a woman to get her in bed, he blurts out the truth or tells them what a hound dog he is."

"I'll do worse than that," Hannah threatened, "I'll make it so he's lousy in bed! Mister Macho Man, the bad boy who couldn't do anything but make fun of me in school. He thinks he's such a lady's man."

"Hannah." Sarah heard the pain in her sister's voice and spoke gently. "You were then, and still are now, so incredibly beautiful and brainy. No one could ever conceive of you being so painfully shy. You hid it well. No one knew you threw up before school every day or that we had to work combined spells to keep you functioning in public situations. They wouldn't know you still have problems. You've faced those fears by doing the things that terrify you and you're always successful. Outsiders see your beauty and brains and success. They don't see what you're hiding in private."

"Someone's coming up the path," Kate said without looking away from Hannah. She held out her hand to her sister. "We're all so proud of you, Hannah. Who cares what Jonas Harrington thinks?"

"It's not Harrington, although he's close by somewhere," Abbey said. "I think it's Sarah's gate crasher. You know, the one she spent the night with. I still can't get over that, and Elle says she wants every intimate detail the minute you get a chance."

"There are no intimate details," Sarah objected, exasperated. "I'm going to install a security system for him. Kate, don't let them read your books anymore, you're giving them wild imaginations."

"It wasn't our imaginations that he was kissing you," Hannah pointed out gleefully. "We *saw* you!"

"And you were kissing him back," Abbey added.

"Well, that part wasn't altogether my fault!" Sarah defended. "He's a *great* kisser. What could I do but kiss the man back?"

The sisters looked at one another solemnly and burst out laughing simultaneously. The dog curled up in the corner lifted his head and whined softly to get their attention.

"He's here, Sarah, and the gate must have opened for him a second time," Kate said, intrigued. "I really have to take a long look at the Drake history book. I want to see *exactly* what that prophecy says. How strange that something written hundreds of years ago applies to us even in this modern day and age."

"Kate, sweetie," Abbey said, "every age thinks it's progressive and modern but in reality we're going to be considered backward someday."

"He's on the verandah," Kate announced and hurried to the front door.

Her sisters trailed after her. Sarah's heart began to race. Damon was not the kind of man she had ever considered she'd be attracted to, yet she couldn't stop thinking about him. She thought a lot about his smile, the way two small dents appeared near the corners of his mouth. Intriguing, tempting little dents. He had the kind of smile that invited long drugging kisses, hot, melting together . . .

"Sarah!" Hannah hissed her name. "The temperature just went up a hundred degrees in here. You know you can't think like that around us. Sheesh! One day with this man and your entire moral code has collapsed."

Sarah considered arguing, but she didn't have much of a defense. If Damon hadn't been such a gentleman and stopped at just kissing, she might have made love to him. All right, she *would* have made love to him. She *should* have made love to him. She lay awake all night, hot and bothered and edgy with need. Darn the man for having chivalrous manners anyway. She smiled and touched her mouth with a feeling of awe. He had kissed her most of the night. Delicious, wonderful, sinfully rich kisses . . .

"Sarah!" All three of her sisters reprimanded her at once.

Sarah grinned at them unrepentantly. "I can't help it, he just affects me that way."

"Well, try not to throw yourself at him," Abbey urged. "It's so unbecoming in a Drake. Dignity at all times when it comes to men."

Hannah was looking out the window. She wrinkled her nose. "Kate, when you open the door for Damon, do let the dogs out for their morning romp. They've been cooped up all night, the poor things."

Kate nodded and obediently waved the dogs through as she greeted Damon. "How nice to see you, Mr. Wilder. Sarah has told us so much about you."

The dogs rushed past Damon. He leaned heavily on his cane, watching the large animals charge the sheriff, who was making his way up the path. Just as the man reached the gate, it swung closed with a loud bang. The dogs hit it hard, growling, baring their teeth, and digging frantically in an effort to get at their prey.

"This isn't funny, Hannah!" Jonas Harrington yelled. "I was *invited* by your sister and I showed up as a favor. Stop being so childish and call off your hounds."

Hannah smiled sweetly at Damon and held out her hand. "Pay no attention to the toad, Mr. Wilder, he comes around every now and then playing with his little gun, thinking he's going to impress the natives." She yawned, covering her mouth delicately. "It's so boring and childish but we have to humor him."

Sarah whistled sharply and the dogs instantly ceased growling, backing away from the fence to return to the house. When the animals were safely by her side, the gate swung open invitingly and the sheriff stalked through, his face a grim mask, his slashing gaze fixed on Hannah.

"What happens if you don't humor him?" Damon asked.

"Why, he throws his power around harassing us with tickets for speeding," Hannah said, holding her ground, her chin up.

"You *were* speeding, Hannah. Did you think I was going to let you off just because you're beautiful?" The sheriff shook hands with Damon. "Jonas Harrington, the only sane one when it comes to Baby Doll's true character."

Hannah flashed him a brilliant smile. Her sisters moved closer to her, protectively, Damon thought. "Why not, Sheriff? All the other cops *always* let me off." She turned on her heel and walked away.

Kate and Abbey let out a collective soft sigh.

"You gave my sister a ticket?" Sarah asked, outraged. "Jonas, you really are a self-centered toad. Why can't you just leave her alone? It's so high school to keep up grudges. Get over it."

"She was the one speeding like a teenager," Jonas pointed out. "Aside from feeding me to your dogs, did you have a real reason for inviting me up here?"

Taunting laughter floated back to them. "Don't flatter yourself, Harrington; nobody *wants* you here."

As Jonas Harrington stepped into the house, the ivy hanging from the ceiling swayed precariously and a thick ropy vine slapped him in the back of his head. Jonas spun around, his hands up as if to fight. He shoved the plant away from him and stormed into the living room, muttering foul curses beneath his breath.

Damon was behind him and stopped immediately, looking warily around the room, then back to the ivy. "Do your plants eat your visitors often?" he asked with grave curiosity as he pushed the vine away from him with his cane. Gingerly he walked around the masses of greenery.

"Only the ones who are mean to my sisters," Sarah replied.

Without warning, startling both of them, Damon suddenly reached out, caught Sarah by the nape of her neck, and dragged her to him. His mouth fastened on hers hungrily. Sarah melted into him. Merged. Became liquid fire. Went up in flames. Her arms crept around his neck. The cane dropped on the floor and they were devouring each other. The world fell away until there was only Damon and Sarah and raging need.

"*Sarah!*" The name shimmered in the air, breaking them apart so that they just stood, clinging, staring into each other's eyes, drowning. Shocked.

Sarah blinked, trying to focus, then looked around and blushed when she saw Jonas Harrington gaping. "Close your mouth, Jonas," she commanded, her tone daring him to make a comment. She'd known Jonas all of her life. Of course he couldn't pass up the opportunity. She waited, cringing.

"Holy smoke." Jonas held out his hand to Damon. "You're a god. Kissing a Drake woman is dangerous, kind of like taking a chance on kissing a viper. You just dove right in and went for it." He pumped Damon's hand with great enthusiasm.

"Ha ha." Sarah glared at the sheriff. "Don't you start, and don't you spread any rumors either, Jonas. I'm already annoyed with you for giving Hannah a ticket."

The smile faded from the sheriff's face. "I don't think because a woman is drop-dead gorgeous she should be treated any differently. She has everything too easy, Sarah. You all treat her like a little baby doll."

"You don't know Hannah at all, Jonas, and you don't deserve to know her. She wouldn't expect you to let her slide because of her looks, you idiot." Sarah threw her hands into the air. "Forget it, I'm finished trying to explain anything to you. If you don't understand friendship by now you never will. Let's get on with this. Damon and I have a busy schedule today." She gestured toward a chair.

Harrington was looking toward the stairs.

"Sit!" Sarah demanded. "This is business. Murder. Right up your alley, Jonas."

Chapter Six

Jonas Harrington listened calmly while Sarah told him the events that had taken place the night before. His dark features hardened perceptibly while she talked. He flicked a smoldering glare toward Kate and Abbey. "Why wasn't I called last night? I might have been able to do something last night. Damn it, Sarah, where's your head? You could have been killed!"

"Well, I wasn't. I saved the rifle for you, hoping you might get prints off of it, but I doubt it." Sarah smiled at him.

Jonas shook his head. "Don't do that; you've been giving me that same smile since kindergarten and it always gets you out of trouble." He gestured toward her face. "Take a long look at her, Damon, because that's going to be her answer every time she does something you don't like." He leaned forward in his chair, his eyes slashing at her. "What about your sisters? Did it even occur to you that you might bring these people down on your own house?"

Furious, he rose, a big man, moving like a jungle cat, pacing restlessly through the long living room. "These men are professionals. You both know that. Whatever you did to bring this on . . . "

"He worked in a high-security job, Jonas, nothing illegal. It isn't drug related so get that right out of your head."

Damon leaned back in his chair, torn between worry that he'd placed the Drake family in danger and feeling pleased that Sarah had turned protective. She immediately had become a fierce tigress ready to spring if the sheriff continued to cast aspersions on his character.

"I want to know what we're up against. And don't start throwing words around like security clearance to me. If we have a couple of men willing to break into a house with a high-powered rifle—"

"They had a tranq dart in it," Sarah interrupted hastily.

"I was kidnapped, along with my assistant, nearly a year ago. My assistant was killed and I barely escaped with my life." As Damon spoke, a dark shadow fell across the room. Outside, the ocean waves thundered and sprayed into the air. "They wanted information that could have affected the security of our nation and I refused to give it to them." Damon passed a hand over his face as if wiping away a nightmare. "I know that sounds melodramatic, but . . . " He slowly unbuttoned his shirt to expose his chest and the whorls and scars left behind. "I want you to know what these people are like."

The shadow lengthened and grew along the wall behind Damon. The shadow began to take shape, gray, translucent, but there all the same, growing in form until a faceless ghoul emerged with outstretched arms and a long thin body. The mouth yawned open wide, a gesture of greed and craving for the addiction Death had developed. The arms could have been reaching for either Jonas or Damon.

Damon hunched away from Jonas, pain flickering across his face, his shoulders stiffening as if under a great load.

Alarmed, Hannah reached out and jerked Jonas halfway across the room out of harm's way. Jonas swore under his breath and planted his feet firmly, thinking she was attempting to throw him out of the house.

Sarah adjusted the blinds at the window, filtering out the light, and returned to Damon's side, touching him gently. That was all. The lightest of touches. She simply laid her hand over his, yet peace stole into him as he buttoned his shirt. The terrible weight that always seemed to be pressing him into the ground lightened.

Kate's eyes filled with tears and she pressed her fingers to her mouth.

Abbey left the room to return with a cup of tea. "Drink this, Damon," she said. "You'll enjoy the taste."

The aroma alone added to the soothing touch Sarah had provided. He didn't think to ask how she had managed to make hot tea in a matter of seconds.

"I could use a cup of tea," Jonas said, "if anyone's asking. And a touch of sanity in the house would be nice, too. Baby Doll was going to huck me right out the door and you all just stood there watching."

"I'll make it for you." Hannah leaned against the door frame and looked up at the sheriff. Her fingers twisted together, the only sign of her agitation. "Do you like it sweet? I'm certain I can come up with an appropriate concoction."

"I think I'll pass altogether. One of these days I'm going to retaliate, Hannah."

She made a face at him as he crossed to the sliding-glass door to stare outside at the pounding waves. "I have a bad feeling about this, Sarah. I know you're used to doing things differently and people have no idea how you do it. Maybe you don't know either, I certainly don't, but I believe in you. I sometimes just feel things. It's one of the things that makes me good at my job." He turned to look at her. "I have a *very* bad feeling about this. Frankly, I'm afraid for all of you."

There was a small silence. "I believe you, Jonas," Sarah said. "I've always known you had a gift."

His gaze moved around the room, restlessly touching on each woman. "I've known this family since I was a boy. Feuds"—his smoldering gaze went to Hannah—"are petty when it comes to your safety. I'm not losing any of you over this. I want to be called if one of you stubs your toe. If you see a stranger or you hear a funny noise. I'm not kidding around with you over this issue. I want your word that you'll call me. You have my private number as well as the number to the office and 911."

"Jonas, don't worry, we'll be fine. I'm very good at what I do," Sarah said with complete confidence.

Jonas took a step toward her, very reminiscent of a stalking panther. Damon was grateful he was too old to be intimidated. "I want your word. Every one of you."

Damon nodded. "I have to agree with Harrington. These men tortured us. They don't play around. I'll admit when I'm around you, I feel magic in the air, but these men are evil and capable of torture and murder. I have to know you're all safe or I'll have to leave this town."

"Damon!" Sarah looked stricken. "They'll just follow you." Worse, he would carry Death with him wherever he chose to go.

"Then cooperate with the sheriff. Give him whatever he needs to stop these men." As ridiculous as it seemed when he'd just met her, Damon couldn't bear the thought of leaving Sarah, but he wasn't about to risk her life.

"I don't mind calling you, Jonas," Kate said readily.

Abbey held up her hand. "I'm in."

Sarah nodded. "I'm always grateful for help from the local law."

All eyes turned to Hannah. She shrugged indifferently. "Whatever helps Damon, I'm willing to do."

Jonas ignored the grudge in her voice and nodded. "I want all of you to watch your step. Be aware of your surroundings and any strangers. Keep those dogs close and lock up the house!"

"We're all over it," Sarah agreed. "Really, Jonas, we don't want any part of men with guns. We'll call you even if the cat meows."

He looked a little mollified. "I'll want extra patrols around here as well as around Damon's house, Sarah."

"Well, of course, Jonas," Sarah agreed.

"It will give me every opportunity to make friends with them," Hannah said. "I don't know many of the new people in town."

Jonas glared at her. "You and your slinky body can just stay away from my deputies."

Hannah made a face at him, raised her hand to push at the

hair spilling across her face. An icy wind rushed through the room, giving life to the curtains, so that they danced in a macabre fashion, fluttering, reaching toward Jonas as if to bind him in the thick folds.

Sarah glimpsed a dark shadow moving within the drapes. Her hands went up in a casual, graceful wave. Kate and Abbey followed the gentle movements with their own. The wind died abruptly and the curtains dropped into place.

Damon cleared his throat. "Does someone want to tell me what happened?"

Jonas shook his head. "Never be dumb enough to ask for an explanation from any of them, Damon. You might get it and your hair will turn gray." His gaze swung to Hannah. "Don't even think about it. Ladies, I can find my own way out."

Damon didn't take his eyes from Sarah. She was looking at Hannah and there was accusation in her gaze. Out of the corner of his eye, he could see Abbey and Kate doing the same thing.

Hannah threw her hands into the air. "I wasn't thinking, okay? I'm sorry."

The silence lengthened, disapproval thick in the room.

Hannah sighed. "I really am sorry. I forgot for just a moment about Dea—" She broke off abruptly, her gaze shifting to Damon. "About the other thing we're dealing with. It won't happen again."

"It better not," Sarah said. "You can't afford to forget for one moment. This is too dangerous, Hannah."

"Wait a minute," Damon interrupted. "If you're talking about me and those men the other night, I don't want your family involved in any way."

"The men?" Kate raised her eyebrow. "Not in the least, Damon, didn't give them a thought. There are things far more dangerous than human beings."

He watched the four women exchange long knowing looks and was exasperated. They knew something he didn't. Something regarding him. "I can understand why poor Harrington gets so frustrated with you."

Sarah rose and blew him a kiss. "He loves all seven of us. He just likes to puff out his chest."

"He was genuinely worried," Damon said. "And I am, too. The things he said make sense. It's bad enough to think of you in danger, let alone all your sisters." He raked a hand through his hair in agitation. "I can't be responsible for that."

To his shock they all laughed. "Damon." Sarah's voice was a mixture of amusement and tenderness. "We accepted responsibility for our own decisions a very long time ago. We're grown women. When we choose to involve ourselves in problems, we accept the consequences." She leaned toward him.

Abbey groaned dramatically. "She's going to do it. She's going to kiss him right in front of us."

"That is so not fair, Sarah," Hannah protested.

"Go ahead," Kate encouraged. "I need to write a good love scene."

When Sarah hesitated, her gaze lost in his, Damon took advantage and did the job thoroughly, not wanting to let Kate down.

Chapter Seven

Damon heard laughter drifting up from the beach as he limped around the corner of his deck to set his teacup on the small table beside his rocking chair. His hip was bothering him more than usual and Sarah wasn't there to make it better. She'd spent the last several days dragging more and more equipment into his house, setting up a security system that might rival Fort Knox.

Jonas Harrington followed him, but instead of taking the chair Damon waved him toward, he stepped to the corner of the deck to watch the figures running barefoot in the sand on the beach far below. "They're up to something."

Damon sank into his chair where he had a great view of that small, private beach. The Drake sisters often were on it, day or night, their laughter drifting on the wind, the sound as soothing as the sea itself.

He missed Sarah. It was silly to miss someone when he saw her every single day. He'd always been a loner and it didn't make sense to him to need to see her quick, flashing smile. He especially loved to watch her eyes light up each time she saw him. He'd take the memory of that expression on her face to his grave.

"I'm beginning to think there really is something magical about the Drake family. I've never needed to be around anyone, but I can't imagine never seeing Sarah Drake again. I thought my life was my work. My brain runs a hundred miles an hour, always sorting through ideas, but she calms me. Don't ask me how." Damon could pick her out easily, her long dark hair blowing free in the wind. She often swept it up in a ponytail, her natural beauty so real to him when she thought nothing of her looks. "She doesn't think she's beautiful. Isn't that strange?"

Jonas shrugged. "I don't think any of them think about their looks all that much, other than Baby Doll. They spoil her and treat her like a little princess." He raked a hand through his hair, frowning. "Well, I shouldn't say that." His gaze remained on the tall, thin blonde with the waves of platinum hair streaming down her back. "Sometimes I think they cater to her—and other times I think they take advantage of her. Don't ask me how, it's just a feeling."

"You like them." Damon took a sip of the hot tea. He never drank tea as a rule, but Sarah had brought him a special blend from Hannah and he found it made him feel better when the weight of guilt and memories seemed to crouch heaviest on his shoulder.

"I love them," Jonas corrected. "They're family. *My* family. I take that very seriously, even if they don't. They spend all of their time getting into trouble, and I don't mean something casual, I mean something dangerous."

"Like me." Damon returned the cup to the saucer and sighed. "Sarah won't back off. She took the job of guarding me and nothing I say will stop her. I've thought a hundred times about leaving so she'd be safe, but . . . " He trailed off, wishing he were a bigger man. He'd never had anyone look at him the way Sarah did and he just couldn't quite make himself give that up.

"She'd just follow you, Damon," Jonas said. "The Drakes are tenacious. Once they sink their teeth into a problem, it gets resolved, because they don't know the meaning of the word quit. Sarah won't quit you, so don't quit her."

Damon didn't flinch away from the steel in Jonas's eyes. "Don't worry, Harrington, I hear your warning. I doubt very much I can hurt Sarah, other than if my past does, but she's in danger of ripping out my heart and handing it to me on a silver platter."

"You've got it that bad?"

"Hell yes, I do. I never thought it would happen to me and in such a short time, too. I can't stop thinking about her." His mouth was dry and his heart pounding just talking about Sarah. He couldn't imagine why a woman so full of life and laughter and love would choose to be with someone so melancholy and dark. He didn't have the least bit of social skills and tended to run roughshod over people with his intellect. He rarely engaged in small, polite conversation and, in fact, knew he was rarely polite. It had never mattered before, but it mattered to Sarah.

"If it helps, I've never seen Sarah really interested in a man before. She dated some, but kept it away from the family and Sea Haven. All the girls probably have dated, but we don't see it here." Jonas frowned and turned back toward the sounds drifting on the wind, his gaze finding the tallest of the Drake sisters.

"What is up with that locked gate they all talk about?" Damon asked.

"The infamous gate." Jonas smirked. "They keep that gate padlocked at all times, like that's going to save them from something."

"Save them from what?"

Jonas shrugged. "I think love. I hear them talk sometimes, but they don't tell me much and in all honesty, I don't want to know. Their house holds generations of power. Real power. I hate talking about this stuff because it sounds too heebie-jeebie for me. I like to deal in facts, not magic, but you can feel the power in the house. A few years back they decided to padlock that gate and it's been kept that way ever since."

"It wasn't locked a week after Sarah came home. When I came up the path leading to the house, it was standing open. I felt like the house was welcoming me. The inscriptions on the bottom of the gate, one in Italian and one in Latin say the same thing."

"You can read Italian and Latin?" Jonas grinned at him. "No wonder Sarah's attracted to you. What does it say? I always wanted to know but wasn't about to ask them."

"'The seven become one when united.' All the symbols have meanings as well. Several are symbols of protection. Do they practice ancient religion?"

"Who the hell knows what they practice. They're magic and

they have very real powers. Libby is a doctor and I've seen her work miracles. Abigail is a loose cannon sometimes. She utters the word 'truth' and everyone around her starts telling every secret they have. Hannah's just plain scary. Elle's very quiet and she doesn't talk much about what she can or can't do, but if she loses her temper, she could probably flatten Sea Haven. It drains them, though, to use their gifts. I've seen them to the point they can't walk or even talk. They drop in their tracks and it takes time for them to recover."

Damon looked up at the worry in the sheriff's voice. "What are you not saying to me? Why do you have that look on your face?"

Jonas nodded toward the beach. "They know something. Sarah has precog. At least I think she does. Every single morning I see her drive to your house."

"She's been working on a security system."

"I noticed. It's state of the art. But she didn't come this morning and she wasn't here this afternoon. And now it's evening and they're on the beach."

"Believe me, I know Sarah hasn't come to see me. It's all I can do not to pick up the phone and call her or go on down to that beach to see what she's up to."

"I think you should."

"Go down to the beach? I looked at the trail, Jonas. I don't think my hip will hold up."

"I'll be happy to help you."

"Why do I have the feeling you're trying to get me into big trouble with those women?"

Jonas flashed another grin. "Better you than me. The sun's

going to be setting soon and they're preparing for that. The moon rising to meet the setting sun. We can make it to the small dunes and sit there and watch them up close and personal. If you want to be part of Sarah's family, you're going to have to just accept that they can do extraordinary things."

"Like walk on water?"

"I wouldn't rule it out."

"You really are a believer. I don't know that I can believe in anything I can't back up with scientific fact."

Jonas's grin grew wider. "You're in for a few shocks, Wilder. Come on, you may as well learn what the Drake family is all about."

Damon wanted to see Sarah. And he was curious about the magic they supposedly wielded. He didn't believe in voodoo and other religions that called on something he couldn't see or feel. Hell, he didn't even know if he believed in God anymore. He had the sneaking suspicion he was beginning to believe there really was something different about the Drakes. And if that were true, where did that leave him? A man of science, grounded firmly in fact.

He stood up, leaning heavily on his cane. "Hell. It would be just my luck to fall in love with a woman who can do some kind of magic. I don't even go to magic shows. I can't enjoy them until I figure out how they do what they do and then it isn't all that impressive anymore."

"Prepare to be impressed and you're not going to find a scientific answer for anything these women do. I wouldn't even bother to try, Damon, you'll just drive yourself crazy. Let's take the car as far as we can and save your leg."

"You're off duty tonight?"

Jonas nodded. "The sisters are home so I figured I might con them out of a home-cooked meal. I like to spend time with them when they're home. They rejuvenate me. Sometimes my job is disturbing. Too many accidents on the highway. The crime in Sea Haven is about nil, but the outlying areas get a bit more. For all their nonsense, the Drakes soothe me."

Damon followed him out to the car, aware, as they walked, Jonas's restless gaze was quartering the area back and forth all around them, looking for danger. Damon ducked his head. He hated that small feeling, so helpless with his damaged hip and damaged soul. He couldn't stop the nightmares and he couldn't prevent others from being in danger just because they were around him.

Jonas started the car and pulled onto the highway. "There's a small dirt road leading to the back of the Drake property. We can reach the very top of the path down to the beach from there. Steps have been dug out and most of the way down there's actually a handrail. I think you'll be safe. In any case, you'd better be or Sarah will have my hide."

"She'll probably have it anyway," Damon said.

Jonas's grin was very much in evidence. "You do know that woman, even on such short acquaintance. She can keep the others in line as well. If you're really serious about her . . . " He glanced sideways at Damon for confirmation.

"Very serious."

"Sarah doesn't put up with nonsense. She likes straight answers. She's very tolerant of people, don't get me wrong, but she's loyal and has integrity and she expects the same from the people she lets into her life."

"Thanks, Harrington," Damon said gruffly.

"For what?"

"For thinking I have a chance with her. I never expected to fall in love. Certainly not this fast. I can't tell if she's just feeling sorry for me because my life's gone down the drain, or if she's genuinely interested."

"She kissed you, Wilder. Sarah doesn't go around kissing just anyone and certainly not in front of her family."

Damon couldn't help the little spurt of happiness that seemed to ease the weight bearing down so hard on his shoulders and chest. There were some mornings when he woke up feeling as if someone was crouched on top of him. On those days, he could hardly get out of bed and only Sarah's smile brought him a semblance of peace.

This morning he had awakened with sweat pouring from his body and the dark specter of death echoing through his dreams. His shower hadn't helped lift the weight and the rest of the day had been long and difficult. He'd been grateful to see Jonas when the sheriff had stopped by to check on him. Part of Damon was afraid he was getting too used to Sarah's presence and already relying on the joy and light that always surrounded her. He brooded over the fact that she hadn't come to see him, hadn't even called him. That scared the hell out of him. He didn't look at Jonas as they drove the small distance to the driveway leading to the Drake's private beach entrance.

Jonas parked the car just above the path leading to the beach below. He stepped out and went around to help Damon. The wind touched his face gently, almost as if fingertips were caressing him, seeking his attention. The sound of the surf pounded below him and the sound of women's voices drifted up with it. He couldn't tell if they were chanting, the voices sounded rhythmic, but for some reason, he felt a chill go through his body.

As Damon stepped out of the car, a dark shadow passed overhead. Jonas glanced up, but there were no clouds, only the setting sun and the rising moon, crossing paths over the wild waves of the sea. He glanced back at Damon and his breath caught in his throat. There was a black shadow on the rising wall behind them. The dark shape appeared to be hovering over Damon, actually crouching on his shoulders. Damon bent over with the weight of the apparition, leaning heavily on his cane.

Ice cold fingers of fear frissoned down Jonas's back. The black shape took on a face, a grinning skull with skin stretched back and bony arms stretching toward Damon. Jonas stepped in front of the other man instinctively. He heard the chant swell in volume, the voices much more clear, carried on the breeze. The sky turned blood red and the boom of the sea was louder as the wind rose to a shriek, ripping and tugging at the black shape in an effort to dislodge it from Damon's shoulders.

Weight settled on Jonas and he watched the black shadow on the rock as it stretched in an effort to encompass his frame as well as Damon's.

"I can't move," Damon said. "And I'm cold all the way through my body." He hunched his shoulders against a terrible weight, his hand absently rubbing his chest, right over his heart. "What's wrong with me?"

"I don't know," Jonas said grimly. But he feared he did know. The Drake sisters were fighting for Damon's life and because he had dared to step between Damon and that shadow, they were fighting for his life as well. He felt helpless standing there with the wind blowing on his face, afraid to move, afraid the shadow would take Damon. The claws seemed stretched with greed, the head of the thing leaning toward Damon as if trying to draw the breath from his body.

The voices swelled in volume—feminine, strong, united. Not just the four on the beach, but the three other sisters reaching from distant places to join so the seven had become united as one. Jonas felt the strength and power pouring through them into him. Small glittering colors sparkled and leapt with life. Small fireworks crackled as they formed a wall between the two men and the apparition.

The shadow drew back sharply, careful to avoid the sizzling lights. Jonas felt the weight on his shoulders lessen. Damon stood a little straighter. The gray lines etched so deep in his face faded.

Jonas drew in a breath as he felt a hand brush his. He looked down, expecting to see someone beside him, gripping his fingers tightly. The sensation was there. Soft. Firm. In control. Yet no one was there. He stood alone with the wind on his face, ruffling his hair and the feel of someone holding him tightly, a feminine body pressed close to his. Everything male in him roared with protest. One of the Drakes—it felt like Hannah—shielded him, and that was just unacceptable.

He made out the shapes of several women with long flowing hair, arms raised to the sky in the midst of the crackling fireworks, insubstantial figures wavering in the air as if they were spirit rather than flesh and blood. Behind him, Damon swore softly under his breath, the actual words unintelligible, but Jonas had the same strong sense of real danger. Damon didn't want to hide behind the women any more than Jonas did.

Jonas tried to move, to step forward, to push his way through that wall of glittering lights and transparent figures to get at the crouching dark shape that was retreating slowly, driven back by the women as they pushed him away from the cliff and out toward the ocean. The soft chant was clear now, the voices strong, blending with the wind and pounding sea, filling Jonas's head with a strange kind of music.

He turned his head to follow the movement of the shadow as it took to the air, the retreat painfully slow as it moved over the sea. A whale breached and three dolphins spun in the air, spraying droplets of water in an arc over the crashing waves, all four silhouetted against the bloodred sky. The shadow's mouth yawned wide as it looked back toward the beach where the four women danced, arms raised, bare feet following a complicated pattern in the sand, arms lifted toward the heavens.

The wind howled, rose to a shriek, and gusted toward the apparition, driving it so far away it was merely a spec on the horizon. Jonas stared at it, blinking. When he looked around, the glittering fireworks were gone and the wind had died down to nothing. He glanced at the beach below and saw Sarah, Kate, Abigail, and Hannah lying unmoving on the sand.

"Get in the car, Damon." Jonas yanked the door open. "Hurry."

Damon did as directed, the echoes of the strange terror still gripping him. "What the hell is going on? I didn't see anything but fireworks, but I was ..."

"Afraid," Jonas finished for him. "I don't know what the hell went on here tonight and I'm not sure if I want to know. Just get in the car. I need to take you home."

"Where's Sarah?"

"She's with her sisters on beach. I'll go down to them, but the things I have to say are better said alone." Grimly the sheriff slammed the door and drove faster than he should have to return Damon to the safety of his home. "Stay inside and use that security system Sarah's always fussing over. I'll call later to make certain everything's all right. My deputy, Jackson Deveau, will drive by several times tonight."

Jonas would have used the siren to return to the beach if it would have gotten him there faster. He was so angry he was certain he shouldn't go, he should stay away from the Drakes until his temper cooled and the fear left his body, but he couldn't just leave them lying exhausted on the beach.

He strode across the wet sand, fury building with every step he took. "What the hell did you all think you were doing?" The sight of their pale faces, worn with fatigue only stepped up his anger. "You were playing with something you sure as hell shouldn't have been playing with."

Sarah lifted a weak hand and waved him away. Hannah didn't look up and Kate and Abbey stared at him, their eyes enormous in their pale faces. He dropped onto his knees in the middle of them, reaching out to run his hand up and down over their arms to rub warmth back into them.

"What was it, Sarah?" he asked.

"Do you really want to know?"

She sounded so utterly weary he nearly kept his mouth shut.

For once, Hannah wasn't sassing him and all of the Drakes looked frightened.

"Hell yes, I want to know."

"Death. You saw death, Jonas. It's how you're connected to us, why you are." Sarah glanced at her sisters and then back at his face. "You have a gift, just as we do. You deny yours and we embrace ours. Death showed you his face and he'll be back. We weakened him, but he'll be back and soon. He has too tight a grip on Damon." She said the last with a small hiccup in her voice.

At once her three sisters put their hands on her in an obvious attempt to comfort her. Jonas moved closer to Hannah and lifted her slightly so she could rest her head in his lap. He dragged Abigail closer as well until she had her head on his thigh. Sarah and Kate followed suit. He listened to the sound of the ocean, allowing the familiar melody to calm his mind and think more rationally.

"Why is death after Damon?" He felt like a fool asking the question. When the Drakes did their magic he preferred to be somewhere distant. He knew what they did and he even accepted it, but he always rationalized anything too spooky. Tonight didn't fit into a neat box and he sure as hell was never going to admit to seeing anything or having gifts or curses or anything else he couldn't find a scientific explanation for.

Sarah shrugged. "I don't think it much matters who death takes as long as he has someone. I don't want that someone to be Damon—or you."

"Me?"

"You stood in front of it. You confronted Death. Why did you do that?"

"Damn it, Sarah. It was a shadow. A shape on the wall and it looked as if it wanted to consume Wilder. I was afraid for him. I just did what seemed right."

"You brought yourself to his attention. You never want to do that," Sarah said. "Some things are better left alone."

"Well, you sure as hell must have his attention. And don't ever protect me like that again. I don't want any of you hurt trying to keep something like that off of me. I don't even know if I believe in all this mumbo jumbo. And if I don't, it can't hurt me." He wanted to shake some sense into them and at the same time he wanted to hold them close where he could protect them. Give him a flesh-and-blood criminal any day of the week, one he could see and fight. He forced calm into his voice when his heart was still pounding in fear for them. "Just don't ever do that again. I protect you. That's the way it's always been with us and that's the way it always will be. I'm taking you all up to the house and making you tea. Unless I decide to drop one or two of you in the ocean. I never want to talk about this again and if you bring it up, I swear I'm denying everything."

He wasn't making much sense but he didn't care. He just wanted them back inside their home where he knew they would be safe. And then he was going to think long and hard about getting drunk.

Chapter Eight

"So, Sarah," Damon said, putting down his glass of iced tea as they sat on his porch. Damon and Sarah spent every minute they could find together. Taking walks on the beach. Working on a security system for his house. Lazy days of laughter and whispered confidences. Damon enjoyed every moment spent in her home, getting to know her sisters. He never ran out of things to say to Sarah and he loved her stories and open personality. There was sunshine in his life and its name was Sarah.

She took a handful of his chips and smiled at him. Overhead the seagulls circled, looking down with hopeful eyes. Damon had had no more unwelcome nighttime visitors and appreciated the regularity of the sheriff driving by to check the neighborhood.

Damon shook his head, dazzled by her smile. She could take every thought out of his head with that smile. "Sarah, are you afraid for me or for everyone else? It's occurred to me that there's always this buffer between everyone we run across and me. I didn't really notice at first, but last night I was thinking about it. I'm getting to know you and I think you prefer that your friends don't see you with me."

Sarah's breath caught in her throat at the hint of pain in his voice. The more time she spent with him, the more she wanted to be with him. And the dark shadow surrounding him gripped him all the harder. "I don't mind anyone seeing us together. You're the one worried about gossip. I'm used to it and it doesn't bother me."

"Then we'll go into town together." It was a challenge.

Sarah let out her breath. The early morning fog had burned off, leaving the sky an amazing shade of blue. She could see clouds gathering far out over the sea. She looked carefully at Damon, inspecting every inch of him. There was no dark shadow around him and his shoulders weren't hunched as if carrying a great weight. "Sounds great, if you're really certain you want to brave it."

He stood up and held out his hand to her. "Come on."

"Right now?" She hadn't expected he would really want to go, but she obediently took his hand and allowed him to help her up.

"Yes, while I have my courage up. Walking with you through town should set a match to the gossips. The story will spread like wildfire."

Sarah laughed softly, knowing it was true. Once they had walked the short distance to the town, she started in the direction of the grocery store, determined to get it over with.

"I feel a little sorry for Harrington," Damon said as he

walked with Sarah along the main street of town. "He drops by the house sometimes and he's very nice." He reached out and tangled his fingers with Sarah's.

"Are you certain you want to do this?" Sarah's voice was skeptical. "Holding my hand in public is going to bring the spotlight shining very brightly on you. Rumors are going to race through town faster than a seagull flies. I know how much your privacy means to you."

"That was before I retired. When I worked from morning until night and had no life." Damon laughed softly. He was happy. Looking at her made him happy. Walking with her, talking with her. It was ridiculous how happy he was when he was in her company. It made no sense but he wasn't going to question a gift from the heavens. "We may as well give them something real to gossip about."

Sarah's laugh floated on the breeze, a melodious sound that turned heads. "Not 'gossip,' Damon, it's 'news.' No one gossips here. You have to get it straight."

Damon listened to the sound of their shoes on the wooden walkway. Everything was so different with Sarah. He felt as if he'd finally come home. He looked around him to the picturesque homes, so quaint and unique. It no longer felt alien or hostile to him; the people were eccentric, but endearing. How had Sarah done that? Mysterious Sarah. Even the wind welcomed her back home. His fingers tightened around hers, holding her to him. He wasn't altogether certain Sarah was human and he feared she might fly away from him without warning, joining the birds out over the sea.

She waved to a young woman on a porch. "They're good

people, Damon. You won't find more accepting people in your life than the ones living here."

"Even Harrington?" he teased.

"I feel a little sorry for him, too," Sarah answered seriously. "Most of the time, Jonas is a caring, compassionate man and very good with everyone, but he just refuses to see the truth about Hannah. He looks at her and only sees what's on the outside. She's always been beautiful. He was very popular with the girls in school, an incredible athlete, tons of scholarships, the resident dreamboat. He thought Hannah was stuck up because she never spoke to him. He made her life a living hell, teasing her unmercifully all through school. She's never forgiven him and he'll never understand why. He's a good man and he wasn't being malicious in school. From his perspective, he was just teasing. He has no idea Hannah is painfully shy and he never will."

Damon made a dissenting noise in his throat. "She's a supermodel, Sarah—on the cover of every magazine there is. She travels all over the world. And, I have to say, she appears very confident on every television and news interview and talk show I've seen her on. I would never associate her with the word 'shy.'"

"She hyperventilates before speaking in public; in fact, she carries a paper bag with her. Most of the talk show hosts and interviewers are careful with her. Because she's painfully shy doesn't mean she allows it to affect her life."

"Why wouldn't you just clue Harrington in?"

"Why should he judge Hannah so harshly, just because she looks the way she does? My sister Joley is striking as well, although not in exactly the same way. Jonas would never dare

331

torment her. All of my sisters are good-looking and he doesn't use that sarcastic tone on them. He only does it to Hannah and in front of everyone."

Damon heard the fierce protective note in her voice and smiled. He drew her closer beneath his broad shoulder. His Sarah. Without warning, fear struck, deep, haunting, sharp like a knife. His breath left his lungs. "Sarah? Are we thinking the same thing? I've never wanted someone in my life before. Not once. I've only just met you and can't imagine the rest of my life without you." He raked his fingers through his hair, his cane nearly hitting his head. "Do you know what I sound like? An obsessed stalker. I'm not like this with women, Sarah."

Her eyes danced. "That leaves wide-open territory, Damon. You're talking about a family with six sisters and a billion cousins. I have a million aunts and uncles. You can't leave yourself open like that or they're going to tease you unmercifully."

They halted in front of the grocery store. Damon faced her, catching her chin in his hand to tilt her face up to his. "I'm serious, Sarah. I know I want a future with you in it. I have to know we're on the same page."

Sarah went up on her toes to press a kiss to his mouth. "Here's a little news flash for you, Damon. I don't compromise my jobs by getting involved with my clients. I don't, as a rule, kiss strange men and spend the night wishing they'd make the big move."

"You want me to make a move on you?"

Sarah laughed, tugged at his hand, dragging him into the store. "Of course I do."

"Well, this is a hell of a time to tell me."

Inez was at the store window with three of her customers, staring at Sarah and Damon with their mouths open. Damon scowled at them. "Is it fly-catching season?"

Sarah squeezed his hand tightly in warning. All the while she was smiling serenely. "Inez! We just dropped in for a quick minute. Kate and Hannah and Abigail are in town for a few days and they can't wait to see you! Joley and Elle and Libby send their love and told me to tell you they hope to get back soon." Her voice was bright and cheerful, dispelling an air of gloom in the store. "You do know Damon, of course."

Inez nodded, her hawklike gaze narrowing in shock on their linked hands. Her throat worked convulsively. "Yes, of course I do. I didn't know you two were *intimate* friends."

Damon glared at her, daring the woman to imply anything else. Sarah simply laughed. "I snagged him the minute I saw him, Inez. You always told me to settle down with a good man and, well . . . here he is."

"I never guessed, and Mr. Wilder didn't say a single word," Inez said.

Damon forced a smile under the subtle pressure of Sarah's grip. Her nails were biting into his hand. "Call me Damon, Inez. I never managed to catch you alone." It was the best excuse he could come up with and sound plausible. It must have worked because Inez beamed at him, bestowing on him a smile she reserved for her closest friends. In spite of himself, Damon could feel a tiny glow of pleasure at the acceptance.

"How is everything lately?" Sarah asked before Damon could warn her it was a bad idea to get Inez started.

"Honestly, Sarah, Donna over at the gift shop is a lovely

woman but she just doesn't understand the importance of recycling. Just this morning I saw her dump her papers right in with plastic. I've sorted for her many times and showed her the easiest way to go about it but she just can't get the hang of it. Be a dear and do something about it, won't you?"

Damon's mouth nearly fell open at the request. What did Inez want Sarah to do? Separate the woman's garbage for her?

"No problem, Inez. I'll go over there now. Damon and I are hoping some of our friends will help us with a small problem. There are some strangers who have been in town, probably for a week or two—three men. We'd like to know their whereabouts, their movements, that sort of thing. Unfortunately we don't have a clear description but one of them has a facial injury, most likely around his jaw. I'm hoping another might have gotten bitten by a tick." She paused, a wicked little grin playing around the corners of her mouth. "Maybe a lot of ticks."

"What have they done?" Inez asked, lowering her voice as if she'd joined a conspiracy.

"They tried to break into Damon's house. Jonas has all the information we could give him. He was going to check the hospital and clinic." She'd turned over the tranquilizer gun to him, too. "If someone spots them, or mentions them to you, would you mind giving me a call? And maybe it would be good to call Jonas, too."

"Now, dear, you know I don't believe in sticking my nose into anyone's business, but if you really need me to help you, I'll be more than happy to oblige," Inez said. "There are always so many tourists but we should be able to spot a man with something wrong with his jaw."

Sarah leaned over to kiss Inez affectionately. "You're such a good friend, Inez. I don't know what we'd all do without you." She turned to look at the three customers. "Irene, I hope you don't mind me bringing Damon when I call on you and Drew this afternoon." She wanted to assess Drew's condition before she brought her sisters over and raised Irene's hopes further. "We just want to visit with him a few minutes," she added hastily. "We won't tire him."

Irene's expression brightened considerably. "Thank you, Sarah; of course you can bring anyone you want with you. I told Drew you might be dropping by and he was so excited. He'll love the company. He rarely sees even his friends any-more."

"Good, I can't wait to see him again. Now don't go to any trouble, Irene. Last time I came to visit, you had an entire lunch-eon waiting." Sarah rubbed Damon's arm. "Irene is such a wonderful cook."

"Oh, she is," Inez agreed readily. "Her baked goods are always the first to go at every fundraiser."

Irene broke into a smile, looking pleased.

The warmth in Damon's heart rushed to his belly, heated his blood. Sarah spread sunshine. That had to be her secret. Wherever she went, she just spread goodwill to others because she genuinely cared about them. It wasn't that she was being merely tolerant; she liked her neighbors with all their idiosyn-crasies. He couldn't help the strange feeling of pride sweeping through him. How had he gotten so lucky?

Damon pushed his sunglasses onto his nose as they mean-dered across the street. He saw they were heading toward the colorful gift shop. "Are you really going to sort some woman's garbage, Sarah?"

"Of course not, I'm just popping in to say hello. Maybe our intruders will buy a memento of their stay or possibly a gift for someone. You never know, we may as well cover all the bases," Sarah replied blithely.

Damon laughed. "Sarah, honey, I hardly think kidnappers are going to take the time to buy a memento of their stay. I could be wrong, but it seems rather unlikely."

Sarah simply grinned at him. She took his breath away with her smile. She should have always been in his life. By his side. All those years working, never thinking about anything else, and Sarah had been somewhere in the world. If he had met her earlier, he might have retired sooner and . . .

"Do you have any idea how perfectly tempting your mouth is, Damon?" Sarah interrupted his thoughts, her voice matter-of-fact, intensely interested.

"Sarah! Sarah Drake! Yoo-hoo!" A tall woman of Amazonian proportions and extraordinary skin waved wildly, intercepting them. An older man, obviously her father, and a teenage boy followed her at a much more sedate pace.

The clouds, gathering ominously over the sea, so far away only minutes earlier, moved inward at a rapid rate. The wind howled, blowing in from the sea, carrying something dark and dangerous with it. Icy fingers touched Sarah's face, almost a caress of delight . . . or challenge. She watched Damon's face, his body, as he accepted the weight, a settling of his shoulders, small lines appearing near his mouth. He didn't appear to notice, already far too familiar with his grim companion.

She moved closer to Damon, a purely protective gesture as the two men approached them in the wake of the woman. The welcoming smile faded from Sarah's face. A shadow moved on the walkway, slithering along the ground, a wide dark net casting for prey. "Patsy, it's been a long time." But she was looking at the older man. "Mr. Granger. How nice to see you again. And Pete, I'm so glad we ran into you. I'm visiting Drew soon. I'll be able to tell him I saw you. I'll bet he'll be happy to hear from you."

Pete Granger scuffed the toe of his boot on the sidewalk. "I should go see him. It's been awhile. I didn't know what to say."

Sarah placed her hand on his shoulder. Damon could see she was worried. "You'll find the right thing to say to him. That's what friendship is, Pete, to be there in good and bad times. The good is easy, the bad, well"—she shrugged—"that's a bit more difficult. But you've always been incredibly tough and Drew's best friend. I know you'll be there for him."

Pete nodded his head. "Tell him I'll be over this evening."

Sarah smiled her approval. "I think that's a great idea, Pete." She touched the elder Granger with gentle fingers. "How did your visit to the cardiologist go?"

"Why, Sarah," Patsy answered, "Dad doesn't have a cardiologist. There's nothing wrong with his heart."

"Really? It never hurts to be safe, Mr. Granger. Checkups are always so annoying but ultimately necessary. Patsy, do you remember that cardiologist my mother went to when we were in our first year of college? In San Francisco?"

Patsy exchanged a long look with her father. "I do remember,

Sarah. Maybe we could get him in next month when things settle down at the shop."

"These things are always better if you insist on taking care of them immediately," Sarah prompted. "This is Damon Wilder, a friend of mine. Have you three met yet?"

Damon was simply astonished. Pete was going to go visit his very ill friend and Mr. Granger was going to see a cardiologist, all at Sarah's suggestion. He looked closer at the older man. He couldn't see that Granger looked sick. What had Sarah seen that he hadn't? There was no doubt in his mind that the cardiologist was going to find something wrong with Mr. Granger's heart.

Sarah asked the three of them to keep an eye out for strangers with bruises on their face or jaw and the trio agreed before hurrying away.

"How do you do that?" Damon asked, intrigued. She was doing something, knew things she shouldn't know.

"Do what?" Sarah asked. "I have no idea what you're talking about."

Damon studied her face there on the street with the sunlight shining down on them. He couldn't stop looking at her, couldn't stop wanting her. Couldn't believe she was real. "You see something beyond the human eye, Sarah, something science can't explain. I believe in science, yet I can't find an explanation for what you do."

Damon was looking at her with so much hunger, so much stark desire in his expression, Sarah's heart melted on the spot and her body went up in flames. "It's a Drake legacy. A gift." Wherever she had been going was gone out of her head. She couldn't think of anything but Damon and the need on his face, the hunger in his eyes. Her fingers tangled in the front of his shirt, right outside the gift shop in plain sight of the interested townspeople.

"The Drake gate prophecy forgot to mention the intensity of the physical attraction," she murmured.

A man could drown in her eyes, be lost forever. His hands tightened possessively, brought her closer to him, right up against his body. Every cell reacted instantly. Whips of lightning danced in his bloodstream while tongues of fire licked his skin, at the simple touch of her fully clothed body. What was going to happen when she was naked, completely bare beneath him? "I might not survive," he whispered.

"Would we care?" Sarah asked. She couldn't look away from him, couldn't stop staring into his eyes. She wanted him. Ached for him. Wanted to be alone with him. It didn't matter where, just that they were alone.

"You can't look at me like that," Damon said. "I'm going up in flames and I'm too damned old to be acting like a teenager."

"No, you're not," Sarah denied. "By all means, I don't mind at all." She half-turned toward the street, still in his arms. "I think Inez is falling out of her window. Poor thing, she's bound to lose her eyesight if she keeps this up. I should have suggested she get a new pair of glasses. I'll let Abigail suggest it. You have to be careful with Inez because she's so sensitive."

It was the way Sarah said it, so absolutely sincere, that tugged at his heartstrings. "I never could get along with people. Ever. Not even in college. Everyone always annoyed me. I preferred books and my lab to talking with a human being," he admitted, wanting her to understand the difference she'd made. He was actually beginning to care about Inez and that was plain damned scary. He was finding the townspeople interesting after seeing them through her eyes.

"Let's go back to my house," he suggested. "Didn't you say there could be bugs in that security system you installed?"

"I'm certain I need to check it over," Sarah agreed, "but I do have to make this one stop first. I promised Inez."

Chapter Nine

The small gift shop was cheerful and bright. Celtic music played softly. New Age books and crystals of all colors occupied one side of the store while fairies and dragons and mythical creatures reigned supreme on the other. Damon had been prepared for clutter after the comments on the shop owner's lack of recycling education, but the store was spotless.

"I think Donna knows her recycling stuff," Damon whispered against Sarah's ear. "She probably brushed up after she saw Inez peering at her through the store window with her lips pursed and her hands on her hips." His teeth nibbled for just a moment, sending a tremor through her. "Let's get out of here while we have the chance."

Sarah shook her head. "I have an especially strong feeling we should talk with Donna today." She was frowning slightly, a puzzled expression on her face.

Damon felt something twist and settle around his heart. Knowledge blossomed. Belief. He was a man of logic and books, yet he knew Sarah was different. He knew she was magic. Mysterious Sarah was back home and with her, some undefined power that couldn't be ignored. He felt it now for himself, after having been in her presence. It was very real, something he couldn't explain but knew was there, deep inside of her.

His knowledge made it much easier to accept the amazing intensity of the chemistry between them. More than that, it helped him to believe in the powerful emotions already surfacing for her. How did one fall in love at first sight? He'd always scoffed at the idea, yet Sarah was wrapped securely around his heart and he had known her for only a few days.

"If you feel we should talk to Donna, then by all means, let's find the woman," he agreed readily. She had changed him for all time. *He* was different inside and he preferred the man he was becoming to the man he had been. If he spent too much time thinking about it, his feelings made no sense, but he didn't want to think about it. He simply accepted it, embraced the opportunity destiny had given him.

Sarah called out, moving through the store with the natural grace Damon had come to associate with her. "Donna's daughter went to school with Joley. Donna is a sweetheart, Damon—have you met her?" She peeked around the bead-curtained doorway leading to the back of the store.

"I've seen her," Damon said, "in Inez's store. She and Inez like to exchange sarcasm."

"They've been friends for years. When Inez was sick a few years ago, Donna moved into Inez's house and cared for her, ran her own gift shop and the grocery store. They just like to grouse at one another, but it's all in fun. The back screen is open. That's strange. Donna has a phobia about insects. She never leaves doors open." There was concern in her voice.

Damon followed Sarah through the beaded curtain, noting the neatly stacked paper tied with cord and the barrel of plastic labeled with inch-high letters. "I'd have to say Donna knows more about recycling than most people."

"Of course she does." Sarah's tone was vague, as if she wasn't paying much attention. "She just likes to give Inez something to say."

"You mean she does it on purpose?" Damon wanted to laugh but Sarah's behavior was making him uneasy. They stepped out of the shop onto a back porch.

The wind rushed them, coming at them from the sea. Coming from the direction of the cliff house. Sarah raised her face to the wind, closed her eyes for a moment. Damon watched her face, watched her body. There was a complete stillness about her. She was there with him physically, but he had the impression her spirit was riding on the wind. That mentally she was with her sisters in the cliff house.

The wind chilled him, raised goose bumps on his arms, sent a shiver of alarm down his back. Something was wrong. Sarah knew something was wrong and he knew it now as well.

Sarah opened her eyes and looked at him with apprehension. "Donna." She whispered the name.

The wind whipped leaves from the trees and whirled them in small eddies of chaos and confusion. Sarah watched the whirling mass of leaves intently. Her fingers closed around his wrist. "I don't think she's far but we have to hurry. Call the sheriff's office. Tell them to send an ambulance and to send a car over. I think one of your kidnappers did decide to shop at Donna's."

She started away from him, toward the small house that sat behind the gift shop. It was overgrown with masses of flowers and bushes, a virtual refuge in the middle of town. "Wait a minute!" Damon hesitated, torn between making the phone call and following Sarah. "What if someone's still there, and what if the sheriff thinks I'm a nut?"

"Someone is still there and just say I said hurry." Sarah flung the words back over her shoulder. She was moving fast, yet silently, lithely, so graceful she reminded him of a stalking animal.

Damon swore under his breath and hurried back inside the store. Inez was standing just inside the beaded curtain. Her face was very pale. "What is it?" she demanded, her hand fluttering to her heart.

"Sarah said to call the sheriff and tell them to hurry. She also said to call an ambulance. Would you do that so I can make certain nothing happens to Sarah?" Damon spoke gently, afraid the older woman might collapse.

Inez lifted her chin. "You go, I'll have a dozen cops here immediately."

Damon breathed a sigh of relief and hurried after Sarah. She was already out of his sight, lost behind the rioting explosion of flowers. He silently cursed his bum leg. He could go anywhere if he went slowly enough but he couldn't run and even walking fast was dangerous. His leg would simply give out.

His heart was pounding so hard in his chest he feared it

would explode. Sarah in danger was terrifying. He had thought there was nothing left for him, yet she had come into his life at his darkest hour and brought hope and light. Laughter and compassion. She was even teaching him to appreciate Inez. Damon swore again, pressing his luck, using his cane to hold back the bushes while he tried to rush over the cobblestones Donna had so painstakingly used to build the pathway between her house and her shop.

A soft hiss to his left gave Sarah's position away. She was inching her way toward the door of Donna's house, using several large rhododendrons as cover. Her hand signal was clear: she wanted him to crouch low and stay where he was. A humiliating thought. Sarah racing to the rescue while he hid in the bushes. The worst of it was, he could see that she was a professional. She moved like one, and she had produced a gun from somewhere. It fit into her hand as if she were so familiar with it, the gun was a part of her.

Damon realized, for all their long talks together, he didn't know Sarah very well at all. His heart and mind and soul wanted and needed her, but he didn't know her. Enthralled, he watched as she gained the porch. Even the wind seemed to have stilled, holding its breath.

Sarah turned back to look up at the sky, to lift her arms toward the clouds. Her face was toward the cliff house. Damon had a sudden vision of her sisters standing on the battlements in front of the rolling sea, raising their arms in unison with Sarah. Calling on the wind, calling on the elements to bind their wills together.

The wind moaned softly, carrying the sound of a melodious

song, so faint he couldn't catch the words but he knew the voices were female. Dark threads spun into thick clouds over-head and the wind rushed at the house, rattling the windows and shaking the doors. The sky darkened ominously, fat drops of rain splattered the roof and yard. Damon tasted salt in the air. The rain seemed to come from the ocean itself, as if the wind, in answer to some power, had driven the salt water from the sea and spread it over the land.

The wind pulled back, reminiscent of a wave, then rushed again, this time with a roar of rage, aiming at the entry. Under the assault, the door burst inward, allowing the chilling wind into the house. Sarah rolled in behind it, as papers and maga-zines flew in all directions, providing a small distraction. She was already up on one knee in a smooth motion, tracking with her gun.

"I don't want to have to shoot you, but I will," she said. The words carried clearly to Damon although her voice was very low. "Put the gun down and kick it away from you." Damon hurried up the porch steps. He could see that Sarah's hand was rock steady. "Donna, don't try to move, an ambulance is on the way." Her gaze hadn't shifted from the man standing over Donna's body.

Damon could see the lump on Donna's head, the blood spilling onto the thick carpet. His fingers tightened around his cane until his knuckles turned white. He transferred his hold to a two-handed grip. Fury shook him at the sight of the woman on the floor and the man he recognized standing over her.

"Damon." Sarah's voice was gentle but commanding. "Don't."

He hadn't realized he had taken an aggressive step forward. Sarah hadn't turned her head, hadn't taken her alert gaze from Donna's attacker, but she somehow knew his intention. He forced himself back under control.

"Why would you attack a helpless woman?" Damon asked. He was shaking with anger, with the need to retaliate.

"Don't engage with him," Sarah counseled. "I hear a siren. Will you please see if it's the sheriff?"

Damon turned and nearly ran over Inez. He caught her as she tried to rush to Donna's side. "You can't get between Sarah and the man who attacked Donna," he said. Inez felt light and fragile in his hands. She never seemed old, yet now he could see age lined her face. She looked so anxious he was afraid for her. Very gently he drew her away from the entrance, pulling her to one side.

The wind whipped through the room, sent loose papers once more into the air. Inez shivered and reached to close the door on the chilling sea breeze.

"No!" Sarah's voice was sharp this time, unlike her.

It was enough to stimulate Damon into action. He held the door open to the elements. It was only then that he felt the subtle flow of power entering with the wind. Faintly he could hear, or imagined that he heard, the chanting carried from the direction of the ocean . . . or the cliff house.

He studied Donna's assailant, one of the men who had tortured him. The man who had pressed a gun to Dan's head and pulled the trigger. Why was he simply standing there motionless? Was it really the threat of Sarah's gun?

Damon had no doubt that she would shoot, but would that

be enough to intimidate a man like this one? He doubted it. There was something else in the room, something holding the killer.

A sense of rightness stole into his heart, carried with it a sense of peace. Sarah was a woman of silk and steel. She was magnificent.

"Jonas is coming," Inez whispered to Damon. "Sarah's going to have a problem. She'll be weak and sick after this. She won't want anyone to see her like that."

Damon could see the acceptance of his relationship with Sarah in Inez's expression. It made him feel as if he truly belonged. Inez's approval meant more to him than it should have, made him feel a part of the close-knit community instead of the outsider he always seemed to be wherever he went.

He nodded his head, pretending to understand, determined to be there for Sarah the way she seemed to be for everyone else.

Jonas Harrington came through the door first, his eyes hard and unflinching. He had Donna's assailant in handcuffs immediately. Sarah sank back on her haunches, her head bowed. She wiped sweat from her brow with the back of a trembling hand. Damon went to her immediately, helping her up, forcing her to lean on him when she didn't want to, when she was worried about his hip and leg.

Sarah went down the hall with Damon's help, found a chair in the kitchen where she could sit. She looked up at him and smiled her appreciation. That was all. And it was everything. He got her a glass of water, helped her steady her hands enough to drink it. She recovered fairly quickly, but she remained pale.

"Are your sisters feeling the same effects?" he asked.

Sarah nodded. "It isn't the same as casting. It takes a tremendous amount of our energy to hold someone against his or her will. It wasn't in his nature to be passive." She held out her hand. "I'm doing better. I need to eat something and sleep for a little while." She sighed. "I promised Irene I'd go visit Drew tonight but I don't have any strength left after this, not the kind I'd need to help them." She pressed her fingertips to her temples. "I can't really do anything for Drew and Irene knows that. Extending his life might not be the best thing. If only Libby were here."

"Sarah." He spoke in his most gentle tone. "Leave it alone for now. Let me take you home; I'll fix you a good meal and you can sleep. I'll talk to Irene myself. She'll understand."

"How did you know my sisters were helping me?"

"I felt them," he replied. "Are you steady enough to talk with the sheriff?"

She nodded. "And I want to make certain Donna's all right."

When they returned to the living room, Harrington already had Donna's assailant in the squad car. Donna burst into tears, clinging to Sarah and Inez, making Damon feel helpless and useless but filled with a deep sense of pride in Sarah and her sisters.

"Why did he attack you, Donna?" Sarah asked.

"I noticed he had your earring, Sarah. The one Joley made for you. He was wearing it. It's one of a kind and I thought you must have lost it. So I asked him about it. He hit me hard and dragged me out of the store back into my house. He kept asking me questions about you and about Mr. Wilder."

Sarah pressed her hand against Donna's wound, just for a

moment. Damon watched her face carefully, watched her skin grow paler until she swayed slightly with weariness. Sarah leaned down and kissed Donna's cheek. "You'll be fine. Don't worry about the store, we'll lock up for you."

"I'm going to the hospital with her," Inez said, glaring at the paramedics as if daring them to deny her. She held Donna's hand as they took her out.

"Sarah?" Jonas Harrington stood waiting against the wall. "You have a permit to carry that gun?"

"You know I do, Jonas," she replied. "You've seen it more than once. Yes, it's up-to-date. And I didn't shoot the man, although I was inclined to with Donna lying on the floor bleeding. And he is wearing my earring. I want it back."

"I'll get it back for you." Jonas was patient. "I know you're tired, but I need you to answer a few questions."

"That's one of the men who kidnapped me. He's the one who killed my assistant," Damon explained. "The other two must be staying somewhere in town. It shouldn't be that hard to find them now that we have him."

"I'll find them." Jonas's voice was grim. "Sarah, will you come by the office later and give me a full statement? I've sent the perp in the squad car down to the office. There's already an outstanding warrant for his arrest and the feds are going to be swarming all over this place as soon as we notify them. They're going to want to talk to the two of you, so you'd better go rest while you can."

Damon circled Sarah's shoulders with his arm. "Can you give us a ride to my place, Sheriff?"

"Sure. Let's lock up and get out of here before Sarah keels

over and her sisters haul us both over the coals. You've never seen them en masse, coming after you." He shuddered. "It's a scary sight, Wilder."

"You're the only one it's ever happened to so far," Sarah pointed out.

Chapter Ten

Damon stared down into Sarah's sleeping face. She was beautiful lying there in the middle of his bed. He had been standing there, leaning against the wall, for some time just watching over her. Guarding her. It seemed rather silly and melodramatic when she was the one with the gun and the training, but it felt as necessary to him as breathing.

Where had such a wealth of feeling come from nearly overnight? Could a man fall deeply in love with a woman so quickly? She was everything and more than he'd ever thought of or dreamed about. How could anyone not love Sarah with her compassion and tolerance and understanding? She genuinely cared about the people in her town. Somehow that deep emotion was rubbing off on him.

She could have been killed. The thought hit him hard. A physical blow in the pit of his stomach. How was it possible to feel so much for one person when he'd just met her? His entire life he'd barely noticed people, let alone cared about their lives.

From the moment he'd heard her name whispered on the wind, he knew, deep down where it counted, that she would change his life for all time.

Their walks together, all the times on the beach, whispering in his house, or hers, even spending time with her family had only strengthened his feelings for her.

Sarah opened her eyes and the first thing she saw was Damon's face. He was leaning against the far wall, simply watching her. She could see his expression clearly, naked desire, mixed with knowledge of their future. His emotions were stark and raw and so real it brought tears to her eyes. Damon hadn't expected to like her, let alone feel anything else for her.

She held out her hand to him. "Don't stand over there all alone. You aren't alone anymore and neither am I."

He heard the invitation in her voice and his body began to stir in anticipation. But he stood there drinking her in. Wanting her in so many ways that weren't just physical.

"You weren't, you know, Sarah. You've never been alone. You don't need me in the same way I need you. You have a family and they wrap you up in love and warmth and support. I never considered the value of family and love. Sharing a day with someone you care about is worth all the gold in the world. I didn't know that before I met you."

She sat up, studying him with her cool gaze. Assessing. Liking what she saw. Damon didn't know why but he could see it on her face. "I'm glad then, Damon, if I gave you such a gift. My family is my treasure."

He nodded. What would it be like to wake up every morning and hear her voice? There was always a caress in her voice, a stroking quality that he felt on his skin. Deep in his body. "And you're my treasure, Sarah. I had no idea I was even capable of feeling this way about anyone."

Sarah smiled. The smile she seemed to reserve for him. It lit up her face and made her eyes shine, but more, it lit up his insides so that he burned with something indefinable. "You brought me life, Sarah. You handed me my life. I existed before I met you, but I wasn't living."

"Yes, you were, Damon. You're a brilliant man. The things you created made our world safer. I watch your face light up when you tell me about other ideas you have and what the possibilities are. That's living."

"I had nothing else but my ideas." He straightened suddenly, coming away from the wall, walking toward her, confidence on his face. "That was how I escaped, into my brain and the endless ideas I could find there." He traced the classic lines of her face, her cheekbones. Her generous mouth. "Take off your blouse, Sarah. I want to see you."

A faint blush stole into her cheeks but her hands went to the tiny pearl buttons on her blouse and slowly began to slide the edges apart. His breath caught in his throat as he watched her. Sarah didn't try to be sexy, there was never anything affected about her, yet it was the sexiest thing he'd ever seen. The edges of her blouse slowly gaped open, to reveal her lush creamy flesh beneath it. She had a woman's body, shaped to please a man with soft curves and lines.

Her breasts were covered with fine white lace. Sarah stood up, her body very close to his. Damon felt a rush of heat take him, a whip of lightning dance through his body. His blood thickened and pooled. His body hardened almost to the point of pain. He embraced it, reveled in the intensity of his need for her.

"You're so beautiful, Sarah. Inside and out. I still can't believe I could go from living in hell straight to paradise."

She reached for him. "I'm not like that at all, Damon. I'm not truly beautiful, not by any stretch of the imagination. I'm not even close. And living with me would not be paradise. I'm outspoken and like my way."

With exquisite tenderness, he bent his head to find her mouth with his. For a moment they were lost together, transported out of time by the magic flowing between them. When Damon lifted his head to look down at her, his gaze was hungry. Needy. Possessive. "You're beautiful to me, Sarah. I will never see you any other way. And lucky for you, I'm stubborn and very outspoken myself. I think those are admirable traits."

"That is lucky," she murmured, allowing her eyelashes to drift down and her head to fall back as he pulled her closer, his mouth breathing warm, moist air over her nipple right through the white lace. Her arms cradled his head as she arched her body, offering temptation, offering heaven.

His mouth was hot and damp as it closed over her breast. Fire raced through her, through him. Sarah gave herself up to sensual pleasure as his tongue danced and teased and his mouth suckled strongly right through the lace. He took his time, a lazy, leisurely exploration, his hands shaping her body, using the pads of his fingers as a blind man would to trace every curve and hollow. Memorizing her. Worshipping her.

Sarah was lost in sensation. Drowning in it. She couldn't

remember him unsnapping her jeans, or even unzipping them. But her lacy bra had long ago floated to the floor and somehow he managed to push denim from her hips. In a haze of need and heat she stepped out of the last of her clothes.

He was never hurried, even as his mouth fused once more with hers and she was trying to drag his shirt from his broad shoulders so she could be skin to skin with him. He was patient and thorough, determined to know her body, to find every hidden trigger point that had her gasping in need. His hands moved over her, finding the shadows and hollows, tracing her ribs lovingly. He allowed Sarah to drag his clothes from his body, not appearing to notice or care, so completely ensnared by the wonders of giving her pleasure. He loved the little gasps and soft cries that came from deep in her throat.

Sarah. So responsive and giving. He should have known she would be a generous lover, merging with him so completely, giving of herself endlessly. Her selfless gift only made him want to be equally generous. For the first time his scars weren't shameful and something he hid. When her fingertips traced them, there was no reluctance, no shrinking away from the ugly memories of torture and murder. She soothed his body, caressing his skin, arousing him further, eager to touch him, wanting him with the same urgency he wanted her.

He lowered her slowly to the sheets, following her down, settling his body over hers. Her face was beautiful as she stared up at him. He kissed her eyes, the tip of her nose, the corners of her mouth.

Everywhere he touched her he left flames behind. Sarah was astonished at the sheer intensity of the fire. He was so unhurried, taking his time, but she was going up in flames, burning inside and out, needing his body in hers. She heard her own voice, a soft plea for mercy as his lips nipped over her navel, went lower. His hands moved with assurance, finding the insides of her thighs, the damp heat waiting for him at the junction of her legs.

"Damon." She could barely breathe his name. Her breath seemed to have permanently left her body. There wasn't enough air in the room.

His finger pushed deep inside her, a stroke of sensuality that drove her out of her mind. Every sane thought she'd ever had was gone. There was a roaring in her head when his mouth found her, claimed her, branded her his. She couldn't keep her hips still, writhing until his arms pinned her there, while his hot mouth ravaged her and wave after wave of pleasure rippled through her body with the force of the booming ocean. Her fingers tangled in his hair, her only anchor to hold her to earth while she soared free, gasping out his name.

Damon moved then, blanketing her completely, his hips settling into the cradle of hers. He was thick and hard and throbbing with his own need. He pushed deep inside of her, his voice hoarse as he cried out as the sweeping pleasure engulfed him. She was hot and slick and tight, a velvet fist closing around him, gripping with a fire he'd never known. Sarah. Magical Sarah.

He began to move. Never hurried. Why would he hurry his first time with Sarah? He wanted the moment to last forever. To be forever for both of them. He loved watching her face as he moved with her. As his body surged deep and her body took him in, her secret sanctuary of heat and joy. Her hips rose to join him, matching his rhythm, tilting to take him deeper and deeper with every stroke, wanting every inch of him. Wanting his possession as much as he wanted her.

The fire just kept building. He was in complete control one moment, certain of it, reveling in it, and then the pleasure was almost too much to bear, hitting him with the force of a freight train, starting in his toes and blowing out the top of his head. His voice was lifted with hers, merged and in perfect unison.

He could feel the aftershocks shaking her, tightening around him, drawing them ever closer. They lay together, not daring to move, unable to move, their hearts wild and lungs starving for air, their arms wrapped tightly around one another. The ocean breeze was gentle on the window, whispering soothing sounds while the sea sang to them with rolling waves.

Damon found peace. She lay in his arms, occasionally rousing herself enough to kiss his chest, her tongue tracing a scar. Each time she did so, his body tightened in answer and hers responded with another aftershock. They were merged so completely, so tightly bound together he couldn't tell where he started or left off.

"Stay with me the rest of the day, Sarah. All night. We can do anything you like. Just be with me." He propped himself up on his elbows to take most of his weight off of her. He wanted to be locked together, one body, sharing the same skin, absorbing her.

She reached up to trace the lines of his face. "I can't think of anywhere I'd rather be or who I'd rather be spending time with."

"Do you wonder why you chose me? I stopped asking myself that question and just accept it. I'm grateful, Sarah."

"I look at you and I just know. Who can say why one heart belongs to another? I don't ask myself that question either, Damon. I'm just grateful the gate opened for you." She laughed with sudden amusement. "It has occurred to me you might be seducing me to try to get the secret of paint preservation."

He tangled his fingers with hers, stretched her arms above her head. "It did seem a good idea. Maybe one of these days I'll be able to speak when I'm making love to you and I'll be able to pry the secret out of you."

"Good plan; it might work, too, if I could manage to speak when you're making love to me." She gasped as he lowered his head to her breast. "Damon." Her body was hypersensitive, but she arched into the heat of his mouth.

"I'm sorry, you looked so tempting, I couldn't help myself. How do you feel about just lying here without a stitch on while I build a fire and cook something for you to eat? I'm not certain I can bear for you to put your clothes back on." His teeth scraped back and forth over her breast. His tongue laved her nipple.

Sarah's entire body tightened, every muscle going taut. "You just want me to be lying here waiting for you?"

"Waiting *eagerly* for me," he corrected. "Needing me would be good. I wouldn't mind if you just lay here on my bed thinking of my body buried inside you."

"I see. I thought it might be better if I just followed you around, looking at you, touching you while you worked. Inspiring you. I have my ways, you know, of inspiring you."

There was a wicked note in her voice that made his entire body aware of how receptive and pliant she was. He was all at once as hard as a rock, thick with need. Damon watched her eyes widen in pleased surprise. Desire spread through both of them, sheer bliss. "I've never felt this way with any other woman, Sarah. I know it isn't possible. I think you really could walk on water."

"For a man who spent a lot of time in a laboratory, you know your way around women," she pointed out. He was moving with that exquisite slowness he used to drive her straight up the wall. The friction on her already sensitive body was turning her inside out. It didn't matter how many times she went over the edge, Damon moved with almost perfect insight, perfect knowledge of what she needed. What she wanted.

"I can read your face and your body," he said. "I love that, Sarah. You don't hold anything back from me."

"Why should I?" Why would she want to when the rewards were so great? If Damon was the man destiny insisted would be the love of her life, her best friend and partner, she was willing to accept whatever he had to give.

Sarah loved the sound of his voice, the thoughtful intelligent way he approached every subject. And she loved his complete honesty. There was that same raw honesty in his lovemaking. He gave himself to her, even as he took her for his own. She *felt* his possession deep in her soul, branded into her very bones.

There was that patient thoroughness and then, when he was fully aroused, his body was a driving force, each stroke hard and fast and insistent, taking them both soaring out over the sea, free-falling through time and space until neither could move again.

Damon held her in his arms, curled next to her, not wanting to end the closeness between them. They were completely sated for the moment, exhausted, breathing with effort, yet there was the same sense of absolute peace. "Sarah." He whispered her name, a tribute more than anything else.

"All those things you feel about me," she said, snuggling closer to him, "I feel about you. I didn't want anyone in my life any more than you did. I sometimes tire of giving pieces of myself to other people, yet I can't help myself. I find places I'm safe, places where I'm alone and can crawl into a hole and disappear for a while."

"Now you have me. I'll be your sanctuary, Sarah. I don't mind running interference in the times you need to regroup." His smile was against her temple. "I've never had a problem bossing people. I've always had a difficult time communicating with people. They never understood what I was talking about and it drove me crazy. Sometimes when you have an idea and it's so clear and you know it's right, you just have to share it with someone. But no one has ever been there."

Sarah kissed his fingertips. "You can tell me any idea that comes into your head, Damon. I admire you." Her smile was in her voice. "And I'm very good at communicating so you'll never have to worry about that."

"I noticed," he said. "Speaking of communication, I made certain the curtains couldn't creep open. I safety-pinned them together just in case any of your sisters decided to go up on the battlements to look through the telescope."

Sarah laughed just as he knew she would. "They know I'm with you. They wouldn't invade our privacy when we're really making love. They simply love to tease me. You'll have a lot of that come morning."

Damon didn't mind at all. He tightened his arms around her and found he was looking forward to anything her sisters might want to dish out.

Chapter Eleven

"Okay, have any of you really read this prophecy?" Kate demanded as they walked along the sidewalk toward Irene's house. The fog was thick and heavy, lying over the sea and most of the town like a blanket. "Because I have and it isn't good news for the rest of us."

"I don't like the sound of that," Hannah said. "Maybe we shouldn't ask. Can ignorance keep us safe?"

"What prophecy?" Damon asked curiously. They had spent the morning together over breakfast, teasing him unmercifully, making Sarah blush and hide her face against his chest. He had felt just as he anticipated—part of a family—and the feeling was priceless.

Sarah laughed in wicked delight. "You all thought it was so funny when it was happening to me, but I had read the entire thing. I know what's in store for the rest of you. One by one you'll fall like dominoes."

Abbey made a face at Sarah. "Not all of us, Sarah. I don't believe in fate."

The other girls roared with laughter. Sarah slipped her hand into Damon's. "The prophecy is this horrible curse put on the seven sisters. Well, we thought it was a curse. I'm not so certain now that I've met you."

His eyebrow shot up. "Now I'm really curious. I'm involved with this prophecy in some way?"

The four women laughed again. The sound turned heads up and down the street. "You are the prophecy, Damon," Kate said. "The gate opened for you."

Sarah gave a short synopsis of the quote. "Seven sisters intertwined, controlling elements of land, sea, and air, cannot control the fate they flee. One by one, oldest to last, destiny will find them. When the locked gate swings open in welcome, the first shall find true love. There's a lot more, but basically it goes on to say, one by one all the other sisters shall be wed."

Sarah's three sisters muttered and grumbled and shook their heads. Damon burst out laughing. "You have to marry me, don't you? I've been wondering how I was going to manage to keep you, but you don't have a choice. I like that prophecy. Does it say anything about waiting on me hand and foot?"

"Absolutely not," Sarah replied and glared at her laughing sisters. "Keep it up—the rest of you, even you, Abbey, are going to see me laughing at you." She tightened her fingers around Damon's hand. "We all made a pact when we were kids to keep the gate padlocked and never really date so we could be independent and free. We've always liked our life together . . . and poor Elle—the thought of seven daughters is rather daunting."

"Thank heavens Elle gets all the kids," Abbey said. "I am

going to have one, and only because if I don't the rest of you will drive me crazy."

"Why does Elle have to have the seven daughters?" Damon asked.

"The seventh daughter always has seven daughters," Kate explained. "It's been that way for generations. I've been reading the history of the Drake family and I've found over the years, from all the entries made, we at least have a legacy of happy marriages." She smiled at Damon. "So far I haven't seen anything that indicated waiting on the man hand and foot but I'll keep looking."

"While you're at it, will you also keep an eye out for the traditional obey-the-husband rule?" Damon asked. "I've always thought that word was crucial in the marriage ceremony. Without it, a man doesn't stand a chance."

"Dream on," Sarah said. "That will never happen. The problem with being locked up in a stuffy lab all of your life is becoming evident. Delusions start early."

They were passing a small, neat home with a large front yard surrounded by the proverbial white picket fence. An older couple was working on a fountain in the middle of a bed of flowers. Sarah suddenly stopped, turned back to look at the house and the couple. A shadow slithered across the roof. A hint of something seen, then lost in the fog. "I'll just be a minute." She waved to the older couple and both stood up immediately and came over to the fence.

Sarah's sisters looked at one another uneasily. Damon followed Sarah. "It isn't necessary to speak to every citizen in town," he advised Sarah's back. She ignored his good judgment and struck up a conversation with the older couple anyway. Damon sighed. He had a feeling he was going to be following Sarah and talking to everyone they met for the rest of his life.

"Why, Sarah, I'd heard you were back. Is everything all right? I haven't seen you for what is it now? Two years?" The older woman spoke as she waved to the sisters.

"Mrs. Darden, I was admiring your yard. Did you remodel your house recently?"

The Dardens looked at one another then back to Sarah. Mr. Darden cleared his throat. "Yes, Sarah, the living room and kitchen. We came into a little money and we always wanted to fix up the house. It's exactly the way we want it now."

"That's wonderful." She rubbed the back of her neck and looked up at the roof. "I see you've got ladders out. Are you re-roofing?"

"It was leaking this winter, Sarah," Mr. Darden said. "We lost a tree some months ago and a branch hit the house. We've had trouble ever since."

"It looks as if you're doing the work yourself," Sarah observed and rubbed the back of her neck a second time.

Damon reached out to massage her neck with gentle fingers. The tremendous tension he felt in her neck and shoulders kept him silent. Wondering.

"I hear Lance does wonderful roofing, Mr. Darden. He's fast and guarantees his work. Rather than you climbing around on the roof, wasting your time when you could be gardening." She turned her head slightly to look at Damon. "Mr. Darden is renowned for his garden and flowers. He wins every year at the fair for his hybrids."

Damon could see shadows in her eyes. He smiled at her, leaned forward to brush a gentle kiss on the top of her head when she turned back to the Dardens. "Lance probably needs the work and you'd be doing him such a favor."

Mrs. Darden tugged at her husband's hand. "Thank you, Sarah, it's good advice and we'll do that. I've been worrying about Clyde up there on that roof but . . . " She trailed off.

"I think you're right, Sarah," Mr. Darden suddenly agreed. "I think I'll call Lance straightaway."

Sarah shrugged with studied casualness but Damon felt her shoulders sag in relief. "I can't wait for the fair this year to see your beautiful entries. I really wanted you to meet Damon Wilder, a friend of mine. He bought the old Hanover place." She smiled sweetly at Damon to include him. "I know you're often in the garden and working on your lovely yard—have you noticed any strangers around that were asking questions or making you feel uncomfortable?"

The Dardens looked at one another. "No, Sarah, I can't say that we have," Mrs. Darden answered, "but then we strictly mind our own business. You know I've always believed in staying out of my neighbors' affairs."

"It's just that with you working outdoors so much I thought you might be able to keep an eye out for me and give me a call if anything should look suspicious," Sarah said.

"You can count on us, Sarah," Mr. Darden said. "I just bought myself a new pair of binoculars and sitting on my front porch I have a good view of the entire street!"

"Thank you, Mr. Darden," Sarah said. "That would be wonderful. We're just on our way to visit Irene and Drew."

The smile faded from Mrs. Darden's face. "Oh, that's so sad, Sarah, I hope you can help them. When is Libby going to come home? She would be such a help. How's she doing these days?"

"Libby's overseas right now, Mrs. Darden," Sarah said. "She's doing fine. Hopefully she'll be able to get home soon. I'll tell her you were inquiring about her."

"I heard the awful news on Donna," Mrs. Darden continued. "Are these strangers involved in her attack? I heard you shot one of them. I don't believe in violence as a rule, Sarah, now, you know that, but I hope you did enough damage that he'll think twice before he attacks another woman."

"Donna's going to be fine," Sarah assured her, "and I didn't shoot him."

Mrs. Darden patted Sarah's shoulder. "It's all right, dear, I understand."

Sarah turned away with a cheery wave. The sisters erupted into wild laughter. Damon shook his head incredulously. "She thinks you shot that man. Even now, with you denying it, she thinks you shot him."

"True." Sarah pinned him with a steely gaze. "She also believes someone saw me walk on water. Now who could have started that rumor?"

Hannah tugged at Damon's sleeve in a teasing way, a gesture of affection for her. "That was a good one, Damon, I wish I'd thought of it."

Kate threw back her head and laughed, her wild mane of hair blowing around her in the light breeze. "That was priceless. And you should hear what they're saying about you. The whisper is, you're some famous wizard Sarah's been studying under."

"Now really," Sarah objected, "at least they could have said *he's* been studying under *me*. I swear chauvinism is still rearing its ugly head in this century."

Damon could feel a glow spreading. He felt a part of their family. He belonged with them, in the midst of their laughter and camaraderie. He didn't feel on the outside looking in, as he had most of his life. Sarah's sisters seemed to accept him readily into their lives and even their hearts. Tolerance and acceptance seemed a big part of Sarah's family. It suddenly occurred to him, even with a threat hanging over his head, that he'd spent less time thinking of past trauma and more about the present and future than he had in months.

"I think I like being thought of as a wizard," Damon mused.

"Sarah says you're a brain." Kate waved at Jonas Harrington as he cruised by them in his patrol car.

"What are you doing?" Hannah hissed, smacking Kate's hand down. "Don't be nice to that idiot. We should make him drive into a ditch or something."

"Don't you dare," Sarah told her sister sternly. "I mean it, Hannah, you can't use our gifts for revenge. Only for good. Especially now."

"It would be for good," Hannah pointed out. "It would teach that horrible man some manners. Don't look at him. And Damon, stop smiling at him. We don't want him stopping to talk." She made a growling noise of disgust in the back of her throat as the patrol car pulled to the sidewalk ahead of them. "Now see what you've done?" She threw her hands into the air as Harrington got out of his car. A sudden rush of wind took his hat from his head and sent it skittering along the gutter.

"Very funny, Baby Doll," Harrington said. "You just have to show off, don't you? I guess that pretty face of yours just doesn't get you enough attention."

Kate and Sarah both put a restraining hand on Hannah's arm. Sarah stepped slightly between the sheriff and her sister. "Did you get anything out of your prisoner, Jonas?" Her voice was carefully pleasant.

Jonas continued to pin Hannah with his ice cold gaze. "Not much, Sarah, and we still haven't located the other two men you say were at Wilder's house the other night. You might have called me instead of charging in on your own."

Hannah stirred as if she might protest. Damon could see the fine tremor that ran through her body but her sisters edged protectively closer to Hannah and she stilled.

"Yes, next time, Jonas, I'll do that: leave the three men with guns trained on the window, sneaking up on the house, while I go find a phone and call you. Darn, those cell phones just don't seem to work on the coast most of the time, do they?" Sarah smiled right through her sarcasm. "Next time I'll drive out to the bluff and give you a call before I charge in on my own."

Jonas's gaze didn't leave Hannah's face. "You do that, Sarah." He knotted his fists on his hips. "Did any of you consider Sarah might have been killed? Or how I might feel if I found her dead body? Or if I had to go up to your house and tell you she was dead? Because I thought a lot about that last night."

"I thought about it," Damon said. "At least about Sarah being killed on my account." He reached out to settle his fingers possessively around the nape of her neck. "It scared the hell out of me."

Kate and Abbey exchanged looks with Hannah. "I didn't think of that," Kate admitted. "Not once."

"Thanks a lot, Jonas," Sarah said. "Now they're all going to be making me crazy, wanting me to change my profession. I'm a security expert."

"It may beat being a Barbie doll, but I think you went overboard, Sarah," Jonas replied. "A librarian sounds nice to me."

Hannah clenched her teeth but remained silent. The wind rushed through the street, sweeping the sheriff's hat toward a storm drain. It landed in a dark puddle of water and disappeared from sight.

Harrington swore under his breath and stalked back to his car, his shoulders stiff with outrage.

"Hannah," Kate scolded gently, "that wasn't nice."

"I didn't do it," Hannah protested. "*I* would have had the oak tree come down and drive him underground feet first."

Abbey and Kate looked at Sarah. She merely raised her eyebrow. "I believe Irene and Drew are waiting."

Damon burst out laughing. "I can see I'm going to have to watch you all the time." Why did it seem perfectly normal that the Drake sisters could command the wind? Even Harrington treated it as a normal phenomenon.

They stopped in front of Irene's house. Damon could see all the women squaring their shoulders as if going into battle. "Sarah, what do you think you can do for Drew? Surely you can't cure what's wrong with him."

Sadness crept into her eyes. "No, I wish I had that gift. Libby is the only one with a real gift for healing. I've seen her work miracles. But it drains her and we don't like her doing it. There's always a cost, Damon, when you use a gift."

"So you aren't conjuring up spells with toads and dragon livers?" He was half-serious. He could easily picture them on broomsticks, flying across the night sky.

"Well . . . " Abbey drew the word out, looking mischievously from one sister to the other. "We can and do if the situation calls for it. Drakes have been leaving each other recipes and spells for hundreds of years. We prefer to use the power within us, but conjuring is within the rules."

"You never let me," Hannah groused.

"No, and we're not going to either," Sarah said firmly. "Actually, Damon, to answer your question, we hope to assess the situation and maybe buy Drew a little more time. If the quality of his life is really bad, we prefer not to interfere. What would be the point of his lingering in pain? In that case, we'll ease his suffering as best we can and leave everything to nature."

"Does Irene think you can cure him?" Damon asked, suddenly worried. He realized what a terrible responsibility the Drakes had. The townspeople were used to their eccentricities and believed they were miracle workers.

"She wants to believe it. If Libby and my other sisters were here, all of us together might really be of some help, but the most we can do is slow things down to buy him time. We'll find out from Drew what he wants. You'll have to distract Irene for us. Have her go into the kitchen and make us lemonade and her famous cookies. She'll be anxious, Damon, so you'll really have to work at it. We'll need time with Drew."

His gaze narrowed as he studied Sarah's serious face. "What

about you and your sisters? Are you going to be ill like you were last time?"

"Only if we work on him," Sarah said. "Then I don't know how you'll get us all home. You'll have to ask Irene to drive us back."

"We should have thought to bring the car," Kate agreed. "Do you think that's a bad omen? Maybe there's nothing we can do."

"Don't go thinking that way, Kate," Abbey reprimanded. "We all love to walk and it's fun to be together. We can do this. If we're lucky we can buy Drew enough time to allow Libby to come home."

"Is Libby coming back?" Damon asked.

"I don't know, Damon," Hannah said, her eyebrow raising, "that's rather up to you, now, isn't it?"

"Why would it be up to me?"

"I thought you said he was one of the smartest men on the planet," Kate teased. "Didn't you design some top-secret defense system?"

Damon glared at the women, at Sarah. "If I did and it was top secret, no one would know, now would they?"

Hannah laughed. "Don't be angry, Damon, Sarah didn't tell us. We share knowledge, sort of like a collective pool. I can't tell you how it works, only that we all have it. She would never give out that kind of information, even to us. It just happens. None of us would say anything, well," she hedged, "except to tease you."

"So why is it up to me whether or not Libby comes home?"

"She'll come home if there's a wedding," Kate pointed out with a grin.

Chapter Twelve

Damon looked around him at the four pale faces. Each of the Drake sisters was lying on a couch or draped over a chair, exhaustion written into the lines of her face. For a moment he felt helpless in the midst of their weariness, not knowing what to do for them. They had sat in Irene's car, not speaking, with their white faces and trembling bodies. He had barely managed to help them into the cliff house.

The phone rang, the sound shrill in the complete stillness of the house. The women didn't move or turn toward the sound so Damon picked up the receiver. "Yes?"

There was a long pause. "You must be Damon." The voice was like a caress of velvet. "What's wrong with them? I can feel them all the way here." The voice didn't say where "here" was.

"You're a sister?"

"Of course." Impatience now. "Elle. What's wrong with them?"

"They went to Irene's to see Drew." Damon could hear the sheer relief in the small sigh on the other end.

"Make them sweet tea. There's a canister in the cupboard right above the stove, marked MAGIC." Damon carried the phone with him into the kitchen. "Drop a couple of teaspoons of the powder into the teapot and let the tea steep. That will help. Is the house warm? If not, get it warm: build a fire and use the furnace, whatever it takes. When's the wedding?"

"How soon can you and your sisters get back home?" Damon asked.

"You know I should be angry with you. Not that burner, use the back burner. That's the right canister."

"I don't see what difference a burner makes, but okay and why should you be upset with me?" He didn't even wonder how she knew what he was doing or what burner he was using. He took it as a matter of course.

"Because I'm concentrating on it, the burner I mean. As for being upset, I think you started something we have no control over. I have no intention of finding a man for a long while. I have things to do with my life and a man doesn't come into it, thank you very much. The infuser is in the very bottom drawer to the left of the sink." She spoke as if she could see him going through the drawers looking for the little infuser to put the tea in.

The house shuddered. Stilled. A ripple of alarm went through Damon.

"What was that?" Elle sounded anxious again.

"An earthquake maybe. A minor one. I've got the kettle on, the teapot is ready with the powder, two teaspoons of this stuff? Have you smelled it lately?" Damon was tempted to taste it. "It isn't a dragon's liver, is it?"

Elle laughed. "We save those for Harrington. When he drops by we put it in his coffee."

"I really feel sorry for that man." To his astonishment the teakettle shrilled loudly almost immediately. He poured the water into the little teapot and tossed a tea towel over it for added warmth. "Are you really going to have seven daughters?" he asked curiously, amazed that anyone would even consider it. Amazed that he was talking comfortably to a virtual stranger.

The house shuddered a second time. A branch scraped along an outside wall with an eerie sound. The wind moaned and rattled the windows.

"So the prophecy says," Elle replied with a small sigh of resignation. "Damon, is something else wrong there?"

"No, they're just very tired." Damon poured the tea into four cups and set the cups on a tray. "And the house keeps shaking."

"Hang up and call the sheriff's office," Elle said urgently. "Do it now."

He caught the sudden alarm in her voice and a chill went down his spine. Damn them all for their psychic nonsense. There wasn't really anything wrong, was there?

The dogs roared a vicious challenge. The animals were in the front yard, inside the fence, yet they were hurling their bodies against the front door so hard the wood threatened to splinter. Damon did as Elle commanded and phoned the sheriff's office for help.

No one screamed. Most women might have screamed under the circumstances but none of them did. When he carried the tray into the living room, all four of the Drake sisters were sitting quietly in their chairs. He ignored the two men standing in the middle of the room with guns drawn. Where before, when confronted with guns and violence, he had panicked, this time he remained quite calm.

He knew they were killers. He knew what to expect. And this time, he knew he wouldn't allow them to hurt the Drake sisters. It was very simple to him. It didn't matter to him if he died, he needed the women to survive and live in the world. They were the ones who mattered, all that mattered. The women *would* remain alive.

Damon set the tray on the coffee table and handed each of the sisters a cup of tea before turning to face the two men. He remembered them in vivid detail. The man with the swollen jaw had taken pleasure in torturing him. Damon was glad he had swung his cane hard enough to fracture the jaw.

Damon straightened slowly. These men had murdered for the knowledge Damon carried in his brain. They had crippled him permanently and changed his entire life. Now they stood in Sarah's home, sheer blasphemy on their part. They had entered through the sliding-glass door and had left it open behind them.

Outside, the sea appeared calm, but he could see, in the distance, small frothy waves gathering and rolling with a building boom on the open water. He felt power moving him, a connection with the women through Sarah. Beloved, mysterious Sarah. He waited while the women sipped their tea. Stalling for time, knowing exactly what he would do.

"You two seem to keep turning up," Damon finally greeted. He took two steps to his right, closer to Sarah, turning slightly sideways so she could see the small gun he had taken from the hidden drawer where Elle had said he would find it. "Do you not have homes and families to go to?"

"Shut up, Wilder. You know what we want. This time we have someone you care about. When I put a gun to her head I think you're going to tell me what I want to know."

Damon looked past the man to the rolling sea. The wind was gusting, chopping the surface into white foam. The waves crested higher. The dogs continued roaring with fury and shaking the foundations of the living room door. Damon calmly raked his fingers through his hair, his gaze on a distant point beyond the men. The sisters drank the hot sweet revitalizing tea. And the power moved through Damon stronger than ever. Around each man a strange shadow flitted back and forth. A black circle that seemed to surround first one, then the other. At times the shadow appeared to have a human form. Most of the time it was insubstantial.

"Would you care for a cup of tea?" Sarah asked politely. "We have plenty."

"Do sit down," Kate invited. She shifted position, a subtle movement hardly noticeable, but it put her body slightly between the guns and Hannah.

"This gun is real," the man with the swollen jaw snapped. "This isn't a party." He grinned evilly at his partner. "Although when it's over we might take one or two of the women with us for the road."

Sarah looked bored. "It's very obvious neither of you is the brains in this venture. I can't imagine that the man in jail is, either. Who in the world would hire such comedians to go looking for national secrets? It's almost ludicrous. Are you in trouble with your boss and he's looking to get rid of you?"

"You have a smart mouth, lady; it won't be so hard to shoot you."

"Do have some tea, at least we can be civil," Abbey said sweetly. There was a strange cadence to her voice, a singsong quality that pulled at the listeners, drew them into her suggestions. "If you're going to be with us for some time, we may as well enjoy ourselves with a fine cup of tea first and get to know one another."

The air in the room was fresh, almost perfumed, yet smelled of the sea, crisp and clean and salty. The two men looked confused, blinking rapidly, and exchanged a long bewildered frown. The man with the swollen jaw actually lowered his gun and took a step toward the tray with the little teapot.

Kate stared intently at the locks on the front door, and the knob itself. Sarah never took her eyes from the two men. Waiting. Watching. The huntress. Damon thought of her that way. Listening, he thought he heard music, far out over the sea. Music in the wind. A soft melodious song calling to the elements. All the while the dark shadow edged around the two intruders.

Hannah lifted her arms to the back of the couch, a graceful, elegant motion. The wind rose to a shriek, burst into the room with the force of a freight train. The men staggered under the assault, the wind ripping at their clothing. The bolt on the door turned and the door burst open under the heavy weight of the dogs. The animals leapt inside, teeth bared. Damon blinked as the crouching shadow leapt onto the back of one of the men and remained there.

Sarah was already in motion, diving at the two men, going in low to catch the first man in a scissor kick, rolling to bring him down. He toppled into his partner, knocking him down so that his head slammed against the base of a chair. Sarah caught the gun Damon threw to her.

The man with the swollen jaw rose up, throwing the chair as he drew a second gun. Damon attempted a kick with his one good leg. Sarah fired off three rounds, the bullets driving the man backward and away from Damon. She calmly pressed the hot barrel against the temple of the intruder on the floor. "I suggest you don't move." But she was looking at the man she shot, watching Hannah and Abbey trying to revive him. Watching the dark shadow steal away, dragging with it something heavy. Knowing her sisters could not undo what she had done. Sarah wiped her forehead with her palm and blinked back tears.

Kate collected the guns. Abbey held back the dogs by simply placing her hand in warning on their heads.

"I'm sorry, Sarah," Damon said.

"It was necessary." She felt sick. It didn't matter that he'd intended to kill them all, or that Death had been satisfied. She had taken a life.

The wind moved through the room again, a soft breeze this time, bringing music with it. Touching Sarah. She looked at her sisters and smiled tiredly. "Hannah, the cavalry is coming up the drive. Do let them in and don't do anything you'll regret later."

Hannah rolled her eyes, stomped across the room, landing a frustrated kick to the shins of the man Sarah was holding. "Thanks a lot, I have to see that giant skunk two times in one day. That's more than any lady should have to deal with."

Abigail leaned down, her face level with Sarah's prisoner.

"You'd really like to tell me who you're working for, wouldn't you?" Her tone was sweet, hypnotic, compelling. She looked directly into his eyes, holding him captive there. Waiting for the name. Waiting for the truth.

At the doorway, Hannah called out a greeting to Jonas Harrington. "As usual, you're just a bit on the late side. Still haven't quite gotten over that bad habit of being late you set in school. You always did like to make your entrance at least ten minutes after the bell." She had her hand on her hip and she tossed the silky mass of wavy hair tumbling around her shoulders. "It was juvenile then and it's criminal now."

Deliberately he stepped in close to her, crowding her with his much larger body. "Someone should have turned you over their knee a long time ago." The words were too low for anyone else to hear and he was sweeping past her to enter the room. Just for a moment his glittering eyes slashed at her, burned her.

Every woman in the room reacted, eyes glaring at Jonas. Hannah held up her hand in silent admission she'd provoked him. She allowed the rest of the officers into the room before she took the dogs into the bedroom. Damon noticed she didn't return.

All the women were exhausted. Damon wanted everyone else gone. It seemed more important to push more tea into the Drake sisters' hands, to tuck blankets around them, to shield them from prying eyes when they were obviously so vulnerable. He stayed close to Sarah while she was questioned repeatedly. The medical examiner removed the body and the crime scene team went over the room.

Each of the sisters gave a separate report so it seemed an

eternity until Damon had the house back in his control. "Thanks, Abbey, I don't know how you managed to get that name, but hopefully they'll be able to stop anyone else from coming after me."

Abbey closed her eyes and laid her head against the back-rest of the chair. "It was my pleasure. Will you answer the phone? Tell Elle we're too tired to talk but have her tell the others we're all right."

"The phone isn't ringing." But he was already walking into the kitchen to answer it. Of course it wasn't ringing. Yet. But it would. And it did. And he reassured Elle he wouldn't leave her sisters and all was well in their world.

It seemed hours before he was alone with Sarah. His Sarah. Before he could frame her face in his hands and lower his head to kiss her with every bit of tenderness he had in him. "There was something I saw, a shadow, dark and grim. I felt it had been on me, with me, and now it's gone. That sounds ridiculous, Sarah, but I feel lighter, as if a great burden is off of me. You know what I'm talking about, don't you?"

"Yes." She said it simply.

His gaze moved possessively over her face. "You look so tired. I'd carry you to bed, but we wouldn't make it if I tried."

She managed a small smile. "It would be okay if you dropped me on the floor. I'd just go to sleep."

He helped her through the hall to the stairs. "Hannah has the turret leading to the battlement, doesn't she?"

Sarah was pleased that he knew. "The sea draws her. The wind and rain. It helps her to be there, up high, where she can see it all. I'm glad you understand."

He went up the stairs behind her, ready to break her fall should there be need. Ready to do whatever it took to protect her. "It surprises me that I feel the power in this house, but I do. I'm a scientist. None of this makes sense, what you and your sisters are. Hell, I don't even know how I'd describe you, but I know it's real."

"Stay with me tonight, Damon," Sarah said. "I feel very weary, like I'm stretched thin. When you're with me, I'm not so lost."

"You'd have to throw me out, Sarah," he replied truthfully. "I know I love you and I want you for my wife. I don't ever want us to be apart."

"I feel the same, Damon." Sarah pushed open the door to her bedroom and collapsed on the large four-poster bed. She looked beautiful to him, lying there, waiting for him to stretch out beside her.

Her window faced the sea. Damon could see the water, a deep blue, waves swelling high, collapsing, rushing the shores and receding as it had for so many years. Peace was in his heart and mind. Soft laughter came from various parts of the house. It swept through the air, and filled the house with joy. Sarah was back. Sarah was home. And Damon had come home with her.

Do you love fiction with a supernatural twist?

Want the chance to hear news about your favourite authors (and the chance to win free books)?

Keri Arthur
S. G. Browne
P.C. Cast
Christine Feehan
Jacquelyn Frank
Thea Harrison
Larissa Ione
Darynda Jones
Sherrilyn Kenyon
Jackie Kessler
Jayne Ann Krentz and Jayne Castle
Martin Millar
Kat Richardson
J.R. Ward
David Wellington
Laura Wright

Then visit the Piatkus website and blog
www.piatkus.co.uk | www.piatkusbooks.net

And follow us on Facebook and Twitter
www.facebook.com/piatkusfiction | www.twitter.com/piatkusbooks

piatkus